BURDEN OF DOUBT

LIANE CARMEN

ISBN: (paperback) 978-1-958610-98-5

ISBN: (e-book) 978-1-958610-99-2

Cover design by 100 covers.

Author photo by Bill Ziady. (www.matchframeproductions.com)

For Adam David,
who is still too sweet and innocent
to know his grandma writes books about murder

1

———————

Maggie liked to begin her day with coffee and murder. An unexplained disappearance would work just as well. After all, no one voluntarily vanished into thin air.

She could still hear her ex-husband's voice as the small kitchen television came to life. *Do we really need to watch this crap before I've even had breakfast?*

After several reassuring sips of a freshly-brewed Morning Blend, Maggie lowered the volume and grabbed her cell phone. Now that she and Todd were divorced, she could watch whatever she wanted, whenever she wanted. Still, she had no interest in listening to his snarky remarks if he heard the ominous narration of her show in the background. *You'll never change, will you?*

A familiar queasiness bubbled up in her stomach. The last thing Maggie wanted to do was start the day talking to her ex. Unfortunately, this morning she didn't have a choice.

Todd always had a way of making Maggie feel like she was the one who was being unreasonable. Hers was a simple request, but he seemed to derive pleasure in making things more complicated than they needed to be.

After several minutes of going back and forth with him, Maggie slammed her mug down against the granite counter. She swore under her breath as the contents sloshed up the sides and over the lip. There should be a rule about not talking to an ex before finishing a full cup of coffee.

"Why are you making this so hard?" she asked, her teeth starting to ache from grinding them so hard. "I just need to make sure you can pick up Jake later after his soccer game. We start deliberating today, and I have no idea how late it will go or when the judge will let us leave."

"I still don't understand how you managed to get picked for a trial." The puff of air Todd released had an undercurrent of disgust. "They ask if you think you can be impartial, and you say 'no.' It's that simple. Not to mention, you have a kid that depends on you. That's an automatic hall pass during jury duty. Not sure how you could have possibly screwed it up."

It had been four months since their divorce was final. Maggie had gotten used to walking on eggshells during her marriage, her ex berating her for making even the simplest mistakes.

She could still remember the time she'd accidentally bought the wrong pretzels. It wasn't like Todd went grocery shopping—ever. When he pulled the bag from the pantry, his face had contorted with disgust as if he were holding a bag of vomit. *Unsalted? Nobody eats unsalted pretzels.* Obviously, some people liked them, or the store wouldn't sell them. Maggie didn't say that out loud. Instead, she stammered an apology and admitted she'd accidentally picked up the wrong ones. He rolled his eyes as if she were hopeless and released an overly dramatic sigh. *I have no idea why I'm even surprised anymore.*

Todd now had to buy his own damn pretzels, but he hadn't stopped trying to make Maggie feel like she couldn't do anything right. She'd been naïve to think a legal document would put an end to that.

"It's like you wanted to get chosen," he said, making no attempt to hide his annoyance that her being selected for a trial was now a predicament thrust upon him.

The truth was, Maggie had felt a slight twinge of anticipation when she'd brought in the mail and found the official-looking postcard. A chance to escape her tedious job at the accounting firm, even for a day? Sign her up. She'd secretly been thrilled when she was chosen for the two-week murder trial, but admit that to her ex-husband? No way.

"I didn't try to get chosen, Todd." She did her best to sound convincing. "I just answered the lawyers' questions honestly, like they make you solemnly swear you'll do." Despite the freezing cold courtroom, Maggie had found herself sweating as the lawyers grilled the potential jurors. She had almost felt like she was the one on trial.

"Come on, give me a break. Anyone with half a brain knows what to say to get out of it. Nobody actually wants to serve. Most of the people I know toss their summons in the trash when they get it."

She pinched the bridge of her nose and drew in a deep breath. "It's illegal to not appear as ordered. It says so right on the card they send you."

Her ex let out an obnoxious snort. "Right. I hear there's a special wing at the prison for the people who pitched their jury duty summons. Besides, I'll bet you were the first one to raise your hand when you heard it was a first-degree murder case."

Maggie dug her fingertips into her temple and closed her eyes before responding. "I didn't just raise my hand and volunteer. It doesn't work like that." Todd would know how the process worked if he'd ever actually showed up when he was summoned.

But her ex-husband wasn't entirely wrong about her enthusi-asm. When they'd passed out the questionnaire to the potential jurors, a wave of adrenaline had run through her when she real-ized the defendant had been charged with premeditated murder. The form asked if committing to a trial expected to last two weeks would present a hardship. It was a no-brainer. Maggie spent more time agonizing most days over what to have for lunch. With a giddy flourish, she had checked the *no* box.

She'd only been called for jury duty once before. That time she'd sat in a large auditorium for most of the day before finally being sent home, her obligation fulfilled.

This time they'd called her juror number, and there was no way Maggie was going to turn down the chance to be part of a real-life murder case. Her job was required by law to allow her the time off to serve—and pay her. A win all the way around. The only flaw in her plan had been thinking Todd would help with their son without complaining. She should have known better.

She lifted her cup to her lips, took a sip, and cringed. Her coffee was cold. This conversation should have been short and sweet, but Todd never made anything easy.

"Well, I don't regret being selected," she said, and she meant it. "The process is fascinating and it's way more exciting than going to the office."

Not to mention, it had given Maggie a sense of satisfaction to imagine her boss trying to manage without her. Harrison Korman could be demanding. Rude even.

But in court? As a member of the jury, she felt respected. Important.

At first, the reverence had caught her off-guard. She wasn't used to being treated that way. Not by her ex-husband. Not by her boss.

"It's no wonder you're having a great time." There was a

distasteful twinge in Todd's voice. "It's like you're living in one of those damn murder shows you're always watching. But this trial isn't a television show to entertain you. Someone was killed, and if that brings excitement into your meager existence, you need to work on getting yourself a life you don't hate so much. Look for a new job. Try to meet someone. Maybe you can pull it together, so you don't wind up single for the rest of your life." He paused. "You should try one of those dating sites for older women."

Maggie snorted mid-sip, and coffee dribbled down her chin. Of all the condescending nerve. Forty-four wasn't that old.

She reached for a paper towel and pressed her lips together tightly. There was no way she'd dignify his comment with a response. She could find someone new if she wanted, which she didn't. Besides, after sixteen years of marriage, it wasn't like she even knew how to date anymore.

Maggie paced back and forth in front of the counter as she nibbled on her thumbnail. They'd gone in circles, and she still didn't have the answer she needed. "Listen, I just need to know. Can you pick up Jake tonight or not?"

Todd heaved an exasperated sigh. "I have an important meeting at four, but I guess I have no choice but to figure something out, right? You're supposed to have primary custody, you know. It's not even my day."

Maggie shook her head in disgust. Most divorced fathers would fall over themselves for extra time with their kids. Unfortunately, she hadn't been smart enough to marry one of those men. Maybe if she had, she wouldn't be divorced.

She rubbed the back of her neck. Todd knew she had no other options, and still, he put her through this. Jake was now in a new school district, so it wasn't even like she knew any of the other parents to ask for a favor.

She threw up a hand and used it to jab at the air in frustration. "What do you want me to do? Tell the judge I need to leave because my ex can't be bothered to pick up his son? All because it's not his day?"

"Calm. Down." Todd said each word slowly and succinctly in that demoralizing way he had that made Maggie's insides boil. "I'm just trying to figure out why I write that big check every month when I always need to bail you out."

He wasn't always bailing her out, and her child support wasn't nearly as substantial as he liked to make it sound to her and anyone who'd listen. Todd had always been cheap throughout their marriage—an absolute penny pincher. Maggie imagined the physical pain it caused him to have to write that check to her every month. It was her one small victory in the divorce.

But then, as if he could see her lips twitch with the hint of a smile, he slammed his imaginary sledgehammer down on her silent gloating. "I suppose Stephanie might be able to pick him up. If she doesn't have a showing, that is."

Maggie's entire body stiffened. *Stephanie.* Big boobs, tiny waist, perfectly manicured nails. A wildly successful real estate agent. His excuse for their divorce grinned at her from bus shelters, benches, and even a freaking billboard. Maggie now had to take a longer route to work just to avoid his girlfriend staring at her. The woman smiled like she was in a damn toothpaste ad.

Maggie desperately wished she had the luxury of pushing back on getting Stephanie involved but she was desperate. There was no one else.

When Jake was in first grade, Todd's job had transferred him to Florida. With visions of palm trees dancing in her head, Maggie had tossed their snow gear, packed up the house, and moved over eleven hundred miles from her friends and family.

She'd never had a reliable support system here. People came

and went. As soon as she made a friend, the next thing she knew, they'd announce they were moving. She'd finally stopped trying.

"That would be great if Stephanie could pick him up," Maggie said in as sweet a voice as she could muster without choking. "She can just drop Jake off at the apartment. I'm sure I won't be home that late."

Todd groaned, just in case his ex-wife didn't comprehend the inconvenience she was inflicting on him. Jake was their son, but the divorce hadn't changed a thing. Any issues were hers to solve. Even more so now than when they were married. In his mind, the check he wrote Maggie financed that scenario. "Fine," he said, dragging the word out so she'd know he was aggravated. "I'll take care of it." Then, he added under his breath, "Just like I always do."

As Jake made his way into the kitchen, Maggie bit back the retort on the tip of her tongue. She tried to keep him out of her battles with his dad. The divorce wasn't his fault. It wasn't hers either.

Jake rubbed his eyes and released a loud audible yawn. After a growth spurt the summer before, her son now stood several inches taller than her. He had an athlete's lean, muscular body and a voice that had deepened overnight. He wasn't quite a man yet, but as much as she hated to admit it, her little boy was gone.

"Okay, thanks, I appreciate it." Maggie's now cheerful tone was a cover for the burning in the pit of her stomach that always accompanied conversations with her ex. "I'll let Jake know you'll text him later to work out the details."

She jabbed at the button to end the call and reached into the cabinet for the industrial-sized bottle of Excedrin. First thing in the morning and her head already throbbed.

"Dad?" Jake asked. Without waiting for a response, he pulled open the refrigerator door and stared blankly at the empty shelves.

"Yeah. You hungry? You want some breakfast?"

He turned and winced at the silver foil package Maggie had pulled from the pantry. "A Pop-Tart? No, thanks."

"I'm sorry. I haven't had time to get to the grocery store. With any luck, the trial will be over today, and life will go back to normal." Not that normal was much better, but they both pretended it was.

Maggie wasn't nearly as picky as her son. She broke off a piece of the pastry and popped it in her mouth.

Jake wrinkled his nose as he watched her. "You're supposed to toast that, you know."

"It's fine just the way it is." She reached for the dregs of her ice-cold coffee and washed it down.

"Better you than me." Jake yawned again as he stretched his arms above his head. "So, do you know which way you're going to vote?"

Maggie spun around. "What?"

"The trial. Do you think he did it?"

"Oh. You know I can't talk about it until it's over." But oh, how she wanted to. It was driving Maggie crazy to keep it bottled up inside. "Every day, the judge makes us solemnly swear we won't share anything about the case. Even with our families." She tipped her head back and swallowed the last sip of her coffee. "We can't even talk about it amongst ourselves until we're allowed to deliberate. At this point, I have no idea what the other jurors are thinking. But I know which way I'm voting."

"Maybe everyone will agree, and you'll be done early. You're going to be able to pick me up after my game later, right?"

"That's why I was on the phone with your dad. We're deliberating today, so I have no idea if I'll finish early enough to make it from the courthouse on time. Your father said he'd try to get you, but he has a late afternoon meeting. If he can't make it, he'll ask—he'll send Stephanie." Maggie worked to veil her disgust at having to say the woman's name out loud. "But if she does pick you up, she'll just drop you off here."

When she spoke with one of her co-workers about her ex-husband's girlfriend, they referred to her as the home-wrecking Barbie doll bimbo. It wasn't necessarily a fair assessment. Maybe the Barbie doll part, but Maggie's marriage was a pile of rubble long before Stephanie and her skin-tight workout gear sashayed into Todd's spin class.

Jake poured the last of the orange juice into a glass, slugged it down, and carefully set the glass on top of a teetering pile of plates in the kitchen sink. "Okay, that works. The new car she got is lit."

"Lit? That means you like it, right?"

"Very good, Mom." Her son flashed her an amused smile. "But yeah, Stephanie always lets me put the top down and blast whatever I want on the radio."

Maggie flinched as if he'd hit her. A little loyalty. Was that too much to ask for from the child who'd put her through twenty excruciating hours of labor and caused her to gain fifty pounds during her pregnancy?

Almost fifteen years later and she'd never been able to lose the extra weight. It had stuck around on her middle and slipped down to her legs, like a bad houseguest who moves into the spare room and then takes over the entire house. If she did decide to date, she'd need a complete overhaul. Not that Maggie could ever hope to look like Stephanie, no matter what she did. The woman didn't have an ounce of fat on her.

"Sorry, Mom," Jake said as he noted the pained expression on her face. "It's just, you always listen to those true-crime podcasts in your car. We never play music."

"Not to mention, I don't have a brand-new BMW."

Her son lifted one shoulder in an apologetic shrug. "Right."

"I get it." *Mom was the boring old sedan. Stephanie was the new flashy and expensive convertible.* "Come on. I'll take you to school on my way to the courthouse. If we leave now, we can hit a drive-through on the way and get you some breakfast." She ruffled her teenager's hair, and a smile flickered on her lips. "No podcast this morning. I'll even let you pick a radio station." She grabbed her purse from the back of the kitchen chair. "But let's go. I can't be late for jury duty. Especially today."

Jake used his fingers to comb his wavy brown hair back into place. "You're going like that?"

Maggie bristled at his words, even though her son's tone was entirely different than her ex-husband's. He seemed amused.

She stared at him, her expression guarded. "Yeah, why?"

Her son used his index finger to draw a circle in front of her. "You might want to check out your shirt."

Maggie stepped into the small bathroom off the kitchen and stared into the mirror. Blotches of coffee had dotted a trail down the front of her blouse.

"Oh, come on. Really?" She reached for the hand towel, ran it under the faucet, and dabbed at the stains. It only made them worse. Maggie let out an exasperated groan.

Laundry had fallen off her radar that week. She'd already struggled that morning to find something that not only fit her but was appropriate for court.

Maggie scrutinized her reflection, and the crease between her poorly groomed eyebrows deepened. Todd was right. She needed to make changes or growing old alone was a strong possibility.

She fished the car keys out of her purse and tossed them to Jake. "Here. Go find a radio station while I find another shirt to wear. I'll be right out."

She hurried to her bedroom in search of something—

anything—that might fit. As she changed, she cursed Todd under her breath. They were divorced, yet she was still letting him ruin her morning.

Maggie had a verdict to get to, and she couldn't wait to see the look on the defendant's face when they read it.

2

———

The twelve jurors filed silently out of the courtroom with their order from the judge to begin deliberations. Once in the jury room, there was a chorus of conversation. A sense of freedom. They were finally allowed to discuss the case.

"Hey, everybody, hang on," Kim said, like a mother hen reeling in her chicks. From the start, she had unofficially put herself in charge of the other jurors. As she'd been quick to remind them numerous times over the last two weeks, she'd served on a jury before. It had been a drug case, not murder. Still, she was the only one who'd been seated on a criminal trial.

"We should start by appointing the jury foreman—or fore*person*." She tucked her blond hair behind her ear and gave the group a knowing smile. "I'll volunteer unless someone objects."

Maggie bit her bottom lip and glanced around the room. No one protested. Most of the jurors were ready for the trial to be over so they could return to their lives. When the alternates were dismissed, a few had even grumbled with jealousy.

Kim rubbed her hands together as if she was ready to get

started. "Okay, that's settled then. How about we take an anonymous poll first to see where we're at." She tore a sheet from her notebook and ripped it into twelve small pieces. "Just write guilty or not guilty," she said as she distributed the slips of paper.

"What if you're still not sure," one of the jurors asked as her shoulders lifted. Jade was the youngest of the group. Only twenty years old. She couldn't even drink yet, but the first jury duty notice she'd ever received had landed her on a murder trial.

Kim's brow wrinkled as if she hadn't considered that anyone would still be unsure. "I guess if you don't know which way you want to vote yet, write undecided." She dumped sugar packets from a Styrofoam bowl she found beside the coffee machine and set the empty bowl in the middle of the table. "Toss it in here when you're done."

Maggie wrote guilty in all capital letters, folded her slip of paper, and threw it in with the others.

Kim's gaze drifted around the table. "That's all of them?" When no one spoke up, she pulled the bowl toward her and read the first vote. "Not guilty." She slid the paper off to the side and unfolded the next one. "Another not guilty." She set the second slip on top of the first and reached for another. "Undecided." When all the votes had been read, she tallied them up. "Eight not guilty, three undecideds, and one guilty."

As a collective gaze drifted around the room to determine who was responsible for the lone guilty vote, Maggie felt sweat coasting down her back. How could she be the only one who saw the truth?

Kim scooted to the edge of her seat and rested her forearms on the table. "Okay, let's get started. I don't know about all of you, but I need to get this wrapped up today. My daughter has a dance recital tomorrow, and I intend to be there." She placed her palm over her chest. "I don't have any issue sharing what I wrote.

I'm one of the not-guilty votes. As far as I'm concerned, the prosecution didn't prove the defendant killed her. Not beyond a reasonable doubt anyway."

Maggie's eyes narrowed. "But do you believe he did it?"

Kim shrugged, then tossed her hands in the air as if what she thought really didn't matter. "I think it's *possible*. But that's not enough. The instructions from the judge were clear. We need to believe the prosecution proved their case beyond *all* reasonable doubt."

A few of the other jurors nodded in agreement.

"The defense attorney said as much in her closing argument." Isaac, a former engineer who was now retired, had been seated in front of Maggie. During the trial, she watched him fill the pages of the notebook they'd been given with the smallest print she'd ever seen. He put on his glasses and read what he'd written. "If we have *any* reason to doubt *anything* the prosecution presented, that's *reasonable doubt,* and we need to vote *not guilty*." He stressed certain words the same way the defendant's lawyer had when she recited them for the jury.

One of the jurors leaned forward, a hesitant look on her face. Joanne appeared to be in her forties, and she'd had the seat next to Maggie in the jury box. "Well, I was one of the undecided votes, but if that's the case—"

"Don't we need to at least go through the evidence?" Maggie asked. She'd never been part of a deliberation before, but she was sure they needed to take a methodical approach if they were going to arrive at a final verdict.

"We absolutely do." Isaac's tone was matter-of-fact. "Especially since we're not all in agreement at this point." He flipped to the first page of his notes. "Maybe we start at the beginning and list the evidence the prosecution presented that was meant to convince us he did it. Then we can decide as a group if they succeeded."

Kim's gaze drifted around the table until it landed on Maggie as if she'd already decided the guilty vote was hers. Her eyebrows lifted. "That work?"

Maggie squirmed uncomfortably in her seat and nodded.

"Fabulous." She aimed her chin at the whiteboard on the wall. "Why don't you take notes?"

"Me?" Maggie's pulse kicked up a notch. The last thing she wanted was to be on display, the buttons on her too-small blouse straining across her chest.

Kim fought a smile. "Why not you?" She clearly knew whose vote had to be turned so they could all go home.

Maggie hesitated, then stood and trudged to the board. After wiping her sweaty hands on her pants, she picked up a marker. She put her back to the room, convinced the heat on her cheeks had colored her face beet red.

"Maybe we should start with a timeline?" one of the jurors said. "You know, for the day of the murder. Then we could compare it to the timeline they presented for the defendant."

Kim gave a quick nod. "Good idea."

Maggie wrote the date of the murder on the board. Next to November second, she added Monday in parentheses. She swallowed hard and then turned to face the group. "Should we start with Grace Hutchinson picking up dinner?"

When she saw several nods, she drew a long line and added a tic on the left side. Underneath it, she wrote 6:00 p.m. "From the surveillance video at the sushi place and the receipt and bag found in the victim's trash, we know she picked up food from Asia Moon about six o'clock the night she was killed." Now in her true-crime element, Maggie's shoulders lowered, her breathing coming at a more comfortable pace.

Kim eyed the other jurors. "Anyone dispute that?"

"She lived less than ten minutes from the restaurant, so we can assume she arrived home by 6:10 p.m." Maggie held the marker in the air, prepared to add the additional observation to the timeline.

"Well, there's no proof that's when she got home." Pablo, a balding man in his thirties, had expressed his aggravation daily about his need to be there. During jury selection, he'd told the judge he installed tile for a living. *If I don't work, I don't get paid.* Much to his annoyance, he'd been selected anyway, going so far as to swear loudly under his breath when the judge announced his juror number.

"Why does it matter what time she got home?" Jade shifted in her seat to face him. "We know she wasn't killed that early because she called the new guy she was dating at 7:15 p.m."

"Ron Brookins," Maggie said to provide clarification. He'd testified, clearly nervous when he first took the stand. He'd stammered a bit at the beginning until he got more comfortable, but Maggie had found him a reliable witness. She turned toward the whiteboard and added his call to the timeline.

Joanne glanced around the table. "And he testified that when they spoke, Grace told him she'd picked up sushi, so that confirms what she had for dinner."

Pablo's annoyed sigh was far louder than necessary. "Which we already knew because of the surveillance footage and the receipt in the trash."

Kim raised an eyebrow at his condescending tone but let it go. "Okay, so we know what the victim had for dinner, and we know all is still well at 7:15 p.m. because of the call to Ron, the new boyfriend."

With a sidewards glance in Pablo's direction, Jade spoke up again. "Grace also called her sister, Pam, at 7:34 p.m. the night she was killed."

One of the jurors looked confused as she paged through her notebook. "I thought she called her sister the night *before* she was murdered? Wouldn't that have been Sunday night?"

"She did call Pam on Sunday, but she also called Monday night." Jade's voice was firm.

The other juror nodded. "Oh, right, Sunday was that cryptic voicemail Grace left that something freaked her out. Then the next night she was dead."

"Exactly," Jade said with a nod. "The weird voicemail was Sunday. Then they played phone tag on Monday about whether Pam could go to dinner that night. She couldn't because she already had plans, so she left Grace a message asking if they could go the next night instead. That's why Grace called her sister back Monday night. To say that dinner on Tuesday would be fine." She gestured at Maggie to add the call to the timeline, looking pleased with herself for contributing to the deliberation process.

Pablo snorted. "That didn't work out so well, now did it? Getting murdered pretty much makes you unavailable for dinner."

"C'mon, really?" Kim shot him a look of disgust. "So, Grace called Pam to tell her they could go to dinner on Tuesday, and they'd talk then. So, we're now at 7:34 p.m. on Monday. The victim is still alive and well and making phone calls." She aimed her attention at Pablo. Her face hardened as if she dared him to comment again.

"That was the last time Grace's phone was used." Isaac consulted his notebook. "She plugged it in to charge at 7:37 p.m."

Another juror nodded. "The new boyfriend testified that he called her to say goodnight at 9:45 p.m., and she didn't answer his call."

Maggie made two additional notations on the timeline. *7:37 p.m. - phone on the charger. 9:45 p.m. - missed call from Ron.*

Kim skimmed her notes and then leaned back in her chair. "There was testimony that she powered on her laptop at 7:40 p.m. and checked her personal email. Then at 7:49 p.m., she logged into a website to buy some candles but never completed the purchase."

"And after 8:02 p.m., there was no more activity on her computer," Isaac said. "I think that's important to add."

Maggie used the heel of her hand to erase the time of Ron's missed call so she could make additional room. She added three more tics and wrote in the times and explanations for Grace's laptop turning on, the visit to the candle website, and the last time activity on her computer was recorded. She then re-wrote the missed call at the end.

Kim stared up at the board and studied it for a moment. "If we look at the timeline, it seems pretty obvious Grace was killed at some point between the time she stopped using her computer and 9:45 p.m. when she didn't answer the boyfriend's call."

"Unless she just didn't feel like talking to him." Pablo smirked as if he knew he was just trying to be difficult. "Or maybe she turned the ringer off and didn't hear the phone. We don't know."

Kim released a heavy sigh, but Jade gave a hesitant head bob as her gaze drifted around the table. "He's right, you know. We don't know for sure she didn't answer because she was already dead."

An older woman, who'd spent most of their downtime in the jury room reading romance novels, piped in. "Well, we heard from her co-worker—the one who found the body. She testified Grace was always at work by nine but didn't show up Tuesday morning." She eyed Pablo. "Grace didn't answer any of her calls either, which is why she got worried and went to the house." She pushed her novel aside and turned to a page in her notebook. "She called 911 at 12:35 p.m. on Tuesday." They'd all heard the painful call the co-worker had made. "The doctor who did the autopsy testified Grace had been dead for twelve to eighteen hours."

"And what about the testimony about the contents of the victim's stomach?" Isaac asked. "The ME testified she'd most likely eaten the sushi an hour or two before her death. That narrows it down considerably."

Jade shrugged. "We know Grace was home by 6:10 or so, but who knows if she ate right away?"

Isaac flipped to another page in his notebook. "The medical examiner listed her approximate time of death to be between 7:30 p.m. and 9:30 p.m."

Pablo rolled his eyes. "She logged onto her computer at seven-forty, so only a moron would say she could have been dead at seven-thirty."

The older man leaned forward to glare at Pablo from across the table. "*Obviously*, and I'm not a moron. I'm just reiterating—"

"What if the killer used Grace's computer?" Maggie cut in before the two men went to blows. It wouldn't necessarily back up her theory that the defendant was responsible for the murder, but she wanted to show Pablo—and the rest of them—that things might not always be what they seemed.

Kim shifted in her seat to face Maggie, an amused expression on her face. "You think the killer decided to shop for candles before he hightailed it out of there?"

Maggie's cheeks tingled as the group waited for her response. "I'm just saying we should keep an open mind. I saw this show once, and that's exactly what the murderer did. He wanted it to look like the victim was still alive, so he used her computer to order something online. He figured that would push the time of her murder back so he could create an alibi." She shifted her weight from one foot to the other as they all stared at her. "I mean, think about it. How many boyfriends or husband kill their significant other but then use their phone to make it seem like she's still alive? They send themselves texts to make it appear they're still communicating even though their wife or girlfriend is already dead. I mean, look at the case of Gabby Petito."

Pablo scowled and threw up his hands. "Who?"

Maggie's head jerked back. But seriously, did he live under a rock?

Before she could answer, one of the female jurors spoke up. "Her boyfriend killed her and then used her phone to send messages to her parents, so they'd think she was okay. Which she wasn't."

"Oh, I did hear about that." Jade winced. "It was really sad. She was so pretty."

Kim thumped her hands against the table to get everyone's attention. "Okay, let's circle back to our case unless you all want to be here longer than necessary. I'd really like to wrap this up today." She pressed her hand against her forehead. "So, where were we? Oh, right." A slight smirk lifted her lips. "Does anyone else think the killer used Grace's computer to shop for candles?"

Maggie's shoulders tensed as the group collectively shook their heads. They'd all missed her point. "That's fine. I was just putting it out there. Sometimes what appears—"

Kim cut her off and gestured at the whiteboard. "That's everything for Grace's night. Draw a second timeline under- neath hers, and we'll look at what was presented about the defendant's activities the night of the murder. What did we learn about Doyle Riggs's whereabouts?"

Jade flipped through the pages in her notebook, then glanced up. "He said he got home from work around 6:45 p.m., but we didn't hear from any witnesses to confirm that."

"But we heard from the guy who delivered the pizza to his house, and Doyle was there to accept it," the older woman said.

Isaac consulted his notes. "That was at 7:40 p.m. So, we know the defendant was home by then."

"What does it matter?" Pablo eyed Jade. "Look at the timeline. The victim was still alive at that point." He shot Maggie an amused glance. "Of course, that's if her killer wasn't actually the one doing a little candle shopping. You know, maybe he was looking for a nice floral scent for his bathroom."

Isaac's eyebrows lifted. His gaze bounced between Pablo and Maggie as he waited to see if she'd respond.

Instead, she stood rigid at the whiteboard, her lips pressed together to prevent anything impulsive from slipping out. Pablo didn't need to believe what she'd mentioned was a possibility, but there was no need to be a jerk about it.

Kim disregarded his comment as if he were a bully harassing the other children on the playground. Maggie could imagine her advising her own kids. *Just ignore him, and he'll realize he can't get to you.* "Let's add the pizza delivery to Doyle's timeline." Kim's gaze drifted around the table, skipping over Pablo. "What else do we have to add?"

Joanne spoke up. "There was the email. The one to his brother at 8:15 p.m."

Ed, a studious-looking man with glasses, had been relatively quiet. He cleared his throat. "The IT guy for the prosecution testified it wasn't actually sent at that time. The defendant sent it earlier in the day but delayed the delivery until 8:15 p.m."

"Which he explained on the stand," Joanne said. "He wanted his brother to read the article after the football game started."

Maggie cocked her head. "Or he wanted it to look like he was home at that time. Maybe it was deliberate to try to establish an alibi."

"That's possible, but people do it more than you'd think," Ed said. "I do it all the time with my emails at work. Especially if someone's on vacation. I delay the delivery of my message until the morning they get back. That way, my email is sitting at the top of their inbox instead of being buried in the middle of a week's worth of messages."

One of the other jurors leaned forward, his forearms on the table. "That's brilliant. Will you show me how to do that?"

Ed shrugged. "Sure, all you do is—"

Kim clapped her hands. "Maybe you two could discuss email tips and tricks over lunch so we can keep going." She gave Maggie a curt nod. "I think we leave the email off the timeline since there's no proof Doyle was home when it was sent."

"What about the call to his partner, the guy he owns the body shop with?" Jade glanced down at her notes. "Manny Perez."

Kim nodded. "Right. What time was that?"

Jade referred back to her notebook. "It was at 9:20 p.m. Doyle was definitely home when he made that call."

"The call ... it's coming from inside the house. Oh, no." Pablo's hands flew to each side of his face. "Of course he was home. His phone pinged off the cell tower by his house the entire night."

"The prosecution really didn't show us any evidence he ever left," the older woman said as she bobbed her head in agreement. "His phone didn't move, and there's no surveillance footage of him leaving once he was home from work."

"Don't you think it's odd there were no cameras in the victim's neighborhood?" Joanne asked, a crease between her eyebrows. "Or in Doyle's?"

Maggie shook her head. "We don't know there weren't any. We only know we didn't see any footage."

"Everybody has a camera on their house these days," Pablo said. "It's obvious they couldn't locate anyone with video that showed Doyle's truck leaving his house or showing up at the victim's or we would have seen it. They didn't find anything because, oh, wait, *he wasn't there.*"

"Let's finish the timelines, and we'll come back to that." Kim dipped her chin at Maggie. "Go ahead and add the call he made to his partner. What about the neighbor walking his dog who had a conversation with the defendant?" She glanced around the table as she looked for confirmation. "What time was that?"

Several jurors flipped through their notebooks.

Isaac came up with the answer first. "It was 10:25 p.m."

The older woman spoke up. "When Doyle testified, he said he took out his trash and spoke to the guy who lived across the street who was out with his dog. The neighbor gave the same approximate time."

"Okay, so there's no conflict there." Kim sounded relieved. She gestured for Maggie to add their encounter in the street to the timeline. "So, let's look at the amount of time Doyle doesn't have an alibi that could be corroborated. We're looking at the window between the pizza delivery at 7:40 p.m. and the phone call to his partner at 9:20 p.m." She glanced around the table. "What's that? A little more than an hour and a half?"

"Grace only lived about thirty minutes away." Maggie capped the marker and returned to her seat, grateful to be out of the spotlight. "He would have had plenty of time to get to her house and back."

Pablo groaned. "Did you miss the part where the guy told us his phone didn't ping anywhere near the victim's house that night? Or near anyone's house but his own? That's what sealed the deal for me. My man's innocent."

Maggie stared at him incredulously, shocked she even had to make this point. "If he was planning to murder someone, do you really think he would have brought his phone? He'd know it could track him." Her eyes narrowed as she challenged Pablo. "Don't you think *your man* would be smarter than that?"

"But the pings go a long way toward suggesting he was home," the older woman said. "There's not a shred of evidence he went out without it. Not to mention, the neighbor said his truck was in the driveway all night."

"But the prosecutor did get him to admit that it's possible Doyle could have gone out and he didn't notice." Maggie crossed her arms tight against her chest. "It's not like he spent the entire night staring out his window at his neighbor's driveway. Besides, if Doyle didn't kill Grace, how did he end up with the football jersey from her house?"

"He explained that on the stand," Jade said. "He bought another one because he didn't want to go through the hassle of getting his back after she broke up with him."

When another juror nodded in agreement, Maggie felt a twinge of defeat. She could see where this was heading.

Were they all under Doyle's spell? She couldn't deny he was a good-looking man, and he'd dressed the part, showing up for court each day in a well-cut suit and tie. He owned a body shop. Was his court attire borrowed? Rented? His defense attorney was certainly trying to present a much different picture. Even his dark hair had been cut to a more conservative length.

Doyle Riggs didn't look anything like the mug shot taken when he was arrested, but Maggie could see where both looks would appeal to some of the female jurors. Still, this wasn't a dating show. It was a murder trial.

Before his attorney called him to the stand, she'd reminded the jury he wasn't required to testify. No, Doyle Riggs did not have to take the stand, she told them in a solemn voice, but her client had insisted. He wanted to tell them all the truth. It had been all Maggie could do to not snort in disgust.

She couldn't argue that Doyle had put on quite the show as his lawyer lobbed questions at him. He admitted he'd been disappointed when Grace broke up with him but claimed that didn't mean he wanted anything bad to happen to her. At one point, he even seemed to cry, which seemed pre-planned and not at all spontaneous. Maggie wasn't sure there were even tears.

Of course, his lawyer ended with the question everyone

wanted answered. "Did you have anything to do with Grace Hutchinson's death?"

Doyle Riggs's gaze had drifted across the jury box as he made earnest eye contact with each juror. "Absolutely not." The words came out of his mouth slowly and firmly as if he was offended he even had to utter them.

Maggie had watched enough true crime cases to see through the prep work done by his attorney, but clearly, some of the jurors had fallen for it.

"I thought we were going to go through the evidence," Isaac said. "What about that partial boot print they found in her blood at the scene?"

"And they did find a credit card charge that showed the defendant owned the same ones," Jade said, her eyebrows raised. "They didn't turn up when they searched his house like maybe he got rid of them."

Pablo huffed. "They couldn't even prove the print came from a boot that was his size. Besides, it's not surprising he'd have a pair of those. He works in a body shop, remember? Nearly every guy who works at a blue-collar job wears those boots. I even owned the exact same ones at one point." He then gave an exaggerated gasp as his hands flew to his chest. "Maybe I'm the killer."

Kim rubbed her temple and drew in a deep breath. "Can we try to stay focused? Let's take each witness in the order they testified, starting with the sister and that voicemail Grace left her the night before she was killed." She stood. "I'll take notes."

When there was no more room to write on the whiteboard, they asked to break for lunch. After they returned, they picked up where they'd left off.

Two hours later, they took another poll. This time all the slips of paper were in one pile except for one—Maggie's.

She wasn't sure why she'd shielded her vote as she wrote. It was no secret she hadn't been swayed.

Kim pressed her lips together and directed her attention across the table. "Are you willing to die on this hill, Maggie? Hang the jury? Make them retry the case?"

"I just—I watch a ton of true crime." Her face grew hot. "Sometimes, these killers are smart. They know what it takes to make it look like they're innocent."

"But you have no *proof* of that." Kim's tone indicated she was becoming exasperated. "They don't even have a real motive. The prosecution claimed he killed her because he was jealous she was dating someone new, but where's the evidence?"

Jade chimed in. "Even her sister, Pam, testified Grace didn't think Doyle wasn't that upset about the breakup."

Kim set her elbows on the table and clasped her hands tightly together in front of her. "Our instructions clearly state we need to determine our verdict based on the evidence they've presented to us. We can't determine our verdict based on what you think could have happened because you saw it in some true-crime show." Her gaze drifted around the table. "To find him guilty, all twelve of us need to believe beyond all reasonable doubt that there's no possible scenario other than Doyle Riggs killed Grace Hutchinson. Is it possible he killed her?" One of her shoulders hitched up in a non-committal shrug. "Sure, it is."

Maggie threw up her hands. "So, why—"

"Stop." Kim leaned in across the table. "A not-guilty verdict doesn't necessarily mean he didn't do it." Her voice was calm but firm. "It only means the prosecution didn't meet their burden to prove it beyond all reasonable doubt."

"C'mon, really?" Pablo asked, a scowl on his face. "He didn't kill her. The dude never even left his house that night."

Maggie's throat tightened. "Just because his phone pinged from his house doesn't mean *he* was there."

Jade tried to reason with her. "Right. But he called his partner—"

"But not until nine-twenty. He had plenty of time—"

The older woman spoke up. "His partner testified that they talked about some of the big plays from the football game. Are we supposed to accept he lied on the stand?"

Joanne nodded. "The neighbor said the same thing. Doyle was talking about the game with him, too."

"Thank you." Pablo bowed to her, then turned his attention back to Maggie. "How could Doyle have known what happened during the game if he wasn't home to watch it?"

"I don't know." She groaned in frustration. "Couldn't he have listened to it on the radio? I'm not really a sports person."

Kim drew in a deep breath. "Maggie, you're grasping at straws. Can you honestly say the prosecution gave you enough evidence to paint an indisputable picture of his guilt? There's no other possibility because you know exactly what happened?"

"Well, of course not. I wasn't there. None of us were."

"There wasn't a shred of evidence in the defendant's truck," Isaac said.

Maggie was beginning to feel attacked. "I know, but—"

Kim held up her hand to cut her off. "Doyle could have used another vehicle. Someone else's gun. We all heard the points you tried to make, but the problem with your version of events is that it's based on assumptions. There's no proof to back any of it up. I know you watch a lot of true crime, but this isn't a television show. It's a legal proceeding. And I'm sorry, but the prosecution didn't convince me that the only possible scenario is that Doyle Riggs killed Grace Hutchinson. Did he care that she was dating someone new? Maybe. Who knows? What I do know is there's no possible way we can send a man to prison for the rest of his life based on what you *think* might have happened."

There were nods from the other jurors.

"And if we're following the letter of the law, we're not supposed to," Kim said softly. "You can still believe he killed her, and that's fine. But the only question that matters is if the prosecution proved it beyond all reasonable doubt. Can you really say you connected the dots they gave you, and they led to no other possibility?"

Maggie sighed. She was sure Doyle was guilty. Still, she was beginning to understand what Kim was trying to say.

"If we're going to follow the judge's instructions, we need to return a not-guilty verdict. Really, it's the only choice the prosecution left us with." Kim shrugged. "If you're unhappy with the outcome of the case, blame them."

Maggie looked around the table. It was written on their faces that the rest of the jurors agreed with her.

"But it's up to you." Kim crossed her arms in front of her on the table. "We can tell the judge we couldn't reach a unanimous verdict. The trial will end with a hung jury, and they'll have to go through the whole thing all over. Grace's sister will have to testify. Cry again on the stand. Her parents will have to come every day to hear all the gory details for a second time. See the photos from the crime scene. Hear about their daughter's autopsy." Kim paused to let the reality sink in. "Or we can tell them we have a decision, and we can all go home." Her head cocked to one side. "So, what's it going to be?"

Maggie heaved a deep sigh and glanced up at the clock on the wall. She wasn't going to convince any of them to see it her way, but if she changed her vote, she might be able to make Jake's soccer game.

3

Maggie lifted her hand to her forehead and shielded her eyes from the late afternoon sun. As she stared down at the soccer field, her shoulders lowered in relief. She'd made it in time. She tucked her phone inside her purse and set off down the path.

There were a respectable number of parents watching the game from the bleachers. Didn't people work? Maggie squinted and looked for a spot where she could slide in unnoticed. There was lots of space in the second row next to a woman sitting by herself. Her gaze was fixed on the field, and she seemed engrossed in the game. Perfect.

Maggie slipped onto the bleachers, then glanced over to see if she'd been noticed. Her stomach sank when the woman's attention shifted in her direction. She offered Maggie a warm smile, then slid down until she sat right beside her.

"Hey, I'm Robin. My son, Charlie, is the goalie for Central."

Maggie hadn't planned on making small talk but didn't want to be rude. She brought her hand to the center of her chest. "Maggie. My son plays for Central, too. Jake Turner. Number twenty-one."

Robin searched for him on the field and gave an enthusiastic nod. "Oh, he's having a great game. They're winning three to one. If they keep this up, that'll be four wins in a row."

"Really?" Maggie gave an embarrassed shrug. "Jake doesn't always tell me the final score, and I, uh, haven't been able to come to any of the games so far. I usually have to work."

"That stinks. I'm a teacher at the middle school, so it works out for me to run over after our dismissal."

A teacher. Maggie could imagine Robin's male students finding themselves with their first crush. She was slender and pretty in the way some women are without even trying. Her long blond hair was twisted in a messy bun on the top of her head, and she didn't appear to be wearing much makeup. She didn't need it.

Maggie shifted self-consciously. "Yeah, I have a hard enough time getting here in time to pick him up when he can't take the last bus home. My boss ... he doesn't have kids. Let's just say he's not very understanding of me wanting to leave early." Harrison Korman wasn't very understanding about a lot of things.

She located Jake on the field, and as she watched, it was as if he could feel his mom's gaze on him. He glanced over at the bleachers, lifted his chin in acknowledgment, and turned his attention back to the game.

"Was he out today?" Robin asked. "Or did you sneak away when he wasn't looking?"

Maggie's forehead creased. "What?"

"Your boss." Robin lifted her oversized sunglasses and perched them on the top of her head. "How did you manage to escape today for the game?"

"Oh, right. I've been on jury duty for the last couple of weeks. We wrapped up the trial today, so I came when they dismissed us. I have to go back to work tomorrow, so I figured I might as well take advantage while I had the chance."

"Jury duty, huh? Was it at least an interesting trial?"

"I thought it was. First-degree murder."

Robin's jaw went slack, and she shifted on the bleachers to face Maggie. "No way. Tell me everything. I live for this kind of stuff."

Maggie studied her to see if she was being sincere. "Really?"

"Oh, heck yeah. My husband's always joking that it's all I watch. He calls it murder-torture-kill TV. Sounds horrible when he says it like that, but I can't help it. I'm obsessed."

Robin's enthusiasm was refreshing. Especially after the day Maggie had spent in deliberations.

"My husband—well, now he's my ex-husband—he used to say the same thing about me." Maggie wagged her finger in the air and mimicked Todd. *"I don't understand how you can stand to watch this stuff."*

"I think men get nervous we might off them and know how to get away with it."

Maggie huffed loudly. "My ex should consider himself lucky I didn't."

"That's only because you didn't have a friend like me to help you," Robin said as she gave her an exaggerated wink.

Maggie was sure she was kidding, but this woman was exactly the kind of person she could see herself being friends with. If she still looked for that kind of thing, that is.

"I'm going to need to hear every last detail about your trial," Robin said, her eyes lit up. "Were they guilty?"

"Well, I was convinced he was." Maggie's shoulders lowered, and she began to relax. It was a relief to talk through the trial with someone who thought like she did. "The rest of the jurors didn't think he did it." She held up her hand to clarify. "Well, they said the prosecution didn't prove it beyond a reasonable doubt." She hesitated, then sighed. "I could see their point, I guess." She pressed her lips together, the truth difficult to admit to this woman she had just met. "I finally voted not guilty, so we could all go home. Well, so I could come to Jake's game."

Robin wrinkled her nose and went silent for a moment. "So, you think he got away with murder?"

"He might have. I don't know about you, but when I watch those shows, I always have a gut feeling about whether they did it or not."

"Oh, *always*."

"This guy ..." Maggie shook her head. "He was a good-looking guy, but he gave me the creeps."

Doyle's expression after the verdict was read was still etched in her memory—a smirk on his lips like he was proud of himself for getting away with murder. He'd glanced over his attorney's shoulder when he hugged her and pinned his eyes on the jury. Even in the afternoon sun, a cold shiver skittered down Maggie's neck. She'd never forget the icy stare he'd given her, as if he knew she'd wanted to lock him up for the rest of his life. Maybe her disgusted scowl when the verdict was read had given away how she really felt about him being set free.

Robin sat back and crossed her legs, her sandal dangling precariously from her foot. "That's terrible they didn't give you enough evidence to convict him. I suppose a gut feeling isn't enough to put someone behind bars for the rest of their life."

"Yeah, that's what the other jurors said, too."

Maggie ran through the highlights of the case as Robin nodded thoughtfully.

"So, he had no real alibi for the window of time when the murder most likely happened? No one who actually saw him?"

"Exactly. Even though the neighbor said he didn't think he went out, it's not like he was watching his driveway all night. And who's to say he didn't slip out the back door to the street behind his and get an Uber. Did the police even check that?"

Robin uncrossed her legs and sat straight up. "You saw that

show where the guy had the Uber pick him up after he murdered his boss, right?"

"I saw it." Maggie huffed, then threw up her hands. "Did the police? You would hope they looked into it, but it didn't even come up. At least not that the jury heard about."

"You know, now that the trial's over, I think all the witness statements and stuff are public record."

Maggie's eyebrows came together. "Really?"

"Oh, yeah. My sister-in-law had to give a deposition in a case once but didn't get called to testify. It wasn't anything nearly as juicy as murder. But still, her stuff was out there. You just need the case number."

"I had no idea. Can you imagine if there were witnesses the jury didn't hear from? Ones who would have made a difference?"

Robin's shoulders lifted and dropped matter-of-factly. "I'd be all over it, but that's me. It would drive me crazy not to know the truth."

"Oh, it already is, trust me." Maggie wrinkled her nose. "But it's not like they could try him again. You know, the whole double jeopardy thing."

"I get that, but who knows? Maybe he's killed before—" Robin clasped her hand over her mouth. "Or maybe now that he sees how easy it was to get away with, he'll murder again." Her gaze drifted to the field, and she nudged Maggie's arm. "Hey. There goes your boy."

Maggie watched as Jake dribbled the ball toward the goal. He lined up the shot and fired. It shot right past the goalie, who dove for it but missed. Score! She leaped from her seat and cheered.

Robin held up her hand and high-fived Maggie when she sat back down. "Told you he was having a great game."

"I'm so glad I was here to see him score. When he used to

play sports on the weekends, I went to all his games. The after-school stuff is hard because of my job." Not to mention the guilt she felt. Other parents showed up for their kids, and Maggie hated that she couldn't be there for Jake.

"My husband doesn't come to many games either," Robin said with a shrug. "He's a general contractor. His company builds million-dollar houses, and if he leaves, everyone stops working. Rich people don't like when their projects aren't ready on time."

"My husband has more flexibility than I do, but he can't be bothered." Maggie's cheeks burned with the slip-up. "I mean, my ex-husband. We got divorced a few months ago. It wasn't exactly my idea."

Robin aimed a compassionate look in her direction. "I'm sorry. What about Jake? How is he handling the divorce?"

"Well, my ex kept the house, so we had to find an apartment. The only decent place I could find was in a new school district, but Jake—"

Robin squeezed her eyes shut, then held up her hand. "Wait a minute, you had to move out of the house? Not him?"

"Please. He's far too lazy to move."

The house had been a sticking point in the divorce proceedings. Maggie had dug her heels in for Jake's sake, but Todd refused to budge. *It's not like your pathetic salary made all the mortgage payments.*

Maggie shrugged. "To be honest, I wouldn't have been able to afford it on my own. Even with my child support." She leaned back and rested her back against the row behind them. "The fresh start was good for me. For both of us. I think it helped that Jake was only a freshman, but he's easy-going." She located her son on the field and gave a slight smile. "I was thrilled when he tried out for the team."

"And he made it. Not to mention, the coach is playing him,

which is amazing. Charlie's a sophomore, but he spent more time on the bench last year than in the goal. So, where did you end up moving?"

"We have a place in Regency Cove. It's not terrible, I guess, for an apartment."

Robin's eyes widened. "Stop it. We're practically neighbors. I live in Sunset Estates. My development is right down the street from you. I walk our dog every night around the lake, and I go right past the entrance to your complex."

The loop around the lake was about three miles and surrounded on both sides by suburban neighborhoods. Maggie's was the only apartment complex on the route.

"When my ex and I were first married, we got a dog. A sweet yellow lab named Bluford." Maggie shook her head and chuckled. "If I had tried to walk him near a lake, I wouldn't have been able to keep him out of it."

The truth was she hadn't walked Blu much. When they moved to Florida, they'd installed a doggie door so he could go out into the backyard whenever he needed to do his business. Her bottom lip quivered as her mind went to their late-night visit to the emergency vet. Maggie's focus was on figuring out what was wrong so they could bring the dog home, but all Todd could talk about was the cost.

"We lost him about two years ago," Maggie said in a shaky voice.

"Oh, I'm so sorry. That's the hardest part of having pets, isn't it?" Robin hesitated and then lifted her shoulders. "I still can't believe you live so close to me. If you're ever running late, I could take Jake home for you."

"Really? That would be—" Maggie's attention drifted over the woman's shoulder. "Oh, you *must* be kidding me."

Robin shifted on the bleachers to follow her gaze. "You know them?"

"Unfortunately. That's my ex-husband. And that's his girl-friend, the woman he cheated on me with."

"Oh." Robin winced and sucked air through her teeth. "Now I see why he's lucky he's still standing." She scowled. "How old is she?"

"Old enough to know better."

Todd and Stephanie stumbled through the grass toward the bleachers, arms wrapped around each other like teenagers. Her ex's hand appeared wedged in the back pocket of his girlfriend's form-fitting jeans. Maybe he planned to hold her up if her four-inch heels couldn't successfully navigate the uneven grass. Was neither of them smart enough to see the sidewalk leading to the field?

They disappeared behind the bleachers and reappeared a few moments later on the side near the path.

Maggie didn't bother with a greeting. "I sent you a text and told you I'd be able to pick up Jake." She aimed her gaze and comment at Todd.

Stephanie offered her the same phony smile she wore on her billboard. "Hi, Maggie."

Her greeting was acknowledged with a curt nod. That's all the woman who'd cheated with her husband deserved. Her distaste for the woman made Maggie's skin vibrate.

"Todd, I texted you that I would pick him up," she repeated. "I thought you told me you had a meeting this afternoon."

"Canceled. I told Steph we should come anyway and catch a little of Jake's game." He waved at the empty space in their row. "Any chance you could both move down and make room?"

When Robin shot her a questioning stare, Maggie bit the inside of her cheek and begrudgingly dipped her head. For Jake. He'd be thrilled if he looked over and saw them all here together.

As Robin slid down, Maggie leaned into her. "Keep going,"

she said in a low voice. They weren't one big happy family, and Maggie's acting skills could only go so far. Even for Jake.

She and Robin shuffled toward the middle of the row—more than necessary. They'd left ample room for the two of them to have their own space at the end.

Todd reached for Stephanie's hand and steadied her as she stepped onto the first metal row. She put one foot carefully down and then the other before letting go. She turned, shuffled noisily to the left, and lowered her heart-shaped butt onto the bleachers. Right beside Maggie.

Perfect. So close she could taste the woman's perfume as it clung to the air. No doubt, Stephanie was one of those women who'd choose the stall right next to the only other person in the ladies' room. Maggie coughed, then dug her fingers into her right temple. Her headache from that morning was back.

Todd's girlfriend seemed oblivious as she stretched out her long, lean legs. She set her black leather pumps on the row in front of her, then crossed her feet at the ankles.

Maggie tried to tuck her own feet—clad in sensible flats meant for the long walk from the parking garage to the court-house—underneath her and out of sight. She sat up straight and hoped her blouse wouldn't look too small if she stopped slouch-ing. Still, her peripheral vision told her what she already knew. Stephanie took up half the space as she did on the bleachers. Todd's girlfriend was put together, whereas his ex-wife was lucky the shirt she'd thrown on that morning hadn't popped a button.

Todd settled next to Stephanie and rested his hand on her thigh. "I know it's not the most comfortable seating, but it's the price to pay if you want to watch your kid, right?"

Maggie's eyes narrowed. Was he kidding? "Well, the game's almost over, and you missed the best part." She stared at the field, refusing to glance in their direction. "Jake scored a goal."

Robin leaned forward to throw in her two cents. "It was quite spectacular."

"Of course it was." Todd's lips parted in a wide smile. "My boy's a superstar."

His boy. As if he was the one with the stretch marks.

He nudged Stephanie. "Jake's a great soccer player. Actually, he excels at all sports. Always has. Gets it from me, of course."

Maggie drew in a deep breath, her inner monologue rebutting his claim in an angry chorus of disbelief. Over the years, Todd, who'd apparently bequeathed his athletic prowess to his son, had never been to a single one of Jake's sporting events. T-ball. Flag football. Indoor soccer. Shuffling him back and forth and cheering from the sideline at weekend games—all Maggie's responsibility. That's what mothers are supposed to do, he'd said once when she complained.

Not once had he offered to help coach one of Jake's teams or played ball with him on the front lawn. Wasn't that what fathers were supposed to do? But no, Todd had his own pursuits, which kept him far too busy. His fantasy football league. Working out at the gym. Cheating on his wife.

Maggie's chest grew tight, breathing painful within their close proximity. She searched the scoreboard for the game clock. Six minutes. That's all she needed to endure. Then she could escape the two of them and pray to never be in this situation again.

She wasn't sure why Todd had bothered to put in an appearance. If he'd been trying to impress his girlfriend with his father-of-the-year routine, it wasn't working. Stephanie seemed oblivious as she stared at her phone and scrolled through emails.

If her ex was bothered by her disinterest, he didn't show it. Instead, he leaned forward to see around her and aimed his chin in Robin's direction. "So, Mags, who's your friend?"

Maggie bristled. His nickname for her rolled off his tongue like it was nothing.

On their first date, he'd asked if anyone called her that. No one ever had. *Well, then it will be my special name for you.* But no more. Todd had lost that privilege when he decided to crawl into bed with someone else.

She wasn't the type to cause a scene, so Maggie pushed down her aggravation. "This is Robin. Her son is the goalie on Jake's team." Her ex-husband didn't need to know they'd just met.

He lifted his hand in the air. "Nice to meet you. Well, from a distance anyway. I'm Todd, Jake's dad." He squeezed Stephanie's shoulder, which brought her out of her email trance. "And this is my girlfriend, Stephanie."

She aimed her fake smile in Robin's direction.

"Good to meet both of you." Robin tipped her head as she stared at Maggie's ex-husband. Her eyebrows scrunched together. "I don't think I've seen you at any of the games before." There was an innocent lilt to her voice, but Maggie felt a subtle pressure against her leg. "Is this the first one of Jake's games you've come to, Tom?"

"It's, uh, *Todd.*" Her ex's cheeks turned bright red. "Not Tom."

"Oh, I'm sorry." When Robin pressed her leg harder against Maggie's, it became obvious the slip-up wasn't accidental. "So, *Todd,* have you been to any of Jake's other games? I'm always here, and I can't imagine how I would have missed seeing you."

Maggie bit back a smile. As Jake's father stammered in his defense, she made a decision. Robin was exactly the kind of friend she needed.

4

Though the verdict had left Maggie frustrated, heading off to jury duty every day had been exhilarating. Each morning, she affixed the badge that announced she was a juror—a warning to those involved with the case to be careful what they said or did around her. She lined up with witnesses and attorneys and made her way through the metal detector.

As she anticipated what witnesses the day might bring, she headed first to get her parking ticket validated and then to the jury room to wait. When the judge announced they were ready, Maggie grabbed the spiral notebook provided to her and lined up with the other jurors.

They filed through the door to the courtroom and stood in front of their assigned seats. Every person turned to face them, their gazes fixed on the jury as if they were the main event. For the first time in her life, Maggie felt important.

Now, the excitement of the past two weeks was over. It was back to reality, where very little in her mundane existence left her feeling the way she'd felt in that courtroom.

She hesitated, then pressed the up button on the elevator.

She wrapped her arm around her middle, physically sick to be headed back to the office after her two-week paid hiatus.

When the doors opened on the sixth floor, she stepped out of the elevator into the plush reception area for the accounting firm where she worked.

She nodded at the receptionist. "Morning."

"Hey, welcome back. I felt so bad when I heard you got sucked into jury duty."

"Oh, don't feel bad. The trial was fascinating. If anything, feel bad I had to come back to work." Maggie nodded at the glass door that led to the offices. "Is he in yet?"

"He was already here when I arrived, so I'm sure he's waiting for you." The receptionist threw Maggie a sympathetic wince. "You might not be able to find your desk with everything he's piled on it."

"Great." Maggie heaved a deep sigh and pulled on the door handle that would make it official. She was back at work.

She hadn't even made it to her desk when her boss came barreling down the hallway, his attention laser-focused on his cell phone.

"Good morning, Mr. Korman," Maggie said loudly, hoping to get his attention before he collided with her.

Harrison Korman looked up just in time, an anxious expression on his face. He always dressed well, but today, he had on one of his more expensive suits. Maggie only knew because he'd bragged about how much it cost the first time he wore it. *You can't put a price tag on letting people see you're successful.*

Maggie wasn't sure hard work had much to do with it. Several years back, the teenage son of a local doctor had raced through a red light and hit Harry as he drove home from work. He wasn't even hurt badly, but she was sure he had played it up for a hefty insurance settlement. Physical therapy appointments. Chiropractors. Several months later, her boss was driving a new Mercedes and preaching about his "success."

Her boss twisted his wrist and stared at the oversized Rolex on his wrist. "You're late, Margaret." His mouth puckered like he'd been sucking on a lemon. "This place has gone to hell while you've been on vacation, so I hope you're prepared to get back to work."

The only other person who called her Margaret was her mother. She'd long ago given up telling her boss she preferred Maggie. He didn't care.

"Sorry." The apology made her stomach churn. Technically, she wasn't late, but he'd gotten to the office before her. To him, that meant his assistant was tardy as far as he was concerned. "But I wasn't actually on vacation. I told you—"

"Right. The jury duty thing." Her boss rolled his eyes so hard Maggie was surprised it wasn't painful. "Just get your desk cleaned up, would you? It's an eyesore. I need to speak urgently with Andrew, but I'll be right back."

Maggie allowed herself a moment of self-pity as she approached her desk. She now saw what the receptionist had warned her about. Piles of client folders leaned haphazardly. Some looked like they'd been flung on her desk like her boss thought he was tossing a Frisbee. Two weeks of mail filled in the random gaps on her desktop. Bank statements. Client payments. Her boss's corporate card bill. There wasn't even an empty spot to set down her purse.

"Oh, geez. Really?"

She heard a muffled voice respond. "I think the emotionless geezer actually missed you."

Her co-worker, Charlene, popped up from the other side of the wall that divided their workspaces.

"Missed me? Doubtful." Maggie let out a huff. "Missed me doing all his work is more like it."

"Well, I'm glad you're back." Charlene rested her forearms on the top of the wall. "The stuff he couldn't handle without you came flying at me while you were out."

"Sorry about that." She glanced back at her desk and released a weary sigh. "I'm going to need more caffeine before I tackle this."

Maggie made her way down the hall.

"Hey. Good morning," she said as she walked into the employee kitchen. An older woman stood over the garbage can peeling an orange. She'd worked for Andrew Mason, one of the founding partners, for years.

"Hey, you're back," the woman said. "I hope you're not looking for coffee because there isn't any."

Of course there wasn't. Maggie was the one who ordered the supplies for the kitchen, and she was sure no one else had bothered while she was out.

"If I can unbury myself, I'll run out later and get some." After seeing the condition of her desk, Maggie wasn't at all optimistic about her chances. "Harry was rushing off to talk to Andy when I came in." The assistants were all required to refer to their bosses in formal terms, but they all used nicknames behind the scenes. "My boss is decked out in his fancy clothes today. Something up?"

The woman shrugged as she pulled on the handle for the employee refrigerator. "Not sure. He flew into Andy's office, and they shut the door." She slid over Tupperware containers and brown bags to make a spot for her lunch cooler. "Unless it's something that involves paying me more money, they could come to work in pink tutus, and I wouldn't care."

"Maybe they've got a big potential client on the hook."

"Anything's possible." She spun to face Maggie, her nose wrinkled in disgust. "By the way, something really stinks in there. Probably been rotting the entire two weeks you've been out."

A year prior, Harry had declared the employee kitchen was Maggie's responsibility. That meant tossing the food people forgot about and didn't include one more penny in her paycheck.

"I'm sure. I'll try to get to that later, too."

It would never happen. The grunt work she'd been assigned would be shoved way down on Maggie's to-do list. Coffee was important, but she had to prioritize client files and mail over expired food, even the stuff that resembled a bad science experiment.

"I'd better get to my desk before Harry comes back and loses his mind that I'm not already bulldozing through it."

On the way back, Maggie peeked into her boss's office and eased out a breath. It was empty. She dropped into her desk chair and cringed when it creaked in protest. She needed some WD40 or twenty-five fewer pounds. Probably both.

She stared at the mess on her desk, unsure where to begin.

"You would think he could have at least stacked the mail in neat piles," she said, her comment aimed at the wall.

Charlene's muffled response came quickly. "He was completely aggravated while were out. Like you'd purposely stayed away to make his life difficult. He flung stuff at your desk with such force, I was surprised some of it didn't come over the wall and hit me in the head. Even Ernie said something to me about it."

Ernest Kinkaide was Charlene's boss. He was lower on the totem pole than Harry but much more likable. And while he might have said something to Charlene about Harry's behavior, Maggie knew he wouldn't dare say anything directly to the source.

"His whole attitude was ridiculous." Charlene sounded

annoyed. "It's not like you wanted to get picked for jury duty. Nobody does."

Maggie didn't respond. Instead, she pulled the trash can from underneath her desk and started with the mail. Important stuff was set aside. Junk went right into the garbage.

She was so focused, she jerked backward when she lifted her gaze and saw Harry standing there.

He stroked his red tie as if he were petting himself. "I need to head to an important client meeting. Do you think you can handle getting your desk under control while I'm gone?"

An important client meeting. That explained the suit and tie. Maybe she'd been right about them courting a wealthy new client.

"Of course. I just need to get it all organized, and then I'll tackle this week's reports."

Maggie had worked for Harry for almost six years. Most days, she was sure she could do his job better than he did.

"Oh, and—" She reached into her purse and pulled out the paper the court had provided her on the last day. Harry had left her a voicemail that if she expected to get paid, she needed a record of her service when she returned. "This is from the court. You know, about the days I was out for jury duty."

He snatched the paper from her hand and studied it, almost as if he needed proof she'd told him the truth about her absence.

His forehead creased. "You served on a murder trial?"

"Yes, sir, I did."

Harry bobbed his head, his thin lips pressed together as he stared at her. "So, was he guilty? Did you vote to lock him up and throw away the key?"

"Well, we weren't sentencing him. Not to mention, we found the defendant not guilty."

His eyebrows shot up to his thinning hairline. "Oh, so he *didn't* do it?"

Maggie offered a non-committal shrug. "A not-guilty verdict could also mean the prosecution didn't prove their case beyond a reasonable doubt."

Harry scowled, looking aggravated at her response. "Margaret, you're talking in circles. Did he murder someone or not?"

"I thought he did, but I was the only one."

"So, you believed the defendant was guilty, but then you caved under pressure from the other jurors?"

Maggie's jaw clenched. "I didn't *cave*. The instructions we were given were very specific. We could only find him guilty if we believed beyond every reasonable doubt there could be no other possible scenario."

Her boss tipped his head to one side. "So, they convinced you someone else could have committed the murder?"

"I was convinced the prosecution didn't prove the defendant was the only possibility. There was no smoking gun if you will. Nothing we could use to definitively say beyond a shadow of a doubt that he did it. So, after we dissected the evidence we were given, I agreed we had no choice but to return a not-guilty verdict."

"I see."

Her boss shoved aside a stack of folders on Maggie's desk and laid down the document from the court. He scrawled his signature, folded the paper in half, and handed it back to her.

"Give this to Helen in payroll. I'll be back in a few hours." His lips curled in disgust as his gaze raked over her desk. "Have this cleaned up by then."

"Yes, sir."

After he walked away, Charlene popped up with wide eyes. "I didn't know it was a murder trial. If you ever get caught up, I want to hear all about it."

WHEN HARRY RETURNED several hours later, Maggie hadn't even made a dent in clearing her desk.

"I have a meeting in the conference room in ten minutes." He thrust a piece of paper in her direction. "Call in our lunch order and go pick it up." Her boss never asked her to do anything. He demanded.

He pulled his company credit card from his wallet and tossed it on her desk. Then without another word, he strode away.

Maggie glanced down at the list he'd handed her. Sandwiches.

Harry stopped mid-stride and wheeled back around. "Order from the deli on Clayton Blvd. They're the only one that knows how to make a decent corned beef on rye. It's located in the strip mall next to the hospital."

Maggie's face fell. She knew where it was. Instead of heading to the sandwich shop right around the corner, she'd now have a twenty-minute drive each way. It would take at least an hour to do Harry's bidding. What about her lunch?

He marched back to her desk as if he dared her to complain.

"Do you know where you're going, Margaret?"

She nodded. "Yes, sir, I do."

Her boss remained frozen beside her desk. Maggie glanced up to see if there was something else he needed.

Harry bent at the waist and leaned toward her, his face encroaching on her personal space. "Go *now*, Margaret. By the time you get there and back, we'll all be famished."

"Right. Sorry." As she gritted her teeth, Maggie reached under her desk. She grabbed her purse and tossed the paper inside. It wasn't like he'd even offered to buy her lunch. He never did. "I'll call the order in from the car."

She hurried past Charlene, who looked up with a grimace and mouthed one word. *Sorry.*

When she got to the parking lot, Maggie's pulse was in overdrive, and it wasn't just the jog she'd taken in her bid to escape. Harry expected she'd use her car. Her gas. As she drove, the responses she longed to give her boss played in her head.

You know what, Harry, get your own damn lunch.

This isn't the job I was hired for, so take your lunch order and shove it.

I'm done with this lousy job. I quit.

She wasn't sure if her imaginary conversation made her feel better or worse. It wasn't like she'd ever say any of it to Harry's face. He treated her like trash, yet she was the one who always apologized. Nodded. Said "yes, sir" like a damn robot. Maggie detested working for him but never took the initiative to stick up for herself or look for something new. Something better.

Then again, she'd done the same thing in her marriage.

When Maggie arrived at the deli, she approached the area designated for call-ahead orders. At least the lunch rush wasn't in full swing yet. No one else was waiting.

"I'll be right with you," the young woman called over her shoulder as she packed up an order on the back counter.

When she was finished, she set the bag behind the register and spun around. "You're picking up? What's the—"

She cut herself off mid-sentence and stared at Maggie, a deep crease between her eyebrows. For a moment, it seemed she was struggling to place her. To figure out why she looked so familiar.

Maggie's breath snagged in her throat. She knew precisely where she'd seen this woman before.

The pretty brunette had been one of the first witnesses the prosecution called to testify. After that, she'd been in the courtroom each day for the remainder of the trial, a stone-cold expression on her face. Her attention had bounced between the witness stand and the jury box—staring at the people who testified and then studying the jury members. She'd pinned her hope, no doubt, on them doling out justice. Which, of course, they didn't. When the not-guilty verdict was announced, the young woman had wailed painfully and buried her head in the shoulder of the man beside her.

Seconds felt like an eternity as they stood frozen and stared at each other. An uncomfortable silence hung in the air.

Maggie saw the instant it all came together, the recognition of who she was evident in the tears that sprang to the young woman's eyes.

"It's you," she said, her voice barely above a whisper.

Maggie's chest tightened, and she lifted her shoulders in an apologetic shrug. "I'm—I'm so sorry."

Then, she turned and ran.

5

"So, what did you say to her?" Robin asked as Duke, her German shepherd, drove his nose into a bush.

After work, Maggie and Jake had demolished the pizza she'd picked up for dinner. She then took her glass of wine to their tiny screened-in balcony while Jake went to his room to tackle his homework.

She stared at the paper she pulled from her purse. Robin's phone number. Was Maggie only supposed to use it if Jake needed a ride home?

No doubt she was overthinking the whole thing. After a certain age, it just seemed so much harder to make friends. To take the first step. And then, if you had nothing in common, what did you even talk about?

Maggie was desperate to share what had transpired at the deli with someone who would appreciate the universe's lousy sense of humor. She'd considered calling her sister, but Stacy had never shared her obsession with crime and murder. At the office, she and Charlene hadn't had five minutes to catch up all day, but even so, Maggie wasn't sure she considered her a friend. Sure, they spoke over their shared wall, but they never spent time together outside of work.

Robin was different. A smile tugged at Maggie's lips as she recalled how sly she'd been when she called Todd out on his nonsense. Who didn't need a friend like that on their side? Not to mention, she had seemed wildly interested in the trial. A fellow true crime addict.

She swallowed her hesitation along with a long sip of wine, then dialed. "Uh, hi," she said when her call was answered. "It's Maggie, Jake's mom. You know, from soccer."

Robin's cheerful response was immediate as if she was happy to hear from her. "Of course. Hi. I guess Jake was able to catch the bus today after practice?"

"Yeah, he did. I had to stay late at work to try to—anyway, you're not going to believe who I ran into today." Maggie took a dramatic pause. "The victim's sister."

"Get the hell outta here." Robin's voice was filled with excitement. "I'm heading out to walk the dog. Can you meet us at the entrance to your complex? We'll pick you up in ten minutes."

It was already dark out. Maggie had hoped to discuss what had happened on the phone but drained her wine glass and agreed. She quickly changed clothes and was waiting when Robin arrived and promised her enormous German shepherd was friendlier than he appeared.

Now, as Duke resumed his pace, Maggie willed her legs to keep up. Her thighs burned. This conversation would have been much more appealing over a bottle of wine.

"You mean, what did I say before I ran out of the sandwich shop with my tail between my legs?" she asked. "Or after I went back in? I mean, I had no choice but to pick up my boss's lunch." Maggie sucked in air. "Not that getting fired would be the worst thing in the world. Of course, then Jake and I would be living in a box under a bridge somewhere."

"You wouldn't because you'd find something better, without a boss who's such a pill." Robin steered the conversation back to the more interesting topic. "So, the sister? Did she mention the trial when you went back?"

"She was waiting on someone else, so I had to get in line." Maggie took in several deep breaths. "I seriously thought my heart was going to explode. I wasn't even going to bring it up, but the way she looked at me when she handed the bag to me ..." Her chest heaved as she tried to talk and keep up with Robin's clipped pace. "I told her the truth."

"Which is?"

Robin stopped again to allow Duke to sniff at an intriguing patch of grass, and Maggie bent at the waist grateful for the chance to catch her breath. This walk made it clear just how out of shape she'd become.

She drew in a lungful of air before responding. "That I believed the defendant did it, but the prosecution didn't give us enough evidence to find him guilty beyond a reasonable doubt. I told her I was sorry. That wasn't a lie." Maggie let out a disgusted snort. "I was sorry the other jurors couldn't see what was right in front of their faces."

"And what did she say?"

Under the glow of the streetlight, she could see the anticipation on Robin's face as she waited for the answer.

"It was awful." Maggie's eyes closed as she shook her head. "She started to cry. Then she said, 'So, I'll never get to be with my big sister again, and that murderer gets to go on with his life like this never happened? I'll *never* be able to accept that he got away with killing her.'" Maggie rubbed the back of her neck and then subtly wiped the sweat from her hand on her pant leg. "And then she looked me dead in the eye and said, 'I didn't have *any* doubt he did it.'"

"Wow. Talk about a guilt trip," Robin offered a sympathetic

wince before she tugged on Duke's leash and resumed her brisk pace.

Maggie took several quick steps to catch up. "Right? It's not my fault the other jurors fell for his act. When Doyle testified—"

"Wait." Robin skidded to a halt and spun to face Maggie. "The defense put him on the stand?"

"Yup. I know sometimes they don't, but the defense attorney told us Doyle felt strongly about getting up there to tell us *the truth*. A few of the jurors said he was very convincing." Maggie shrugged. "They believed his version of events."

"The prosecution didn't rip him to shreds when they had the chance?"

"Would you believe they didn't even question him?"

Robin's eyes went wide. "What?"

"I was shocked. It was like they didn't even care. I guess maybe the prosecution felt they had already proven their case."

The huff of disbelief Robin released was long and loud. "And didn't they feel silly after the verdict? Grace's sister should be pissed at the proscutor, not the jury." She was silent for a moment and then resumed walking. "But what if he didn't really kill her? What if we could figure out who did?"

Maggie's brow crinkled. "But he did do it, and there's nothing anybody can do about it now. He was acquitted. End of story."

"I know that's your gut feeling, but isn't it possible the police just latched onto him because he was the ex-boyfriend?" She glanced over, her head tilted. "C'mon, we've both seen shows where they arrest someone even though they have almost no compelling evidence."

Maggie couldn't deny that was true. Sometimes she even yelled at the television when she learned the jury convicted them. But Doyle was different. Robin hadn't seen the smug expression on his face when they announced the not-guilty verdict. That man knew he'd gotten away with murder.

"Maybe there was even stuff you didn't get to hear," Robin said as they crossed the street and approached the sidewalk that would take them past the lake. "They arrested him, but clearly they didn't have enough to convince the rest of the jury. What if there was evidence that pointed away from the defendant? The prosecution would never have presented any of that."

Maggie was silent for a moment before she gave a hesitant nod. "I guess it's possible."

"We could dive into what's public record to see what we can figure out. And hey, if you're still convinced he did it, then you're right. There probably isn't much we can do with double jeopardy, but at least you could stop wondering."

"That might be worse. Then I'll know I should have tried harder to convince the other jurors." Maggie gave an embarrassed shrug. "But I was more interested in getting out of there to make it to Jake's soccer game."

"You can't beat yourself up over it. You said yourself they weren't going to budge. What's done is done, and hey, if he testified under oath and it turns out he's guilty ..." Robin gave her an expectant stare.

"That means he committed perjury on the stand."

"Correct. No idea how much time you get for that, but at least it would be something." Robin clicked the button on the retractable leash. As Duke trotted off to explore the bank of the lake, she turned, her eyebrows lifted. "Don't you think doing our own investigation would be kind of—I don't know, exciting?"

Maggie did miss jury duty, and the idea of having something to balance out the dreary reality of dealing with Harry enticed her. Still, she barely had time for Jake and her job. Grocery shopping. Laundry and cleaning the apartment. Where was she supposed to find the time to fit this in, too?

Robin's nudge to her arm interrupted her concerns.

"Can you imagine if we did end up solving the case? We could start our own podcast and talk about it."

"A podcast? Us?" Maggie considered the ones she listened to in the car or through her earphones while doing housework. The hosts sounded confident and professional. She could never pull that off. "Don't you need to have some sort of training?"

"Oh, come on." Robin dismissed her concern with a flick of her wrist. "Everyone's got a podcast these days. We could totally do it. Some people use them to make a lot of money. Then you could tell that boss of yours you're out of there."

"You know how much I'd love to tell Harry where to go with his corned beef sandwich and his job."

Maggie imagined the satisfaction she would have if she could quit. An even bigger thrill would be delivering the news to Todd. A *true-crime* podcast. It would be proof her obsession wasn't as worthless as he'd always claimed. Wouldn't it be ironic if his girlfriend wasn't the only one with a billboard?

"I might be crazy to think I could do it." Her lips parted in a slight smile. "But I can't say I don't love the idea."

everal days later, Robin called to get together to talk about the case. Maggie had been intimidated when she'd first walked into her house—it was in a different league than the one she'd lived in with Todd.

"Don't be too impressed." Robin waved her hand dismissively as she noticed her looking around. "You should see the stuff those rich people decide they don't want anymore. Our entire kitchen is courtesy of the person who bought a three-million-dollar house on the bay but decided he didn't like the Italian cabinets."

Maggie eyed the white lacquered row of doors with a bit of jealousy. She had stubbornly refused to take much from the house she'd shared with Todd, and her second-hand shopping hadn't yielded anything nearly as impressive. "They're beautiful."

Robin gestured at a round glass table littered with papers. "We can work here."

She pulled a chilled bottle of wine from behind one of the cabinet doors. "You'd never even know it's a wine refrigerator, right?" She set two glasses down on the table and poured half a glass of Chardonnay in each. "So I used the case number you gave me and printed all the witness statements so we can reference them." She handed one glass to Maggie. "Good thinking making a copy of your paperwork from the court before turning it in at work."

"Well, it was mostly because I was sure they'd claim they never got it and refuse to pay me even though I handed it to the lady in payroll myself."

Robin took a long sip of her wine, then set the glass off to the side. "So, what do you think the jury's biggest problem was?"

Maggie set her elbow on the table and rested her chin in her hand as she considered the question. "They weren't convinced Doyle went out because his phone pinged from the tower by his house the entire night."

"Which just means his phone was there."

"Exactly." Going over the facts of the case with Robin was a welcome change from the jury room. "If you're going to kill someone, you get a prepaid one that can't be tracked. I mean, that's just murder 101."

Robin nodded in agreement. "Of course, especially if it's premeditated. What about the defendant's vehicle? Was that at his house, too?"

"Another issue for the jury. No proof it ever left once he got home from work, and they didn't find a shred of evidence inside linking it to the crime."

Robin frowned as she sifted through the statements she'd printed. When she found the one she was looking for, she pulled it from the pile. "What about this witness? Melody Kaplan? She told the police she saw a white sedan run a stop sign as it sped out of Grace's neighborhood. She remembered the car because it almost hit her." She handed the paper to Maggie. "Is that what Doyle drives?"

"A white car? We never—" Maggie's mind raced as she

skimmed the woman's statement. "We never heard anything about a white car. Doyle drives a black pickup." She shook her head in disbelief. "I can't believe we didn't even—"

Robin tapped the table with her index finger. "See, this is what I was talking about. The prosecution wouldn't want you to hear from this witness, but I'm surprised the defense didn't call her."

"Well, the burden of proof belongs to the prosecution." How many times had Kim spewed that fact in the jury room? "It's possible the defense didn't feel they needed to put her on the stand. Considering the verdict, they weren't wrong." Maggie remembered the arguments in the jury room. Without surveillance video of the driver, her testimony might not have even made a difference. "The white car could just as easily have been a Door Dash driver racing to his next food delivery."

Robin rubbed her lip thoughtfully with her index finger. "Except the timing is coincidental. This woman said she saw the car around 8:05 p.m. That falls in the window of time for the murder, right?"

"It would have been tight, I think. Doyle was definitely home at 7:40 p.m. He had a pizza delivered."

Maggie reached for her wine glass. As she sipped, she tried to visualize the timeline she'd written on the whiteboard in the jury room. She wished she had the notes she'd taken during the trial. The jurors hadn't been permitted to take their notebooks when they left.

She wrinkled her nose and set down her glass. "Another problem. The IT guy testified that Grace was on her computer until 8:02 p.m."

"Shoot, that is too tight." Robin's eyebrows shot up. "Unless she wasn't the one using it."

Maggie threw her hands in the air. "Thank you. I suggested the same thing, but the other jurors acted like I was crazy."

"It's also possible the witness was wrong about the time she saw the white car." Robin's shoulders lifted. "You never know. Any idea how long the drive is from Doyle's to Grace's?"

Maggie remembered the prosecutor driving home the point that Doyle had plenty of time to get to Grace's and back in the window of time he couldn't account for. "About thirty minutes. Maybe a little less."

"So, if the witness's timing is off even a little bit, it's still possible." Robin's eyes narrowed. "Didn't you say Doyle owned a body shop? Who's to say he didn't take a customer's white car home that night and use it to drive to Grace's house?"

"I considered that, too. I even brought it up in the jury room because the lack of evidence in his pickup was another sticking point."

"But it makes sense if Doyle used another vehicle. There would be nothing to find in his truck."

Maggie gave a hesitant nod. She'd made the same point during deliberations. Still, there had to be a reason this witness's information was discarded as irrelevant. "Since this witness was never called to testify, I guess the police either found out the white car was unrelated, or they found nothing at the body shop that raised their suspicions." She slumped back in her chair. "Besides, if Doyle drove a customer's car home, how did he get his truck home? The neighbor testified the black pickup was in his driveway."

"All night?"

"He thought it was but couldn't say for sure. He had a security camera near his front door, but a post on the porch blocked the view of Doyle's driveway."

"Of course, it did." There was a trace of sarcasm in Robin's voice. "Still, the camera would have captured the truck if it drove away, no?"

The defense had asked the neighbor the same question on

the stand. As Pablo had pointed out repeatedly in the jury room, there clearly wasn't footage of Doyle's pickup leaving, or they would have shown it.

"Apparently, the street is a big circle. Doyle could back out of his driveway and go either way to leave his development. If he went one way, yes, the camera would have caught him. If he went the other way, no."

Robin's eyebrows scrunched together. "There were no other cameras on the block? That seems impossible to believe."

"I agree, but if there were, the jury didn't hear about them."

Robin folded her leg underneath her and pressed her fore-arms against the table. "So, you're telling me the jurors just accepted the neighbor's testimony that he believed Doyle's truck was there all night?"

Maggie sighed and offered a slow nod. In the absence of evidence to prove otherwise, that's precisely what most of them had done. "He said the black pickup was in Doyle's driveway when he got home from work around seven and then again when he went out to walk the dog at about ten-thirty. Doyle was taking out his trash cans, and they chatted in the street for a few minutes. The neighbor confirmed he was wearing a Bucs jersey, and they talked about the football game." Maggie shrugged. "According to him, Doyle was acting completely normal."

"Yeah. That's what they said about Ted Bundy, too." Robin rubbed her chin thoughtfully. "What if the pickup blocked the white car so he didn't see it?"

"Even so, how would Doyle have gotten both vehicles home?" Maggie rested her head on the back of the chair and stared up at the ceiling. "Let's say Doyle didn't drive the white car home. He leaves after the pizza's delivered. The neighbor admitted he wasn't staring out his window all night."

"Right. Why would he be?"

"Doyle goes to the body shop. He swaps out his pickup for

the white car and then heads to Grace's house. After the deed's done, he drives back to the body shop, drops off the other vehicle, and picks up his truck." Maggie rubbed her hands together. "He's back before anyone realizes he left." Her smile fell away. "Of course, that's assuming there was a white car there to take. One that the police didn't check into or didn't know about."

Robin looked skeptical as she shook her head. "That whole scenario would have taken too much time." Her shoulders sagged. "I guess the white car was just a coincidence. The police probably figured out it wasn't related."

"Which would explain why the jury never heard about it." Maggie set the paper off to the side. "Well, not sure that witness was much help. Anyone else's statement look interesting?"

Robin sifted through the stack and pulled one out. "There was this guy. Ron Brookins."

"That's the guy Grace started seeing after she broke up with Doyle, but they only had one date. He testified at the trial." Maggie gave a half-shrug. "Seemed believable."

Robin drummed her fingers on the kitchen table as she looked over his statement. "This guy—Ron—he picked Grace up at her place for their date." She glanced up and cocked her head thoughtfully. "Conveniently puts his fingerprints and DNA in her house."

"Doyle's too. Even if he didn't murder her, they dated for a couple of months."

"I assume they took fingerprints from both men to use as a comparison. Did they find any other prints?"

"Just an unidentified partial palm print on the front door. The *inside* of the front door."

Robin's eyes narrowed. "Really?"

"Yeah, but we had no way of knowing if it was the killer's. One of the jurors even suggested a delivery person might have left it."

Robin snorted. "On the *inside* of the door?"

"She claimed the FedEx guys always bring the heavy boxes inside for her."

The older woman informed the rest of the group that she regularly had large bags of dog food delivered and was a generous tipper. The woman insisted the delivery guys not only brought her boxes into the house but also set them in her kitchen for her. The whole scenario was a Dateline episode in the making as far as Maggie was concerned.

"I hate to say it, but they might have a point," Robin said reluctantly. "There's no way of knowing when or how that palm print got there."

"No DNA found on Grace's body or clothes either, but she was shot in the back of the head. Just once. The murderer didn't need to lay a hand on her, so how much DNA is he going to leave?"

Robin wrinkled her nose. "So sad. Sounds like she was trying to get away."

Most of the jurors could barely look at them, but Maggie could still visualize the crime scene photos. The bottoms of Grace's bare feet. Arms outstretched in front of her. The stark contrast of the blood against the white tile.

"She was found on the floor next to her kitchen table. We figured she was probably running to the back door to try and escape. The ballistics expert testified that from the bullet's trajectory, it seemed like she tripped."

The prosecution had presented an animation that showed the jury their theory of where both parties had been when Grace was shot. *The path of the bullet can tell us exactly how this happened, ladies and gentlemen.* "Whoever shot Grace stood over her and fired before she could get to her feet. The witness testified it had to be someone who was about six feet tall."

"Did the prosecution say how tall our friend Doyle is?"

"He's just under that by about an inch."

Robin pursed her lips. "Close enough. What about the new guy?"

No one had even asked the question, but Ron Brookins wasn't the one on trial. Maggie remembered when they called his name to testify. He seemed petrified. His shoulders had been hunched over as he made his way to the stand, his eyes pointed at the floor. It would have been hard to judge his height based on his entrance, but when his testimony was over, he seemed relieved. She'd watched as he strode out of the courtroom and was sure he'd been fairly tall with an athletic build hidden under the navy suit he wore.

"I'd say he's about the same height as Doyle," she said.

"Interesting."

"The killer also stepped in Grace's blood in a pair of Timberline boots. Not a full print, so they couldn't tell us exactly what size they were. Doyle purchased the same style about a year before the murder." A copy of a credit card receipt with his signature scrawled on the bottom had been shown to the jury.

"Did they find the boots when they searched Doyle's house? Was Grace's blood on them?"

"They weren't there."

"Isn't that convenient?" Robin turned her attention back to Ron's statement. "Okay, so the new guy mentions that before they left for their dinner date, he noticed a Buccaneers football jersey hanging over the back of one of Grace's kitchen chairs." When she glanced up, there was a confused crease between her eyebrows. "That seems like an odd thing to bring up."

"It was Doyle's. I'm sure the police asked Ron about it because earlier that day, Grace had sent Doyle a text message about returning it. Ron testified that he's a huge Bucs fan, so he asked if the jersey was hers. Grace told him it belonged to a friend, and she was planning to return it."

"A *friend*?" Robin's head tipped to the side. "Maybe she didn't want to bring up an ex to the new guy." She slugged down the last of her wine and set her glass out of the way. "So, the jersey was at Grace's house when Ron was there on Sunday. Then the next night, she's murdered."

"And the jersey's gone."

Robin's eyebrows lifted as she leaned forward over the table. "Tell me more. How do we know Ron didn't take it?"

"Well, the neighbor said Doyle was wearing a Bucs jersey when he took out the trash the night of the murder, and the police found it when they searched Doyle's house. Ron testified it appeared to be the same one he'd seen at Grace's. Brady. #12. Size extra-large."

Just then, the door from the garage opened and a tall man with salt and pepper hair called out, "Hey, hon, I'm home."

Robin stood and strolled over to kiss him hello. She waved her hand in the direction of the table. "This is Maggie. Her son Jake's on Charlie's soccer team."

He lifted his hand in a wave. "Juror on the murder trial, right?" he asked as his eyes took in the papers scattered across his kitchen table. "I'm David." His gaze drifted toward Robin, but unlike the contempt Maggie aways saw in Todd's eyes, there was acceptance and a hint of amusement. "I'm the husband. My lovely true-crime addict here told me all about your case."

He pulled open the refrigerator, took out a bottle of beer, and twisted off the cap. "I'll leave you two to whatever you were doing."

"Hang on." Robin reached for his arm as he walked away. "You might be able to help with something sports-related. The defendant left a Buccaneers jersey at the victim's house. After she was killed, the police searched his house and found it. But don't they all look alike? How would the police know it was the same jersey?"

"Same color and player, right?" David asked. "What about the size?"

"Red and white Brady jersey. XL."

He smiled. "Of course. It wasn't autographed or anything?"

Maggie shook her head. "It wasn't."

Robin's husband sipped his beer thoughtfully. "Obviously, there might be forensic evidence that would differentiate them." He winked at his wife, clearly proud of himself for throwing that tidbit out there. "But just by appearances, if it was a replica jersey in the same size, they'd look exactly alike." He shot Robin a sheepish look. "You know, provided one didn't have a big mustard stain or something on it."

"You mean the way you like to wear your condiments?" Robin rolled her eyes, but it was clear it was all good-natured fun. She aimed her chin at the refrigerator. "Charlie and I ate when he got home from soccer practice, but I left you a plate. We're almost done here."

Her husband kissed her on the cheek. "Take your time. I'm going to grab a shower."

Robin's lips were pursed as she sat back down. "Even if they did look alike, I still can't believe none of the jurors thought it was a big deal that the one found at Doyle's house looked exactly like the one missing from the murder scene."

"Doyle's story was that he bought two, except he couldn't produce a receipt for the second jersey. He claimed he paid with cash and tossed the receipt."

"How tidy of him." Robin leaned back and crossed her arms against her chest. "David's right about the forensic evidence, though. There wasn't gunshot residue or blood spatter on the jersey they found? Even if Doyle washed it, that would be hard to get rid of completely."

Maggie shook her head. "Nope. And that was a sticking point, too, especially since Ron saw it hanging over the back of

Grace's kitchen chair the night before. She was shot and killed right by the table."

Robin frowned. "It just seems hard to believe Doyle would have killed Grace to get his jersey back. Especially since she sent that text and offered to return it. And it makes no sense that he'd want two jerseys that were exactly the same."

"Well, he testified that after Grace ended things, he wrote off the one he'd left at her house. He said he was convinced Brady would take the team to the Super Bowl, so when he saw one at the sporting goods store, he snatched it up."

"So, it's just a coincidence he found one in the same colors in an XL?" Robin asked with a scowl.

"The jersey manufacturer testified at the trial." Maggie reached for her phone and pulled up a sporting goods apparel website. She slid the phone across the table toward Robin. "These are the three colors they offer for their jerseys, but the guy who testified said the red and white one is the most popular. It outsells the other two by a significant margin. He also told us that by that point in the season, they were difficult to find. The Bucs online shop where Doyle bought the first jersey was sold out."

Robin's expression said she was still having a hard time accepting Doyle's version of events. "If that's true, why wouldn't Doyle just agree to see Grace again to get his back? It wasn't like she was trying to keep it."

"On the stand, he made it sound like it was just one of those things." Maggie remembered the casual way Doyle shrugged when asked about it. "He testified that it was only after he'd already found the new one that Grace sent the text and offered to return his."

"So, he didn't need to respond."

"Right. Supposedly, he wasn't angry, just ready to put the relationship behind him."

"So, he says. Did he sound bitter?"

Maggie's shoulders lifted. "Not really. That was a big part of the problem during deliberations. The other jurors didn't think Doyle had any real motive to kill Grace. They'd only been out four or five times, so it wasn't like it was a long, serious relationship."

Robin was quiet for a moment, a slight furrow between her eyebrows. "Aside from the jersey, it doesn't sound like they really had much on him."

It was true that most of the evidence was circumstantial, but pieced together, Maggie was convinced it told the story of Doyle's guilt. "Well, the cops found the message offering to return the jersey on Grace's phone, but he had deleted it on his. Like he was trying to hide the fact that they'd actually met up."

Robin leaned forward, the lines on her forehead deepening. "But if he didn't respond to her text, was there a phone call between the two of them?"

"We asked the same question in the jury room because we never saw anything about a call. A few of the jurors were convinced they hadn't spoken, or the prosecution would have shown us the proof they did."

"So, if they didn't text and didn't speak by phone, there was no evidence they planned to meet up." Robin's gaze drifted thoughtfully. "Doyle's story about buying another jersey allowed him to claim he had no need to see Grace."

Maggie nodded in agreement. "Right. Confirming he met up with her would have put him right back in the cone of suspicion."

"One hundred percent. So, let's just say Doyle's story is true." Robin whipped up her hand. "Not that I believe it for a hot minute, mind you, but let's just say it is. Then what happened to the jersey Ron saw at Grace's house the night before she was killed?"

"One of the jurors suggested that when she didn't hear from Doyle, she could have dropped it in a thrift shop bin on her way to work. Or tossed it in the trash."

Robin scrunched up her face. "Come on. You're kidding?"

The frustration Maggie had felt in the jury room returned. "Now you see what I was dealing with. They also suggested someone else might have been at her house that night, and she gave the jersey to them."

"Because of the palm print on the door?"

"Potentially, but also in the pictures from the crime scene, there were two wine glasses on the coffee table that looked like there had been wine in them." Maggie had studied that photo in the jury room with a heavy dose of skepticism. Two perfectly placed long-stemmed glasses side by side had just the slightest tinge of burgundy at the bottom. They looked staged.

Robin pursed her lips as she contemplated this new information. "Maybe she and Ron had wine the night before, and she hadn't cleaned up."

"He testified they didn't have anything to drink at the house before they left, and here's the part that's really suspicious. They found no DNA or fingerprints on either wine glass."

Robin cocked her head, her eyes squinting. "You mean, no usable DNA or fingerprints?"

Maggie shook her head. "No, I mean they found nothing. Not even Grace's fingerprints."

The jurors had all agreed the lack of forensic evidence was suspicious. They just weren't convinced it implicated Doyle.

Robin rested her index finger on her lips as she bobbed her head. "Someone wiped them clean. Was there a wine bottle?"

"Empty, but no forensic evidence there either. Oddly enough, the cork from the bottle was missing. It wasn't even in the trash."

"Probably wanted something to keep as a souvenir," Robin said matter-of-factly. "Dahmer used to do that."

Maggie grimaced. "Uh, wine cork, body parts. Not exactly the same thing. But here's something else that's strange. Grace's purse was spilled on the floor by the front door."

"Anything missing?"

"No one knows for sure. There was still money in her wallet."

"Geez." Robin shook her head in disgust. "It's like whoever killed her couldn't decide if they wanted to stage a robbery or a rendezvous. Where did she meet the new guy?"

"At a club in Ybor City the weekend before."

"So, she meets this guy while she's out drinking and then invites him to pick her up at her house for their first date." Robin's eyes narrowed. "Doesn't that seem a little risky? I wonder why the police didn't consider him as a possible suspect."

"He testified that he was at his dad's house watching the Bucs game the night of the murder."

Robin's hand flew up into the air. "Wait, what? His dad was his alibi?" she asked incredulously. "Wouldn't most parents be willing to lie for their kid?"

"The police must have believed it. Otherwise, Ron might have been the one on trial."

Robin pinched her lips together and eyed Maggie. "He was watching the football game, huh? Makes me wonder if he has one of those red and white Brady jerseys, too."

"It didn't come up." Maggie sat back in her chair and gave her head a slight shake. "I just don't know what motive Ron would have had to kill Grace. They only had one date."

Robin flashed Maggie a knowing stare as she gathered all their papers into a neat pile. "Unless he's some sick serial killer.

I'm sure you listen to the same podcasts I do. Most of them just kill for the thrill of it. That's their motive."

Maggie still wasn't convinced. "Anything's possible, I guess, but Doyle didn't have a single person who could back up his story that he was home during the possible window for the murder."

"Other than his phone pinging from the tower near his house all night." Robin pushed her chair back from the table and stood. "Which we both know means nothing. Come on, let's go walk the dog. Tomorrow night we'll do a test run. I want to see how long it would have taken Doyle to drive from his place to the body shop and then to Grace's house."

When she lifted Duke's leash from the hook in the hallway, the dog came running, his nails clicking against the tile.

"I also think we should make a plan to talk to Ron Brookins." Robin's eyebrows lifted. "Or better yet, maybe we need to speak to his alibi."

7

"I just can't make sense of the pineapple in her digestive system." Robin glanced at the navigation screen on the dashboard, then hit her blinker to indicate the upcoming right turn. "If JonBenét ate it before she died, then who fed it to her?"

"Obviously not an intruder." Maggie relished having someone to dissect her favorite cases. "It proves she wasn't sleeping when she got home from the Christmas party like the parents said."

"I just can't believe they'd write that ridiculously long ransom note. I see people sitting around a table contributing all those movie lines. You know, like a joint effort. I think that's why it was three pages long."

"You see that? Like you're a psychic?" Maggie asked, a slight smile tugging at her lips. "Then ask your crystal ball how the ransom note was written on paper that came from a notepad inside the house." Her eyes narrowed. "Not to mention the kidnapper put the pad and pen right back where they belonged."

"Maybe they prided themselves on being an exceptionally

tidy criminal." Robin pulled the car over to the curb in front of the house across the street from Doyle's. "Well, it's not quite the Ramsey mansion, but that's it." She pointed out the driver's side window.

His porch light was on, and the lawn appeared to be lush and recently cut. A few small palm trees were tucked into a bed of mulch surrounded by terracotta-colored bricks, but that was the extent of the landscaping in the front. Doye's black pickup discussed at the trial was parked in the middle of the driveway, and a light shone through the slats of the closed blinds in the large front window.

Robin squinted into the darkness. "It doesn't look like a murderer's house."

"What's a killer's house supposed to look like?"

"I don't know. Creepier. Not so ... normal."

Maggie craned her neck to see around Robin. "It doesn't look like he uses the garage for his truck."

"I wish he wasn't home." Robin's brow crinkled as she stared longingly out her window. "I'd love the chance to walk around the house. Take a look at what he's got in his backyard."

"You'd be taking the tour alone." There was no way Maggie was getting out of the car and chancing an encounter with Doyle Riggs. "But since he is home, how 'bout you kill the headlights?"

"Oh, good idea," Robin said as if it hadn't occurred to her that they shouldn't call attention to themselves as they watched the house of a potential murderer. She hit a button and the street in front of them went dark.

"Besides, what are you expecting you'd find back there?" Maggie fought a smile. "Do you think he has a big shed with a sign that says 'where I keep the stuff to murder people?'"

"Maybe he does," Robin said with a straight face. "And now we won't know for sure. But seriously, when we record the podcast, we need to be able to make our listeners feel like they're here with us." She gave Maggie a sinister smile. "I want them to feel the danger of being so close to *a cold-blooded killer*." She dragged out her description for effect.

When Maggie turned to look out the back window, she felt an unexpected jab in her side. She sucked in air and threw her body against the back of her seat as she glared at the source. "Are you crazy?"

Robin giggled. "No, but that was fun. I can't believe you're so jumpy."

"I have no interest in being Doyle's next victim." Maggie's heart was still racing. "If he comes out that front door, you'd better turn on the car and hit the gas."

Robin leaned back in her seat and seemed unconcerned. "This is a public street. What's he going to do if he sees us?"

Maggie had spent almost two weeks just feet away from him in the courtroom, but the thought of facing Doyle Riggs on the darkened street in front of his house made her shudder. "If it's okay with you, I'd rather not find out."

"Listen, if he wants to cross paths with you, he could easily find you. It's not like the names of the jurors aren't part of the public record."

Maggie shrank back in her seat. "What?" she choked out. "My name is out there?"

"I thought you knew. It's not like it's a big deal. You found him not guilty." Robin gave Maggie's arm a reassuring pat. "If anything, Doyle should send you all thank you notes."

The inside of the car suddenly felt unbearably stuffy and hot. Maggie let out a deep breath and wiped a bead of sweat from the side of her face.

"Did anyone testify at the trial about whether he even owns a gun?" Robin asked.

Maggie whipped her head in her friend's direction and swallowed hard. "Why? Are you thinking he might shoot me?"

"Of course not. I'm just making conversation." Robin gave her a hard stare. "We're conducting an investigation here, remember?"

"Oh, right, sorry." Maggie exhaled loudly. "He did have a gun registered to him at the time of the murder." She stole a nervous glance at Doyle's house. "But he claimed he kept it at the body shop. For protection."

"Oh, *really*?"

"Don't get too excited. Doyle owned a nine-millimeter, and the bullet that killed Grace was a twenty-two. I learned more at the trial than I ever wanted to know about guns."

Robin ran her hand thoughtfully around the steering wheel. "Still doesn't mean Doyle didn't have access to a gun that wasn't registered to him."

This is why she and Robin were meant to be friends. "I said the same thing." Maggie couldn't resist a slight smile. "He probably keeps the other one in that murder supply shed in his backyard."

Robin reached over the center console and gave her a playful swat on the arm. "You know what I mean. If you're planning to kill someone, you don't use the gun registered to you to commit the murder. That's just stupid."

"I agree." Maggie glanced out the passenger side window and aimed her chin at the house they were sitting in front of. "This must be the neighbor who testified at the trial. The one who saw Doyle taking out his trash the night of the murder."

Robin let out a huff. "I'm sure he tossed his bloody boots right into the can for the garbage men to pick up the next morning. They're probably buried in the landfill by now."

"No kidding." Maggie eyed the front porch. "But now I can see why their view of his driveway was blocked. See the posts on either side." She released her seatbelt and gestured toward the back window. "If Doyle backed out of his driveway and went that way, their camera wouldn't have caught him leaving."

"And there's only a few houses between him and the exit. Let's go back out the way we came in." Robin started the car and pulled to the left side of the street to turn around.

As her headlights aimed into Doyle's front window, Maggie flung her hands in the air. "Why don't you just shine a spotlight into his house?"

"Would you relax? The boogeyman isn't going to come out and get us."

Maggie sucked in a sharp breath. "I swear I just saw his blinds move."

Robin put the car in reverse and shot her an exasperated look. "You're imagining things."

She completed the three-point turn and coasted the car down his street. "See any cameras?"

Maggie stared instead out the back window, fully expecting to see Doyle racing out his front door.

Robin snapped her fingers. "C'mon, stay focused. I need you to help me look."

Maggie let out a breath and squinted into the darkness. "I don't see any."

"Okay, then let's get out of here."

Maggie jabbed the button on her phone to start the timer. "Okay, go."

"Did you tell Jake what we were doing tonight?" Robin asked as they drove. "I tried to tell Charlie a little bit, and he was instantly bored. Of course, he's sixteen, so pretty much every-thing I tell him is of little interest to him."

"Jake's not that bad yet, but he's with Todd tonight. He has him every Wednesday night and every other weekend."

"A little court-ordered father-son bonding time?"

Maggie shrugged. "I guess. Believe it or not, he spends more time with him now than when we were married." Her phone beeped with a notification, and she glanced down. "It's just the Ring app."

"Someone strolling by the door of your apartment?"

"No, it's one of those neighborhood alerts." Maggie opened the message, and her eyebrows shot up. "Ohhh. It's a good one." She read from her screen. "Just heard what sounded like gunshots. Anyone else hear them?"

Robin cocked her head to the side. "Interesting. Where?"

"Almost three miles away. I guess that's not too close to where we live." Maggie used her fingers to zoom in on the map. "We probably need to avoid the area around Fourth Street when we go home." She shot Robin a look. "Unless we want to go that way to try and see what's going on." She loved having a friend who was as interested in crime-related situations as she was.

"Sure, *that* you want to check out, but back there ...."

"Well, it's different if someone's shooting at *me*. Not to mention, Doyle gives me the creeps. But it's not like I need to rush home." Maggie sat silent for a moment thinking about her empty apartment. "I think the worst part of the divorce is that Jake actually likes Stephanie." She wrinkled her nose the way she always did when she said Todd's girlfriend's name. Like the sound of it gave off a putrid odor.

"Ugh. So how long was that going on before you found out?" Robin glanced over with an apologetic wince. "I mean—if you're okay talking about it."

Maggie waved her hand to dismiss her new friend's concern. "It's fine. I don't mind sharing the gory details. They met at the gym. I should have known something was up when Todd started going more than usual. Shaving before he left. Wearing cologne. I started having my suspicions, but—" She hesitated, unsure how much of the truth she was willing to share. When she glanced over at Robin, compassion was etched on her face. No judgment. "Part of me was just relieved he wasn't around as much. Then, one day when I came home from work, I went into our bedroom to change and smelled perfume. I also had a Ring camera installed on my old house, so I checked the footage. Lo and behold, there they were on my front porch together. My husband and his mistress. They were trying to squeeze in a quickie before I got home."

"No, they were *not*." Robin grimaced. "In your bed?"

"Yup. Todd's way too cheap to pay for a hotel, and Stephanie's condo is on the water."

Robin lifted a hand from the steering wheel and reached for Maggie's arm. "That is awful. I hope you kicked his cheating ass to the curb that night."

The back of Maggie's neck grew warm. She hadn't. She'd let it continue for three more months. Ignored what was right in front of her. Part of her had hoped the affair would end on its own, and she could just pretend it had never happened. It wasn't that she wanted to be with Todd or was even angry about his betrayal. Mostly, it was because she was terrified of the other option. Getting divorced. Trying to survive on her own.

"I decided to bide my time," Maggie said instead. "I needed to figure out how I wanted to use what I knew."

Robin bobbed her head. "Smart." She huffed. "Me? I would have lost it on him right then and there."

The truth was her hand had been forced when another mother at Jake's school confided she'd seen Todd and Stephanie together having lunch. Well, not just eating, she'd said, lest Maggie write it off as an innocent business outing. *If my husband were canoodling like that with someone else, I would want someone to tell me. Right out in the open, too, like he had nothing to hide.*

She'd then patted Maggie's arm in consolation and strolled away, satisfied she'd lobbed the ball of knowledge into someone else's court. A private indiscretion Maggie might have been able to live with. But flaunting it like that? Word spread like a bad rash, and everywhere she went, other mothers stared. They shook their heads in pity. Todd had left her with no choice but to confront him with what she knew.

"It took a little while, but I finally had it out with him. It wasn't like he could deny he'd been cheating on me. I had the footage where he practically had his tongue down her throat while he unlocked our front door."

Maggie didn't mention it had been more than that one time. Even now, her insides churned as she wondered what their neighbors had seen. Maybe they figured she was too stupid to realize what was going on.

Robin shot her a quick glance. "I would have loved to have been a fly on the wall when he found out you caught him red-handed."

When it first happened, Maggie had wondered if Todd wanted her to see them together. An attempt to make her jealous. But when she'd showed him the video, her husband had seemed genuinely surprised—not to mention moderately aroused—that his antics with Stephanie had been captured. He'd shown no remorse whatsoever.

"Oh, you would have been a very disappointed fly." Maggie shook her head. "He was very blasé about the whole thing. Tried to say the affair was my fault because I wasn't interested in going to the gym with him."

Robin whipped her head in Maggie's direction. "*Your* fault?" She grunted in disgust. "Oh, that man is so lucky I didn't know you then, or I would have totally helped you off him." She slapped her palm against the steering wheel. "We could have buried Tom's cheating ass in the woods. Someplace where no one would ever find him, but where the animals could pick the meat off his bones like they were at the all-you-can-eat barbecue buffet."

Maggie couldn't help but laugh at the image Robin portrayed. "When you called him by the wrong name at the soccer game, I almost died."

"We women have to stick together," Robin said as she waved her hand between the two of them. "He's lucky I didn't know then what I know now." She gave Maggie a conspiratorial wink and dipped her chin. "But if you're still mad about it, you just say the word."

"I'll keep that in mind." Maggie leaned back in her seat, and a warm feeling swelled up inside her. Someone was on her side. Unconditionally. It was nice to have a friend again.

They arrived at the darkened body shop a few minutes later, and when they pulled into the parking lot, Robin turned to Maggie. "How long?"

"Twelve minutes and ten seconds."

"And how far are we from Grace's?"

Maggie punched the address into Robin's navigation system. "At least fifteen minutes."

"That far, huh?" Robin turned the car around and pointed at Maggie's phone. "Okay, start the timer again."

As they drove, Maggie couldn't help but notice Robin's gaze repeatedly lifting to her rearview mirror.

"Don't freak out," she said finally. "I'm not sure, but I think someone's following us."

8

M aggie spun around in her seat to see if there was a car behind them. "Come on, stop joking around. You know I'm nervous enough."

Robin glanced over with a serious expression that indicated her concern was legitimate. "Pause the timer. "I'm going to make the next right and see if they keep going." A moment later, she yanked the wheel hard and punched the gas. "Did he turn too?"

Maggie's chest heaved as she stared into the darkness behind them. No headlights. "I don't see anyone."

Robin exhaled loudly, and when she pulled over to the side of the road, she swatted Maggie's arm. "See, now you're making me paranoid, too, but it was nothing. We're almost there. I'm going to turn around, so restart the timer."

A few minutes later, they made the turn that would send them down Grace's street.

Maggie stole a look behind them and stiffened when she saw headlights. "There's a car behind us."

"Other people are allowed to use this road, too, you know." Robin didn't even bother to check her rearview mirror this time.

"I shouldn't have said anything, but I promise you, we're not being followed. You can relax."

Easier said than done.

When Robin pulled the car up in front of the house where Grace had been murdered, she sat silently but gave Maggie an expectant stare.

"What?"

Robin eyed the phone gripped tightly in Maggie's hand.

"Oh." Maggie eased out a slow breath and pressed the button to end the timer. "Sixteen minutes and twenty seconds from the body shop to here, which makes the total trip time ..." She did the simple math in her head. "Twenty-eight and a half minutes. Plus, Doyle would have needed additional time to go inside to kill her. Remember, her body was found in the kitchen."

"That seems to put our white car timeline in peril." Robin frowned as she put the car in park. "It's interesting that Grace's place is on a dead end. With only one way out of the neighborhood, you'd think whoever killed her would have been nervous they'd get trapped."

At the moment, Maggie felt the same way. She unclicked her seatbelt and swiveled in her seat. As she checked out the area around them, she couldn't resist a glance back up the road. Robin was right. No one had followed them.

Robin squinted at the small sign affixed to the fence in front of them. "Looks like the side of the house butts up against a protected preserve." She shut off the engine and plunged the dead end back into darkness. Her nose wrinkled as she gave Grace's house a wistful stare. "I guess someone new lives there now."

The small white house had a perfectly manicured lawn and colorful flowers in pots by the front door. It was hard not to notice the two SUVs in the driveway or the warm lights behind sheer curtains hanging in the front window. Despite the somber reason for their visit, Grace's old house now looked cheerful and alive.

Maggie pointed toward an oversized box beside the trash can on the side of the house. "Looks like the new people have a baby." She cringed as she imagined the family inside. "I wonder if they even know someone was killed here."

Robin shifted in her seat and glanced out the back window. "I get that her house was at the end of the block, but I can't believe none of the neighbors heard the gunshot. Someone should have been able to verify the time Grace was killed."

"There was no testimony at the trial about it."

Robin started up the car and used the driveway of the house across the street from Grace's to turn around. She put the car in reverse and then slammed on the brakes.

"Uh, is it my imagination, or do they have a camera by their front door?"

Maggie followed her friend's gaze. "That's definitely a camera. It's the same one I have."

Robin turned to Maggie, a deep crease between her brows. "Wouldn't the police have asked for their footage?" She gestured at the front porch. "No posts in the way here. They would have had a perfect view of the front of Grace's house."

Maggie stared out her window at the car parked right beside her. "And we're probably on their camera right now. Sitting in their driveway."

Robin stomped on the gas pedal. The car lurched backward, and Maggie's head flew back against the headrest.

She flashed Maggie a sheepish look. "Sorry." As she inched the car forward, she shook her head. "I just don't understand how there isn't any video footage of the killer if the people across the street have a camera."

"Maybe it didn't capture Doyle's black pickup, so the prosecution didn't want the jury to see it." Maggie's mouth pulled tight. She didn't want to believe the police had video of someone else but had arrested Doyle anyway.

Robin slowed the car to a stop. She leaned toward Maggie's window to study the house next to Grace's. "What about these people? There's no camera, but they didn't hear anything? Really?"

"The one thing I always notice from some of those Ring notifications is that people can never seem to tell where the gunshot's coming from."

"But right next door? That would be hard to miss."

Maggie peered into the darkness. "There are no cars in the driveway, although I guess they could be in the garage. But it doesn't look like anyone's home." She glanced at the clock on the dashboard. "It's about the same time of night as when the murder happened. Maybe whoever lives there works nights. I would assume the police knocked on doors and spoke to Grace's neighbors."

"I suppose." Robin continued to let the car drift up the street, braking periodically to stare out the windows. "I know the timeline's messed up, but what about the white car speeding through the stop sign. Where did that happen exactly?"

"Oh, let me look." Maggie pulled the file with the witness statements from her tote bag and sorted through them. "Here it is. Melody Kaplan said the white car came barreling down 77th Drive and didn't even slow down at the stop sign at Oak Street."

"Grace's house is on 77th. Did we pass Oak yet?" Robin squinted out her window.

"You drive. I'll look." Maggie peered into the darkness as the road curved to the right. When they got to Pine Street, she shook her head. "Not yet."

Robin came to a stop, then continued driving.

The next sign said Maple. "Nope. This isn't it either." A few moments later, Maggie saw the street she'd been looking for. "Stop!"

Robin slammed on her brakes. "Well, I almost went through it, too." She looked in both directions, went through the intersection, and pulled the car over to the curb.

"It's too bad the person in the white car didn't slam right into Melody Kaplan."

Robin admonished her with a disapproving scowl. "*Maggie*."

She held up her hands in protest. "I'm just saying. Then we'd know for sure if the white car was related."

"Well, that would be—"

Knuckles rapped loudly on the driver's side window, and Maggie drew in a stuttered gasp.

Robin squinted in the dark looking for the button on the car door handle. When her window rolled down, a police officer stood beside the car.

"Sorry about that, Officer." Robin brought her palm to her chest. "You startled me."

He leaned in her window, and his gaze swept the inside of the car. "Ladies, can I help you with something?"

Maggie gulped down a steadying breath. They weren't doing anything illegal, but her cheeks were on fire. One look at her flushed face, and the cop would assume they were guilty of something.

"We were just, uh, looking for a friend's house." Robin sounded far more casual than Maggie felt. "We seem to have gotten lost."

Maggie's pulse raced as she waited to see if the officer would ask for the address they were supposedly looking for.

"I'm going to need to see some ID," he said instead. He gestured at the passenger seat. "From both of you."

Maggie reached into her wallet and attempted to slide her driver's license out of the clear compartment. It was stuck. She tugged at it until it finally came free. Her hand trembled as she handed it to Robin, who silently passed both of their licenses to the officer.

He switched on a light and waved it over Robin's ID in his hand. A moment later, he tucked the flashlight under his arm and moved Maggie's to the top. Her heart thudded as she watched him hold his light over her driver's license and then bring it closer to scrutinize it. It was more than the cursory glance he'd given Robin's. He couldn't have any way of knowing Maggie hadn't made the time to get a new license after the divorce. A form of denial, maybe. It still had her old address listed.

After several long agonizing moments, the officer glanced up and aimed his flashlight at the passenger seat. "Maggie White?"

How did he know her maiden name? Maggie winced as she stared into the blinding light. She leaned on the console between the two front seats and used her hand to shield her eyes as she attempted to see the person behind the voice.

"Yeah, that's me." She squinted in his direction. "But I can't really—"

"Oh, sorry about that."

The police officer lowered his light, and Maggie blinked hard as she tried to clear the spots still dotting her vision.

"It's, uh, Matt Winters," he said. "We went to high school together. In New Jersey."

As if Maggie needed the reminder. She'd had a massive crush on him sophomore year that had gone nowhere.

She nodded in recognition as he came into focus. "Right. We did."

"You haven't changed much. You look just like you did in Mr. Foreso's history class."

She released a nervous chuckle. "Oh, I don't know about that."

Robin turned and shot her a curious look, so Maggie explained their connection. "White's my maiden name. Matt sat behind me." She gestured at herself and then him. "White. Winters. We were seated in alphabetical order."

"Not just that class," Matt said as he handed Robin back her ID. "Our lockers were side by side. We even sat next to each other at graduation. So, how long have you been in Florida?"

"About eight years. My husband got transferred down here. Although technically, I guess I am Maggie White again." She lifted and dropped her shoulders. "I just got divorced."

"Oh, sorry to hear that. Me too. Well, about a year ago." Matt leaned in the car window and reached past Robin to hand Maggie back her license. "Not everyone can handle being married to a cop." He set his forearms on the frame of the driver's side window.

"I'm sure."

In the darkness, Maggie couldn't see the entirety of how Matt Winters had aged, but the arms resting on the car seemed tan and muscular. His hair had a bit of gray—and there was certainly less of it than she remembered—but her high school crush still looked good. Really good.

"Sorry for the inquisition, but I've watched you two drive around here like you're casing the block. We've had a bunch of car thefts in the area, so you know, gotta check out anything that looks suspicious." Matt laughed. "You two ladies aren't out stealing cars tonight, right?"

Maggie's hand went to her chest. "Us?" She shook her head. "No, it's nothing like that." She exchanged a glance with Robin, then admitted the real reason for their visit to this neighborhood. "Actually, you know that house at the very end of the block. The little white one?"

Matt's eyes narrowed, his head now cocked to the side. "Yeah, what about it?"

"You know someone was murdered there, right?"

"I do, but how did you know about it?" he asked, his tone turning suspicious.

Maggie raised her right hand in the air. "Juror number eight."

"Ah." His face hardened. "Is this an unofficial visit to the scene of the crime? I sincerely hope the trial's over." Gone was the friendly cop who had recognized Maggie from high school. "Otherwise, the judge isn't going to be very happy to hear about this. I'd have no choice but to—"

Maggie waved her hand in the air to interrupt his warning. "No, no. The trial's over. We—we found the defendant not guilty. I just—there were things I still had questions about, so I wanted to see the house and the neighborhood for myself."

His eyes narrowed as he rubbed the stubble on his chin. "It's a little late to be questioning your verdict, don't you think? If you let him off, there's not much you can do about it now."

"Oh, I know. Double jeopardy." Maggie threw the term out so he'd know she was familiar with how the system worked. "I just need to know if he got away with it. Not that we had a choice. The jury, I mean. The prosecution—" She stopped herself and gestured at Robin. "We're just looking into it because if he didn't do it, then the person who did is still out there."

The cop's mouth pulled tight. "A piece of advice, if I might. Bad guys don't generally like people checking upon them. For any reason." His gaze bounced purposefully between Robin and Maggie. "I'd hate to see you two get in over your heads. Trust me, these things never end well for amateur detectives. You need to leave the investigating to the professionals." He waited a moment for his words to settle, then gave the window frame two thumps with his hand to indicate the end of his lecture. "Take care, Maggie. It was good to see you again after all these years."

"It was good to see you, too."

The officer gave Robin a hard stare. "I'm going to drive off now, and I expect your car will be right behind me. We clear?"

She nodded and held up her right hand. "One hundred percent. We're leaving, too."

After the cruiser pulled away, Robin shifted to face Maggie. "Okay, I'm not sure how well you could see from the passenger seat, but your friend from high school is all grown up and very handsome." Her eyes lit up. "And single. You know, in case you missed the comment about his divorce."

"I think I heard him mention something about that." Maggie aimed her chin at the road. "Come on, you promised him we'd get out of here."

Robin wasn't wrong about how well Matt Winters had aged. For the first time in as long as she could remember, Maggie couldn't stop smiling.

She'd forgotten all about her fear that someone had been following them.

9

The next night Maggie gave Jake a brief rundown of what she and Robin had done the night before while he was at his dad's. He'd been moderately interested in what had transpired since the verdict, and she enjoyed talking about their investigation with someone who had a neutral point of view.

"Do you still think he did it?" he asked as he slid into a chair at the kitchen table.

Maggie pulled the chicken she'd defrosted from the refrigerator as she considered the question. "I'm—I'm not sure."

Her brow wrinkled as she glanced around the kitchen for her purse. She spotted it hanging on the back of Jake's chair and tapped his shoulder. When he leaned forward, she pulled the recipe she'd printed at work from her bag.

"So, you think the jury made the right decision? You know, to let him go?" He planted his elbows on the table and lowered his chin into his hands.

Maggie hesitated only briefly before nodding. "Based on the evidence they gave us, yeah, it was the correct verdict. I can see that now."

After setting the oven to preheat, she squinted at the sheet of paper and compared the ingredients she needed with what she'd laid out on the counter. Since moving, Maggie hadn't often cooked dinner for the two of them, but she was determined to turn over a new leaf—one that didn't include a drive-thru or a pizza box. She reached into the sparsely-filled cabinet next to the oven and pulled out the salt and pepper.

"Since Robin and I started looking into the case, I discovered that there was stuff the jury didn't hear about. Evidence that could potentially point to someone else."

"Really?" Jake asked, sounding confused. "I don't understand. Why wouldn't they give you everything they had?"

Maggie pulled the one large knife she owned from the utensil drawer. Now that she was planning to cook more often, she regretted leaving an entire kitchen full of necessities with Todd.

"Well, Robin and I aren't aware of everything the police uncovered. But we found out they interviewed a witness who saw a white car speeding away from the murder scene. Doyle, the defendant, drove a black pickup."

Jake was silent for a moment as he seemed to consider this new information. "So, most likely whoever was driving the white car did it." His tone was matter-of-fact. "Not your guy."

As if it were that simple.

Maggie shrugged as she began chopping garlic. "It's possible. Or maybe the person driving that car wasn't related to the case." She glanced over her shoulder at him. "What if they were just in a huge rush to get somewhere that night? Or it could be they were simply a terrible driver with no regard for stop signs."

"So, because they can't prove the person in the white car was the one who killed her, they decided not to tell the jury about it?" Jake tossed his head from side to side with a scowl. "That's messed up."

"I agree, but like I said, we don't know everything the police do. They must have been convinced Doyle did it, or they wouldn't have arrested him." Maggie used the knife to slide the garlic from the cutting board into the pan with the chicken. "Besides, if they couldn't prove the white car was relevant or that the defendant had access to a white car, it wasn't evidence that helped their case. After all, the trial was to try and convict him."

"Which they didn't do."

"No, they didn't." Maggie's lips pulled tight, and she eased out a slow breath as she recalled her frustration in the jury room. "You have to get twelve people to all agree. That's not so easy either. Especially if the prosecution doesn't give you all the information to work with."

"I get it, I guess. At least now you don't have to feel guilty about letting him go. You and Robin can go back to being moms instead of private investigators."

Maggie stiffened, then wheeled around to face him. "We weren't looking into the case because I felt guilty."

"Oh." Jake sat up straight and looked surprised. His head fell to one side as he stared at her. "But I thought you said you felt bad when you ran into the lady's sister."

Maggie's cheeks warmed as she grabbed a handful of cherry tomatoes and ran them under the faucet. She had said that. "I did feel bad." She grabbed a paper towel from the roll and wrapped them inside to dry them off. "But also, Robin and I— we're thinking of doing a podcast. Something true-crime-related." She pulled the first tomato and sliced it in half. "You know, like the stuff I always listen to in the car." Maggie still wasn't sure she was cut out for it, but at least it justified the time she was spending with Robin investigating.

"Oh. That's kind of cool, I guess." Jake hesitated. "But why do you like all this murder stuff anyway? Doesn't it depress you?"

Maggie spun around again and shook her head. "Not at all.

It's like solving a mystery. I love trying to put all the puzzle pieces together to figure out who did it or why someone disappeared."

"But your shows don't always have the answer at the end." Jake let out an exaggerated groan. "I know. I've been forced to listen to them in the car."

Maggie pressed her lips together to keep from laughing. "That's true. Some of the cases people cover are unsolved. I might think I know what went down, but I don't always get to find out if I'm right. But that's why Robin and I discussed doing the podcast. We figured we'd start with this case. Investigate it for ourselves and talk about what we find. Hopefully, in the end, we'll have the answers about what really happened."

A smile twitched her lips. "Then, if a listener's teenage son is forced to listen to us, he'll know how the case ended. If it goes well, maybe we move on to another unresolved crime for the next series of episodes."

"Are you going to quit your job?" Worry crept into Jake's eyes. "To do this podcast thing?"

She placed a reassuring hand on his shoulder just as the oven beeped that it was ready. "I wish, but I could never afford to do that. Not yet anyway. Besides, I'm still not positive the podcast is going to happen. Right now, it's just an idea we have."

Maggie went back to the counter to finish prepping dinner. She added the rest of the ingredients and sprinkled everything with salt and pepper. After setting the timer on the microwave, she moved the pan to the oven.

"You're not scared it could be dangerous?" Jake asked. "The investigating part, not the podcast."

As Maggie slipped into the chair across from him, she remembered how she'd felt sitting outside Doyle's house. That was different. The sinister look he'd given her after the verdict was still fresh in her memory.

The idea that he might have followed them the night before sent a burst of fear rippling through her insides. But she would never tell her son any of that. To answer his question, she reverted to the way she'd felt before the trial—before she'd ever known anyone as evil as Doyle Riggs.

"That's the beauty of watching true crime shows," she said. "Seeing what happens to people who get themselves in trouble makes you hyperaware of what you need to do to stay safe. That's why I'm always telling you how important it is to be aware of your surroundings." Maggie nudged his cell sitting on the table. "Not to walk while you stare at your phone. You know that if someone tries to grab you, you yell as loud as you can and try to get away."

Jake's eyes glazed over. "When I was little, I'll never forget how many times you told me to never get in a car with anyone who offered me candy or said you sent them to get me. I still remember the code word you gave me." He jabbed his finger in the air and mimicked her. "*If I ever need anyone to get you in an emergency, they'll use the word broccoli. If they don't say it, I didn't send them. Scream, kick 'em where it counts, and run away.*"

Maggie fought a smile. Her son's imitation of her was spot on. "Hey, it worked, didn't it? You made it to fifteen safe and sound. But it's good advice, not only for little kids but adults, too. Most criminals won't grab someone determined to draw attention to the situation. That's a fact. You never want to get in a car with someone hoping they'll eventually let you go. If someone takes you to a second location, it's almost certain they're going to kill you."

"Way to be morbid, Mom."

Maggie shrugged. "It's reality. It's not that different from preparing for an active shooter at school. It's horrible to imagine, but it's the world we live in. You need to know what to do if it ever happens."

"If I can't escape, then hide." Jake recited the words mechanically, a reflection of how many times it had been drilled into his head. "Don't trust anyone who says they're the police unless I can see them. Don't reveal myself unless I'm one-hundred percent positive the danger has passed."

Maggie gave him a firm nod. "Exactly. Staying safe is a matter of being smart, but unfortunately, that also means walking around with a bit of mistrust. That goes for—"

"I know," he said in a weary voice. "Online, too. Never believe anyone is who they say unless they can prove it."

"It's true. What better place to be a predator than in those games you play? Anyone can say they're a fifteen-year-old boy." Maggie's eyebrows lifted as she stared at her teenage son. "Or a girl."

Jake reeled back as if he was insulted. "Come on. I would never run off to meet someone I met playing Xbox. Give me a little credit."

Her eyes narrowed as she stared at her son. "I hope not. I can't help worrying because I know what could happen. Kids disappear every single day." That was the flip side of being obsessed with true crime. How often had she heard a child had gone missing only to learn later they'd trusted the wrong person, and it had cost them their life? "One stupid, impulsive decision—"

Jake's groan interrupted her lecture. "Trust me. I get it. You can sleep easy, Mom. You've raised me to be paranoid about everything and everyone."

"Not paranoid. Careful." Maggie jabbed her index finger in his direction. "There's a difference. Besides, I'm sure Charlie gets the same speech from Robin."

"I'm sure he does. It's like you two are the same person sometimes." He held her gaze and offered a slight smile. "I'm glad you met her. It's nice for you to have a friend, and she's been good for you." His shoulder lifted in a half-shrug. "I mean, she's got you out walking every night, and you're making chicken for dinner."

Maggie laughed. "I know, right? No more fast food around here." She'd started to enjoy getting healthy. Not because Todd shamed her into it, but because she'd now accepted she deserved to feel better. She stood and pulled a package of mixed vegetables from the freezer. "And you like Charlie, too, right?"

Jake nodded, then his hand flew to his mouth as he teased her. "Oh, no, Mom. We do play Xbox. Are you sure it's okay for me to meet up with him?"

Maggie shot him an aggravated look. "Yes, because you already know who he is in real life."

"Ohh." His face turned serious. "I like spending time with them. It's kind of like we have family here."

Maggie pulled a dish from the cabinet and dumped the vegetables into it. "Maybe at some point, I'll even meet someone I want to date."

Her son chuckled. "Doubt it."

Maggie wheeled around, surprised by his reaction. "Why wouldn't I? I mean, your dad and I are divorced. He's got Stephanie."

"I guess maybe someday you might want to." Jake folded his arms in front of him on the table and rested his chin on them. "Like when I go to college." The corners of his mouth lifted in a sly smile. "Otherwise, you'll miss me too much."

She raised her eyebrows. "Oh, so I have to wait until you leave me to date?"

Maggie didn't tell him she already had a prospective candidate in mind.

10

"I tracked down the pizza delivery guy today," Robin said as they made their nightly walk with Duke around the lake. "He confirmed Doyle's black pickup was in the driveway, and he was pretty sure he wasn't wearing a Bucs jersey when he answered the door."

"Well, the game hadn't started yet. But I thought we already confirmed Doyle didn't have enough time to swap vehicles and commit the murder if the woman saw the white car at 8:05 p.m."

"I tracked her down, too. And I left a message for Ron Brookins."

"Really?"

Robin shrugged. "No school today."

"That's not fair." Maggie scowled. "I had to deal with Harry's crap all day."

"Sorry. Anyway, Melody Kaplan is in her seventies. When I asked her how she knew what time she saw the white car, she told me she was on her way home from playing bridge with friends. Apparently, she usually likes to get home earlier, but that night she stayed for dinner ... and a glass of cabernet." Robin gave a knowing nod. "Or two."

Maggie's eyes narrowed as she walked. "So, she was older, and she was drinking." Maybe Doyle had the opportunity to commit the crime after all. "Was she positive about the time?"

"When I pressed her, she admitted it might have been later. Not by much, according to her, but even twenty minutes and Doyle could be back in the running as our prime suspect."

"I don't know." Maggie planted her hands on her hips as she walked. "I still think if the police could have proven Doyle had access to a white car, they would have put her on the stand."

Robin's face scrunched up. "Melody Kaplan would have made a terrible witness. The defense could have claimed she was drunk or too old to see well at night."

Duke came to an abrupt stop, a low growl in his throat. His attention was riveted to the clump of trees up ahead. They fronted a canal, and at the right time of day, the orange glow of the sun setting would reflect off the water in a picture-perfect moment. But at night, the entire area was shrouded in an eerie black haze.

"What's the matter, buddy?" Robin tugged at the leash, but the dog refused to move. She peered into the darkness. "Don't be silly. There's nobody there."

Maggie took a step backward. "What if someone's hiding?" She wished Robin had never told her about her name being made public.

Robin spun to face her and jabbed her index finger in the air. "Don't make my dog paranoid, too."

Then just as quickly as he'd frozen in place, Duke relaxed and resumed his usual pace.

"See," Robin said pointedly. "It was nothing."

Maggie squinted to see for herself. She gulped down a steadying breath as the group powered forward.

With the dog walking briskly beside her again, Robin picked up where she'd left off. "Anyway, when I asked Melody Kaplan

about the white sedan, she had no idea of the make and model."
She waved her finger in the air and spoke in a high-pitched
voice. "I think it was one of those expensive ones, but, honey, I
don't know much about cars. Nor do I care, as long as the one I
have gets me to my bridge game."

As they got closer to Robin's house, Duke strained at the
leash. "You're going to get water soon," she said. "We're almost
home."

"I need some, too." Maggie wicked the sweat from her forehead with her fingertips. "How is it still so humid out?" Though
at first she'd huffed and puffed trying to keep up every night, it
was getting easier. She slid her finger into the waistband of her
pants and found room that hadn't been there previously. "I'm
actually losing weight."

"That's because you're finally doing things that make you
happy. When you were married—well, nothing has more calo-
ries than stress and misery." Robin unclipped the dog's leash
and pulled open her front door. "Not to mention, Duke and I are
such good company. Come in, and I'll get you a bottle of water. I
have something to show you."

"Oh, okay." Maggie's mind was already spinning on how she
was going to get home. Usually she walked back to her apartment complex from Robin's house, but Duke's growling had
made the hair on her arms stand up. She wasn't sure she wanted
to go back the same way alone. "I actually have a bit of a surprise
for you, too."

Maggie slugged down half a bottle of water while Duke
emptied his bowl. He sprawled out on the cool tile, his tongue
hanging out, chest still heaving up and down.

"I get it, buddy," she said as she watched him. "I'm thinking
of lying down next to you."

"Not yet, you don't." Robin stood from the kitchen table.
"Come on." She gestured for Maggie to follow her.

They trudged up the stairs and past Charlie's room. He didn't even notice them, his attention laser-focused on his television as he played a video game.

Maggie shook her head. "I swear he looks just like Jake."

"He'd better have his homework done," Robin said, her voice abnormally loud for her son's benefit before she waved Maggie into the guest bedroom at the end of the hallway.

"Are you inviting me to stay over?" Maggie asked. "I wasn't really going to nap on your kitchen floor with Duke."

"You can sleep anywhere in the house you want, but this is what I wanted you to see." With a flourish, Robin pulled open a set of double doors and flipped a light switch. "This *was* the walk-in closet."

Maggie peeked inside and then shot Robin a curious stare. Her spare room closet was practically empty, with no shelves or clothes hung on bars. It was almost as big as Jake's bedroom at the apartment.

Robin stepped inside. "Come in."

While the bedroom was tiled, the oversized closet was carpeted. Two leather office chairs sat on either side of a square wooden table. A few boxes of what appeared to be electronics were piled on top. Maggie ran her hand along the inside wall, the texture squishy under her fingers. All four walls and the ceiling were covered with gray tiles made of foam.

"Are you planning to kidnap someone?" She was only half-joking. "That thing about Todd ..."

"Don't be ridiculous." Robin stroked her fingers slowly against her chin and spoke in a low, raspy voice. "Unless, of course, you've decided he needs to be taught a lesson about respect."

Maggie couldn't help but laugh. "Well, he could absolutely use the lesson, but I don't know. This seems a bit extreme."

Her friend's face twisted in disgust. "I wouldn't waste all this on that cheating sack of you-know-what. My husband sent one of his guys over yesterday to set this up. It's for us."

Maggie's forehead creased. "For us? Why?"

"For recording our podcast. They soundproofed the room, so we don't have to worry about Charlie screaming at his video games or Duke barking." Robin moved to the table and slid a box toward Maggie. "This is your microphone." She relocated the other two boxes to the other side of the table and dropped into one of the leather chairs. "This one's mine, and I have a way to plug us into my laptop so we can record and edit." She gestured at the chair on the other side of the table. "Check it out. They're super comfortable."

Maggie pushed the chair back from the table, no easy task against the plush carpeting.

"We can bring the listeners in as we go through Doyle's case," Robin said. "Then we can bring up other cases and analyze them. We can find sponsors."

"You're serious?"

Robin flinched, her surprise at her friend's ambivalence written all over her face. "Weren't you?"

Despite what she'd told Jake, Maggie hadn't really considered they might actually pull it off. Her shoulders lifted in a helpless shrug. "I thought it was an interesting idea, but I can't— I mean, I don't know how to be a podcast host. And how much time would something like this take?"

"It's just you and me talking. The only difference is we'll be doing it in here instead of while we're walking the dog. We'll recap what we find out about the case. Where we plan to go next. We don't have to release the episodes until we solve it. At this point, we'll just record them as we go along."

Maggie's head was spinning. This was a crazy idea, but maybe they'd never even release the episodes. She wouldn't be very good at it, but at least she could say she tried. She uncapped her water bottle and took a long sip to buy herself some time.

"I know you listen to tons of true-crime podcasts, just like I do." Robin's face turned serious as she studied Maggie. "Why do you think those people can do it, and we can't?"

"I mean, I'm sure we *could*. It's just—it's just—" As she stammered, Maggie realized she didn't have a good answer as to why she wouldn't be willing to try. It was the least she could do after Robin had gone to all this effort to set up the space to record. "It's just—you're great at talking off the cuff. I don't know that I would be very good at it."

"It'll take practice. For both of us." She gave Maggie a stern stare. "You just have to silence all that nonsense Todd used to fill your head with. You'll be great at it if you give yourself a chance."

Her friend was right. This was precisely the type of thing her ex-husband would have told her not to waste her time attempting because she'd fail. Maggie hesitated and gave herself a quick internal pep talk. What would be the harm in trying? It was time to do something for herself. Something she enjoyed.

Robin took Maggie's silence as proof she was considering it. "So, are you in?" She looked like she was about to burst.

What would be better than talking about true crime with someone as obsessed as she was? Maggie rolled her water bottle between her hands and then nodded slowly. "Yeah, I'm in."

Robin squealed and came to her side of the table. "This is going to be amazing." She leaned down to hug her. "You'll see. Maybe you can even finally tell that boss of yours to shove it." She tipped her head to the side. "That's not your news, is it? Did you get some fabulous job offer for twice as much money?"

"Please. No one is knocking down my door to give me a new job." Maggie bit back a smile. "But it might be something even better. I got a very interesting call last night."

"Oh, yeah, from who?" Robin asked casually as she plopped back down in her leather chair.

Maggie could see her friend had no idea what was coming. "A certain police officer called me." She tried to resist the urge to grin like a lovestruck teenager. It was impossible. "He asked if I wanted to have dinner with him this week. To catch up."

Robin's eyes lit up. "Stop it. You said, yes, of course."

Maggie's hand covered her mouth. She still couldn't believe she'd agreed to have dinner with Matt Winters. "I did." Her hand moved to her forehead. "But now I'm freaking out. Is catching up—is it a *date*?"

"He's single. You're single. Hell yeah, it's a date."

"I don't know how to do that." Maggie let out a soft whimper. "It's been more than sixteen years."

"Obviously, he's interested." Robin rubbed her hands together. "We'll go shopping tomorrow night to find you something perfect to wear."

Maggie's phone buzzed. She slid it from her back pocket and Jake's name was on the screen. "Hey, what's up?"

"You coming home soon? I need you take me to the store to get something for school."

"Tonight?"

Her son hesitated. "Yeah, I need it for class tomorrow."

"Come on, Jake, really?" She sighed. "Okay, I'm leaving now."

Maggie was tempted to ask Robin for a ride, but she could just picture her eyes rolling at the request. *You're being ridiculous. There's no one hiding in the bushes.*

As she headed out into the darkness, Maggie's nerves were already on edge. As she turned onto the sidewalk outside Robin's development, the glow of the streetlights cast eerie shadows that danced on the sidewalk in front of her. She'd never noticed them on their nightly walks, but now that she was alone, the slightest movement sent her heart galloping into her throat.

Her chest heaved in and out with long, deliberate breaths, and she picked up her pace. When she'd gotten safely past the trees that had drawn Duke's attention earlier, her shoulders lowered in relief. Robin was right. Maggie had let Doyle and this case get under her skin, but she needed to stop imagining he was lurking around every corner.

But what if he was?

Maggie ran the rest of the way home. Just in case.

11

Maggie gathered her work into a pile and tossed it into her inbox. She had just reached into her purse and pulled out her car keys when Harry flew out of his office. It was almost as if he'd been watching her. Waiting for the moment she'd dare to pack up to leave for the day.

"I hope you're not trying to sneak out early." His beady eyes were riveted to the keys in her hand. "I have a meeting tomorrow morning with Surbhi and Partners, and I need their quarterly report."

It was after five, and this was the first she'd heard about any meeting. As Maggie's heart thudded, she glanced at the clock on her computer. She could never finish what he needed and still make her dinner with Matt.

"I—I can't stay."

Her boss stared at her, his head tilting as if he wasn't sure he'd heard her correctly. "Excuse me? What did you say?"

Maggie had been looking forward to her dinner with Matt all week. The new outfit she'd purchased with Robin was laid out on her bed waiting for her. No way would she cancel.

"I can't stay tonight." Sweat dripped down her back. Silently, she cursed Harry and his report. "I, uh, have somewhere I need to be. An appointment."

She'd never use the word "date," even if she were sure that's what her dinner with Matt was supposed to be. Not that it would matter to Harry. In all the years Maggie had worked for him, she'd never known him to be in a relationship or noted even a hint of female companionship. Or any companionship, for that matter. She wasn't sure if being single was Harry's choice, but she also couldn't imagine anyone volunteering to spend time with such a miserable man.

Her boss's eyes narrowed into tiny slits as he glared at her. "What exactly do you propose I tell the client? That my assistant was too busy to do the job she's paid for?"

The job she had been hired for included working until five. Normally, Maggie caved to her boss's unreasonable demands because it was easier than standing up for herself. Not tonight. She had every intention of walking out the door in the next few minutes.

"I can come in early tomorrow and get it done." Jake was with Todd, so she wouldn't have to worry about getting him to school in the morning. "It shouldn't take me more than an hour."

Harry uttered a grunt that didn't sound like gratitude. "So, now I have to arrive early as well to ensure it gets done?" His tone indicated he felt the need to babysit because Maggie's word wasn't good enough.

She clenched her jaw to prevent blurting out her indignance. "You don't have to come in early—I mean, I'll make sure the report's ready for your meeting. I'll be here at eight to get it done."

Harry's eyes bore into her as if he were throwing down an

ultimatum and daring her to protest. "Seven," he said. He pronounced each syllable as if it was its own word.

Maggie flinched. "What?"

"Common sense dictates you arrive early enough to allow time for something to go amiss. If the report will take an hour, and I have to conduct my meeting at nine, do you have any cushion—any cushion *at all*—with your half-baked plan to arrive at eight?"

She pressed her lips firmly together, anger in the pit of her stomach. Maggie had offered to come in early. She wasn't obligated to show up a minute before nine, but of course, her boss hadn't shown the slightest amount of appreciation. Instead, he'd insulted her.

Harry answered his own question when he realized Maggie wouldn't. "No. Your plan includes no margin for error whatsoever. If your printer fails or you jam the copier, I'll be the one who looks like a fool in front of the client. Clearly, that will not be permitted to happen." He slammed his hand down on her desk like a child throwing a tantrum. "You either stay to complete it tonight, or I expect to see you in the morning— sitting at your desk not one minute later than *seven o'clock*." He said the time slowly and crisply as if he didn't want to take the chance she'd misunderstand.

Maggie's eyes narrowed as she stared at him. Years ago, she'd decided Harry must have been bullied in school. She had no doubt he'd been the kid who ate lunch alone and had his books knocked from his hand as he walked down the hallway. At some point, he must have made a vow to make people pay. To turn the tables when he was the one with the power. There was no other answer for the perverse pleasure he took in making Maggie's life difficult.

She plastered a fake smile on her face, willing to do and say anything that would allow her to leave the office to get to her dinner on time. "Yes, sir. You're right, of course. I will absolutely be here at seven."

Instead of saying thank you, Harrison Korman released a disgusted hiss through his tight, thin lips. "I hope whatever it is you're choosing over your job is worth it."

He spun on his heel, stormed back into his office, and slammed the door.

HER UNGRATEFUL BOSS was the last thing on Maggie's mind as Matt pulled out her chair at the restaurant. She caught a whiff of his cologne. An effort to smell that good had to mean he considered their dinner to be a date.

"I still can't believe I found a fellow Warrior in Florida," he said as he took the seat across from her. "It's like finding a little piece of home. Can you believe it's been twenty-seven years since we graduated high school?"

"I know. Crazy, right?"

When the waiter appeared with menus, they placed a drink order and took a moment to peruse their dinner options.

Finally, Matt closed his menu and set it off to the side. "I don't remember seeing you at the twenty-fifth reunion. Were you there?"

Maggie shook her head. She hadn't even mentioned the invitation to Todd, and she would never have had the guts to go by herself. "I, uh, couldn't get out of work. You know, to travel up there."

She drew in a deep breath hoping to slow her heart which seemed to be thudding loud enough for the whole restaurant to hear. She was a grown woman, but Matt Winters made her feel like she was back in high school.

"My wife couldn't get out of work to fly up on Friday either."

He cupped his hand around his mouth as if he was imparting a secret. "I'm pretty sure she just didn't want to go. I went alone and had a blast." He shrugged. "It was sort of the beginning of the end."

The waiter dropped their drinks off, and a grateful Maggie lunged for her Pinot Grigio. She took a long sip and willed it to calm her as the cool liquid traveled down her throat.

"Is that why you got divorced?" she asked. "Did your wife not enjoy doing things together?"

In the last few years of their marriage, Todd acted as if Maggie's sole purpose in life was to embarrass him when they went out. *Is that what you're wearing?* Finally, he didn't need to worry anymore. Maggie refused to go anywhere with him.

She couldn't imagine Matt treating his wife that way. Even in high school, he'd always been very kind. It was one of the reasons for her crush all those years ago.

Matt took a thoughtful sip of his beer, then set his mug back on the table. "I suppose the best answer is we grew apart. We never had kids. Not really our original plan, but—" he shrugged in a matter-of-fact way that indicated he'd come out on the other side of acceptance. "What can you do, right? That's the hand we were dealt."

Maggie couldn't help but offer a sympathetic wince. "Still, that's tough. Especially if you both wanted children." Despite her difficult marriage, she'd never once regretted having Jake.

"Yeah, we both wanted 'em. Just had different ways of dealing with the realization that it wasn't going to happen. I threw myself into work. The overtime pay was nice, but I was' never home." Matt wrapped his hands around his beer mug before lifting it to take a sip. "Eventually, she found someone else."

Maggie was surprised there was no bitterness in his voice. She couldn't even utter Stephanie's name without wanting to choke on it. She sipped her wine, relieved her pulse had slowed to a normal pace as the alcohol worked to settle her nerves.

"So, what made you decide to become a cop?"

"I had been selling insurance up north." Matt leaned back in his chair and raked his hand through his hair. "It was going okay. Not great, but okay. Then, about ten years ago, my ex's parents moved here." His shoulders lifted and dropped. "At that point, we thought we'd have kids, so she wanted to be near her family."

"Makes sense."

"After we got here, I started reevaluating what I wanted to do with my life. It wasn't selling insurance." Matt glanced off as if he needed to choose his words carefully. "I wanted to make a difference and help people," he said when his gaze settled back on Maggie. "What about you?"

"My divorce or my job? Or why I moved to Florida?"

"All of it." Matt offered a smile of encouragement. "If I have to unpack my baggage from the last couple of decades, it's only fair you do it, too."

Maggie took one last sip before setting her wine glass back on the table. "Well, Todd—my ex-husband—he had a chance to get a promotion, which is how we ended up in Florida. After the divorce, I wanted to go back to New Jersey to be near my family." She cast her eyes down at the table, the memory of their fight playing in her head. "He told me I could go, but there was no way I could take our son."

So many times, Maggie had considered whether she should have called his bluff. Told Todd she would take him up on his offer to let her move back without Jake. Her ex talked a good game, but he couldn't have handled being a single parent full-time, and he knew it. Maybe if he married Stephanie, but there had never been any talk of a proposal. None that Maggie had heard about anyway.

"No chance your family will move here?" Matt asked.

Maggie twisted her cocktail napkin in her hand. "I've been trying to get them to move down here for years. My mother's convinced alligators and giant mosquitos roam the streets, and my sister—" She shook her head, thinking of Stacy's last trip. *How in the world does anyone have decent hair in this place?* "Every time she comes for a visit, she spends the entire time complaining about how the humidity here is a fiasco her curly hair could never survive."

"Your sister's younger, right?"

"Yeah." Maggie cocked her head to the side, and her eyes narrowed in suspicion. "How did you know that? Did you do some sort of cop research on me?"

Matt's casual chuckle seemed to come easily. "Not at all. I remember your family from graduation. They seemed so nice and—normal. My parents were divorced and acted like it was torture to be in the same place for a few hours." He crossed his arms on the table in front of him. "How long have you been trying to get them down here?"

"Since the day I left about eight years ago." Maggie thought about how different her life would have been if she'd had them nearby. Maybe she would have had the strength to end her marriage when it all went downhill. "It was hard not to have a support system here, especially with my son."

"I can understand that. It's not easy to pack up and move far away from the people you love." He picked up his beer mug. "Did you have a job set up here? You know, like your husband?"

Maggie shook her head. It had taken her so long to find something that Todd had suggested she might need to wait tables. She had never interviewed well. Her nerves always got the best of her until all she could think about was getting out of there.

"I started temping, and eventually, I ended up being offered a position at an accounting firm." Her cheeks grew hot at the implication that it was anything more than an office job. "I'm not a CPA or anything like that. I'm an assistant to—" Maggie thought about her exchange with Harry earlier that day. "To a complete jerk. I'm convinced he was picked on when he was young, so now he takes his unresolved anger out on me every day."

Matt set down his beer and frowned. "Well, that's not okay. Why do you stay?"

He'd thrown a loaded question at her. Why didn't she leave? Try to find something else?

Over the years, Todd had been less than supportive. *It's not like you'll ever make the effort to find a new job, but with your attitude, who would even hire you?*

"I guess that leads me to my divorce."

Matt reeled back slightly, his eyes narrowed. "Your ex wouldn't let you quit?"

"No, it wasn't that." Maggie looked away, the truth hard to admit. "I just—I've never had the confidence to look for something else. To go out and compete for a job. Interview and hope they choose me." It hadn't gone well when they'd first moved to Florida, and she had no reason to think it would be any easier just because she was older.

"I guess I have a hard time with change." She gave a helpless shrug. "Even the divorce. I was miserable, but—" Maggie's confession came easier after hearing his story. "It wasn't my choice. My husband found someone else, too."

"I'm sorry." Matt's eyes filled with sympathy as he reached across the table and rested his hand on top of hers.

Maggie flinched, caught off guard by his act of compassion. His warm hand covered hers completely, and she hoped he wouldn't realize his touch had sent her pulse racing. She wondered with a twinge of jealousy if he had dated anyone else since his divorce.

The waiter appeared with a basket of bread and made a motion to set it in the middle of the table. When Matt pulled back his hand, Maggie allowed herself a few stuttered gulps of air. As he stood poised to take their order, Matt gestured at her to go first. Another new experience. Todd had never done that when they went out to eat. Not even in the beginning.

After their waiter walked away, Matt tipped his head, an amused smile lifting his lips "So, I noticed something when I picked you up tonight. Your address doesn't match what was on your driver's license."

Heat prickled Maggie's face. "Oh, right. I, uh, didn't change my address after the divorce. I need to make time to do that."

"More of that not liking change stuff, huh?"

She reached for her wine, but the glass was almost empty. "I guess at first, maybe."

His eyes met hers. "Sometimes change is a good thing, Maggie. My parents divorced when I was a toddler, so I felt I had something to prove when I got married. I was determined we'd make it because I'd seen the other option. Then I had—" Matt pressed his lips together as he seemed to be searching for a way to explain. "I had an epiphany, I guess you'd say. Life's too short to spend it being unhappy."

Matt ran his index finger under his chin as if trying to decide how much he wanted to share. "Don't get me wrong. I was bitter about it all in the beginning. Her affair. The divorce. It took me a long time to accept that nothing is just one person's fault. We both stopped caring enough to try to make it work." He picked up his beer mug and held it in Maggie's direction. "But you can't go backward, right? You have to take what you learn and move on."

She nodded in agreement but wasn't sure her situation had been the same. Maggie's parents were still happily married, but that wasn't what kept her with Todd. It was fear. Fear of the unknown. No idea how she'd manage to take care of herself and Jake on her own.

"It was probably easier for you to walk away because you didn't have kids together," she said without thinking. Her hand flew to cover her mouth. "I'm sorry. I didn't mean it like that. I just—I just meant you don't have to share custody and—"

"It's okay, and you're right. It did make it less complicated."

Matt held out the bread basket in her direction, and despite how good it smelled, Maggie shook her head. He set a piece on his small plate, and his cheeks turned rosy-red as he slathered a thick layer of soft butter on it.

"I'm supposed to be watching my cholesterol. You can see how well that's going for me." He took a bite before setting it down. "So, what would you do if you weren't the assistant to a bullying jerk? You've already made one big change with your divorce. Why not jump off the ledge? Step out of your comfort zone and look for something different?"

She gave an uncomfortable shrug. "At my age, I'm too old to think about starting over."

"Uh, we're the same age, and I don't think that's true. You really want this guy to bully you for the next twenty years? There must be something you'd rather do."

"Oh, I don't know." The idea of starting something new terrified her.

Matt leaned forward and held her gaze. "You know when you watch a football game?"

Sports weren't her thing, but Maggie wasn't sure she wanted to admit that to him just yet. "Um, sure."

Apparently, her half-hearted response didn't fool him. "You don't watch football?" He sounded disappointed. "Okay, we'll need to work on that."

We'll need to work on that. What did that mean?

"Still, I'm sure you know the basics of the game, right?" he asked. "Four quarters? Halftime?" Matt's expression was intense as he waited for her to confirm.

"Yeah, well, that I know."

"Well, sometimes the first two quarters go horribly wrong. Then, the players head into the locker room at halftime, right? That's when a good coach rallies his team. He gets them to believe in themselves again. He knows that if his players change their mindset—if they don't give up—it can be a whole new game in the second half." Matt tipped his head to the side, his eyebrows raised. "See what I'm getting at?"

Maggie wrinkled her nose. "Not exactly."

"I guess what I'm trying to say is the score at halftime isn't nearly as important as people think. What matters is how the game ends. So which half is more important? The first half or the second?"

Maggie bobbed her head as the point he was making became clear. "So, the point I'm at now in my life—you're saying this is my halftime?"

"That's exactly what I'm saying. What's happened up till now?" Matt waved his hand in the air dismissively. "Forget it. Well, not your son, of course. But it's up to you to change your mindset—to make the second half matter. Figure out what you really want to do for the next twenty years. There must be something."

Maggie hesitated, but Matt wasn't Todd. He wouldn't ridicule her. "I'm sort of obsessed with true crime. Not that I could ever be a cop or anything like that." She leaned in over the table and lowered her voice. "Don't tell anyone, but I was excited when I got selected for jury duty. Especially once I found out it was a murder trial."

"People who use the word excited in the same sentence as jury duty are few and far between. Trust me, crime isn't that exciting when you live with it every day. You become numb to a point, but some days, some situations." He drew in a deep breath, then exhaled it as a prolonged sigh. "They're rough."

"Well, I think it's fascinating. Do they ever let you take anyone on a ride-along?"

Matt's lips lifted in an amused smile. "You want to ride with me?"

Her eyes lit up. "Am I allowed? You wouldn't have to worry about me because I can handle whatever you dish out. You should have seen them in the jury room with the autopsy photos. I've seen way worse in bed at night scrolling through my phone. All I need is someone in a Reddit forum warning people not to look at certain crime scene photos on the internet, and I just have to see them. Nothing bothers me."

Matt polished off the last bite of his bread. "I'm not sure that's anything to brag about."

"Oh." Maggie shrank back in her seat as her enthusiasm dissipated. "I'm not—I'm not bragging."

"What I meant was—as cops, we need to become immune to some of the horrible stuff we see, or we wouldn't sleep at night. But there are real people attached to these stories. If you lose sight of that—if you can't feel empathy for what people are going through, it hardens you. I pray I never get like that." He reached for his beer and drained the last of it just as the waiter appeared with their dinners.

When he asked if she wanted another glass of wine, Maggie hesitated, then shook her head.

Matt ordered another beer, and then his attention was back on her. "So, tell me what your trial was about," he said as he picked up his fork.

She thought for a moment. "Jealousy, I guess."

Matt bristled and then took a bite of his lasagna. "You mean that's why the victim was murdered?"

"Well, the victim and the defendant dated for a while, but

she broke up with him," Maggie said as she slowly cut the chicken on her plate. "The prosecution tried to convince the jury he killed her because she started seeing someone new right away."

"Is that what you thought?"

Maggie finished chewing before she responded. "I think it was a possibility, but did they prove it?" Her shoulders lifted. "Not really."

"Was there any history of domestic violence between the two? Any calls to the cops?"

"None that we heard of."

Matt pursed his lips. "That doesn't always mean anything. Lots of times, victims of DV suffer in silence. Even their families don't know." He stared down at his food as if he were a million miles away. "Sometimes, by the time someone realizes what's happening, it's too late."

Maggie could only imagine what he'd seen as a cop, but she wasn't sure it applied to her case. "There wasn't any testimony that suggested that was the problem. Apparently, Grace—that was the victim—she was ready to settle down and get married. The defendant wasn't in the same place, which was why she broke up with him. Her sister even testified that Grace told her the defendant wasn't that upset about it."

"Could have been an act." Matt's shrug indicated he didn't believe there couldn't have been more to their relationship bubbling beneath the surface. "With these guys, it's about power. Control. He might not have wanted to give her the satisfaction of knowing how he really felt."

"Or he stewed about it afterward." Maggie thoughtfully dipped her fork into the potatoes that accompanied her dinner. "I thought maybe he saw her out with the new guy, and that set him off."

"Very possible," Matt said with a nod.

"The prosecution didn't give us much. Mostly just a few pieces of circumstantial evidence, which wasn't enough for the rest of the jury to convict him. I didn't understand what they were thinking at the time, but now I do. They were simply following the judge's instructions." Maggie lifted her napkin from her lap and wiped her mouth. "But I'm convinced he got away with murder."

Matt pressed his lips together and shook his head. "That poor girl's family."

"Well, that's why my friend Robin and I are looking into the case. I—I ran into the victim's sister, and my friend convinced me—" Prepared to give Robin all the credit for pursuing the truth, Maggie caught herself. "I just need to know if we let a murderer go free. Or maybe I'm wrong, and someone else did it." She fought a smile. "If that's the case, two amateur detectives are going to rock that guy's world if he thought he was going to get away with it."

Matt laid down his fork and gave her a pointed stare. "I remember telling you I didn't think poking around was such a great idea."

Maggie dismissed his concern with a wave of her hand. "We're fine, really. We're actually recording a podcast about what we find."

His eyes narrowed. "A podcast?"

"Yeah." Maggie's nod was filled with pride. Despite her initial misgivings, she had started to enjoy recording the episodes. "Mostly, we talk about what we've found in our investigation, where we'll go next. That kind of thing."

"You're investigating a guy who was acquitted and talking about it in a podcast?" Matt's words came out slowly as if we were trying to make sense of it.

"Lots of podcasts talk about true crime cases, including ones where the main suspect was found not guilty." Maggie's cheeks burned as she became defensive. "Do you know how many shows are out there about Casey Anthony? Besides, it's not like any of our episodes have aired yet. We've recorded them, but we're waiting until we see where the case nets out. Obviously, our investigation isn't finished."

Matt ran his hand over his face as if he was still confused. "But even if—"

"I know they can't charge him again," Maggie said quickly. "We still think her family deserves to know the truth."

"I agree with that. It's just—" Matt glanced at the tables around them and then leaned toward her. Concern flickered in his eyes as he lowered his voice. "Maggie, there's not a murderer out there who'd appreciate someone checking up on them. I'm not sure it matters if he can't be charged again."

She recalled what Robin had said when she panicked about the names of the jurors being made public. *You found him not guilty. If anything, he should send you all thank you notes.* Maggie had finally reassured herself that Doyle wasn't after her. Her friend was right. It didn't make sense that he'd even bother to give her a second thought.

"I'm sure he gratefully took the verdict and went back to his life," Maggie said. "He was acquitted, so he'd have no reason to think anyone would still be investigating him."

Matt leaned back in his chair and blew out a deep breath. "Let's hope so."

She resumed eating, determined to change the subject. "So, have you found anyone else we know who lives in Florida?"

She forgot about Doyle and the case as they reminisced about high school and their hometown. Matt was easy to talk to, and she found herself laughing and having a wonderful time.

"I wonder if that Italian bakery next to the Chili's is still open." Matt smacked his lips. "Man, I used to love those cookies they had."

"The ones with the sprinkles?"

He bobbed his head with enthusiasm. "Exactly. You know the ones I'm talking about."

"I do. My dad used to bring those home all the time, and every time there was a birthday, that's where we went to get a cake."

Matt released a sigh. "I miss that place. And just try to find decent pizza down here. I remember back in high school. The was nothing like Gino's Pizzeria for a slice and a Coke."

When the waiter asked if they wanted dessert, Matt convinced Maggie to share tiramisu with him. As she savored the rich goodness, she glanced up and caught him staring at her. He dug his fork into their dessert for another bite, then offered a slight smile before bringing it to his mouth.

"What?" she asked. "It's good, right?"

"It is good. *Really* good."

Maybe he wasn't just talking about their dessert.

It had been so long since Maggie had been out with a man that she wasn't sure what to expect when he pulled his car into the parking lot of her apartment building and shut off the engine. Her pulse fired up when Matt reached for his door handle.

"C'mon, I'll walk you up."

When they got to her doorway, Matt shoved his hands into the front pockets of his jeans. "I'll be honest. I wasn't sure what to expect tonight." He cleared his throat. "I still can't believe how long it's been since we last saw each other."

"I know, right?" Maggie shifted her weight awkwardly from one leg to the other.

"I had a great time."

"Me too." She hoped Matt couldn't see the sweat on her forehead, the anticipation of what might happen in the next few minutes almost more than she could bear.

"I'd like to see you again." Matt ran his tongue across his bottom lip as one shoulder hitched up. "If you're up for that."

Maggie managed a nervous smile as butterflies raced through her stomach. "I would love it." She could barely breathe as she waited to find out if this was a friendly dinner amongst old friends or something more.

Matt slipped his hand from his pocket and placed it on the side of her face. His lips brushed against hers in a gentle kiss that lingered just long enough to give her the answer she'd hoped for.

"Goodnight, Maggie," he said softly.

After saying goodnight, she let herself into her apartment and plopped down on the couch, unable to wipe the sappy grin from her face. She leaned back, her hands clasped behind her neck, and allowed a contented moan to slip from her lips. Maggie could still smell his cologne. Feel Matt's lips on hers. It had definitely been a date.

The teenage girl in her squealed. After all these years, her high school crush had kissed her. It had been worth the wait.

———

12

"I haven't been able to stop thinking about you since I saw you here," Maggie said when Grace's sister approached their table. She'd called Pam and apologized profusely for running out of the deli with Harry's lunch. "We appreciate you taking the time to meet with us on your break."

Robin crossed her arms in front of her on the table, her eyes filled with compassion. "I'm very sorry about your sister."

Pam dipped her chin. "Thanks." She held a small tray with three cups of coffee and spoons. "I figured we could use this." She gestured at the collection of condiments at the end of the table. "There's sugar and creamer if you need it."

"Thanks so much." Maggie pulled one of the cups toward her and gestured to her left. "This is my friend Robin. Now that the trial is over, we're both—well, we're trying to get to the truth about what happened to your sister." They had agreed not to bring up the podcast yet.

"Obviously, you both heard all the testimony at the trial." Robin reached for the caddy with the sugar packets. "But it's all new to me, so I've been reading some of the statements and trying to piece it all together." She dumped two packets into her cup and picked up a spoon. "Maggie said your sister left you a voicemail indicating something was wrong."

"She did. The night before—" Pam reached into her back pocket and pulled out her cell phone. "I still have her message." She dragged her finger down the screen, hit the speaker button, and set her phone on the table.

As Grace began to speak, Maggie's skin prickled. The transcript of the call had been read in court, but hearing her actual voice felt entirely different. The volume was low, so Maggie leaned in closer. She didn't want to miss anything.

Hey, Pammy. I'm sorry to call so late, but I had to charge my phone. Grace let out a chuckle. *Stupid battery. I know, I know. I promise I'm gonna go get a new phone this week.* There was a hesitation before she spoke again. *Anyway, I was kind of hoping you were still up. Something happened tonight. I mean, I'm fine, so don't worry. I'm just—well, I'm a little freaked out.* Her voice changed and became high-pitched. Nervous. *I don't know. Maybe it's nothing, and I'm just overreacting. I feel like I need another opinion. Can you meet me for dinner tomorrow night? We can eat at that Italian place by my office that you like. Just let me know. Oh, and I had my date with Ron. It went well, I think. I'll tell you all about it when I see you. Love ya.*

"What time did she leave that message?" Robin pulled out a pen and her small notebook.

Pam didn't even look at the screen, as if the time had been forever etched in her memory. "It was 10:49 p.m."

Robin scribbled on the page, then glanced up. "Does she normally call that late?"

"Not usually. I was already sleeping." Pam slugged down a long sip of her black coffee. "Mondays are my early day at the deli. I work breakfast."

"So, this was Sunday, the night she went out with Ron Brookins, right?" Robin asked as she tapped the end of her pen against the table. "The casual way she mentions their date at the end didn't sound like whatever she was calling about was related to him."

Maggie nodded in agreement. "At least not something he did specifically."

"Now that the trial's over, everything about the case is public record," Robin said. "Even the depositions that were taken from witnesses that weren't called to testify." She twisted in her seat and turned to Maggie. "Did you bring the folder?"

"I have it." Maggie rummaged around in her bag, pulled it out, and laid the file on the table. She thumbed through the statements until she came to Ron's. She moved it to the top of the pile and skimmed the first page. "Ron said he picked Grace up at her house around seven on Sunday evening. That's when he saw the football jersey that was—"

"The jersey that magically appeared back at Doyle's house after my sister was killed? The one he was wearing later that same night?" Pam's voice dripped with bitterness. "That's how I know he killed her. The jersey was there Sunday night and gone after Grace's murder. Where else would it have gone?"

Maggie had asked the same question in the jury room.

"Well, your sister sent him that text." Robin sipped her coffee. "It wasn't like she didn't intend to return it. Do you think there's a chance Doyle stopped by to get it on Sunday night and saw her with Ron? I mean, the Bucs were playing Monday night, so he probably wanted to wear it while he watched the game."

"In his living room? By himself?" The words came out clipped and harsher than Maggie intended.

Robin shot her friend a look to ease up. "I don't watch sports. All I know is my husband didn't watch a single Gators game last season without his lucky T-shirt. Maybe that jersey was Doyle's good luck charm, and he was paranoid they'd lose if he didn't wear it."

An embarrassed heat burned Maggie's cheeks. "Sorry. I was just never convinced the jersey was as important as the prosecution made it out to be." She peeled back the top of a creamer pod and dumped it into her coffee. "I do think there could be some truth to the jealousy angle they presented." The metal spoon clinked against her cup as she stirred, and her shoulders hitched upward. "It's possible he decided if he couldn't have her, no one could."

When Robin's eyes widened, Maggie noticed the pained expression on Pam's face.

She slumped back in her seat. "I'm sorry. I didn't mean—" Maggie wasn't used to discussing a case with someone from the victim's family sitting there. "I'm just saying that was the story the prosecution tried to sell. They didn't do a convincing job because, in the end, there's no proof Doyle found out about Ron." She took a small sip of her coffee. "That's part of the reason the other jurors had a problem finding him guilty. They couldn't connect the dots the way the prosecution hoped we would."

"But they're right," Pam said in a soft, barely audible voice. "The prosecution, not the other jurors." Her gaze drifted between Maggie and Robin. "It had to be Doyle. There's just no other reasonable answer. My sister—everyone loved Grace."

Robin stared at her notebook with pursed lips. "Still, let's go back to Ron for a minute." She looked up. "He picked up your sister at seven, and they went to dinner, right?"

"Yeah. They went for Mexican food. The place near the mall."

"And after that?"

"Ron testified that Grace wanted to get some makeup at the mall after they ate." Pam's smile was wistful. "It sounds just like her. My sister loved getting all done up to go out." Her voice shook, and she drew in a stuttered breath. "He said they walked around and shopped until it closed."

Maggie confirmed her story with a quick nod. "The police found the makeup she bought and the receipt. On the kitchen counter." Her eyes flickered in Pam's direction, unsure if she could explain further. "It was documented in the, uh—in the photos."

Pam bristled, and Robin patted her hand. "If this is too difficult for you, we understand."

Her shoulders drooped with a sigh. "No. I want to know what happened to my sister more than anyone. I *need* to know."

"Okay," Robin said with a subtle nod before shifting in her seat to face Maggie. "What did Ron say they did after leaving the mall? He drove her home, right? Did he go back into Grace's house?"

"He didn't. He said they sat outside in his car for a bit." On the stand, Ron had testified he and Grace had been talking and laughing until he finally had to leave. According to him, their first date had gone exceptionally well.

Robin's head cocked thoughtfully to one side. "Maybe they weren't just talking. What if that's what Doyle saw?"

It would have made for a better story, but Maggie didn't believe it had gone down that way. "His phone didn't ping from Grace's house that night." She could still hear the defense attorney as he cross-examined one of the witnesses. *Isn't it true that the last time Mr. Riggs's phone pinged anywhere near the victim's house was twelve days before the murder?* "It doesn't make sense he would have shown up without his phone that night. It's not like he knew another guy would be there."

"I suppose." Robin eyed the statement on the table. "What else did Ron say?"

Maggie lowered her gaze to the paper in front of her. "He told the police he left Grace's house a little after ten because he had a twenty-five-minute drive home and an early meeting on Monday. He claims he watched her walk into her house before he drove away but didn't see anything out of the ordinary."

"*Claims?*" Pam sat up straight, and her gaze volleyed between Maggie and Robin. "You think Ron was lying about that?"

Maggie held up her hand. "Not necessarily. I just think there's no way to prove he did or didn't watch your sister as she went into the house. After what happened, it serves him much better to say he did."

Pam swallowed hard. "From what I saw on the stand, he seemed like a decent guy."

"No, I agree." Maggie attempted to redirect the conversation. "Let's work from the assumption that he told the truth."

"Which brings us back to Doyle." Robin turned to face Pam. "Is it possible he was waiting for your sister inside her house?"

She hesitated only briefly. "I don't see how. Grace always locked her door, even when she was home. I think I'm the only person who ever had a spare key to her house, and that's only because her AC died. She had a meeting she couldn't miss, and she begged me to wait there in the sweltering heat for the guy to come fix it."

"So, you're sure she wouldn't give a key to a guy she was dating?"

"Positive. My sister was very safety conscious. She even carried Mace in her purse in case—" Pam's bottom lip quivered with the realization that the worst *had* happened. "Clearly, she wasn't careful enough."

Robin sipped her coffee to give Pam a moment. After setting her mug back on the table, she scooted forward in her seat. "Let me ask you something. Do you think Grace would have gone back out at that time of night? A quick run to the store? Gas for the next day so she wouldn't have to stop in the morning?"

"I don't think so, but—I guess it's possible."

Robin turned to Maggie. "I wonder if the police looked for receipts or credit card charges. If they found something, anything, it would show she went back out after Ron dropped her off."

"It never came up at the trial which probably means they didn't find anything. And her phone wouldn't have pinged because Grace mentioned she needed to charge it."

Robin released a defeated sigh. "Oh, right." She wrote in her notebook, then turned to Pam. "Was that a common thing? For your sister to let her phone die?"

A sad smile worked at the corners of Pam's mouth. "It was. Grace's phone was old. I kept telling her she needed to get a new one because it wouldn't hold a charge anymore. If it was in her purse while she was out to dinner with Ron, she probably didn't even realize it was dead."

"But if she went out after their date, she could have charged it in her car," Maggie said, her voice lifting.

"All I know is she charged it somewhere—at least enough to call me."

"Because something freaked her out." Robin's shoulders sagged with her sigh. "But we still have no idea what that was."

"The voicemail could just be a red herring." Maggie leaned forward to explain to Pam. "It seems like it's important in uncovering the truth, but it's just a coincidence. In the end, what freaked Grace out wasn't relevant to what happened. Maybe it was nothing."

Pam's blank stare and silence suggested she wasn't convinced.

"Grace said herself that maybe she was overreacting," Maggie said. "When you met up for dinner and discussed it, she might have realized whatever happened wasn't as bad as she thought."

Pam's mouth pulled tight, and pain raced across her face. "Since that opportunity was stolen from us, I'll never know."

"We know. It's not fair," Robin said gently.

"That voicemail had something to do with Doyle." Pam's voice was firm. "I'm sure of it."

Robin studied her for a moment. "What do *you* think happened?"

"I believe Doyle stopped by unannounced on Sunday night to get his jersey and saw my sister with Ron. Probably when they were leaving to go to dinner. He got jealous, pissed even, that she was dating someone new so soon after she broke things off with him. Later that night, he came back. He was creeping around outside Grace's house, waiting to see what time she got back from her date. Then when she sat in Ron's car for a while, he couldn't get out of there without being noticed, so he had to hide. Maybe Grace saw him somehow, or she heard noises outside her house after Ron left. Either one of those things would have freaked her out."

Something about her theory gnawed at Maggie. "At the trial, you testified that your sister didn't think Doyle was upset about her breaking up with him."

Pam's face hardened. "That defense attorney practically bullied me into saying that. Grace didn't specifically say he was angry about it or threatened her in any way. That's true. But if Doyle saw her with a new guy so soon? I think that changed everything. The more he thought about it, the madder he probably got. He decided to go back the next night to see if he'd find Ron at her house again. When he saw Grace was alone, I think he decided to confront her. And then ..." Pam pressed her lips together as her eyes welled up with tears.

"If Doyle was at your sister's house on Sunday night, then he wasn't hiding someplace where he would have heard her leave that voicemail to you, or he would have known—" Maggie caught herself, but the look on Pam's face told her she'd had the same thought.

"No, you're right," she said with a sad nod. "I think about that all the time. If I had just met my sister for dinner on Monday, she wouldn't have been home. I would have known what had her so worried. She might still be alive."

Robin reached for her hand. "This isn't your fault. You can't blame yourself."

"You didn't talk to Grace that day, right?" Maggie asked. "On Monday?"

Pam shook her head. "No. We played phone tag. I tried to call her between the breakfast and lunch rush to tell her I couldn't have dinner with her that night. I got her voicemail which wasn't unusual when she was at the office. I left a message and told her I had already made plans with one of the girls from work. I asked if we could meet for dinner Tuesday night instead." Her gaze drifted between Maggie and Robin. "But I did ask her to call me back and tell me what had happened. You know, explain why she'd left me that weird message the night before."

"And she didn't call?" Robin asked.

Pam's eyelids fluttered and closed. When she opened them, her eyes were wet again. "No, she did. Just as my friend and I were heading into a movie." She reached for a napkin. "Of course, now I want to kick myself that I let her call go to voicemail."

As Pam dabbed at her tears, Robin laid her hand on Pam's arm. "You had no way of knowing."

"But Grace left you a message, right?" Maggie could picture it on the timeline she'd drawn on the whiteboard in the jury room.

"She did, but she just said she'd see me for dinner the next night, and we'd talk about it then. That was the last call made from her phone."

"That's how the prosecution created the window for—" Maggie cut her thought short. "If I remember correctly, she made that call around 7:30 p.m."

Pam sniffled and swiped at her nose with the napkin. "Right."

"And did you call her back when you got home that night? From the movie?" Robin asked.

"I tried, but she didn't answer." Pam drew in a deep, shuddering breath. "I didn't leave a message. It was late—around eleven. At the time, I figured Grace had probably gone to bed, and I would just talk to her at dinner the next night."

"Did your call go right to voicemail?" Maggie asked. "Like her phone was dead again?"

"It rang several times before her voicemail picked up, but the police said Grace's phone was on the charger in the kitchen when they—" Pam pressed her lips together. "My missed call was on her screen. Along with a call from Ron and about ten from her office the next day wondering where she was."

"And other than the jersey missing, was there anything in the house that seemed out of place?"

Maggie answered. "Just her purse spilled by the front door."

Robin sat silent for a moment and then turned her attention to Pam. "You said your sister carried Mace in her purse. If she realized she had a problem, maybe she was trying to get to it."

"I thought the same thing, and we did ask the police about it. They found it, still attached to her keychain inside her purse. If she was reaching for it, her bag fell before she had time to grab it."

Maggie considered the information about Grace shopping for candles. She could still hear Kim's snide remark in the jury room. *Does anyone else think the killer used Grace's computer to go candle shopping?* "Do you still have your sister's computer? The laptop they found on the coffee table?"

Pam nodded. "Yeah. The police gave it back to us. Why?"

"I was just wondering about one of the settings. Did your sister do a lot of her shopping online?"

"Oh, yeah." Her lips lifted in a wistful smile. "The Amazon Prime delivery guy was a regular visitor at Grace's house."

Robin offered a smile of her own. "That's all of us, right?" She gazed off thoughtfully, then turned to Maggie. "Weren't there wine glasses also found on the coffee table? Was the computer next to the glasses?"

"Close enough." Maggie could still visualize the photo shown to the jury. Two wine glasses were placed side by side, while Grace's laptop seemed shoved to the upper right corner of the rectangular table. One wrong move and it would have hit the tile floor.

Pam pulled her lips tight and shook her head. "I still didn't understand how they found no fingerprints or DNA on either of those glasses. How is that even possible?"

"It's not possible unless someone wiped them clean." Robin shot Maggie a look. "You'd only do that if you had something to hide."

Maggie bobbed her head in agreement. "I argued in the jury room that someone staged the scene to make it look like something else had gone on." She heaved a deep sigh. "Unfortunately, no one agreed with me." Pablo had been the most vocal. *We don't know this chick didn't have a whole string of guys. Who's to say she didn't invite one of them over, and he killed her after a few drinks?*

"If Doyle had stopped by to get his jersey without calling or texting, would Grace have let him in?" Robin asked.

Pam was silent as she considered the question. "Probably, but I doubt she would have poured him a glass of wine and invited him to stay."

"If Doyle knew about Ron, it could be he was trying to make it look like the new guy was responsible," Maggie said. "He staged a cozy get-together by setting out two glasses. He figured he could claim that he's the ex-boyfriend, so it's not like he would have been at Grace's house drinking with her."

Robin hesitated, then drew in a deep breath as if she was about to say something they wouldn't like. "I know you're both convinced it was Doyle, but did Grace have any exes before him? Someone else who maybe wasn't over her?"

"Not over her? I don't think so." Pam leaned back in her chair. "My sister did have a serious boyfriend for a few years. She kept waiting for him to propose, but every birthday, every holiday, he never did. When she gave him an ultimatum, he took the opportunity to bail. But that was over two years ago. He seemed genuinely upset when Grace died."

The jurors hadn't heard a word about this guy at the trial. "How do you know he was upset?" Maggie asked.

Pam's shoulders lifted and dropped matter-of-factly. "He was at her funeral."

Maggie and Robin exchanged a knowing glance.

"What?" Pam asked as she eyed both of them.

"In many cases, the killer shows up at the funeral," Robin said in a soft voice. "It's an opportunity to find out what the police are telling the family."

"Oh." Pam held her head in her hands as she seemed to be considering the idea that her sister's murderer might have been there pretending to grieve with everyone else. Finally, she shook her head as if her sister's ex-boyfriend wasn't a possibility. "I really don't think he had anything to do with it. We spoke that day. He told me he's been dating someone, and it sounded serious."

Robin held her pen over her notebook. "What was his name?"

"Scott Pierson, but really, he and Grace had parted ways and moved on with their lives," Pam said confidently. "My sister bought the house after they broke up. Scott didn't even know where my sister lived."

"I hate to ask, but did you and your parents go inside?" Robin asked. "You know, afterward?"

Pam closed her eyes as she shook her head. "The police wouldn't let us in the house until after they processed the scene, and by then, we couldn't—we just couldn't bear to go inside."

Robin gave a sympathetic nod. "I understand."

"About three months later, we had to go in to clear it out. My parents decided to put Grace's house on the market." Pam's sigh slumped her against the back of her chair. "None of us wanted to ever think about that place again."

"I can't say I blame you."

"Three months later," Maggie said thoughtfully. "That's a pretty long time, but I guess the police had finished combing it for evidence."

"We had to pay someone to come in and clean. There was black fingerprint powder everywhere."

"But they didn't find anything, right?" Robin asked.

"The defense brought up a random palm print that was found on the inside of my sister's front door. You know, to suggest someone else could have been there that night. The truth was the police have no idea who it belongs to or if it even means anything. All they told us was that it didn't match anyone they tested."

"And you said Grace always locked her front door, yet there was no sign of forced entry?"

Pam confirmed with a nod. "That's why I keep coming back to the fact that it had to be someone my sister knew. She wouldn't have opened the door otherwise."

Robin's shoulders sagged. "We know it wasn't a food delivery because she picked up dinner. Supposedly, Ron had a solid alibi. You were at the movies. Any friends that would just stop by?"

"My parents and I asked everyone we could think of. Nothing."

Robin released a sigh. "I can see why the police suspected Doyle. He can't prove where he was for about an hour and a half. And based on all the evidence, that's the window of time the police were looking at. It had to be him stopping by unannounced to pick up his jersey."

Pam bobbed her head. "I agree. I think he started grilling my sister about dating someone new, and it pushed him over the edge."

Maggie pursed her lips as she crossed her arms against her chest. "I don't think so. To me, the whole thing screams premeditation. Doyle's phone pinged from his house, so if it was him, he left it behind. Deliberately. Who does that unless they're trying to be deceptive about where they really are? There was also the email he sent to his brother." She'd fought hard with the other jurors about its importance. "The one about the Bucs and their chances of getting to the Super Bowl."

"What was that about?" A groove appeared between Robin's eyebrows as she leaned in over the table. "I don't remember seeing anything about an email."

"Doyle forwarded a link about the Bucs to his brother. The timestamp on his computer showed it was sent at 8:15 p.m."

"Wait." Robin's eyes went narrow. "Not from his phone?"

"Nope. It was sent from his laptop."

Robin threw up her hands as if this fact changed everything. "So, he was home at eight-fifteen? Then he couldn't have—"

"Slow down." Maggie held up her hand and pulsed it in her friend's direction. "An IT guy testified at the trial and said it was scheduled to be sent at that time. Like Doyle sent it earlier but delayed the delivery."

Robin jerked backward in her chair, her face twisted in shock. "Stop it. You can really do that?" Then, her mouth gaped as she realized what he'd been trying to accomplish. "He was trying to cut down the window of time he was unaccounted for. Trying to give himself an alibi that he was home at that time."

"Of course," Maggie said. "That's what I thought, too. Although when the defense questioned him about it, he testified he'd only sent it that way so he wouldn't forget. On the stand, Doyle claimed he didn't want his brother to read it earlier because they usually made a side bet on the game that had to be locked in right before kickoff. His brother gets home from work at about eight-fifteen, which is allegedly why Doyle chose that time."

Robin huffed in disbelief. "Yeah, okay. Did the brother back up his story? About the bet?"

Although there had been spectators in the courtroom, the jury had no way of knowing who they were. The only clues they had were from reading their responses to certain testimony, but it seemed obvious most of the audience was there for Grace's family.

Maggie's gaze drifted to Pam, and she slowly shook her head. "I'm not sure he was even there to support Doyle. He didn't testify."

Robin flung her hands up. "I'm blown away. I can't believe that email wasn't enough for the jury to convict him."

"Trust me. I tried. Doyle did also place one outgoing call that night from his cell phone. Around 9:20 p.m."

"Any idea to who?"

"His partner in the body shop, a guy named Manny Perez. He testified at the trial that their four-minute conversation was about the football game. We know the call was made from Doyle's house because it pinged from the tower near there the entire night." A fact the other jurors had reminded her of time and again during deliberations. Maggie flashed an apologetic look in Pam's direction and eased out a slow breath. "And now we're back where we started. We believe Doyle is responsible for Grace's murder, but we're missing that one piece of indisputable evidence that proves it."

Pam stood and reached for the empty tray she'd left behind her. As new tears prickled her eyes, she gathered the dishes and trash from their time together. "I don't know if today was even helpful, but I have to get back to work."

"We're not giving up, I promise," Maggie insisted with a side glance at Robin. "If you think of anything that could be helpful, give me a call. Even if you're not sure it means anything, it could be important. You never know."

"Okay. I really appreciate everything you're both doing." Pam reached up to wipe the tears from her cheek. "I'm—I'm lost without my big sister, and every day I wonder if I could have changed what happened to her. I need to know the truth because I just don't understand. Why did Doyle have to kill her?"

13

R obin gave Maggie an expectant look as her finger hovered over the button to begin recording. "We'll cover what we found out last night, but we'll talk about it like we just got back but couldn't wait to update our listeners. Ready?"

Maggie put her hands over her earphones and nodded. For the first few podcast episodes they recorded, her nerves had gotten the best of her. It was getting easier with practice.

"Welcome back to Moms and Murder. I'm Robin."

"And I'm Maggie."

Robin played their prerecorded opening, during which Maggie spoke first. "We're both moms."

Then Robin. "Who are obsessed with true crime."

"And we need answers," they announced simultaneously. "Even if it means finding them ourselves."

Robin always kicked off their episodes. "So, when we ended last week's episode, we promised to tell you about a white car reportedly seen speeding out of the neighborhood the night of Grace Hutchinson's murder."

Maggie scooted forward in her seat to lean closer to her

microphone. "Which I never heard a thing about during the trial."

"Right, but as we discussed, it wouldn't fit the prosecution's agenda to tell you about it. The defendant didn't have a white car, but you and I wondered if maybe he had access to one. He is co-owner of a body shop, after all. But we knew he was home at seven-forty the night of the murder."

"Right," Maggie said. "The pizza delivery. But the witness said she saw the white car at 8:05 p.m. It flew through a stop sign, headed away from Grace Hutchinson's house, and almost hit her."

"Correct. So, we started discussing it, and we questioned whether the defendant could have swapped his truck somehow for a white sedan. You and I took a trial run to see if we could make the timeline fit."

"Which it didn't," Maggie said.

"No, it didn't. But then I went to talk to the witness and found her, dare I say, not very reliable." Robin's lips lifted in a satisfied smile. "She admitted it could have been a little later."

Maggie gave a quick glance down at her notes. She didn't need them but was comforted that she had them in front of her in case her mind went blank. "Which means the timeline we were working from might not be accurate."

"And if that's the case, it could change *everything*. So, then we started thinking. There had to be someone in the victim's neighborhood with a surveillance camera. I mean, doesn't everyone have one these days? Those Ring cameras are so affordable."

Maggie piped in as they'd planned. "I have one."

"A lot of people do. We knew we needed to go back to Grace Hutchinson's neighborhood," Robin said into her mic. "Take a look around. We wanted to see if we could find a house with a camera that might have captured something we could use."

Maggie cringed as they prepared to report on their repeat

visit to the place where Matt had first told them to let the case go. They'd blatantly ignored his advice.

"And lo and behold, what do you think we found?" Robin asked dramatically. "We found a few cameras. But the road to answers doesn't always run smooth, does it?" She pointed her index finger at Maggie to cue her response.

"Well, it certainly didn't today, Robin."

She gave Maggie an enthusiastic nod and thumbs up. "No, it certainly didn't. When we went back and looked around, we were shocked to see a camera located in a pretty relevant location. It was on the house right across the street from the victim's. I mean, seriously? As we told you in a previous episode, Grace Hutchinson's house was at the end of the street. A dead end. To say we were pretty excited is an understatement. Maggie, do you want to share what we found?"

They'd discussed ahead of time that she would be the one to tell the story and introduce their interview with Grace's neighbor, Mrs. Henry. From the very beginning, Robin had insisted the two of them needed to be equals on the show. *We're not going to be like some of those podcasts where you're just the sidekick who asks inane questions as if you've never heard a thing about the case.*

Maggie's small notebook was opened up on the desk in front of her. When they'd gotten back from Grace's neighborhood, she'd added notes for the podcast before she could forget anything important.

"I couldn't believe it when we saw that camera," Maggie said, leaning close to her mic. "Right across the street, no less. And yet, the jury didn't hear about—or see—any surveillance footage. And trust me, when we were deliberating, we asked ourselves why. We felt like there had to be a camera somewhere that caught something the night of the murder. So why didn't we hear about it? Or better yet, see it? Some of the jurors suspected it was because the footage showed something the prosecution didn't want us to see."

"And now we know the answer." Robin's eyebrows lifted as she smiled mischievously. "The camera across the street caught something all right."

"That it did," Maggie said. "Robin and I spoke to the woman who lives there—a nice older woman named Sarah Henry. She told us a little about Grace, and it was helpful to hear about her from another person's perspective."

Robin scooted forward in her seat. "What she told us was in line with what we've heard from others who knew her. No one has any idea why someone would have wanted to kill her."

"Right," Maggie said with a nod even though only Robin could see her. "Grace's neighbor even admitted she's still a little nervous living there. As our listeners know, no one has been convicted of the crime, and a heinous murder occurred *right across the street*." As planned, she spoke the last words slow and ominous for effect.

"I think I'd be a little nervous, too."

"No kidding. When we told the woman we were trying to help Grace's family figure out what really happened—"

"Which is the truth," Robin cut in.

"It is, and Sarah Henry wanted to help. Grace's neighbor agreed to talk to us and invited us into her home."

"Now, she did tell us the police came to see her as well. The day after the murder."

"They did," Maggie said. "They noticed her camera—same as us—and asked about her footage. So, as we're sitting there in this woman's living room, all I can think about is why the prosecution kept what they found from the jury. Did it record the white car we've been wondering about, and that's why they didn't want us to know about it?"

Robin bobbed her head in agreement. "I was thinking the

same thing." She pointed toward her laptop, which was the cue to introduce the audio clip.

Maggie dipped her head in acknowledgment. "We asked the victim's neighbor if we could tape our conversation and play it back for our listeners. She agreed, so take a listen."

Robin hit a button on her keyboard to play the audio she'd transferred. It was her voice they heard next. "So, the police came to you, right? They asked if the camera on your front door had captured any footage from the night of the murder?"

"They did." The older woman had sat wringing her hands in her lap. "Of all the nights. If I had known ..." She looked up, a somber expression on her face. "Who could have imagined something so terrible was going to happen?"

Maggie heard the hopeful lift in her own voice, despite a start to their conversation that seemed less than promising. "Were you able to provide any video for the police? Anything that would help the investigation?"

There was a moment of silence. "No," the woman said finally, her voice soft. "I didn't have anything the police could use."

Maggie's stomach sank when she'd first heard the words, and it did again as she listened to it now.

"I was crushed," Sarah said. "Not only did I want to help, but there was a substantial reward offered for any information that led to the arrest of the person who killed Grace."

This was the first they'd heard of money being offered. Had someone offered up Doyle in exchange for the payout?

"Your camera—it just didn't record?" Robin's tone conveyed the disbelief they both felt. "Or did you somehow—somehow erase it?"

Grace's neighbor hesitated before she responded. "The camera wasn't on the door. I'd—I'd taken it off earlier that day."

Robin exchanged a defeated glance with Maggie. "Why was that? Did it need to be charged?"

"Not exactly." The older woman leaned back on the couch as if she was settling in to explain. "You see, there was this cat."

"A *cat*?" Robin asked, her head tilted to the side as if perhaps she hadn't heard correctly.

"She was a neighborhood cat, I guess," Mrs. Henry said. "Gray and white. Just as sweet as can be. I don't know where she came from, but I started feeding her." She leaned forward and gestured toward a sliding glass door on the back wall of her kitchen. "Outside on my patio. It wasn't long before two other cats started showing up for meals. The little gray one would just hang back, and at first, the other ones gobbled up all the food and left her with nothing."

Maggie heard the sigh she emitted on the audio as it started to make sense. "So, you moved the camera to the back of your house? To keep an eye on her?"

"Not exactly," the woman said again. "After I realized what was happening, I always made sure she got her fair share. So, when she looked like she started putting on a little weight, I was happy."

It had taken everything Maggie had not to roll her eyes. She now knew exactly where this story was headed.

The older woman's cheeks reddened. "Yup, the bigger she got, the less I could deny it. That sweet girl was pregnant. I left the sliding door open one morning when I went in to make my coffee. I turned around, and there she was. She wound herself around my leg and looked up at me with these big green eyes like she was pleading with me to help with her babies."

"So, you kept her inside?" Robin asked.

Mrs. Henry nodded. "First, we took her to the vet. Found out she was carrying four kittens, and she only had a couple of weeks to go. My husband was a little paranoid she'd end up in the corner of our closet giving birth." She gave a helpless shrug. "We moved her into our guest bedroom. I set up a nice cozy box for her to have her kittens in when the time came. Most days, I just hung out in there with her. Reading or doing needlepoint."

Maggie remembered the frustration she'd felt during the interview. Nothing Grace's neighbor told them so far had explained why the camera had been removed from the front door.

"My husband said I was obsessed with waiting for her to have those babies. I guess I was, but it was kind of exciting."

Robin hit a button on her keyboard and turned off the mics.

At that point in their interview, the woman had reached for her cell phone and scrolled through her photos. Then, she'd turned her phone around so they could see what was on the screen. It was a photo of a gray and white cat lounging on a bed, her round stomach leaving no doubt her time was coming close.

"This was Mona a few days before she gave birth." She chuckled. "My husband called her that because he used to say, 'she's gonna Mona like an injured basset hound when she has to get those babies out of her.'" The woman stared at the picture with a wistful smile. "She was huge, right? But still so beautiful."

Maggie wanted to wave her hands in the air to encourage the woman to get to the point. Instead, she nodded, like she understood the anticipation the woman must have felt waiting for those kittens.

Since their listeners couldn't see the picture and it wasn't relevant, they'd agreed to cut that portion of the interview from the show and pick up where Robin had tried to get their conversation back on track.

With a nod at Maggie, she turned their mics back on when they heard Robin's voice again on the audio. "So, I take it the cat —Mona—was expecting her kittens around the time Grace was killed? But I'm still unclear how that connects to the camera on the front door."

"Oh, right," Mrs. Henry said as if she'd forgotten the whole point of their conversation. "Well, we were still waiting for her to give birth, but my husband and I had agreed to watch the grand-kids. My son and daughter-in-law live right in St. Pete. You know, not far. They had tickets to the Bucs game, but those Monday night games go so late. Usually, my husband and I just spend the night in their spare room and come back in the morning. I left Mona plenty of food and water, but it was killing me to leave. After all that time I'd spent waiting, I figured it would be just my luck she'd decide to have those babies while I was gone."

The missing puzzle piece dropped into place. "So, you took the camera off the door and aimed it at the box in your guest room." Maggie's tone was matter-of-fact, more a statement than a question.

"I did. But don't you think for one second I planned to tell my husband about it. I figured I'd put it back up when we returned, and he'd never be the wiser. But then, of course ... well, you know." Her voice softened. "That was the night Grace was murdered. We weren't even home."

Robin hit the key to stop the audio. "So, there you have it. It looked like we had the perfect opportunity to find out exactly who was at Grace Hutchinson's house the night of her murder."

"Not that it always matters," Maggie said. "I mean, look at the Delphi murders. The police had video and audio of the suspected killer. You'd think that would have been a slam dunk arrest right after it happened."

"That's true." Robin scrunched up her face. "But anything would have been better than the footage of those kittens being born."

"And just in case our listeners are wondering if maybe Grace Hutchinson's neighbor had something to hide, she insisted on showing the video to us." Maggie grimaced. "That cat was pretty tough, though." She crossed her arms on the desk in front of her.

"I don't know about you, Robin, but four births and no epidural? Uh, no thank you."

"I'm with you," she said as she wrinkled her nose. "And for all our animal lover listeners who want to know what happened after the kittens were born, you'll be happy to know that after the interview, we met Mona. She's quite content living as an inside cat now."

"Mrs. Henry's husband even let her move out of the guest bedroom."

"I'm pretty sure Mona rules their house now." Robin pointed at the clock to indicate they were nearing the end of their time.

Maggie gave a nod. She knew how she was supposed to cover the end of the story. "Three of her four kittens were adopted by friends and other family members. But the fourth one got to stay with Mona. We had a chance to meet her after our interview as well. Of course, she's no longer a kitten, but she grew up to be a beautiful cat." As planned, Maggie paused for effect. "The Henrys named her Gracie."

"That really choked me up when she told us that." Robin's eyes were glassy even now. "Apparently, Grace knew Mona was pregnant, and she'd expressed interest in adopting one of her kittens. She was hoping for a little girl." She leaned toward her mic. "Maggie, we've gone off on a sentimental tangent here today on Moms and Murder, so we probably need to reel it back in. Bring our listeners back to the case at hand. As you all just heard, our hopes that there might be footage from the night of the murder went nowhere with the house across the street from our victim."

"I certainly got my answer as to why the jury never heard anything about it."

"We did find another surveillance camera on the house a few doors down from Grace," Robin said. "But that didn't go any better."

Maggie shook her head. "No, it didn't. We learned they didn't have it at the time of the murder. But as they told us, 'when someone on your block gets killed, it makes you realize you need to beef up the security on your house.'"

"Yeah, and we got the same sentiment from a couple of the other houses. So, all in all, we didn't find anything useful today in Grace's neighborhood." Robin held Maggie's gaze and dipped her chin.

"Well, that's not entirely true," Maggie said as she played her part in their preplanned ending to this episode. "We did get answers to some of the other questions we had."

"That's true we did. As you all heard, we were crushed to learn Grace's neighbor had removed the camera from their front door the day she was killed." Robin cocked her head, and the corners of her mouth lifted slightly. "But then we asked if there was footage ..." She hesitated for a moment as planned before she continued. "From the night *before* the murder."

Maggie bit back a smile at Robin's suspenseful delivery. "That's right. We wanted to know if Grace's new boyfriend, Ron, had told the truth about their date."

"And we absolutely needed to see if we could use it to figure out what Grace had been so worried about that night. If you recall, she'd left that voicemail for her sister. Told her something *freaked her out*. Was someone lurking in the bushes outside her house? We knew that footage could prove useful to our investigation." Robin's eyebrows shot up as she pointed at Maggie. They had decided she would provide the zinger for their audience.

"And it was all there." Maggie paused dramatically. "Just waiting for us in the cloud."

Robin's face broke into a grin and she pumped her fists in the air.

Then she regrouped, and her expression turned serious. She

stared down at the desk as she spoke into her microphone. "And not only did that video footage give us some of the answers we were looking for, but we learned Grace did something unexpected the night before she was killed." She lifted her gaze. "I don't know about you, Maggie, but I'm still not sure what to make of this new information."

"I agree. It certainly adds yet another layer of mystery to this case." With her part of the show completed, Maggie's shoulders relaxed. It was getting easier, but she still felt tense until she was finished recording.

"It sure does give us something new to dive into," Robin said. "But we're going to get to the bottom of this case, and as always, we'll take our listeners right along with us. No matter what we find. Thanks for joining us for this episode of Moms and Murder. Join us next week when we discuss what shocking information the surveillance footage revealed and what it could mean to our list of suspects."

Robin hit the button to end the recording and let out a celebratory whoop. "You're really getting the hang of this. You were so good tonight. I know a lot of it was about the cat stuff, but still. The ending made it all worth it."

Maggie removed her headphones and crossed her arms on the table in front of her. "Now, we just need to figure out where Grace went that night after Ron left."

14

"Do we need to walk off the margaritas?" Maggie asked as Matt slipped his credit card into the leather folio with their check. A warm sensation filled her insides as she took one last sip from her oversized goblet. Feeling slightly tipsy, she leaned hard against the back of her chair.

Jake was with Todd, and Maggie needed to sober up before she returned to her empty apartment. She and Matt had talked on the phone every day since their first date, but she wasn't ready to invite him in. Not yet anyway.

Matt caught the waitress's eye, then turned his attention back to Maggie. "We could take a stroll around the mall if you want. It's right next door."

"Perfect." A smile stretched her lips as the server picked up the folio. "You know it's too bad the waitress didn't card me tonight for my drinks." Maggie pulled her wallet from her purse and flashed her new license in his direction. "How about me? I'm accepting change."

He glanced at it and gave an approving dip of his chin. "Look at you. It's not so bad, right?"

It certainly wasn't. If it meant being with Matt, change was an extraordinarily good thing.

When he had asked where she wanted to go for dinner, the Mexican restaurant where Grace had gone on her first—and last—date with Ron slipped from Maggie's mouth before she could stop herself.

She wasn't sure what answers she thought she might find, but it was worth a shot. She'd spend her night the way Grace had and hope something jumped out at her. A clue. Some indication of what might have happened that night that caused her to leave that cryptic voicemail for her sister.

When they entered the mall near an ice cream store, Matt flashed Maggie an inquisitive look. "Want dessert?"

"No, thanks. I'm full."

He reached for her hand, and Maggie's heart skipped in her chest as his warm fingers intertwined with hers.

"Do you remember that ice cream place on Route 46?" he asked as they strolled hand in hand. "The one by the dairy farm."

"Oh, I used to love that place." When she was younger, summer nights often found Maggie's family sitting at the picnic tables, where she and her sister would try to finish their cones before they melted. They never succeeded. "Were the cones huge, or did they just seem that way because we were smaller back then?"

"Both, I think."

Maggie couldn't wait to give him the surprise she'd gotten him. They already had a lot in common simply because they'd grown up in the same town.

Matt must have had a similar thought. "I feel like we skipped through all the awkward getting to know you stuff." He rubbed his thumb across the top of her hand. "Officially, it's only our second date, but if you count all the classes we had together over the years, it's more like our two hundredth date."

Maggie was in awe of how at ease she felt. The margaritas had left her feeling brave enough to utter a confession. "I probably shouldn't tell you this, but I had a huge crush on you in high school."

The corners of Matt's mouth lifted. "Why wouldn't you want to tell me?"

She shrugged, an embarrassed flush warming her face. "It's humiliating to tell someone you pined for them twenty-something years ago."

Matt's eyebrows shot up, and then his lips parted in a wide grin. He pulled her out of the pedestrian traffic and wrapped her in a hug.

"Pined for me, huh?" His voice was soft but smug in her ear.

Maggie scrunched up her face and wiggled free. "See, I shouldn't have told you."

"Why didn't you say anything back then?" Matt gestured toward a bench by the fountain. "Maybe we wouldn't have divorces and baggage to talk about."

As she sat, Maggie's eyebrows came together, her lips pinched. "Come on. You weren't interested in me back then, and you know it."

Matt gave a firm shake of his head. "Not true. I always thought you were cute. I just didn't have the nerve back then to do anything about it." He leaned over and kissed her. "Now, I got all sorts of game going on. Were you surprised when I called you?"

"I was a bit ..." Maggie hesitated as she searched for the perfect word to explain how she'd felt to answer the phone and find Matt Winters on the other end. "It was a bit surreal. I can't say I ever expected you'd call, but I was happy you did. Very happy."

"Don't you think it's a crazy coincidence we both ended up moving to the same place?" He held her gaze as his fingertips trailed down her forearm. "I know we ran into each other under some odd circumstances, but the timing was perfect. We're both divorced and available." He leaned over and kissed her again, then gave her a wink. "I think it was meant to be."

Maggie couldn't help but smile. She'd said the same thing to Robin.

Matt dug into his pocket, then held out a penny. "Wanna make a wish?" He leaned into her. "Actually, I have no idea if this is that kind of fountain, but it can't hurt, right?"

Maggie lifted the coin from his palm and stood. She squeezed her eyes shut, not sure she needed to waste her wish on their relationship. Everything she hoped for was already coming true. Instead, she recited a silent prayer that Grace would get the justice she deserved and opened her eyes. With an underhanded toss, the penny flew from her hand, made a tiny splash as it hit the water, and sunk to the bottom.

"So ..." Matt's eyebrows lifted as she reclaimed her spot on the bench. "Care to share what—"

The muffled sound of her phone ringing in her purse interrupted the moment. She'd been spared from revealing the truth about her wish.

"I should—it could be Jake." Maggie pulled her cell from her purse and checked the caller ID. "It's my sister. She probably wants to know how our second date is going." When she'd told Stacy she had a date with Matt Winters, her younger sister had squealed so loud Maggie had to move the phone away from her ear. *Try not to drool. You know, the way you did in high school every time you saw him.*

Maggie hadn't drooled. Okay, maybe she had.

No doubt, Stacy also wanted to know how her surprise had gone over.

Maggie silenced the ringer on her phone. "I'll just call her back tomorrow with all the dirt."

Matt pressed his hand against his mouth in mock horror. "What? You're going to kiss and tell?"

"That depends." Her head tipped to the side as she gave him a coy smile. "You going to kiss me?"

Matt leaned over and brushed his lips against hers, sending a shiver through her. "And if you're good, there's more where that came from. You just need to promise me you'll tell your sister what a good kisser I am."

"Oh, I don't think you have to worry about that." Maggie reached for his hand. "I probably couldn't have handled you back in high school anyway." She was embarrassed to admit she didn't remember much about Matt's family, even though she must have seen them at their graduation. "So, I know you said your parents were divorced. Are they still in New Jersey? Do you have any brothers or sisters?"

He drew in a deep breath. "My dad's remarried. Still lives up north. My mom moved down here about ten years ago. I have—" His mouth pulled tight, and he looked away. "I *had* a sister. She died."

The air deflated from Maggie's chest, and she squeezed his hand. "Oh, Matt, I didn't know. I'm so sorry."

He gave a clipped nod, then stood and extended his hand to help her up. His face hardened as if he'd said all he was going to say on the subject. "Mall's closing soon. I suppose I need to take you home."

They walked along in silence until they got to his car in the parking lot.

"I know it will take longer," Maggie said when he opened her car door. "But would you mind taking Branson Boulevard instead of the expressway back to my house?"

Matt opened his mouth to say something, then closed it and

gave her a quizzical stare as she slid into her seat. "Trying to save me toll money? I promise that penny wasn't all I have."

Maggie managed a thin laugh. "I, uh, heard about a store I wanted to check out, but I'm not exactly sure where it is." It wasn't like she could admit she had no idea what she was looking for.

He hesitated, then nodded. "Okay then. I'll go slow so you can keep an eye out for it."

Like a tour bus operator, Matt pointed out points of interest along the way. "That electronics store? A guy stole a $2000 computer but ran out of the store so fast that he dropped his wallet." He looked over and grinned. "Easiest arrest ever." He then aimed his chin toward Maggie's side of the car. "Oh, and see that restaurant coming up on the right? A customer there claimed he found a piece of a finger in his burger."

She screwed up her face. "That's disgusting."

He gave a matter-of-fact shrug. "We figured maybe the cook in the back didn't like the guy. After all, it was the *middle* finger."

Maggie groaned, then shot him a skeptical look. "You're kidding, right?"

"Nope. I'm going to take you there on our next date."

She playfully swatted Matt's arm. "There's no way we're eating there. Gross."

"Hey, you said you could handle whatever I dished out."

As his eyes scanned the road for his next story, the mischievous smile slipped from his face, and he went silent.

"What is it?" she asked. "Something worse than a finger in a burger?"

Matt gave a slow nod and pointed down the street they were passing. "About nine years ago, there was an accident at the next intersection. A guy was chasing his girlfriend in her car, and he slammed into the back of her vehicle. He had a gun in the car, and when her car burst into flames, he used it to kill himself."

Maggie drew in a sharp breath. "Oh, wow. At least he didn't shoot her first."

"She died anyway." Matt pressed his lips together. "People tried to help, but there was just no way to get her out of the car. The fire. It was too intense." His gaze drifted down the road. "I haven't been up this way in a long time, but there used to be a memorial. A big wooden cross someone painted purple."

Maggie's eyebrows shot up. "Wait a minute. I feel like I saw that just recently. It was faded, but it sounds like the one you're talking about." She swiveled in her seat. "I have been here." She pointed down the road. "That's where the defendant from my trial works. Well, actually, I think he's a part-owner."

Matt glanced over at a small strip mall as they passed it. "The pizza place?"

She waved her hand in the air to indicate it was farther away. "No. The white building, just past the drug store. It's a body shop. You know, to fix cars."

Matt arched an eyebrow and shot her a look. "Is that so?"

"Oh, right." She grabbed his arm. "Sorry. I'm sure you know what a body shop does."

"Did they actually bring you there during the trial?"

"No. Robin and I came here on our own. The same night we saw you by the victim's house." Maggie stared out her window. "We were trying to time how long it would have taken Doyle to get to her house on the night of the murder if he stopped by his work first."

"Doyle? I presume that's the defendant's name. Why did you think he went by the body shop?"

"A witness saw a white car speeding out of the victim's neighborhood the night of the murder, but she wasn't called to testify. Doyle drives a black pickup. Robin and I thought maybe he used a customer's car."

Matt cocked his head as he considered the possibility. "A

reasonable theory, but I'm sure it was looked into. The prosecution probably decided the car wasn't relevant."

"Shouldn't the jury have heard from her anyway? It could mean someone else did it."

"But *someone else* wasn't on trial. The defense could have called her, I suppose, if they thought her testimony was necessary to sway the jury, but the burden rests with the prosecution. My guess is she wasn't a great witness, so both sides decided she had nothing to contribute."

Maggie murmured in agreement as they passed the darkened building, long closed for the day.

Grace and Ron had most likely driven the same route the night of their date. They'd passed Doyle's body shop on the way back to Grace's house. The following day, she was murdered. It didn't feel like a coincidence.

When Matt parked in the lot at her apartment complex, Maggie wasn't nearly as nervous as she had been after their first date.

He shut off the car. "Come on, I'll walk you up."

He held her hand as they strolled toward the sidewalk that would take them to her building, but Maggie skidded to a stop. "I can't believe I almost forgot. I have something for you. A surprise."

An amused smile lifted his lips. "For me?"

"Stay here. It's in my car." Maggie took off at a fast clip. There was no assigned parking, and her car was parked on the far side of the lot.

She'd begged her sister for a favor—cookies from the Italian Bakery Matt had talked about on their first date. Stacy had gone to get them and shipped the box to Maggie's office address. Now that she lived in an apartment, she was never confident a package left outside her front door would still be there when she got home.

Maggie unlocked her car and reached for the package she'd carefully placed on the floor behind her passenger seat. She tucked it under her arm, slammed her door, and took off through the parking lot.

She could see Matt in the distance as he waited patiently on the sidewalk. She weaved through the vehicles and headed back toward the open asphalt that stood between her and him. As she got closer, she could see the curious expression on his face. She bit back a smile as she anticipated the reaction he'd have when he opened the box and realized what was inside.

With her gaze anchored on him, Maggie raced out between two parked cars. For a brief moment, her feet faltered. She took a last-second cursory glance to her left just as Matt's booming voice cut through the darkness. A warning. There wasn't time to swing her head in his direction. She sucked in a sharp breath as the sound of a revved-up engine ripped through the night air. Her arm flew up to shield her face, her eyes protesting the pair of bright white lights. They were heading right for her.

Blinded, Maggie stumbled backwards as the high-pitched squeal of the car's brakes stole the air from her lungs. The cardboard box tumbled from her hands. It rolled several times against the pavement before coming to rest sideways against the oversized tire of a large SUV.

In several seconds, Matt was upon her. "Are you okay?"

She leaned heavily on a stranger's car as she gulped down several steadying breaths. "I'm—I'm fine," she choked out.

"What the hell were they thinking?" Matt's hands were clenched into tight fists at his side as he frowned in the direction of the exit.

"It was my fault. I—I wasn't paying attention, and I stepped out—"

"He shouldn't have been driving that fast through a parking lot," Matt said firmly as his eyes flashed with anger. "I wish I had gotten the license plate. Trust me, I would have aimed a few choice words in his direction the next time I was in uniform."

It had all happened so quickly, the vehicle a blur in Maggie's memory.

Had Matt seen the car that almost hit her? Or was it a pickup truck? The question was on the tip of her tongue, but Maggie wasn't sure she wanted to know the answer.

15

Maggie's hands trembled as she retrieved the box from the ground and dared to hope Matt's cookies had survived the fall.

"So, I, uh, got you a surprise." The close call in the parking lot had subdued her excitement.

"Hang on." Matt lifted the box from her hands and set it on the hood of the car beside them. "That can wait." He wrapped his arms around her and pulled her in close. "I need to make sure you're all right."

Maggie was sure Matt felt her heart hammering against his chest. She drew in a deep breath and eased it out slowly. "I'm fine. Just a little shaky."

The tension lessened in her shoulders as she breathed in the now familiar smell of Matt's cologne. She had no proof that what happened was a deliberate act by the driver. Yes, the person behind the wheel had been driving too fast, but Maggie had darted out from between the parked cars. She was partially to blame.

She offered him a weak smile. "I guess this is what you get when you live in an apartment, right?"

Matt pulled back, his face stern. "It's not okay. I may have to place a call and ask someone to patrol this place. Someone needs to scare these people into slowing the hell down before someone gets hurt."

Maggie couldn't admit she'd feel better if she knew someone was keeping watch. If she mentioned any suspicion her near-miss might have been related to the case, Matt would be even more insistent they halt their investigation. They couldn't bow out now. After what she'd seen on their ride home, Maggie felt more confident than ever. She was close to uncovering a large piece of the puzzle of what had happened the night before Grace was killed.

He kissed her gently and his expression softened. "I'm glad you're okay." His eyes drifted to the package on the car beside them. "So, you mentioned a surprise?"

"It's just—just a little something I know you'll like."

Matt reached for the cardboard box and studied the return address label. "So, is this from you ... or your sister?" An amused smile quirked his lips. "Did she pine for me, too?"

"Don't get too crazy. I asked her to send it."

After he'd worked through the packing tape Stacy used to seal the box, Maggie was relieved to see a layer of bubble wrap inside. Maybe the contents were intact after all.

Matt's mouth dropped open when he made it to the white bakery box tied with thin red and white string. He ran his fingers over the gold sticker with the name of the bakery. "Tell me my favorite sprinkle cookies aren't in here?"

"Okay." Maggie laughed. "There's no sprinkle cookies inside."

"It's been years. I used to dream about these." He lifted his eyes to meet hers. "I can't believe you had these sent for me," he said softly. "You're amazing, you know that?

"So are you."

Matt reached for her hand. "Come on, I need to deliver you safely to your door this time."

As they stood outside her apartment, he kissed her and thanked her over and over. "I swear I'm not going to go home and eat this entire box."

Maggie was tempted to invite him in, but she still wasn't sure she was ready to take that next step. Besides, Matt was scheduled to work early in the morning.

When she entered the apartment, her cheeks still warm from their long goodbye in the hallway, Maggie reeled back.

"What are you doing here?" she asked.

Jake looked over at her and removed his headset, his face offering no clue he'd heard anything other than the video game he was playing. "Dad dropped me off. He needs you to take me to school in the morning. Something about having an early meeting."

No call. No text. Her annoyance with her ex-husband escaped in a long hiss through the crack in her lips. Good thing she hadn't come into the apartment with Matt strolling along behind her.

"You look nice. Were you at Robin's?"

"No. I uh, went to dinner with—with a friend." Maggie plopped down next to Jake on the couch. "By the way, be careful in the parking lot out there." The bus from school dropped Jake near the complex entrance, and he had to make his way across the parking lot to their building. "People drive like maniacs."

"No kidding. That's why I stay on the sidewalk."

Apparently, her son was smarter than she was. Maggie pulled her laptop from the coffee table and rested it on her thighs as she typed the name of Doyle's body shop in the search bar.

Jake gave her a sidewards glance. "What are you looking for?"

Maggie pursed her lips and stared at her computer. "I'm not sure. Something freaked out Grace the night before she was killed. She left her sister that voicemail I told you about, but she died before anyone could find out what it was about. On the way home from dinner tonight, we drove by the defendant's body shop, and I'm convinced it's connected somehow."

"In what way?"

"I don't know yet." Maggie squinted at the search results. "They have at least a four-star rating on all of the review websites that came up. This one's actually 4.6 stars." She slid her finger along the tracking pad and double-clicked. Her gaze drifted down the list of comments. "I don't see any customer complaints. This lady even wrote—" She cocked her head. "Wait a minute."

Jake had just put his headphones back on but took them off again. "What is it?"

"There's a review on here and the date—it was written four months after the murder." Maggie read what the woman had posted out loud. "'I've been negligent in not leaving a review sooner about the outstanding service I received from D & M's body shop. Last October, an inconsiderate lug left a large dent in the driver's side door of my Toyota Camry. I brought my car in, and the owner told me if I left it, they could fix it first thing Monday morning. Over the weekend, I got called out of town for a family emergency. When I got the call that my car was fixed, I explained my situation and asked if I could leave it for an additional day. I was told it wasn't a problem, and they sent me the pictures below of my repair. They did a great job! The owner even had my car detailed for me. When I picked it up the next day, it looked brand new. That's five-star customer service. Here's hoping no one decides to hit me again, but if they do, I'll be back.'"

Jake shrugged as Maggie gave him an expectant stare. "So,

the guy who might be a murderer is also a good businessman?"

She shook her head and sighed. "Maybe he is, but that's not the point. Grace Hutchinson was killed on a Monday. The first Monday in November. So, if the reviewer brought her car in at the *end* of October ..." Maggie waved her hand in the air to encourage Jake to make the connection.

Instead, her son groaned. "Mom, you're talking in circles. I don't get why this one review is so important. Can't you just tell me?"

"Maybe you need to see it." Maggie turned her laptop around and tapped on the screen. "See, this is Meredith B's review."

Jake held out his hands. "I see it, but—"

She moved her index finger lower. "These are the pictures she attached. One is the before picture with the dent, and the other is the after picture when it was fixed."

He leaned in and gave an appreciative nod. "Wow. They really did do a great job. You can't even tell—"

"It's not about the dent, Jake. It's about the color of the door." Maggie leaned against the back of the couch and ran her finger across her lips. "If the dates line up the way I think they might, it means there could have been a white sedan at the body shop the night of the murder. Just like the one the witness saw speeding through Grace's neighborhood the night she was killed." The crease between her brows deepened as her gaze landed on her son. "Not to mention, it's a little odd it was detailed before this woman picked it up. What body shop does that just because?"

"Oh, I see what you're saying." Jake aimed his chin at her laptop. "Maybe he borrowed that lady's car to commit the murder."

Maggie bobbed her head slowly. "Maybe he did."

Her plan to follow the path Grace had taken on her date with Ron had worked. She couldn't wait to tell Robin she'd found the elusive white sedan.

16

The next night, Robin sat at Maggie's kitchen table and stared in disbelief at her computer screen. "Wow. How did the police miss this?"

Maggie slid into the chair across from her. "She didn't leave the review until months after her car was fixed. By then, Doyle had already been arrested."

"And none of the other reviews mentioned having their car detailed at no charge?"

"None that I could find."

"Interesting. Very interesting." Robin wrenched her gaze from the laptop and cocked her head thoughtfully. "Now, how do we figure out who this Meredith B is so we can go talk to her?"

Maggie's shoulders hitched. "I have no idea. Her profile listed her location as Tampa." She stood slightly to reach her computer and pulled it to her side of the table. "She has a picture on her profile, but I'm not sure how we could find her without a last name."

Robin tucked her leg underneath her and leaned forward. "Click on her name and see if she has other reviews."

"Oh, there's lots. Apparently, Meredith B is very opinionated." Maggie scrolled through the reviews she'd read the day before. "She must eat out a lot. She's reviewed a ton of restaurants." She chuckled. "This one was my favorite. It says *I'll have Maria's Tacos cater my funeral.* She's pretty funny in some of these."

"Good. Sounds like our new friend has a sense of humor. With any luck, that means she's not some uptight stick in the mud who won't want to talk to us. Look for any place she's reviewed where they might know her last name. Someplace she visits regularly. You know, like a dentist. Or a chiropractor."

"How about a nail salon?"

Robin's eyes lit up as she gave an enthusiastic nod. "Yeah. That might work."

"She gave Main Street Salon five stars." Maggie scanned her review. "According to this, she gets her nails done there every two weeks by a woman named Noreen."

The corners of Robin's mouth lifted in a satisfied smile. "Sounds like we need a couple of appointments."

ON SATURDAY MORNING, they sat side by side getting pedicures.

Robin turned to Maggie with a well-rehearsed comment. "Meredith was right. This place is amazing."

Noreen glanced up, the brush from the bottle of coral-colored nail polish in her hand now frozen in the air. "Did someone refer you to the salon? If they did, we usually give them five dollars off their next service."

"Oh, really?" Robin waved her hand at Maggie, who sat in the pedicure chair next to hers. "Well, my friend and I went out to dinner, and while we were waiting to be seated, I couldn't help but notice this woman's nails. I asked her where she got them done because they were so pretty. She said her name was Meredith."

Noreen's brow crinkled. "Meredith Mann? Older woman with silver-blond hair?"

"No, I'd say she was in her forties. Brown hair that came to about here." Robin brushed her hand across her shoulder. "Cute wispy bangs."

The nail tech working on Maggie piped in. "Meredith Brinkley."

"Oh, you're right," Noreen said as she bobbed her head. "She does have the best hair, and her daughter, Morgan, looks just like her. It's uncanny."

"Oh, that's so funny." Robin threw a hand in the air and shot Maggie a look. "We said the same thing, right? Her daughter was with her that night. When we left, it looked like they were sharing a dessert." Her gaze cut sideways to Maggie again. "Remember how jealous I was?" Robin smacked her lips. "It was chocolate, and it looked ridiculously delicious."

Maggie bit back a smile. Improvisation was her friend's forte.

Noreen looked surprised. "Oh? Meredith's always talking about how her daughter never wants to go anywhere with her anymore." She shook her head and groaned. "Teenagers."

Maggie nudged Robin's arm. "We hear that, right?"

"I have a daughter who's a junior in college," Robin said. "And we both have teenage boys in high school. A freshman and a sophomore."

Noreen's attention was back on polishing Robin's toenails. "I think boys are easier, and Meredith's getting a little freaked out because Morgan's a senior. Time is ticking. You know, once they go off to college, nothing's ever the same."

Robin heaved a sigh. "Ain't that the truth?"

Maggie's chest tightened. She didn't want to think about Jake going away. The divorce had been hard enough, and on the weekends when he was with Todd, the silence in the apartment was unbearable. "I'm hoping my son doesn't want to go too far when the time comes," she said. "Anywhere in-state is fine. At least I can hop in the car to go see him."

"Yeah, no such luck for Meredith. Morgan's got her hopes pinned on Auburn." Noreen laughed. "I think she's afraid if she doesn't get far enough away, she'll end up working at her parents' store for the rest of her life."

When Robin's eyebrows lifted, Maggie could almost see her wheels spinning. "Oh, what kind of store do they own?"

"Pool supplies. They're in that strip mall behind the 7-Eleven and the Wendy's. You know, on Fletcher."

"Oh, yeah." Robin gave a slow nod. "I know exactly where it is. My son's orthodontist was in that plaza. I've passed by her store, but my husband takes care of our pool. I'm so lucky. All I have to do is pull up a lounge chair."

Maggie pressed her lips together to keep from laughing. Her friend didn't have a pool.

"Yeah, Morgan works there a couple of days a week after school. It can't be an exciting place for a teenager, but Meredith says the store does well and pays the bills." Noreen glanced up and shrugged. "Not to mention, it covers her mani/pedi every two weeks."

"Can't ask for anything more, right?" Robin eyed Maggie as a slow smile spread across her face.

Forty minutes later, their freshly pedicured toes strolled into the pool supply store.

Robin ran her finger under her chin as they stared at Meredith Brinkley from the other side of the front counter. "You look really familiar."

"Maybe I just have one of those faces," the woman said with a shrug. "You've never been here before?"

Robin shook her head. "Nope. First time." She tipped her

head to the side and pretended to study Meredith thoughtfully before she waved her finger in the air. "Wait a minute. I know this might sound crazy, but did you write a review for Maria's Tacos?"

When Meredith laughed, it was an infectious giggle that matched the tone of her reviews. "I did, and I wasn't kidding. My husband knows. If I kick the bucket, you call the coroner first, and the next call needs to be to Maria to tell her to get ready to cater my funeral."

Robin's nod was slightly more exaggerated than necessary. "Hilarious. My husband and I were looking for a Mexican place, and after I saw what you wrote, I had to read your other reviews. I followed you."

Meredith crossed her hands against her chest. "Look at me. I'm famous."

"Seriously. You should write a restaurant review column for the paper or something. My husband and I were cracking up. I even remember the one you wrote for an auto body place because my husband said only a pretty woman could get their car detailed for free. Is it even a service that place offers?"

"Oh, D & M Body Shop? Yeah, I don't know if that's a thing they do."

"Were you in a car accident?" Maggie hoped to get her talking about her experience with Doyle.

"I wasn't even in the car when it happened." Meredith expelled an annoyed sigh. "Some idiot must have cut their wheel too tight as they pulled out of the parking spot next to mine. Or maybe they just decided to ram my car with their shopping cart. I mean, seriously. I ran into the supermarket for five minutes to get Halloween candy." She threw a hand in the air as her gaze drifted between Maggie and Robin. "Who wants to be the house that turns out the porch light and pretends they're not home, right? So, I come out of the store with an industrial-sized bag of chocolate, and there's a huge dent in my door. Naturally, the jerk who did it didn't bother to hang around to apologize—" She scowled. "Or give me their insurance information."

Robin huffed in solidarity. "They probably didn't even have insurance."

"Probably not." Meredith's lips pursed in disgust. "Anyway, someone recommended that body shop, so I took it in. He gave me a reasonable price, so I didn't even file an insurance claim. Who needs that headache, right?"

Robin gave a knowing nod. "No kidding. You have insurance, but then if you make a claim, they jack up your rates."

"Exactly. Anyway, I left it for the weekend, and it was supposed to be fixed that Monday. Then my husband's clumsy mother decided to fall down the stairs, and we had to run out of town." Meredith shook her head as if she still couldn't believe what happened. "We weren't even home for Halloween. And you know who ended up eating all that damn candy." She rubbed her rounded belly. "Me."

"Was your mother-in-law okay?" Robin's face held an expression of concern.

"Broke her leg in three places, and they had to do surgery to put in a metal plate."

"Oh, that's terrible."

"For me?" Meredith asked as she pointed to her chest. "I was the one who got stuck sitting at the hospital all day. When they called to say my car was finished, I had forgotten I even dropped it off. But the owner was so nice. Doyle, I think, was his name. I guess he's the D in D & M. Anyway, he said he would text me pictures of the completed work, and I could leave it there until I got home the next day."

"I saw the pictures in your review," Robin said. "After it was fixed, I couldn't even tell there had been a dent."

Meredith bobbed her head in agreement. "I know, right? They did such a great job that I gave him my credit card over the phone to pay for it." She gave a slight shrug. "I guess maybe the guy felt bad for me. You know, the situation with my mother-in-law. I was shocked when I picked up my car. It looked amazing —inside and out. Like new, really."

"It's so hard to find good customer service these days." Maggie rested her forearms on the counter. "It's nice you took the time to leave a review." She and Robin appreciated the gesture more than Meredith could possibly know.

"Since I have my own business, I know how important they are. Some days, it feels like it's only the disgruntled ones who take the time to blast you."

"Everyone's so brave when they're hiding behind a computer screen, right?" Robin asked.

"Isn't that the truth?" Meredith's gaze drifted between the two women. "So, what can I get for you today?"

"Oh, just some ..." Robin glanced around the store. "Some chlorine. My husband didn't have time to get any, and we have family coming over this weekend. I'm sure the kids are going to want to go swimming."

"Tablets or liquid?"

Robin clearly hadn't anticipated the question, but to her credit, she flinched only slightly before answering. "Um, liquid."

Meredith strolled over to one of the shelves, then lobbed the heavy bottle onto the counter.

She laid her hands on the glass. "Anything else?"

"Nope, that's it." Robin eyed Meredith's manicure as she pulled out her credit card. "Your nails look so pretty."

She held out her hands to admire them for herself, then ran the card. "Main Street on Wiles Road. Tell them Meredith Brinkley sent you, and I'll save five bucks at my next appointment."

"Will do." Robin tucked her wallet back into her purse and grabbed the jug of chlorine. "Thanks."

As they exited the store, Maggie took a quick glance around. She hadn't mentioned the parking lot incident to Robin, who would no doubt write it off as a coincidence. Maybe it was, but she wasn't taking any chances. She scanned her surroundings, but nothing seemed out of the ordinary. Not a black pickup in sight.

"So, that's it," Maggie said in a low voice as they strolled to Robin's car. "Doyle used Meredith's white Camry to commit the murder. Then, he had it detailed to destroy any evidence. Melody Kaplan must have been wrong about the time."

"And maybe since Meredith paid for the job, the body shop's system closed it out which made it look like the car had been picked up. That could be why the police didn't see it as a possibility." Robin popped the trunk and dropped the jug of chlorine inside with a grimace. "Not quite sure what I'm going to do with that." She clicked her key fob and unlocked their doors. "There's just one more thing we need to confirm."

"What's that?"

Robin didn't respond until they were both settled inside. "We need to make sure the body shop doesn't offer detailing services. That would make it even more suspicious that they had Meredith's car done, sympathy for her family emergency or not."

"I guess we could call and just ask." Maggie reached for her seatbelt and clicked it into place.

Robin hesitated, then shook her head. "I think we need to look around his place." She started up the car and shrugged. "We might notice something useful. You can't do it because he knows what you look like from the trial."

That was fine with Maggie. She had no desire to run into Doyle Riggs. Day or night.

"But I could go in and pretend to be a potential customer." Robin glanced up at her rearview mirror.

Maggie scrunched up her face and adjusted the vent until she felt a bit of cool air blowing on her. "I guess you could, but don't you think Doyle might get suspicious? It's not like your car needs any body work."

Robin gave a thoughtful nod, then shifted into reverse and pulled out of her parking space. Instead of heading toward the exit, she drove around slowly as if she were looking for something.

Maggie frowned. "What are you—"

Robin held up her index finger, then put the car in reverse again. She slowly backed up until the car stopped with a thud.

Maggie spun around in her seat and her gaze landed on the light pole the car had backed into. Her eyes flew open. "Are you nuts?"

Robin waved away her concern. "Oh, I didn't hit it that hard. They'll be able to pop that right out."

"You'd better hope so, or your husband's gonna freak."

"Sometimes, you do what you need to do in the name of justice." She put the car in drive and shrugged. "It isn't the first light pole I've backed into, but this dent has Doyle Riggs's name on it."

17

When she heard the knock at the front door, Maggie tripped as she ran to let Robin in.

"Tell me everything," she said as she ushered her into the apartment. "What happened at the body shop?"

Robin dropped into the armchair as Maggie sat next to Jake on the couch.

"I did just what we talked about. I went in and said I needed to fix a dent on my bumper. I told him I had a little run-in with a light pole."

Jake's head whipped up from his video game. "You hit a pole?"

Robin shrugged. "Well, yeah, but I did it on purpose. I needed some damage on my car, so I could go check out Doyle's body shop."

The teenager's confused gaze drifted between the two of them, and then he shook his head. "You guys are weird."

Maggie dismissed him with a wave of her hand. "Yeah, we know. Feel free to play your game." Then, her attention was back on Robin. "Did he look at you like you were a moron?"

"Nah," she said with a flick of her wrist. "I'm sure he hears it all."

"So, did you talk to Doyle or someone else?"

"Oh, it was him. He was wearing one of those blue mechanic's shirts with his name on it. I can see why the jurors fell for his act. He's pretty cute, and he was actually very nice when I first got there. I told him if the cost was reasonable, I wouldn't put in a claim through my insurance. Same as Meredith did."

Maggie leaned forward, her arms on her thighs. "So, he was cool with that?"

"Yup, he said that's what most people do unless it's a ton of damage. He said fixing my bumper probably wouldn't even meet my deductible." Robin released a giggle. "I told him I thought it was easy to fix, but my husband isn't very handy." She huffed a breath. "Even with this ruse, that's probably the most ridiculous thing I've said all day."

"So, he went out to look at the car? Did he agree?"

"Not necessarily. But you're skipping past the good part."

"Oh, sorry." Maggie made a motion to zip her lips.

"While I was standing there, I noticed a motorcycle on the other side of the glass." Robin's head tipped to the side. "So, I said, 'Oh, you fix bikes, too.' And Doyle told me they don't. He said ..." She paused, then raised her finger to make her point. "'That one's mine. It was so nice out, I decided to ride it to work today.'"

"What?" Maggie sat straight up, her voice brimming with excitement. "Doyle has a motorcycle?"

"One that's usually at his house, apparently. He probably keeps it in the garage, or maybe in that backyard shed I didn't get to see." Her eyes narrowed. "You know, the *murder* shed."

Jake's head jerked up, deep lines on his forehead. He eyed the two of them for a long moment but said nothing.

"Robin's just being dramatic. Doyle doesn't really have a murder shed in his backyard."

"You don't know he doesn't," Robin said, her expression deadpan. "Anyway, no matter where he keeps it, the takeaway is that if he took the motorcycle to pick up Meredith's car the night of the murder—"

"His truck would have never left the driveway," Maggie said, finishing her thought. "I can't believe the police didn't figure this out."

"No kidding. But here's the best part."

"There's more?"

"When Doyle was writing up the estimate, he said he'd need my car for a day or two. So, I asked if I could have it detailed before I got it back, and it was like a switch flipped. His eyes got all squinty and pissed off." Robin mimicked Doyle's deep voice. "We don't do that here, ma'am."

Maggie's eyes widened. "He must not know Meredith wrote that in her review."

"Well, if he didn't, he does now. I told him I saw a review for the shop, and the person said their car was detailed before it was returned. I mentioned I thought it was such an awesome service to provide."

"And what did he say?" Maggie held her breath as she waited for Robin's response.

"For a minute, he just stared at me, almost like he was trying to figure out who I was or what I was up to. I was a little nervous he might come over the counter."

"He was that mad?"

"Not mad so much as—suspicious. You know, like, who the hell is this lady? Then he said, 'There was one time when a mechanic spilled his coffee in a customer's car. Maybe he took it in.'"

Maggie snorted. "Right, *coffee*."

"Exactly. He looked like a deer in headlights trying to come up with a story to explain Meredith's review." Robin leaned back in her chair. "Then he crumpled up my estimate. Said they were so backed up that there was no way they'd be able to get to my car anytime soon. He suggested I call Dent King. He told me they'd come right to me and fix it in my driveway."

"Are you kidding? I can't—"

Maggie was interrupted by Robin's cell phone skittering across the coffee table.

"Oh, I turned the ringer off while I was there." She glanced at the caller ID. "No clue who this is, but perhaps a certain body shop owner changed his mind about wanting my business." She pressed the accept button. "Hello." A pause. "This is she."

Robin stood and gestured for Maggie to follow her into the kitchen. She laid her phone on the counter and tapped the speaker button.

"I hope it's okay that I'm callin' y'all," the man said. "But Sarah Henry gave me your number. She was putting up some signs in the neighborhood about a cat that's gone missin'. Anyway, we got to talkin' about that poor girl at the end of the block."

"Grace Hutchinson?" Robin exchanged a glance with Maggie.

"Right," the man said. "The girl that was murdered. She told me y'all are trying to do some investigating. You know, to help the family. I guess the guy the cops arrested wasn't the right guy after all."

"Well, he was found not guilty," Robin said into the phone. "That doesn't necessarily mean—"

"Well, I got some information. I tried to give it to the police way back when, but they didn't seem much interested in what I had to say."

Robin's eyebrows shot up. "Well, if you'd like to share it with me, I'd love to hear it."

"That's why I'm callin'. The night that girl was killed—it was a Monday night, and I was coming back from my AA meeting at the church on Parkside Drive."

Robin dramatically dropped her head. "Uh, huh."

"I was waiting to make the right onto 77th Drive. I have no idea why there was so much traffic that night, but there was this car waiting at the stop sign. The guy had his left turn signal on —which, you know, you're really not supposed to make a left there. Anyway, I was keepin' an eye on him because I thought for sure he was gonna make that illegal turn when I tried to come down the street. I figured he'd smash right into me if I wasn't careful."

Robin propped her elbow on the counter and used her palm to hold up her head. "He didn't, did he?"

"Nah. I waved him on and let him go. I don't need no accident on my record. Hadn't even had my license back for very long."

"So, mister ..."

"Jenkins. Roy Jenkins.

"Well, Mr. Jenkins, I appreciate the call, but I'm not sure how this relates to Grace's murder."

"There was something about that guy that seemed off. He was wearin' gloves. In Florida. Right there, that's suspicious."

Robin pressed her lips together and shot Maggie a look. "I agree. That does seem odd."

"I thought the same thing. When I heard about that girl gettin' killed, I called the cops and left a message. Must say I was mighty surprised no one cared enough to call me back."

"What exactly did your message say?"

"I told them I saw a suspicious guy drivin' a white Toyota Camry the night that girl was killed."

At the mention of the white car, Robin's eyes widened, and she poked Maggie's arm. "You're sure it was a Camry?"

"Damn near positive. I'm pretty good with car stuff. Used to be a mechanic before the drinkin' got bad."

Mr. Jenkins, do you remember what time you saw that car?"

"I certainly do. Our meeting ends by 8:30 p.m. Normally, I stay after and get me some of the free coffee and cookies, but the Bucs were playin' that night. I wanted to get on home to watch the game."

"And how far is the church from your house?" Robin asked.

"Only 'bout ten minutes."

"So, you would say you saw the white car at about 8:40 p.m. that night?"

Yup. That's what I said in my message to the police."

"This is actually very useful information, Mr. Jenkins. When the time comes, we'll make sure you get a chance to tell the police what you saw."

"Someone killed that girl. They need to pay for what they done."

"I couldn't agree more. Thanks for calling. I have your number on my caller ID, and we'll definitely be back in touch." Robin disconnected the call and let out a squeal. "Looks like our first witness had one cabernet too many. She was wrong about the time."

"Or this guy is wrong." Maggie held up her hand before Robin could protest. "Just playing devil's advocate here. Why do you think the police never called him back?"

"They couldn't connect Doyle to a white car, so they had no interest in hearing from anyone who saw one. Especially when this guy's time didn't match what Melody Kaplan said. They probably figured neither one of them meant anything."

"I guess that's possible," Maggie said, but she wasn't convinced.

"Since we spoke to Meredith, we know he had access to her white Camry the night of the murder. And if Mr. Jenkins saw it at 8:40 p.m., that gave Doyle plenty of time to accept the pizza delivery at his house and then hop on his motorcycle to drive to the shop to pick up her car." Robin's forehead creased. "There's just one thing he said that has me confused. The gloves. It sounds like Doyle was trying to prevent leaving his fingerprints in Meredith's car, but why would that matter? He could always claim he left them there while the car was being fixed."

"Maybe they were motorcycle gloves or he wore them to break into Grace's house or—" Maggie winced. "Maybe he wasn't sure he was going to shoot her—we still don't know whose gun he used. If he strangled her instead, maybe the gloves were to make sure he didn't leave his DNA on the body."

Robin jabbed her finger in the air. "Oh, good point. But I still don't understand why he needed to get the car cleaned."

"Don't forget, there was a partial boot print at Grace's house. Doyle must have stepped in her blood, and he was probably worried some of it got in Meredith's car. That would be impossible to explain away."

Robin nodded thoughtfully. "He didn't want to take a chance she'd notice it and ask questions. Now it makes sense why he got it detailed before he gave it back."

"But when you asked him about that service, he turned down your business."

"Correct."

"Sounds to me like Doyle just wanted to get rid of you."

Robin gave her a knowing smile. "Sounds to me like he used Meredith's car to try and commit the perfect murder."

"Where in the world are you taking me?" Maggie stared out the passenger side window of Matt's car, but nothing looked familiar.

"I told you, it's a surprise," he said. "I still can't believe you were able to get out of work today."

She turned her head and heaved an exaggerated cough. "Yeah, well, I called in sick." Maggie flashed an innocent smile. "It's not a complete lie. Most days, Harry makes me feel like I want to throw up."

Matt's expression changed as a scowl crossed his face. "I hate that you let him get away with treating you the way he does. We need to figure out a way to get you out of there." He hit his blinker to indicate a left turn, then placed his hand on her arm as he waited for the light to change. "Okay, close your eyes."

Maggie complied, then felt Matt's warm breath on her cheek. "No peeking."

"I'm not, I swear. But I have no idea where we are, so even if I could see, I'm not sure that would help me."

After a few moments of driving, the car stopped and the engine quieted. "Hang tight for a second." The driver's side door creaked, then slammed shut. A moment later, Matt's hand gripped hers. "I'll help you get out of the car. Just keep 'em closed."

As Maggie held onto the crook of Matt's arm, he led her into a building. At least she assumed they were inside. She was sure she'd heard a door squeaking as it opened, and then her skin prickled with a sudden change of temperature. Air conditioning. Matt kept her at arm's length and spoke to someone in a soft voice with words Maggie couldn't quite distinguish.

A moment later, there were new voices—all male. More hushed conversation.

Matt reached for her hand again and tugged her gently forward. "Come on. We're almost there."

She shuffled along beside him, taking one cautious step after another until they came to a sudden stop.

"Okay, you can open your eyes."

Maggie's eyelids fluttered as she took in her surroundings. They were in some sort of office building. Tile floors. Long endless hallways. The walls were painted white with small brown signs outside the offices. The wall in front of her held framed photographs of people.

The groove between Maggie's brows deepened as she tried to make sense of where he'd taken her. "I don't understand."

"Oh, geez, really?" Matt reached for Maggie's arm and spun her around until she faced the wall that had been behind her.

She took in the round green logo and black painted outline of a body and let out a squeal. "We're at the crime lab? How? Who—"

"I called in a favor. Told them you were a little, um, obsessed."

"That's an understatement." Matt understood and accepted her in a way Todd never had. Maggie wrapped her hands around his neck and hugged him tightly. "Thank you. This is the best surprise ever."

Matt swung his gaze to the two men standing with them. "See, I told you. You want to impress most women, you bring them flowers, a box of candy. Not my girl. Give her crime and a bit of murder. Some evidence to uncover. She's happy as can be."

My girl. Maggie's insides swelled with happiness.

She stared in awe as the two men—Roberto and Joe—started the tour.

They led her to what looked like an office. Roberto twisted his key in the lock, and when the door opened, Maggie stared into a cavernous space with packed metal shelves that went from the floor to the ceiling.

"Evidence storage," he said.

"Ever hold a million dollars in cocaine?" Joe asked as he dropped a bag filled with white powder in Maggie's outstretched hands.

Her mouth gaped as she shot Matt a look of disbelief. "You have to take my picture. Robin's never going to believe this."

From there, they went on to the ballistics room, where she learned firsthand how every bullet fired had markings unique to the weapon that discharged it. Rows and rows of tagged guns hung in a steel cabinet. Across from that was an enormous metallic cylinder. Maggie leaned over to read the tag on the side. *Bullet Recovery Tank.*

When Joe thumped his hand against the side, it made a hollow metallic ringing sound. "If we need to test a weapon against a bullet we have from a crime, we fire it into this. It's filled with water."

There was the garage with a stolen car, a session where she learned how to pull fingerprints, and they were now giving her a lesson on how to detect the presence of blood. Maggie had started to feel like a genuine CSI.

"So, what do you think?" Roberto asked.

She chewed on her bottom lip as she held up the swab. It had turned a light shade of pink. "Even though I couldn't see it, there was definitely blood on that tile."

"Exactly," he said. "Even if it's been wiped off, we can still do a presumptive blood test using phenolphthalein. There was hemoglobin present, so when you added the hydrogen peroxide, the reaction turned the swab pink."

A woman wearing a polo shirt that had Crime Scene Investigator stitched on it bustled into the area where they were testing the samples. She stooped over and pulled some supplies from under the counter where Maggie was standing.

"I'm sorry." Maggie stepped back. "Am I in your way?"

"Nope, you're fine," the woman said as she secured the flap of the large envelope with red tape from a special roll. She whipped out a black pen and signed her name on the seal. Amy Fuller.

"Is that evidence?" Maggie asked, finding it impossible not to stare. "Like from a real case?"

Amy's eyebrows came together as she shot Roberto and Joe a look of confusion.

"This is Maggie," Roberto said as he waved his hand in her direction. "Joe and I are giving her a tour of the crime lab today."

"Oh." Amy bobbed her head. "Gotcha. Yeah, these are fingerprints from the garage door at a house where a couple was murdered this morning."

Maggie's eyes lit up. "And you think they belong to the person who did it?"

The CSI eyed Joe with a slight smile. "I sure hope so. That would make this one of the easy cases, huh?"

Maggie considered the investigators that had gotten up on the stand during Doyle's trial. "If they arrest this person, will you have to testify in court about what you found?"

"Maybe," she said with a shrug. "Honestly, I'd rather be in the field than in a courtroom any day, but we do what we need to do to lock up the bad guys." The woman's face grew serious. "The families of the victims depend on us. The work we do could make the difference between them getting justice and the person who committed the crime going free to do who-knows-what to someone else."

Maggie nodded as she pressed her lips together. She understood exactly what she was saying and couldn't help but wonder if this woman had worked on Grace's case.

"Gotta go." She retrieved her sealed envelope of evidence. "Have, uh, fun? I guess this is a cool place to hang out if you're into this kind of stuff."

Maggie grinned. "Oh, I'm into it. I work in a boring accounting office. You pretty much have my dream job."

The CSI's eyebrows shot up. "Oh, wow. Okay, then let me go back to it. Gotta get those bad guys off the street. Enjoy."

Ten minutes later, Matt rejoined her in the hallway outside the captain's office. "Having a good time?"

"You have no idea. I watch shows on television, but this is how it all happens in real life." Maggie couldn't wipe the smile from her face. "Robin is going to be so jealous."

"Try not to rub it in too much. You have one last stop today, but Roberto and Joe had to run to a new case, so I told them I'd take you." He gave her a quick peck on the cheek and then gestured with his hand for her to follow him.

They strolled down the long hallway until he stopped and opened the door beside a sign that read *DNA Lab/Chemistry*. Inside, they were greeted by a woman who introduced herself as Christa.

She pointed at a line of tape placed on the floor just outside the glass door that led to the lab. "I can't let you go much farther than my workspace because, well, we don't want your DNA to show up on evidence we're testing for a crime, right?"

From the required distance, Maggie checked out the people working inside. They wore hairnets and masks, while white cloth jumpsuits covered their clothes. She bit on her bottom lip as she watched their gloved hands cut samples from clothing and other items. They carefully dropped them into test tubes using long metal tweezers. It could have been any science lab with its metal counters and impressive equipment. Except these people were in the process of helping solve crimes.

Maggie eased out a long breath. "So cool."

"DNA is like the holy grail." Matt shot a knowing glance at Christa. "Hard to prove you weren't at the scene of the crime when your DNA says otherwise, right?"

"Absolutely. Even I'm amazed at how far we've come using it to solve crimes." She glanced around at the row of office cubes and relocated two chairs to the space next to her desk. "Have a seat."

Matt pushed the chair closest to Christa toward Maggie and claimed the other one for himself.

Christa's gaze dipped to a folder on her desk, and she removed a sheet of paper. "We had a case where a woman was raped in her own home by a guy with a knife. The perpetrator didn't kill her, but he covered her eyes with blacked-out swim goggles so she couldn't identify him. He wore gloves and was smart enough to use a condom. He probably thought he was being super careful to not leave any evidence behind."

Maggie perched on the edge of her chair, anticipation on her face. "Not careful enough, I'll bet." Otherwise, they wouldn't be sitting in the DNA lab talking about him.

"The woman mentioned to the police that she thought he was allergic to her perfume. The guy sneezed." A smile tugged at Christa's lips. "DNA jackpot."

"So, did you catch him?" Maggie asked breathlessly.

"His DNA wasn't in CODIS—that's the national database. So, we had no match."

Maggie moaned. "That must have been so disappointing. So, there's nothing you can do with it?"

"Well, if he commits another crime, we could have a match at some point down the line. But for this case, we enlisted help from a company that does phenotyping." When Maggie's forehead wrinkled, Christa explained further. "They take the DNA we find at a crime scene and create a composite of what the person might look like." She waved her finger in the air. "Now, it's not exact, but it gives us a good idea of hair color, eye color, and race. That kind of thing." She passed the paper to Maggie. "This was what we got back on our mystery DNA."

Maggie reached for the document and studied it as Matt looked over her shoulder. "So, according to this, they're almost ninety-eight percent confident your suspect has blonde or brown hair."

"A huge starting point, right?"

Maggie gave a hesitant nod. "Right. He most likely has blue or green eyes because eye color has a ninety-two percent confidence score. His skin is fair or very fair. That's an almost eighty percent confidence rating."

"So, based on all these characteristics, we know the man we're looking for is white."

Maggie pointed at the image on the sheet of paper. "This is what they predict he looks like?"

Christa bobbed her head. "Yup. Now, of course, his hair could be longer or shorter. He could have a beard or a mustache. It also doesn't tell us his age. But we have a lot more to go on than we had when we started the investigation."

Maggie exchanged a glance with Matt before her gaze drifted back to Christa. "So, did the profile help?"

Christa's face lit up. "It sure did. Our perpetrator was convicted a couple of months ago, and he's now sitting in prison where he can't hurt anyone else. Want to see what he looks like in real life?"

Maggie's eyebrows shot up. "Absolutely."

Christa handed over a copy of the convicted rapist's mugshot.

Maggie's jaw hung open. The resemblance between the two pictures was incredible. "Wow. "I can't believe how much he looks like the photo created from his DNA." She passed the picture to Matt.

"He does." Christa leaned back in her chair and crossed her legs. "They don't all look this close, but that one was pretty amazing. When we showed it to the victim, she thought it resembled the maintenance guy at her apartment building. He hadn't been working there long, but he'd been in her place to fix something a week or two before the rape. The detectives followed him around for a couple of days until he dropped a soda can in the trash. They compared the DNA from the can to the sample we had from the victim's shirt. Bingo. He was our guy."

"That's incredible."

Matt handed Maggie the photo to return to Christa.

"It's just one technique we're using." She leaned forward to accept the picture and filed both the DNA snapshot and mugshot back into the folder on her desk. "They're also doing incredible things with investigative genetic genealogy. That's where they load the DNA into a public site to look for related family members."

"That's how they finally caught the Golden State Killer, right?" Maggie's cheeks warmed as she offered an embarrassed shrug. "I devoured Michelle McNamara's book the day it came out. I felt terrible she didn't get to see him convicted after she invested so much into catching him."

"Impressive," Christa said as she gave Maggie an appreciative nod. "I guess I don't need to tell you how valuable DNA is becoming to catch these guys and close out cold cases."

"It's hard to believe anyone gets away with anything anymore."

And yet, somehow, Doyle was walking free.

"It is getting harder, that's for sure. Even perps like the Golden State Killer—guys who thought they'd gotten away with crimes from years ago are getting that knock at the door."

"Now, whatcha gonna do, buddy?" Matt said.

Christa laughed. "You got that right. These new advances mean they need to keep looking over their shoulders, because we're not giving up on locking them away."

"DNA lasts a long time, huh?" Maggie couldn't stop thinking about Grace's case.

"If it's collected and preserved correctly at the time of the crime, yeah," Christa said. "Of course, lots of environmental factors kick in if it's exposed to the elements for long periods. Heat, water, moisture. Not the perfect scenario, but sometimes we get lucky."

Maggie's lips pursed. "Can you wash DNA off clothing?" If the jersey taken from Doyle's house had Grace's DNA on it, it would prove he'd taken it from the murder scene.

"Not easily, but it also depends on the source. Is it coming from blood or another bodily fluid? That's pretty difficult to get rid of completely. If it's touch DNA that comes from someone simply handling the item, it depends." Christa's shoulders lifted. "Sometimes there just isn't enough to form a complete DNA profile, and that's even before it's washed."

Maggie nodded thoughtfully. "This has been incredibly informative." She extended her hand in Christa's direction.

"Thank you so much for taking the time to explain all this to me."

As they walked out of the building, she looked back in awe. The day had been worth the misery Harry would inflict on her for calling out sick.

"Did all that crime-solving make you hungry?" Matt asked as he opened her car door. "If you want, we can go back to my place, and I'll make us an early dinner. I have to be at work at seven tonight."

This would be the first time Maggie had been to Matt's house, and nerves and anticipation coursed through her. As if he sensed her hesitation, he glanced over and held her gaze. "Unless you'd rather not. That's fine, too."

His concern for her feelings was so genuine that she couldn't help but smile. "No, I'd love to see your place." She slid her cell phone from her purse. "Let me just text Jake." He didn't know she hadn't gone to work, and she wouldn't be home much later than usual.

As Matt grilled steaks on the small deck outside, Maggie rummaged around in his kitchen and found half a bag of frozen vegetables and a large potato she cooked in his microwave.

When he came back in and saw what she'd prepared, he shrugged. "I guess I should have made sure I had more food in the house before I invited you over for dinner, huh?"

"No, this is great." She eyed the perfectly cooked steaks, and her mouth began to water. "I don't have a grill at the apartment, so this is a treat."

He leaned down and kissed her, then embraced her in a hug. "I'm just glad you're here."

"Me too."

"You want wine? His head swiveled as he looked around the kitchen. "I do have some of that around here. Unfortunately, you'll have to drink alone since I'm working tonight."

She shook her head. "Water's fine."

As they sat at Matt's kitchen table, he held up his glass, and she did the same. "To our first dinner here. The first of many, I hope." His lips twitched with a sheepish smile. "I promise I'll go grocery shopping next time."

"I don't care what we eat. Today was amazing."

Matt clinked his glass against hers. "You're amazing."

"I've never been lucky at anything. How in the world did I find you again?" Maggie took a sip of water and set her glass down to cut her steak.

As they ate, she filled Matt in on the parts of her tour he'd missed while he was sitting in with the captain.

"I love that they're using all the stuff in the lab to prove who committed the crime." Her forehead wrinkled. "I just wish some of that had made a difference in Doyle's trial. Grace's family didn't get justice, and I can't imagine how that must feel. For both her family and the people who investigated the case."

"I understand, more than you know, but it's not your crime to solve. Digging into Doyle's life—it won't be appreciated if he finds out about it. He could be dangerous, and for you and Robin to put yourselves at risk for a podcast. It's not worth it."

Maggie threw a frustrated hand into the air. "So, we just let him get away with murder? How is that fair to Grace's family?"

Matt laid down his fork. His gaze wandered while an awkward silence hung in the air.

"It isn't fair," he said finally, the anger in his voice catching her by surprise. "But sometimes that's just the way it is." He stared at her like he wanted to say something else but instead lowered his eyes to his plate.

Maggie's mouth opened, and a confused breath escaped. She pushed her dinner away and stared at him, bewildered, as he finished his steak without saying another word.

Her stomach swirled until she couldn't stand it anymore. "Matt," she said softly.

When he brought his gaze up, his face was cold and unreadable.

She crossed her arms on the table and leaned toward him. "I'm sorry."

His expression slipped into a frown. "What are you sorry about?"

"I don't know, but—I feel like—"

Matt let out a breath and shook his head. "It's not you." He pushed his plate off to the side and reached for her hand. "Do you remember when you asked me why I became a cop?"

"Uh, huh. You said you wanted to help people."

"I did—I do, but there was more to it."

He stared at their clasped hands for a long moment before continuing. "After I moved to Florida with my ex, my mom and sister decided to follow me. Beth—that's my sister—she started dating this guy. They'd only been dating a few months when she took my mom and me out to dinner and announced she was moving in with him."

The twinge below his cheek betrayed how hard his jaw was clenched. "I can't explain it, but I didn't have a good feeling about him. I told her I thought she should wait, get to know him a little better. Beth laughed and told me I was being an overprotective big brother."

A slight smile quirked Maggie's lips. She'd been a recipient of his worry as well. "I can see that as a possibility."

"Yeah, well, I was right." Matt's face hardened. "It wasn't long before my sister stopped calling. Me or my mom. We saw her less and less until I finally showed up at her apartment one day. She claimed everything was fine, but I knew my sister." He drew in a deep breath. "When I pressed her, she admitted things had been rough. She wanted out. I said I would help her, and she could move in with my wife and me if she needed to."

The mention of his ex-wife stung a little, but Maggie kept her expression neutral. "I'm sure she appreciated the offer."

He pulled back his hand and raked it through his hair. "When she broke the news that they were over and she was moving out—he went nuts. Beth called the police. They showed up, took some information, and basically told the two of them they should figure out a way to separate for the night." Matt's eyes grew glassy, and he shook his head. "They just left him there with her. I don't know why she didn't call me to come and get her—" He choked back a sob. "She got in her car and left." He swiped at his tears. "I'm sorry. This isn't something I ever share."

"It's okay. You don't have to—"

He put up his hand and his eyes bore into hers. "I do. I need to tell you what happened, so you understand where I'm coming from."

Maggie bit her bottom lip and gave a hesitant nod. "Okay."

"Remember that accident I told you about? The purple cross by the side of the road?"

Her body went rigid. "Oh, Matt, no."

"Purple was my sister's favorite color." He tightened his jaw again as if the pressure gave him the strength needed to tell her the rest. "When Beth left the apartment, her boyfriend followed her and chased her like she was prey. He rammed her from behind at the red light and propelled her car into the intersection." He winced as if he was in physical pain. "A box truck slammed into her."

Maggie could still hear snippets of the story he'd told her on the way back from the mall. *Her car burst into flames. People tried to get her out. The fire was too intense.*

Maggie stood, came around the table, and wrapped her arms

around him. "Oh, honey. I'm so sorry you had to go through that."

"We lost Beth, and we didn't even get to tell her boyfriend what a piece of shit he was. He stole that from us." Matt pulled back and looked her directly in the eye. "So, I do understand what you're saying about Grace's family. We didn't get justice either."

"You have every right to be angry. What he did was horrible."

"Maybe my sister would still be here if the police had done something different that night. But that's when I decided what I wanted to do, and it had nothing to do with selling insurance. I wanted to help people like Beth."

Maggie pressed her hand to the side of his face. "And I'm sure you have."

"I like to think so." His eyes searched hers. "But now there's you," he said softly.

The realization hit Maggie squarely in the chest. The reason he shared his story. Why he was so worried about their investigation. "But I'm not dating Doyle."

"I know that." Matt's mouth pulled tight. "I also know his type, and I'm well aware what a loss of control does to someone like that. If he really did kill Grace for breaking up with him ..."

Maggie reached for his hand. "I'm sorry if I've made you worry about me."

"I can't lose you, too. A guy like Doyle isn't worth it, and he can't be held accountable even if you could prove he did it. The two of you nosing around in his life—you could be poking a hornet's nest. Then what happens?" His eyes pleaded with her. "Promise me, Maggie. Promise me you'll let this go."

19

When Maggie exited her office building, Robin was already waiting for her.

"Hey," she said as Maggie pulled open the passenger side door. "I can't believe the miser is letting you escape for lunch."

"Oh, Harry wasn't happy about it. Not at all. Especially since I called out sick yesterday." Maggie reached back for her seatbelt, then clicked it into the buckle. "I'm pretty sure he was just about to ask me to go get his lunch, but I didn't give him a chance. You should have seen his face when—" She bit back a smile. "Well, looks like you'll get your chance."

Her boss had exited the building, his thin lips pursed in an aggravated grimace.

Robin shifted in her seat to get a better look. "That's him? You're right. He does look super annoyed."

Maggie glanced at Harry and snorted. "He always looks like that."

"I pictured him differently." Robin studied him in her rearview mirror. "He's flashier than I expected."

"Oh, he's all about appearances. He wasn't always this bad, but he's stepped up his game in the last few years. Stopped smoking. Got himself a wardrobe of fancy suits. An expensive watch. I swear, the man's like a broken record." Maggie pinched her lips together as she mimicked him. "You can't be a success if you don't look the part." She huffed. "You can imagine how he feels about how I present myself."

Robin shot her a disapproving glance. "Don't worry about what he thinks. You look great."

"Well, I'm a work in progress. Let's put it that way."

"He seems like the kind of guy who thinks a designer suit can hide the fact that he's really an insecure nobody," Robin said as she backed out of the guest parking spot. "Same reason he orders you around. He needs to feel important."

She pulled forward. Harry was on the driver's side as he marched to his car, the scowl still on his face. As if he could feel Robin's eyes on him, he whipped his gaze in her direction.

She lifted her hand. "Wave goodbye to Mr. Nobody. I hope he doesn't hurt himself getting his own lunch."

As they drove away, Maggie shifted in her seat to stare out the back window. Her boss stood rigid beside his car as he watched them. He squinted into the sun, then reached into the inside pocket of his suit. He pulled out his expensive designer sunglasses, observed Robin approach the exit to the lot, and then disappeared inside his car.

Maggie pressed a hand against her mouth and groaned. "As fun as that was, I'm sure I'll pay dearly for it this afternoon."

"Screw him." Robin scrunched up her face. "You get a lunch hour. You're allowed to get something to eat. Besides, I wanted to go over some stuff before I go on vacation."

Maggie followed Robin's lead when they placed their orders at the restaurant. "I'll have the market salad as well." She handed the waitress her menu. "Grilled salmon on top and the house dressing on the side works for me, too."

Maggie glanced around the almost-full dining room. It was a luxurious feeling to escape the office with no obligation to do Harry's bidding. "So, when's your flight?"

"Day after tomorrow. We leave at the crack of dawn. My daughter will fly directly from Miami and meet us there."

"Spring break in Cancun." Maggie issued an audible sigh. "Lucky you."

"Hey, I invited you and Jake to come with us."

"I know you did, but I just couldn't pull it off. Money's tight, even with my child support."

"You have to see this place. It's gorgeous." Robin pulled out her phone, pressed a few keys, and passed it across the table.

"Sure, rub it in." Maggie scrolled through the pictures on the website and pushed down a pang of jealousy. "This place looks amazing. Have one of those fruity drinks for me."

"It's all-inclusive, so there will be plenty of cocktails." Robin's bottom lip jutted out. "I really wish you were coming, but since you're not, I appreciate you offering to take care of Duke. He loves you now and will be just as happy to stay in the house and have you visit him."

It was nice to have a dog again, even if Maggie was just the surrogate dog walker. Other than the one time he'd growled, there had been no other issues. Still, she felt better having him along, especially at night. "Don't worry. We're buddies, and I would miss our walks now that I'm in the groove."

"You mean now that you're looking hot."

Maggie's cheeks warmed. She couldn't remember the last time anyone had complimented her appearance. "Let's not get crazy."

Robin's gaze drifted thoughtfully. "You know, I was thinking maybe I'd show Melody Kaplan a picture of a white Toyota Camry like Meredith's. See if she thinks that's what almost hit her."

Maggie reached for her water glass and took a sip. "I thought you said she didn't know anything about cars."

"I know, but I figured it's worth a shot. And I find it odd I never heard back from Ron Brookins. I called him twice and I left a message for his dad. Neither one of them will call me back. I know it looks like Doyle's a sure thing, but can you imagine if we found out Ron had access to a white car?"

Maggie could still picture him on the stand, sweat beading on his forehead as Doyle's attorney questioned him. "The poor guy was a nervous wreck when he had to testify at the trial. I mean, seriously, they had one date and he got caught up in this whole nightmare. I'm sure he just wants to put the whole thing behind him."

Robin pressed her lips into a firm line as she shook her head. "Still. I don't like that his dad is his alibi. And if he has nothing to hide, why won't either of them return my call?"

Maggie's lips twitched with a slight smile. "You still think he might be a secret serial killer?" He seemed like such a normal guy, but then again, Robin hadn't seen him on the stand. Maybe if she met him, it would convince her he had nothing to do with Grace's murder.

"You never know. Lots of killers look normal on the outside. They don't all look like John Wayne Gacy. It's no wonder I'm afraid of clowns." Robin squeezed a slice of lemon in her water and took a sip. "By the way, David's truck will be at the airport while we're gone. He's going to take me tomorrow to drop off my car so the bumper can be repaired while we're out of town." She gave an irritated hiss. "Obviously, I'm not taking it to Doyle's place."

"David couldn't fix it?"

Robin's cheeks turned pink. "Apparently, the bumper on this car isn't as easy to fix as the last one I dented. They have to replace the whole thing, so we can never tell him I hit that pole on purpose. Deal?"

Maggie pressed her hand to her forehead. "Oh, geez. Yeah, it's a deal." Their lunches appeared, and she leaned back in her seat to allow the waitress to set her salad in front of her.

Robin took a bite of her salmon, then glanced up. "I was thinking that when I get back, we should also try to find Grace's ex-boyfriend, the one Pam told us about. It can't hurt to feel him out and see what kind of vibe we get."

Maggie was silent as she drizzled dressing over the top of her salad. "Do you think that's necessary?" she asked finally, avoiding eye contact. "Pam said he moved on a long time ago."

"I know, but I feel like we should cover all the bases." Robin reached behind her and pulled her small notebook from her purse. Let me make a list." She released an evil chuckle. "A hit list." She turned to an empty page and made a note. "It'll give us another episode for the podcast. It's not like we have to use it if it turns out to be nothing."

Maggie gave a curt nod, but her stomach felt queasy. She wanted to honor Matt's request. Really, she did. But it was also hard to let go of something she'd been working toward—uncovering the truth about Grace's death. Despite her initial misgivings, she'd gotten more comfortable co-hosting the podcast. She enjoyed it and didn't want to walk away.

"We need to dig into Doyle's past, too," Robin said as she ate. "You know, are there exes that could tell us what he was like when they dated him? Maybe he has a history of jealousy." She set down her fork for a moment and scribbled in her notebook. "There's got to be a way to find out if Doyle was ever married, or maybe we could find out if anyone ever filed a restraining order against him."

Matt's words rang in Maggie's head. *Promise me you'll let this go.* It hadn't been easy for him to share the story about his sister, but he'd done it so she would understand his concern.

Robin stabbed at her lettuce. "Did he have any character witnesses at the trial?"

"Not really. Just the neighbor across the street. And I didn't get the impression they were friends."

Robin wrote in her notebook. "We should talk to him, too."

Maggie cringed, then set down her fork. Now she wanted to get Doyle's neighbor involved? What if he mentioned they were still looking into the murder?

"Something wrong?" Robin asked, a slight furrow between her brows. "You still sick?"

"I was with Matt yesterday. He had the day off."

Robin eyed her suspiciously. "So, you weren't really sick?"

"Sick of listening to my boss bark orders at me, maybe." Maggie couldn't contain her smile as she thought about the previous day. "It was totally worth the evil eye I got from Harry this morning."

Robin's eyebrows lifted in anticipation as she leaned forward. "Well, are you going to tell me how it was?"

Maggie realized the assumption her friend had made and couldn't resist the chance to have a bit of fun. She brought her hands to her chest and plastered a love-struck smile on her face. "Matt took me to a place I've only dreamed about."

Robin's fork clattered against her plate as it fell from her hand. She pushed her salad away and crossed her arms in front of her on the table. "Tell me everything. Absolutely everything."

Her anxiety about their investigation was forgotten as Maggie burst out laughing. "Matt called in a favor and got me a tour of the county crime lab yesterday."

Her friend sat straight up and slapped her palms on the table. "Stop it right now."

"It was incredible." Maggie recapped the previous day and shared the pictures on her phone as Robin grunted with jealousy. "Then we went back to his place, and he made dinner."

Robin tipped her head. "Just dinner?"

Maggie's cheeks got hot, but she had no intention of sharing all the details of the previous day. "He had to work at seven." She left it at that as if there wasn't anything more to tell.

Disappointed, Robin resumed eating. "It seems like it's getting serious."

Maggie had never felt this way, even when she first met Todd. Matt had opened up to her, and their connection felt stronger every time they were together.

"I really like him." The corners of her mouth turned up. "I haven't been this happy since—maybe ever. It's just—" Maggie's smile faded as dread pushed down on her. Robin wasn't going to like what she needed to say. "Matt's not thrilled about us investigating this case. He's worried we're in over our heads. Afraid we're going to poke a hornet's nest by digging into Doyle's life."

Robin stared at her with pursed lips. "Like Doyle has a posse?"

"He didn't say those words specifically." Maggie's shoulders lifted. "He's just afraid our nosing around will be noticed, and it won't be appreciated. He thinks it's dangerous."

"But why?" Robin's forehead creased as if she didn't understand why Matt was making such a big deal about it. "Even if we can prove Doyle committed the murder, he can't be tried again. I highly doubt he'd risk coming after us over a perjury charge."

Maggie eased out a sigh as she remembered their conversation the night before. She couldn't deny Matt had made some strong points. "We still have no idea why he killed Grace or if she's his only victim." She threw up a hand. "What if he thinks we've found proof of a different murder—one he hasn't already been acquitted of? That changes the stakes completely." She squirmed in her seat and tried to push the incident in her parking lot from her mind. "If Doyle comes after us, we don't have a way to protect ourselves. That's what Matt is worried about."

Robin gave a slow nod. "I can understand his concern, I guess. Does he think we should get ourselves guns?"

Maggie's head jerked back. "Get ourselves guns?" As the occupants of the table next to theirs stared, she realized her words were louder than she intended. She leaned in and lowered her voice. "I'm pretty sure that's not going to make Matt feel better about this. I don't even know how to use one. Do you?"

"No, but we can take lessons." Robin's tone was matter-of-fact. "Get concealed carry permits."

Maggie held her head in her hands. This wasn't where she'd expected the conversation to go. She glanced around before responding. "I'm not comfortable getting a gun," she whispered tersely. "I'm not sure I could fire it, even if someone were after me. What if I panicked and shot the wrong person?" She shook her head. "No way. I am not the type of person who should have a gun."

Robin was quiet for a moment, then a pained look crossed her face. "So, what are you saying? You want to bow out of the investigation? Not be part of the podcast anymore?" She searched Maggie's face as if she was looking for her to say Robin had misunderstood. When that didn't happen, she let out a breath. "I can't believe you'd want to bail, especially at this point."

Maggie slumped back in her chair. "I don't want to quit. Really, I don't. But I'm also not sure I have a choice." She scrunched her shoulders against her neck and lifted her hands helplessly. "Do I want to be with Matt or continue with the investigation and the podcast?"

Robin's cheeks turned red. "That's not fair. You haven't even been dating him that long. He can't just give you an ultimatum."

Maggie straightened up in her seat to protest. "He's not. Matt hasn't said it's him or the investigation." Her shoulders sagged as she shook her head sadly. "Not yet anyway."

How could she possibly explain this to make Robin understand? It wasn't fair to share Matt's story about his sister. He'd confided in her that he never told anyone what happened to Beth.

"Everything is perfect between us until we start talking about this case. I can already see it has the potential to—" Maggie's voice softened. "If it breaks us up, I'll be crushed." Her eyes pleaded with her friend to understand. "Do you know how long it's been since I felt like someone cared what happened to me? I'm just not sure I'm willing to risk losing that for Doyle Riggs."

"I understand, but it's not just about Doyle." Robin looked her firmly in the eye. "It's up to you to create the life you want to have, Maggie. You can't deny you've enjoyed doing the investigation. The podcast. You're really good at all of it."

Her friend wasn't willing to give up so easily. "What if I did the investigating, and I just filled you in on our nightly walks with Duke? We could still record together as if you were part of it. Matt can't possibly believe there's any danger hanging out in my spare room closet, right? I mean, c'mon, we're moms obsessed with true crime. *Moms*. Plural." Robin's lips pushed forward into a pout. "I don't want to do this without you."

Maggie sat silent as she contemplated her offer. "Maybe that would work. Let me talk to him while you're on vacation, and I can let you know when you get back. Is that okay?"

Robin gave a reluctant nod. "At least I know you won't work

on the case without me while I'm gone." She glanced around for the waitress. "We probably need to get the check."

Maggie inhaled sharply when she checked the time and realized she'd been gone almost an hour and a half. "I had no idea how late it was. Harry's going to make my life a living hell when I get back."

20

"Why was Harry crankier than usual yesterday?" Charlene asked as Maggie made herself a cup of coffee in the employee kitchen.

"I left to have lunch with a friend, so he actually had to go out and get himself something to eat." Maggie stirred in a splash of creamer and shrugged. "Not to mention, I lost track of time and was gone for almost two hours."

"That explains why he dumped so much on you when you got back." Charlene pulled the foil off the top of her yogurt container and reached for a plastic spoon. "What time did he actually let you leave last night?"

"After seven. At least Jake's off for spring break, but he was starving by the time I got home. I can't wait until he has a license and can get around on his own."

"Maybe the Barbie doll bimbo will let him drive her convertible."

Maggie released a hiss of air. "He would love that. I haven't heard much about Stephanie lately, which is fine with me." Her shoulders hitched in an embarrassed shrug. "I'm dating someone, so I don't care what Todd does anymore."

Charlene's eyebrows shot up as she held her spoon frozen in the air. "Oh, really?"

"Yeah, he's a cop, and I—I think it's getting serious." Just the mere mention of Matt made Maggie smile.

"Oh, good. You deserve to be happy. Especially after all that BS your ex pulled." Over the years, Charlene had heard quite a lot from the other side of their shared wall. "Now, if you could just figure out a way to get away from Harry, your life would be perfect." She leaned in and lowered her voice as if someone might hear. "I heard Jason's assistant isn't coming back from maternity leave. He's going to be hiring someone new."

Maggie sipped her coffee thoughtfully, then shook her head. "I'd never get it. You know Harry would badmouth me and tell him how awful I am."

"Harry doesn't like anyone." Charlene's lip curled in disgust. "While you were out, that man was so condescending. I mean, if you're going to ask for help while your assistant's out, the least you could do is be nice about it."

"Yeah, that word isn't exactly in my boss's vocabulary. I'm sorry you got stuck dealing with him and had to do some of my work."

Charlene scraped her spoon against the bottom of her yogurt cup. "It wasn't *that* bad—just the bi-weekly payroll for Surbhi & Partners and Czarnowski. Oh, and some freight company, but that one was easy. Must be a small place."

"A freight company? That's not one of Harry's clients."

Charlene cocked her head as she eyed Maggie. "Really? That's odd. He said he was drowning while you were out and needed me to pick up some of your work." She closed her eyes and tapped her finger against her lips. "Martin Freight," she said when she opened them. "I'm pretty sure that was the name of the company."

Maggie shook her head. "Never heard of them." She had to be mistaken.

Charlene shrugged. "Well, someone's been doing their payroll. Maybe he tried to foist someone else's work on me while you were out."

"Harry did leave me a message trying to tell me I should come into the office every day after jury duty, but I ignored it. Like I'm really going to sit in court all day and then come to the office. What about my kid?"

"Good for you." Charlene stood and tossed her trash in the garbage can. "So, how was jury duty?"

Maggie wrapped her hands around her coffee cup. "A welcome break from this place."

"And it was a juicy murder trial?"

Maggie nodded. "The process was fascinating, even if the outcome was a little disappointing."

She shot a quick glance at the clock on the wall and gave her co-worker an abbreviated version of the case. "So, in the end, we had to vote not guilty. But I'm not so sure he didn't get away with murder."

Charlene shook her head. "Wow. That's terrible. Imagine if he goes out and kills someone else because he's not in prison."

"Tell me about it. Especially since he saw how easy it was to get away with it. He really went out of his way to cover his tracks and it worked. There was even a witness who saw a car racing from the scene. She told the cops, but—"

Maggie faltered as Charlene's gaze drifted over her shoulder and she got to her feet. When she spun around in her seat, Harry was in the doorway, an angry scowl on his face.

"So, this is where you're hiding instead of working," he said. "I hate to disturb your little coffee klatch, but I was trying to confirm whether Geoff Brown made his quarterly tax payment."

He rolled his eyes dramatically. "Your filing leaves much to be desired."

Her boss couldn't have looked very hard. Maggie had made a copy of the check the day before and it was right inside the folder where it belonged. Cheeks burning, she rose from the table. "Sorry. I'm coming now. I can show you the copy of the check, but the original was mailed to the IRS yesterday."

She trailed behind Harry down the hallway toward her desk like a scolded child about to be locked in her room. Charlene didn't even look up as they passed her desk. A minute later, Maggie pulled the photocopy of the check from the folder to show Harry, but he brushed her hand away and stormed into his office.

"I don't know how much longer I can stand to work for such a miserable human being," she muttered under her breath as she tossed the folder in disgust onto her desk.

A muffled "I'm sorry" came from the other side of the wall.

As Maggie went about her day, she couldn't stop thinking about the company Charlene had mentioned. It seemed odd Harry would have her coworker doing someone else's work, and he hadn't bragged about a new client. He'd been locked in his office all morning, but he finally emerged without so much as a glance in her direction. As Maggie watched him stomp off down the hall, she seized the opportunity to search the shared server containing the firm's client files. Sure enough, there it was—Martin Freight.

She clicked on the folder to open it, but a message flashed on her screen. *You do not have access to this account.* Maggie pursed her lips as she stared at her computer. She'd never been restricted from viewing any of Harry's client files. He was up to something, and she was determined to figure out what it was.

She stood slightly and peered over her wall. Charlene was away from her desk.

Maggie picked up her office phone and dialed Andrew Mason's assistant. "Hey, is Harry in with Andy?"

"Yup, they're in there with the door shut. Need me to get him?"

Her pulse quickened. "No, that's okay."

After one last look down the hallway, Maggie slipped into Harry's office. His computer was locked, and the firm's logo flashed on the screen. Unlike her desk, his was neat and organized and his leather planner sat in the upper left corner. With one finger, Maggie flipped open the cover. An oversized index card with Harry's handwriting was tucked into the inside pocket. His passwords. Maggie slid her cell phone from her pocket and snapped a photo. Maybe she could access the client files from her computer if she used his login information.

She had just closed his planner when she heard a noise behind her. Harry cleared his throat again—louder this time. As Maggie's heart hammered in her chest, she slowly turned around.

His beady eyes were locked on her. "What the hell do you think you're doing in my office?"

"I—I was just looking for a file. I'm sorry." She bowed her head and scurried back to her desk.

Harry was right behind her. "If you need something in my office, you ask me. Under no circumstances do you just help yourself. Is that understood?"

Her face burned. "Yes, sir."

He thrust a piece of paper in her direction. "Go get my lunch." He yanked his corporate credit card from his wallet and threw it at her.

"Yes, sir," Maggie said again, leaning down to pick up his card, which had landed on the floor. She glanced down at the paper in her hand. Her boss had no issue going all out on the company's dime. He wanted a steak from Morton's, and he'd written medium rare in capital letters, underlined, with an exclamation point at the end.

"And while you're at it, get coffee for the kitchen." He threw a look of disgust in her direction. "We're almost out again. That is your responsibility, you know."

Maggie nodded and reached for her purse. "Yes, sir. I'll pick it up while I'm out."

"Do I need to tell you to get the coffee first, Margaret, so my lunch doesn't get cold? There's nothing worse than a cold filet mignon. And before you leave the restaurant, make sure it's medium-rare. If it's not, refuse it, and have them make a new one."

As she hurried off down the hallway, Maggie's internal monologue was loaded with sarcasm. *Oh, medium-rare. Is that how you want it done? I had no idea.* Was she supposed to cut his steak to see how it was cooked? He'd lose his mind if she touched his lunch.

Maggie didn't even stop to get herself something to eat, and when she returned, Harry was in his office. His door was closed.

She buzzed his phone. "I'm back with your food."

He came out, snatched the bag from her desk, and returned to his office. The door slammed behind him.

Maggie was about to stick her head over the wall to vent to Charlene when her cell phone rang. Jake's name and picture flashed on the screen.

"Hey, Mom," he said when she answered. "Can I go to a movie later?"

"I guess. How are you going to get there?"

"My friend's mom said she'd take us if you can pick us up when it's over. Are you working late again tonight?"

Maggie felt like she'd regularly disappointed her son between her job, the case, and spending time with Matt. She stared at Harry's closed door. "I—no, I'll figure it out. What time?"

She grabbed a piece of scrap paper and jotted down the details.

"There's some cash in the cabinet with the drinking glasses," she said. "Take the twenty, and you should have enough to also get some popcorn."

Just then, Harry's door opened.

"Margaret, can you come in here, please." He'd asked rather than demanded and said please. That was unusual.

"I gotta go, sweetie," Maggie said in a low voice as she pressed the phone tight against her ear.

"Mom, wait. You're *definitely* going to be able to pick us up, right?"

Harry stared incredulously from his doorway, stunned that she dared to finish a personal call after he'd summoned her.

"Yeah, I'll be there. I promise. Have a good time."

Maggie's breath caught in her throat as she entered her boss's office. He wasn't alone.

Heidi from Human Resources sat at his small conference table. Her expression was stone cold as she gestured at the empty chair across from her. "Have a seat."

Maggie's legs shook as she walked.

There was no way this was good.

When Maggie pulled into Robin's driveway, she was just walking out her front door.

Maggie hit the button to roll down her car window and poked her head through the opening. "You heading out?"

"Yeah. I need to pick up David's prescription before we go on vacation." Robin strolled toward the car and leaned in the open window. "Shouldn't you be at work?"

Maggie glanced at the bag on her passenger seat. The only items she'd grabbed before she was escorted from the building were the pictures of Jake from her desk. "I got fired."

Robin backed away from the car as Maggie pushed open the door and stepped out.

"Because you were late coming back from lunch with me yesterday?" Her friend scowled. "That's ridiculous. Harry can't use that as grounds to fire you."

"He claims that I've been distracted ever since I came back from jury duty, and my work is suffering. He told HR I've been late every morning, and I'm always in a rush to get out at the end of the day. He mentioned my *extravagantly indulgent* lunches. I'm gone for more than an hour one day, and it's a regular occurrence all of a sudden. But oh no, it's fine when I'm out picking up his lunch."

"I can't believe HR would—"

"There's more. Harry set me up." Maggie leaned against her car and heaved a deep sigh. "He accused me of making a payroll mistake for one of his biggest clients."

At first, she wondered if she'd somehow made the error. Harry wasn't wrong that she had a lot on her mind. But the more Maggie thought about it, the more she knew the change had to have been made manually after the checks were issued. If not, the system would have kicked it back.

Maggie pressed her lips together and shook her head. "I didn't do it, but HR believed him."

"Why would he do that?"

"Well, he hates me, so there's that." Maggie's cheeks burned. "He also caught me in his office this morning. I was snooping."

Robin flinched, appearing surprised she'd do something so brazen. "Really? For what?"

"I had a feeling he was up to something shady. Now that he fired me, I'm convinced I was right. One of the other assistants mentioned she did some of my work while I was out on jury duty. Payroll for a company I never heard of."

"Maybe it's a new client," Robin suggested with a shrug.

"That's what I thought, so I looked them up. The files are there, but I don't have access to them. They're restricted. I snuck into Harry's office because I wanted to check them out on his computer."

"Are you kidding?"

"I wish I was. He walked in and caught me." Maggie groaned and held her head in her hands. "I know. It was stupid. I just—something's up with this client. I've never not had access to one of Harry's accounts. He's hiding something. I figured if I caught him doing something sketchy, maybe I could even get him out of there." Her eyes welled up. "Instead, I'm the one who got fired. I have no idea what I'm going to do."

"Well, it's not the ideal way to go, but you should thank him for forcing you to find something better." Robin laid her hand on Maggie's arm. "You'll be fine."

"I hope so."

"By the way, I was going to tell you when we walked Duke later, but I tried to call Melody Kaplan. You know, to see if I could show her the picture of the Camry."

"Oh, yeah. What did she say?" Maggie wasn't sure why they needed her to confirm the car she'd seen was Meredith's. At this point, it seemed obvious.

"Like I said, I *tried* to call her. I didn't get to talk to her because … well, she's dead."

"What?" Maggie eked out. Her stomach lurched as she thought of the car that had almost hit her. She'd finally convinced herself it had nothing to do with their investigation. A mere coincidence. But if Melody Kaplan had met a similar fate, that changed everything. Her breath caught in her throat. "How did she die?"

"I didn't ask, and her daughter didn't say. She seemed pretty upset, so I didn't want to pry. She wasn't that old, but I guess when it's your time, it's your time."

Maggie was about to respond when she heard an unfamiliar beeping. "Did you hear that?" She leaned into her open car window. When she heard the sound again, she opened the door and grabbed her cell phone from the passenger seat. She frowned as she stared at the screen. "I've never seen this message before."

"What's it say?"

Maggie read the notification. "Air Tag Found Moving with

You. Your current location can be seen by the owner of this Air Tag."

Robin held out her hand and stared at the message when Maggie passed her the phone. "This isn't cool. I've heard about them being used to stalk people."

"Are you kidding me?"

"I'm afraid not." Robin scowled. "I wonder if Doyle's neighbor ratted us out that we wanted to talk to him." Her face was serious as she handed Maggie back her cell phone. "You need to figure out where that thing is and disable it."

"Great. How do I do that?"

"I don't know." Robin offered her an apologetic wince. "I hate to say it, but you might need to ask Matt. He probably knows more about these things than either one of us."

"I didn't think this day could get any worse." Dread gnawed at Maggie's insides as she pulled open her car door. "I was wrong."

22

Maggie pulled out of Robin's driveway feeling like a weight was on her chest. How could she tell Matt that not only had she been fired, but she was also potentially being stalked? She held the phone in her hand, an ache in the back of her throat. She wasn't ready. Instead of dialing, she headed to the liquor store.

Knowing the bottle of wine was in her trunk made her feel better. She'd be home in five minutes. A full glass two minutes later. She gulped down a deep breath, hit the speaker button, and called Matt.

He answered on the second ring. "Hey, how's it going?"

Maggie gripped the steering wheel. At the sound of his voice, she felt helpless to stop the sob that choked her words. "I got fired."

"Oh, I'm so sorry." His voice filled with compassion. "What happened? It wasn't because you called out sick, was it?"

She couldn't bring herself to share the details—the truth. "My boss is just a jerk. You know that. He's had it out for me for a long time."

"I know, but he can't just fire you for no reason. What did they say?"

"Just that my work has suffered since I came back from—" Maggie cut herself off, but it was too late.

Matt finished her thought. "From jury duty? Which is when you started doing all this stuff with Robin on the side. I told you there was nothing you two could do about Doyle. I begged you to let it go." His voice was now laced with the disapproval she'd expected. "Now that it's cost you your job, will you stop?"

"I did talk to Robin about bowing out of the investigation, but—" Maggie swallowed hard, but she had no choice. She needed his help. "There's something else." She wrapped an arm around her stomach, but it didn't ease the sharp pain stabbing her insides. "I got this—this weird warning on my phone. I don't know what it means."

After she read him the message, the line went silent.

"Matt, you there?"

His prolonged sigh brought Maggie no comfort about the situation.

"This isn't good," he said in a serious voice. "Someone could be using the device to track you. Did you find the Air Tag?"

"I don't—I don't even know what it looks like."

"Where are you now?"

"I stopped at the store, but I'm on my way home right now."

"Bad idea. Don't go back to your apartment."

Maggie's stomach clenched. "You're scaring me. Do you think someone might follow me there?"

"Well, you don't want to lead someone to where you live."

If Doyle was the driver who'd almost hit her in the parking lot, he already knew where Maggie lived.

"We need to find that thing and disable it. I'm at work, but meet me here, and I'll help you look for it. It's not a bad thing for them to see you're at the police station."

"Okay." Maggie made a U-turn the next chance she had and tried to remain calm. At least she didn't have to deal with this alone.

When she pulled into the parking lot, Matt was waiting for her. He waved her into a spot near the entrance.

After she opened her car door, he leaned in, gave her a quick kiss, and held out his hand. "Let me see your phone." He hit a few buttons as she watched and pulled up the screen with the notification. "It says it was first seen with you at 12:22 p.m. today." He glanced down at her. "Where were you at that time?"

Maggie licked her lips as she thought about it. "Um. I think that was about the time I left work to get coffee at the office supply store. From there, I went to pick up my boss's lunch."

She could still hear the irritation in Harry's voice. *Do I need to tell you to get the coffee first, Margaret, so my lunch doesn't get cold?*

Matt snorted as he studied Maggie's phone. "Your boss had Morton's for lunch?" He held up his hand. "Sorry. Okay, so let me show you something."

She stepped out of her car, and he turned the phone around so she could see.

"These red dots show your movement." He used his thumb and index finger to zoom in. "See, here's you at Morton's. Then, it shows you traveled back to your office. This dot shows you at ..." He squinted at the screen.

"Probably Robin's house. After that, I went to the store. I, uh, needed a few things." When he gave Maggie a quizzical stare, her cheeks warmed. "Okay, wine. I needed a bottle of wine." Her sigh was loud and heavy. "It's been a rough day."

Matt rested his hand on her arm. "It's okay." He turned his attention back to her phone. "From the store, it looks like you were driving to your apartment but then changed course."

"Because I headed here."

"Right." He pointed at her screen again. "See the last dot—

this is where you are now." He used his fingers to zoom in again, and Maggie could now see the red dot hovering over the police station. "So, at some point, before it started tracking your movements, someone slipped it into your purse, or more likely, it's on your car somewhere. I'm not sure if I can disable it." He pressed a button on the phone and frowned. "Yeah, that's what I thought. It says the server is unavailable. We probably don't have permission to disable it because the tracking device doesn't belong to you."

Maggie felt sick. "So, what do I do?"

"Hang on." Matt pulled out his phone and made a call. "Hey, it's me. Yeah, I think she's got one somewhere. You have a few minutes?"

"Who was that?" she asked after he hung up.

"One of the detectives. He's much more experienced with these than me, so he offered to come out and help us."

A few minutes later, a man strode purposefully toward them in the parking lot.

"Hey, I'm Detective Franklin. Sounds like someone dropped an Air Tag on you, huh?"

Maggie shrugged helplessly. "I guess. I have no idea what any of this means."

"Okay, let's start with your clothing." He looked her over. "You weren't wearing a jacket today, right?"

"A jacket?" It was eighty-five degrees outside. "No. This is what I've been wearing all day."

"Okay, doubtful they would have had access, but check the pockets of your pants."

She certainly would have known if someone had their hand in her pocket, but Maggie pulled out the lining of each so he could see. They were empty.

Detective Franklin opened her driver's side door and gestured at the seat. "Can you dump your purse here?"

After Maggie unloaded the contents, he reached into his pocket and pulled out a pair of latex gloves.

Sweat dripped down her back as she watched the detective sift through her belongings. When he picked up the small notebook and shook it, she prayed he wouldn't look inside. The last thing she needed was Matt seeing the notes she'd taken as she and Robin investigated Grace's murder.

"It's not here." The detective reached for the purse itself. "Can I look?" He patted it down, unzipped each inside pocket, and rooted through them before handing the bag back to Maggie. "You can put everything back. Most likely, the tag is in or on your vehicle." He shot her a pointed stare. "Do you normally lock your car when you leave it?"

Maggie nodded as she stuffed her belongings back into her purse. She added her cell phone and set her bag on the driver's seat.

"Yeah, I always lock it."

Almost always. Unless she was in a hurry.

"That's good. It's easier if we don't have to search every nook and cranny inside the car."

Detective Franklin strolled to the front of Maggie's car. She slammed the car door shut and followed him.

"They're tiny, but it's not always easy to slip an Air Tag into someone's bag without them noticing." He ran his hand under her bumper. "When you leave your car in a parking lot, it only takes a second for them to hide it somewhere on the vehicle and walk off."

The detective worked his way methodically around her car, shining a small flashlight up into the wheel wells.

Matt reached for Maggie's hand and gave it a squeeze. "It'll be okay. Don't worry."

Several minutes later, it was Matt who looked concerned.

"Nothing?" he asked when it seemed the search was almost complete and hadn't yielded anything.

"Not yet." Detective Franklin laid down on the concrete behind Maggie's car and aimed his flashlight under her back bumper. Sweat glistened on his forehead. When he got to his feet, he wicked it off with his fingertips and crouched in front of the license plate. He held his cupped hand underneath and jiggled the frame. A small white disc dropped into his palm.

As Maggie's mouth went slack, Detective Franklin gave them a satisfied nod. "Found it." He got to his feet with a grunt and handed the Air Tag to Matt.

"That's it?" Maggie stared at the tiny tracker. "That little disc?"

The detective brushed the dirt from his hands. "Yup."

She shook her head in disbelief. "How would I have ever found that? Especially the way it was hidden behind my license plate."

The detective glanced around before his gaze settled on a trash can. "Probably what they were counting on," he said over his shoulder as he peeled off his gloves and tossed them inside.

Matt shot her a look. "Or maybe someone wanted you to know they were keeping an eye on you." He turned to Detective Franklin. "The notification her phone sent said it was first seen with Maggie at 12:22. Does that mean that's when it was put on her car? She was at work, and—"

The detective held up his finger. "I wouldn't take that time as gospel. That's why it says the time it was first seen. If the owner of the Air Tag isn't with it, it depends on the Bluetooth signal from other iPhones to help track it. It's possible it was placed on the car before the time shown. Someone could have even put it there in the middle of the night. Right in her driveway."

"Well, I live in an apartment complex."

The detective tipped his head. "Even worse. They might have

gotten your car confused with someone else's. Maybe it wasn't even meant for you. Did you stop anywhere on your way to work this morning?"

Maggie shook her head. "No, I was—I was a little late." She avoided eye contact with Matt. Maybe Harry was right to fire her after all.

"Okay, so you parked your vehicle at work and went inside your office building, right? At that point, if there wasn't an iPhone with a Bluetooth signal near your car, it wouldn't be able to update your location to send to the person tracking the tag. That is until people started going out to lunch. Or if you had your Bluetooth turned on, it could have happened when you got back to your car to go out."

"So, I have no way of knowing exactly when it was placed on my car?"

Detective Franklin shook his head. "That's why these things can be a problem. It can take time before the Air Tag realizes it's moving with somebody other than the owner. That's when it sends the notification. By the time you figure out it's on you, someone's been watching your every move for hours. Some people don't even get a notification until the next day."

Maggie was stunned. "What? Are you kidding me?"

The detective shook his head. "Nope, 'fraid not. And that's if you have an iPhone. You don't get the same warning if you have an Android. There are now ways to check if you have one following you, but most people don't even know these things exist."

"Thanks for your help." Matt held out his hand, the disc in the middle of his palm. "What do we do with this now?"

Detective Franklin reached for it. "If it's okay, I'll take it. We might be able to trace the serial number to the owner. Worst case, I'll remove the battery to disable it." He turned to Maggie. "For now, I would turn off the location services on your phone. If they realize this one's no longer working, they could get an idea to put another one on you." He dipped his head and met her concerned gaze. "Be hypervigilant for a little while. If someone hid this on your car at your apartment complex, they already know where you live. And where you work."

Maggie blew out a deep breath, a queasy feeling in the pit of her stomach. "Okay, I will."

She remembered her conversation with Jake. She liked to think she was always aware of her surroundings, but someone had put this on her car without her even knowing. If not for the notification on her phone—and Detective Franklin—they'd still be monitoring her every move.

She thanked him again, and as he headed back toward the station, Matt gave her arm a quick squeeze. "Be right back."

He trotted off after the detective. They spoke for several minutes, and when Matt returned, his face was stone cold.

She squirmed under his hard stare. "I know what you're thinking."

"And what's that?" His expression told Maggie he wanted to hear her say the words.

"Doyle knows I'm investigating him," she said reluctantly. "You're convinced he put this on my car to keep tabs on me."

Matt was silent for a long moment. "That night in your parking lot. Maybe he already knows where you live."

"That was my fault. I don't think—" She cut herself off when the look he shot her said her argument was pointless.

"You and Robin. Did you let this go like I asked you to?"

Maggie chewed on her bottom lip, but she couldn't lie to him. "Not completely."

Matt's eyes narrowed as he stared at her. "What are you not telling me?"

"We—we reached out to Doyle's neighbor yesterday. To see if he would be willing to talk to us."

Matt groaned. "Then, o*f course*, Doyle put this on your car." He ripped his eyes from hers and stormed off, holding his head in his hands.

Maggie chased after him and grabbed his arm. "You heard Detective Franklin. Maybe the tracker wasn't even meant for me. Or—who knows? Maybe my lunatic boss wanted to make sure I picked up the coffee before his steak so his lunch wouldn't get cold."

Matt wheeled around. "Really, Maggie? Stop."

"What? Anything's possible. We don't know for sure it was Doyle."

Matt ran his hand over his face and exhaled a long breath. "Listen, it's like I've told you from the beginning. Bad guys. Don't like people. In their business." He punctuated his words to get his point across. "You should be grateful Doyle started with the Air Tag because at least now you know. He's on to you. He knows you're talking to people and trying to prove he committed a crime he's already been acquitted of."

When Maggie opened her mouth to argue, Matt put up his hand. "I'm serious. Consider yourself lucky you got a warning." He held her gaze to ensure she was listening. "I'm not asking you anymore. I'm telling you. Stop investigating this guy. *Let it go*." His words were crisp and sharp.

She'd known it would come to this, but Maggie's throat grew tight. "I actually talked to Robin about it yesterday at lunch."

Matt bobbed his head, his lips set in a firm line. "Good. I'm glad you two are starting to see reason."

"She's willing to continue the investigation alone, but—" Maggie ran her tongue over her bottom lip as he stared at her. One shoulder lifted in a hesitant shrug. "She still wants me to record the podcast with her." How could Maggie make him understand the pride she felt that she was getting good at it?

That they had something worthy of being listened to. "I want to keep doing it."

"So, Doyle thinks you're still involved?" The way Matt shook his head told her there was no way he'd support the idea. "No way."

"I know we're close to figuring this out." She gripped his arm and attempted to plead her case. "Obviously we are if Doyle's so nervous he's hiding a tracker on my car. Besides, we've already recorded a bunch of episodes. When we put it out there, we can't just leave the listeners hanging."

Matt yanked his arm free. "You're acting like this investigation is for your entertainment, like it's a television show." He released a grunt filled with frustration. "This is real life, and I'm telling you, you're messing with the wrong people."

"I know it's real life. But what about Grace's family? Don't they deserve to know what happened? Don't they deserve justice?"

"It's too late. The jury found Doyle not guilty." Matt gave her a pointed stare. "*You* found him not guilty. You were part of that decision, remember?"

Maggie flinched as if he'd slapped her. "I had no choice."

"That's not entirely true, but still, you can't change your mind after the fact. That isn't how it works. No one can be tried twice for the same crime."

"I know that."

"But what you and Robin are doing is attempting to try this guy again." Matt's voice escalated. "Even if Doyle confessed to you. Told you every last detail about how he chased Grace through the house before he executed her with a bullet to the back of her head. You still wouldn't be able to do a single thing about it. It's over, Maggie. You have to accept it."

"But he got up on the stand and testified. Couldn't they get him for perjury and—"

Matt threw up his hands with a frustrated groan. "That means nothing. Perjury is a third-degree felony. The most he might get is five years. Maybe not even."

"At least it would be something."

He gripped Maggie's shoulders and locked his eyes on hers. "The best you can hope for is karma. Maybe Doyle doesn't decide to walk the straight and narrow path. He commits another crime and ends up locked up after all."

She stared at him in disbelief. "I have to hope he kills someone else?"

"Uh, I was thinking of a pretty famous case. Aren't you a true crime buff?"

"Oh," she said as she made the connection.

Maggie wrenched her gaze away, a sick feeling in the pit of her stomach. Doing what Matt wanted meant breaking her promise to Pam. Disappointing Robin. She'd be letting herself down that she wasn't going to see this through to the end.

"Don't you think Grace's family deserves to know the truth about why she was killed?" she asked in a soft voice as if a gentler tone could change his response. "So many of these true crime shows end without the answer, but we don't want to do that. Robin and I—"

Matt's jaw went slack, and he tossed his head back and forth. "I don't—I don't think I can keep doing this."

Maggie stumbled backward and caught her breath. "Doing what?"

He slumped against her car. "I can't keep having this same conversation with you. I'm worried because I care about you. I let you in. I told you about my sister so you would understand." A muscle twitched near his jaw. "What if that car in your parking lot wasn't a coincidence? Can you imagine if you'd been mowed down while I stood there and watched?"

Maggie opened her mouth to protest again, but the look on his face stopped her.

"I can't wonder every time we're apart if this is when Doyle does more than put a tracker on your car. Maybe next time he sends someone else to teach you a lesson about minding your own business?" Matt's hands sliced through the air as he tried to make his point. "You're trying to prove the man murdered someone. Why are you so sure you couldn't be next?"

"I could say the same thing about you. You go out every day and chase bad guys." Maggie put her arms around him. "I worry, too, you know."

"But I'm trained to take that risk. You're chasing a story for a podcast, but you don't know the first thing about what you're doing!"

Maggie flinched, stunned at the harsh tone of Matt's voice.

He let out an exasperated moan. "I didn't mean it like that. What I meant was you're not part of law enforcement. You're an assistant at an accounting firm—"

Her face hardened. "Not anymore, I'm not."

"Exactly. This investigation got you fired. Now what? You need to find another job and forget about this case. You have a son to take care of. You should put your attention—"

"Oh, no, Jake." Maggie's stomach clenched. "I was supposed to pick him up at the movies." Panic set in. "Where's my phone? What time is it?"

Matt peered into her car window. "Is it in your purse?" He opened the car door and handed her bag to her.

Maggie yanked out her cell phone and moaned when she checked the time. She was supposed to pick up Jake and his friend over an hour ago. Now, she was letting her son down, too.

She slid into the driver's seat. "I have to go." She shut the car door and hit the button to roll down the window. "I'll—I'll call you later."

Matt leaned in her car window but instead of kissing her goodbye, he pressed his lips tightly together. "It's either me or this case, Maggie. I can't keep worrying that I'm going to lose you. I just can't." There was pain in his eyes as he held her gaze. "Take some time and think about what you want."

Her throat tightened. Maggie opened her mouth to respond, but no words came out. Was he breaking up with her? While she stared in disbelief, Matt turned and walked off.

Fighting back tears, she drove away and dialed Jake's number. It rang several times, then went to voicemail.

When she was out of the vicinity of the police station, she pulled into an office parking lot to check her notifications. There were several missed calls and texts from Jake. A missed call from Robin. Three new voicemails. Maybe he'd been able to get a ride from the other parent.

Maggie hit play on his first message. Jake sounded slightly annoyed. *Mom, where are you? You said you'd come to pick us up. You promised.*

She swiped at her tears with the back of her hand. She had told him she'd be there, and she'd disappointed him. Made him look bad in front of his friend. Maybe Matt was right that she needed to stop worrying about Doyle's case and instead spend her time taking care of the things—and people—that mattered.

She hit play on the second message, and her son's voice was now bitter. Ice-cold. *Don't bother coming to get me. I finally had to call Dad, and he's on his way.* There was a momentary pause. *He's going to take me back to his house. I think I want to live with him for a while.*

23

First Matt, then Jake. The tears dripped from Maggie's eyes and blurred her vision as she drove to Todd's. She had to make this right.

It felt odd to pull her car into the driveway of her old house —like nothing had changed. But everything was different now.

Maggie pulled tissues from her center console and wiped her face. There was no way she'd give Todd the satisfaction of seeing she was upset.

She hesitated at the front door, then realized the camera that had been her ex-husband's downfall was still in place. As her stomach churned, Maggie shifted her weight from one foot to the other. She drew in a stuttered breath, then rang the doorbell of the house she used to live in.

When Todd answered, it seemed obvious he'd hoped to see someone else. The way his face fell made it clear he still had no idea he could use the security camera app to screen who was on the front porch.

"Hey, Mags." His eyes dropped from her face and raked over her entire body. "You lose weight?"

Her skin prickled under the scrutiny of her ex-husband.

"Yeah, a little." Her shoulder lifted in an uncomfortable shrug. "Can I, uh, can I come in and talk to Jake?"

Todd held open the front door.

"He's actually not here," he said as Maggie stepped inside. "He went to play soccer with his friends from the neighborhood. They're thrilled he's back." A cocky smirk lifted his lips. "You know he wants to stay here, right? With me."

Maggie blinked hard to keep from crying and gave a curt nod. "I know," she said when she gathered her composure. "He mentioned that in his voicemail."

She glanced around the house, familiar and yet foreign at the same time. Their wedding picture and some family photos that included her had been relocated. The trash, perhaps. Other than that, Todd hadn't changed a thing. The house looked the same as it had the day she moved out.

"Jake was pretty pissed. What happened to you?" Todd plopped down into his leather recliner. *His* recliner. Maggie hadn't dared sit in it when they were married. "Beer?" he asked as he reached for a bottle. Several empties littered the top of the coffee table.

She shook her head. "No, thanks."

"If you got stuck at work, you could have at least called him. Or me." Todd tipped the beer bottle back and took a long sip.

He said it so matter-of-factly. Like all Maggie ever needed to do was call Todd, and he'd come running to help her out. If she wasn't so miserable, she might have burst out laughing.

"I didn't get stuck at work. I—actually, I got fired today." She had no idea why she felt the need to share what had happened with her ex.

Todd ran a hand through his hair and exhaled a long puff of air. "Oh, wow. That's rough. But I'm not surprised. Your attitude always reflected the fact that you hated that place."

What did he mean by that? The issues she had at work were her fault and had nothing to do with her boss being a bully?

"Yeah, well—I'll—I'll find something else."

"I mean, you're going to have to. If Jake wants to live with me, we'll need to go back to court to, uh, modify the custody and support." He fought a smile. "Obviously, you'd need to pay me."

Maggie's pulse quickened as panic set in. "Pay you child support?" Her legs wobbled underneath her, and she lowered herself onto the couch.

"Well, of course. If I have primary custody, you'd have to pay me. Why would it be any different than when you had it?"

Maggie could barely afford her bills now, even with the money she got from him every month. Now, she wouldn't even have a paycheck. She needed to find a new job as soon as possible, but how much would she need to earn to make up for losing her child support and having to pay Todd? She'd never find anything that paid that much.

"I don't understand why you look so surprised." His voice was smug as he lifted and dropped his shoulders matter-of-factly. "It's meant to support the child, so if I have the child ..." Todd left Maggie to finish the thought as he picked up his beer from the coffee table and guzzled it.

Damn him. It was like he was celebrating her downfall.

There was no way Maggie would let Todd see his news had knocked the wind out of her. Instead, she took a different approach.

"Oh, I'm not surprised about the money." She worked to keep her shaky voice from betraying her. "I'm just unclear how you'll manage with Jake here full-time. Picking him up after soccer. Homework. Making dinner every night. Won't that cramp your style with Stephanie?" Distracted by dollar signs, Todd hadn't considered how a teenager would impact his new lifestyle.

He averted his gaze and slumped against the back of his recliner. "We broke up."

"Oh." Maggie leaned forward and perched on the edge of her seat. "Was it, uh, mutual?"

Todd winced, shook his head, and took a long swig of his beer.

"I'm sorry." It was the perfect opportunity to gloat about the fact that she was seeing someone, but that could backfire. After her conversation with Matt earlier, Maggie had no idea where they stood anymore.

"Stephanie's just—" Todd gestured in Maggie's direction with his bottle. "She's not like you, Mags. She likes expensive clothes and fancy dinners out. She would never stay at a job she hated for as long as you did. She's a woman who makes things happen for herself, and she expects—well, she wants someone who can keep up with her."

Maggie ignored his veiled insults in hopes of gaining more information about Todd getting dumped. It was the only positive thing that had happened all day.

"And that's not you?" She tried to sound casual.

He pursed his lips, then shrugged. "I thought it could be." He took a thoughtful sip of his beer. "I realize now I'm better suited to be with someone more grounded. Like the way you were when we were first married ... before you got so down on yourself."

Maggie's eyebrows came together. "I didn't—I wasn't—"

"Oh, come on. You got to the point where you wouldn't do anything to help yourself. You hated your job, but hell would have frozen over before you tried to get a new one. But then again, who would have hired you?" Todd shook his head. "I could barely stand to see what you were doing to yourself. At least with Stephanie, that's not an issue." He held his beer bottle to his lips and issued a pitiful sigh. "Well, it wasn't anyway." He drained the bottle and added it to the rest of the empties on the coffee table.

Maggie sat silent while she stewed about her ex seizing the opportunity to kick her while she was down. Why was she surprised?

Todd waved his hand in her direction. "At least our divorce looks like it's been good for you. Are you not eating as much because you're stressed about being single, or is it that you can't afford to buy that crap you used to load the pantry with here? It can't possibly be that you finally realized you should hit the gym." He ran his finger under his chin as his eyes studied her in a way that made her skin crawl. "You're not in shape like Stephanie is, but you look a heck of a lot better than you did when we were together."

Maggie shrank back on the couch. In an instant, Todd had transported her back to the insecure woman she'd been when she lived here. Stress eating while she pretended to do laundry. Avoiding his stare while she got dressed.

"I'm just—I've started walking every night. Eating better."

Todd let out an annoyed huff. "It figures."

He lifted himself from the recliner and ambled toward the kitchen. When he returned, he held a new beer in his hand.

"You always fought me. No matter what I said, you were determined to do the opposite. Just to spite me."

"That's not true," Maggie said, but the words rang hollow even to her own ears. It was true.

"I don't know how we got to the point where you hated me so much." Todd set his bottle on the end table. "We were so happy in the beginning." He pressed his knee into the couch cushion beside her, his leg up against her hip as he leaned closer. "Remember?" His eyebrows lifted, a suggestive smile playing on his lips. "What about our trip to Cape May?"

As Maggie pressed herself against the back of the couch, he gave his head a slight shake. "What happened to that girl?"

Cape May. It had been the last waning moments of summer in New Jersey, and Todd had surprised her with a weekend getaway. During a moonlight stroll on the beach, he'd proposed. To celebrate, they'd gone skinny dipping in the ocean, then drank copious amounts of wine on their balcony. Around two in the morning, the occupants of the hotel room next to theirs had begged them to take their celebration inside.

Todd fell onto the couch beside her and moved closer, his breath hot on her neck. "That's who I thought I was marrying," he whispered into her ear. "Do you know how much I wanted that girl back over the years? What happened to her?"

Maggie squeezed her eyes shut. His touch was both familiar and uncomfortable. Was he right that she had been the one who changed? Had she pushed him away?

"Come back to me, Mags. We can be that couple again." Todd cupped the sides of her face with his hands. "Think about how happy that would make Jake. We could be a family again."

Maggie opened her mouth to protest, but nothing came out. She was sitting in the same spot on the couch where she'd confronted Todd about sleeping with Stephanie in her bed. As she'd cried about the end of their marriage, he'd shown a complete lack of remorse. And now? Had he really changed his mind about wanting to be with her, or was this a reaction to being dumped?

She shook her head. "I don't—"

Todd placed his finger on her lips. "Shhh." He moved in and kissed her.

Her internal monologue was one of disbelief, punctuated by screams of disgust.

"Move back in," he said softly. "We can forget all this nonsense about custody and child support. The time apart was good for us. We can start over, and you won't have to worry about paying me a penny."

Maggie struggled to breathe. In her head was a kaleidoscope of voices that played like a recording on a loop.

It's either me or this case. Matt was who she wanted to be with, but had she already lost him?

She could still hear the anger in Jake's voicemail. *I want to stay with Dad.* Paying child support to Todd would be impossible. Without a job, she wouldn't even be able to cover her own bills.

Still in shock she'd gotten fired, she recalled HR's by-the-book delivery. *We regret to inform you that your employment is being terminated. Effective immediately.*

Maggie sat rigid as Todd's question hung in the air. In the silence, she was sure he heard the chaotic thudding of her heart.

His eyebrows lifted. "You wanted to go back to New Jersey, right? You need to find a new job anyway, and I'm sure I could find something up there." He leaned in close, his voice in her ear. "We could go back. Together."

Maggie's head spun with the offer he'd set in front of her. She could leave Harry and the job she'd hated behind. Start fresh. Have her family nearby.

But it meant being with Todd again, and her inner voice vehemently rejected the idea.

Her ex stared at her, his face etched with confidence. "So, what do you say, Mags? Are we doing this?"

Inside, she screamed her answer. *Absolutely not.* Maggie wanted Matt. Her friendship with Robin and the podcast. The feeling of accomplishment she'd have when she found a new job. A better job. As much as she wanted to be near her family, she needed to prove to herself that she could make it on her own.

When Todd leaned in to kiss her again, Robin's voice

boomed in her head. *The only person who can give you the life you want is you.*

Maggie pushed him away. "No, stop. I don't want this," she said firmly in a voice that now matched the one in her head. She scrambled off the couch and wheeled around to face him. "I don't belong here. This house—you. This isn't my life anymore." She planted her hands on her hips. "There's someone else."

Her ex sat up and perched on the edge of the couch. "What?"

"I don't want to start over with you. Here or in New Jersey. I've been dating someone."

"You have?" Todd eyed her suspiciously. "For how long?"

Maggie flinched and wrinkled her nose. "Not as long as you've been dating Stephanie if that's what you're implying. But it doesn't matter. We could never go back to the way we were. Too much has happened. I didn't—" The realization hit her. "Someone wise told me it's never one person's fault a marriage falls apart, and they were right. I don't blame you for being disappointed with me while we were married. I realize now the woman I was when I was with you—she wasn't someone I liked either. But I'm not her anymore. I've changed. My life's not perfect, but I'm happy."

"So, this new guy, he's why you lost the weight?" Todd's eyes narrowed into angry slits. "You would never do it for me, but you did it for him?"

"I didn't do it for him either." Maggie thumped her hand against her chest. "I did it for *me*." She gave him a hard stare. "And don't worry, I'll find a job. A better job. Something I enjoy doing this time." She reached for her purse and threw the strap over her shoulder. "What I won't do is give up on Jake. Please tell him to call me when he gets back."

She spun on her heel, and before Todd could say another word, Maggie yanked open the front door. Her jaw set with a new resolve, she refused to look back, even if it meant she missed the chance to relish in the stunned expression on her ex-husband's face.

When the door slammed behind her, there was a certain satisfaction in the sound it made—a finality.

Todd and this house were her past. Maggie didn't ever want to come back here again.

24

Maggie's hands shook as she fumbled with the keys to start her car. What had just happened?

Whoever said you can't go home again had known what they were talking about. Being in her old house had thrown Maggie back in time, threatened to return her to the insecure wife she'd been with Todd. That woman now felt as unfamiliar as the charm he'd tried to lay on her.

It all seemed so clear now.

Maggie wanted a husband who loved her unconditionally. No matter what she weighed or how much she hated her job. She'd wanted him to accept her the way she was instead of ridiculing the things she enjoyed. Her resentment had built over time like she was existing in a pressure cooker.

Rather than explode, Maggie had chosen the path of least resistance. It had been easier not to care, but Todd was right. Eventually, she had refused to do what he wanted. Strictly on principle. And in the end, those decisions had hurt her, too.

In his desperation to avoid being alone after getting dumped, Todd had revealed his answer as to why their marriage had fallen apart. *That's who I thought I was marrying. Over the years, do you know how much I wanted that girl back?*

But how could Maggie have remained as carefree as she'd been when they were first married? It wasn't possible. They had a son who depended on her, and it wasn't like Todd offered much in the way of assistance. He was able to live his life the way he wanted, unfettered by the responsibilities that had fallen on her.

Despite how miserable she was in her marriage, Maggie had been insecure and more afraid of being alone. It had taken time for her to find her way, to see her true worth, but what had terrified her the most had also set her free. Maybe getting fired from the job she despised would do the same.

She couldn't deny there had been a twinge of truth in Todd's statement. Her attitude had reflected how much she hated her job. Maggie was now desperate to do something she loved. Something she was passionate about. The podcast was part of that, but she wanted to do the investigating, too.

But where did that leave her relationship with Matt? She didn't want to repeat her mistakes, but this wasn't the unconscious defiance she'd shown Todd. This was more about Maggie becoming who she was meant to be.

There was the faint sound of ringing. Her cell phone. As she rooted around in her purse, she said a silent prayer Jake was calling. Or, with a little time, maybe Matt had reconsidered his parting words to her.

Her sister's name flashed on her screen.

Maggie had been in a hurry to escape Todd's house but had no idea where she was heading. She entered a fast-food restaurant parking lot and pulled into a parking space.

"Hey, Stace. Everything okay?"

"Yeah, I had a little car accident yesterday, but—"

Maggie threw the gear shift into park and turned off the

engine. "Are you okay?" Her hand flew to her forehead. "I swear the drivers up there are almost as bad as—"

"No, no, I'm fine, and at least the kids weren't with me."

Maggie heaved a sigh of relief, then considered Melody Kaplan and the white sedan that had almost plowed into her. "Did someone run a stop sign or a red light? You called the police after it happened, right? Do I need to get on a plane because—"

"No, I don't need you to come here and throw down with anyone." Her sister released an embarrassed chuckle. "Unless you want to beat me up. The whole thing was stupid and completely my fault."

Maggie's shoulders lowered and she leaned back in her seat. "Oh. You need to be more careful. How's your car?"

"Totaled. Mom said she'd watch the kids so we can go car shopping this weekend."

"A car can be replaced, but I'm just grateful you're okay. I can't even imagine—"

The realization hit Maggie like a punch to the gut. The idea that the accident might have been someone else's fault had incensed her. She'd been prepared to do battle with anyone who might have hurt her sister.

Pam didn't have that option. Someone had taken that privilege away from her and left instead a painful void in her chest where some measure of justice should have lived.

"Hey, I'm glad you're okay," Maggie said into the phone. "I have something I need to do that can't wait. Is it okay if I call you back in a little bit?"

"Sure. I'll be here." Her sister released a defeated hiss of air. "It's not like I have a car to go anywhere."

Maggie hung up and dialed another number. "I was just wondering how you were doing," she said when Pam picked up. "How's everything in your world?"

"As good as it can be, I guess. It's funny you called. I was just thinking about what you said that day we met at the deli. You know, about some small detail that might not make sense."

"Right." Maggie sat up straight. "Did you come up with something?"

"Well, I'm not sure if this means anything ..."

"Whatever you have, we'll take it. You never know whether something could be important or not." Even something Pam deemed insignificant could turn out to be a missing piece of the puzzle.

"Well, my parents sold most of Grace's furniture. We had to empty the house before the closing. You know, for the people who bought it."

Maggie gnawed absent-mindedly on her thumbnail. "Okay."

"When the guy who bought the couch came to pick it up, my mom found something tucked underneath. It was something that seemed a bit odd to all of us. Not to mention out of place."

This had promise. "What was it?" Maggie asked.

"It was a shriveled-up flower. Not like the kind you find in potpourri. It had a long stem, like an actual flower that had dried up over time." Pam blew out a deep breath. "By then, it had been about six months from the time—since my sister had been in the house. Since anyone had been in that house."

Maggie's forehead wrinkled. Most people probably didn't have a dead flower under their couch, but she was struggling to tie it to the murder. "You said Grace was in that house for what? Almost two years? Isn't it possible someone she dated brought her flowers?"

"I guess," Pam said, but there was skepticism in her voice. "It still wouldn't explain how it ended up under her couch. But here's the thing."

There was a thing. Maggie held her breath.

"It was a *daisy*. My sister wouldn't want to hurt anyone's feelings, but if someone brought her daisies, I'm sure she would have refused to accept them. She would have never brought them into the house."

"Did she have something against cheap flowers?"

"What? Oh, no," Pam said when she realized the point Maggie was making. "My sister had a ton of allergies. Most flowers bothered her, but daisies were the worst. I mean, they're really a weed."

"So, anyone who knew Grace well wouldn't have given her flowers," Maggie said thoughtfully. "But what about Ron? He might not have known about her allergies."

They'd never heard back from him, but after seeing the Henry's surveillance camera footage, they knew he didn't drive a white car. At least he didn't the night of their date. Robin still didn't trust his alibi, but even if he'd been the one to bring Grace flowers, it didn't mean Ron murdered her. If anything, it was probably just his attempt at a sweet gesture for their first date.

"I guess I can call and ask him." Pam was silent for a long moment. "But I don't remember seeing any flowers—you know, in the pictures the police took."

Maggie thought back to the crime scene photos they'd been shown at the trial. She didn't recall any flowers in the house either.

"Maybe Ron took them home with him when he realized Grace was allergic, but at some point, a daisy fell out of the bouquet. What if he tucked it behind her ear as a joke or something?"

"Grace would have needed a Benadryl before they even left the house for dinner," Pam said with conviction. "She would have been miserable and sneezing all night otherwise."

In his statement and on the stand, Ron hadn't mentioned anything about Grace being out of sorts.

Maggie rolled down her window to let some air into the car.

She wrinkled her nose as the smell of fast food wafted in. She was hungry, but the idea of a greasy burger and fries no longer held any appeal. Still, the aroma had her thinking. "What about candles?"

"What?"

"You said your sister had allergies. Did Grace light candles in her house?"

Pam didn't take long to respond. "I don't think so. Most things with scents were an issue for her. Perfume. Even some shampoos. Why do you ask?"

"The testimony about her computer. Supposedly, the last thing she did was visit an online site for candles."

"Yeah, I heard that, too." Pam hesitated. "I thought maybe she was looking for a gift for someone."

It was possible, but Maggie wanted to be sure. "At the deli, you said you still have her laptop. When you get a chance, can you check the sleep setting? I want to see how long it could have sat unused before the screen locked."

"I don't understand. You—you think someone else was on her computer?" Pam sounded confused.

"I'm just trying to cover all the bases. Like with the flower. Maybe there's a good explanation for how the daisy got under her couch, but if you don't mind trying to get a hold of Ron to ask him what he knows, that would be helpful." Maybe he wouldn't have a problem returning Pam's call.

"Okay, and I'll try to pull it together to check her computer. It's—it's in the back of my closet. I could never make myself open it after she died." Pam's voice shook and it was clear how much pain she was still in over losing her sister. "Most days, I can't believe she's gone."

"I know," Maggie said gently. "After we met with you at the deli, Robin and I—we went by Grace's house."

"Oh." Pam released the word with a soft breath. "I've thought about driving by there, but I can never bring myself to go back. To see the place where ... you know."

"I understand, but the people who live there now—" Maggie hesitated, not sure if her update would be helpful or cause more pain. "They seem to be happy in the house," she said softly hoping the news might help Pam in some way. "They planted pretty flowers in pots by the front door. It even looks like they might have a new baby or one on the way. When we were there, we saw a box for a crib."

"Oh, wow. They're probably using the bedroom in the back for the nursery. When Grace bought that house—" Pam released a small chuckle. "Oh, she was so proud of herself. It wasn't huge, but it was all hers. She had a great job, good friends." Her voice turned wistful for what her sister would never have. "More than anything, Grace wanted to be a wife and a mom. I'm sure she's looking down and smiling about a baby growing up there."

Maggie shifted in her seat as she stared up into her rearview mirror and watched a family exit the restaurant. "You think so?"

"I do. My sister would never want the legacy of that house to be her murder. Hopefully, the new people can erase the horror of what happened to her there. You know, replace the bad with something good instead."

"That's a nice way to look at it." Maggie paused. She had more she needed to share. "Robin and I went there to talk to the lady who lives across the street."

"Mrs. Henry?"

"Right."

"She's very nice, but Grace sometimes called her the crazy cat lady."

Maggie snickered as she recalled the video she'd shown them during their meeting. "Yeah, we found that out the hard way. Did you know she named one of her cat's kittens after your sister?"

"Really?" Pam sounded surprised and touched by the gesture. "That's sweet. My sister told me she was thinking about adopting one of the babies."

"Mrs. Henry mentioned that. Robin and I actually went to talk to her because we noticed she had a camera on her front door. Apparently, she did have it at the time of the murder, but she'd taken it down the night your sister was killed."

"The police told us the same thing."

Maggie wondered if the detectives had to watch the footage of Mona giving birth, too.

"It's super frustrating because obviously, their video could have solved the whole case. You know, if they had captured the person—" Maggie cut her thought short. "Obviously, that was a bust, but as we were getting ready to leave, Robin and I asked if there was any chance she had footage from the night before."

Pam inhaled sharply. "And did she?"

"She did. Her husband downloaded all the footage from the week before the murder, and it was saved to his drive in the cloud. Mrs. Henry mentioned there had been a reward, so they both pored over what they had, but they didn't see anything they deemed suspicious."

"There was a reward, a pretty substantial one. My parents and Grace's company contributed to it. It was never claimed, and then the police arrested Doyle. So ..." Pam hesitated as if she was nervous about what Maggie might tell her. "What did you find out? Was Doyle there that night?"

"I don't think so. At least there was no sign of him that we saw. Ron was there, and everything he told the police about that night checked out. He and Grace sat in his car for about twenty minutes. Of course, we couldn't see what they were doing, but they were parked in her driveway."

The video had shown Ron drove a red hatchback at the time,

a fact Maggie had been quick to point out to Robin. *I'm pretty sure a secret serial killer would have a more low-key car.*

"Ron even waited until your sister was in the house before he pulled away. It seemed like he did it to be chivalrous, not because he was worried about her." The video had shown Grace turning and casually waving before unlocking her front door and going inside. "Whatever she was talking about in her voice-mail to you—it doesn't appear to be anything that happened outside the house."

"So, Doyle got inside her house somehow." Pam's tone was matter-of-fact. "Although it still surprises me that—"

"I don't think so," Maggie cut in before Grace's sister went too far in the wrong direction. "On the video—Robin and I saw something we didn't expect."

"What? What did you see?" Pam asked in a shaky voice.

Maggie took a deep breath. "Your sister did go out that night. About ten minutes after Ron left."

"Really? Where did she go?"

"We're not sure. Grace left with a bag. When she came back about thirty minutes later, she still had it with her."

"What kind of bag?" Pam asked. "Like a duffel bag?"

"No, nothing like that. It was a plastic grocery bag. The handles were tied together, and we couldn't tell what was inside."

Pam eased out a slow breath. "So, wherever Grace went— whoever she went to see—that person did something to her. Something that freaked her out."

In the dark interior of her car, Maggie nodded in agreement. "I thought the same thing. I'm convinced that trip has something to do with the voicemail she left you. Do you have any idea where she would have gone at that time of night?"

"No, none." Pam's high-pitched answer sounded like she was

on the verge of tears. "I feel like I'm never going to learn the truth about what really happened to her."

Maggie thought again of her own sister. "I can't even imagine how you feel." She could still hear Matt's voice pleading with her to let the case go, but as the sound of soft weeping came over the line, she knew that wasn't an option. "We're going to find out what happened to Grace. I promise."

After she hung up, Maggie stared at the call log on her phone, but nothing had changed. She found it hard to believe Jake was still playing soccer with his friends. It had been dark for hours. Had Todd even relayed her message?

Maggie had missed their nightly walk with Duke, and she expected to be chastised when she hit play on Robin's voicemail.

Hey, it's me. David just followed me so I could drop off my car at the body shop. You're not going to believe this, but there was a note folded up inside my door handle. It said ... She paused as if she was getting the note to read it verbatim. *It says, Give up. There's nothing you can do about it now.*

Maggie sucked in a breath, hit pause, and tipped her head back against the headrest of her seat.

She hit play again on Robin's message with hopes there was more to the warning Doyle had given, but as the message continued, it appeared she'd read the note in its entirety.

It's a good thing David didn't see it, or he'd probably be just as freaked out as Matt. I'm sure the dust will settle while we're on vacation, but it certainly sounds like Doyle's telling us to back off. Well, me, I guess, if you're bowing out of the investigation. He's obviously getting nervous, so that tells me we must be close to finding out the truth. I hope Matt helped you figure out where he hid that damn Air Tag. I'm still packing, but come over if you want to go walking with Duke. She laughed. *You don't have to worry. No one's going to mess with us if he's around.*

Guilt made Maggie's chest tighten. The note on Robin's car

was her fault. The Air Tag had tracked her there earlier, and now Doyle knew where they both lived.

Robin had David to protect her, and they were getting ready to leave town. Was it safe for Maggie to go home? She was now relieved Jake was at his dad's, but her heart hammered in her chest at the idea of being in her apartment alone.

She wanted to call Matt but didn't know what to say. He had tried to warn them from the beginning. Maggie could still recall the words he'd said the night he tapped on Robin's car window. *I'd hate to see you two get in over your head. These things never end well for amateur detectives.*

But if she and Robin were close to proving Doyle's guilt, they weren't the inexperienced sleuths he thought they were. A steady diet of true-crime shows had taught the two of them well. They just hadn't accepted their investigation could turn dangerous. It was impossible to deny they were now in over their heads. Way over their heads.

Rubbing her temple, Maggie brought the phone to her ear and replayed Robin's voicemail. She wanted to ensure she heard every word and listening to it again brought her to the same conclusion. Her initial reaction had been spot-on. The note didn't make sense.

She reached into her purse and removed the small notebook with her information about the case. When she found the page she needed, she tapped the button for the overhead light. This was too important to trust her memory.

As she studied her notes, she was convinced they explained what had happened the night before Grace was killed. Why she left the house so late. The voicemail to Pam.

Maggie released a deep sigh and rested her head against the steering wheel. *Let it go.* Matt's words played in her head over and over.

She couldn't give him what he wanted. She'd made Pam a

promise, and she intended to keep it. Matt was worried about her, but Maggie needed to see this through to the end. To finish what she and Robin had started. All she could do now was hope the cost wouldn't be a broken heart.

There had to be a way to prove her theory was correct. Maggie tossed her notebook onto the passenger seat and started up the car.

She didn't have much time. She needed to go shopping.

25

After her errands were complete, Maggie parked her car on the side of the drugstore that faced Doyle's body shop. She drew in a deep breath and grabbed the bag from the passenger seat.

A row of shrubbery divided the two properties. After a quick glance around the parking lot, she strolled casually, then broke into a jog, until she was hidden behind an overgrown hedge looking down the grassy incline. From her vantage point, Maggie observed a row of cars parked across from the three bay doors. Most had visible dents or crushed front ends. They appeared to be vehicles customers had left to be repaired.

She squinted into the darkness. The building extended farther back than it appeared from the road, but it was pitch black toward the rear. In the faint din of leftover light from the drug store parking lot, Maggie saw the outline of several vehicles pulled up alongside the building. One was a pickup truck.

Hidden from view, Maggie allowed her gaze to drift along the length of the building. No cameras she could see. She lowered her head and descended the small hill toward a set of bushes not far from the truck. It was definitely Doyle's.

She laid her bag on the ground and prepared what she needed, cursing quietly when the darkness made it more difficult. As her heart thumped wildly, she crouched and scooted toward the bed of the pickup. Using electrical tape, Maggie affixed the Air Tag she'd just purchased underneath the bumper.

"Two can play at this game. Let's see how much fun you have with it."

Maggie turned, prepared to race back first to the safety of the bushes and then to her car. Her feet froze at the sound of muffled voices. She ducked down behind the truck, then stood slightly as her gaze flew nervously around the parking lot. Matt was right. She should have let this go. If Doyle caught her, there was no telling what he might do.

She closed her eyes for a moment to try and focus, to listen for something other than her heartbeat thudding in her ears. The voices got louder. Despite the darkened building that appeared closed, people were inside. It didn't sound like they were far from the spot where Maggie cowered.

Her eyes scanned the building in front of her until they landed on a tiny sliver of light. Two additional bay doors at the back of the building had panes of glass painted black, except for one small area where the color hadn't gone all the way to the edge.

Maggie sucked in a deep breath and sprinted back to the bushes. She grabbed her bag, then darted back to Doyle's truck. Hunched over, she made her way around it until she was at the first bay door painted black. She leaned closer and could hear them on the other side.

"Listen, we need to lay low for a bit." It was Doyle's voice.

"Don't be a pussy, man." Was that Manny? Maggie had only heard the partner speak when he testified at the trial, but he had a slight accent. It had to be him.

Something scraped against the floor, like a chair being shoved backward. "Oh yeah, you're not the one who almost went to prison for something you didn't do. You're lucky I even—"

Manny's voice escalated. "I already told you, man. It wasn't me."

Doyle growled in response. "And I've already told you, I know you're full of shit."

"Listen, man. If you didn't pop her, then someone else did you a solid, but gettin' arrested? That's on you. The cops would of had nothin' 'cept you had to grab that damn jersey."

"Yeah, well, if she was still alive when I got there, I wouldn't have stepped in her blood when I grabbed the fucking bag off the table."

"You should of just left that mess in the bitch's car. Let the cops think she had somethin' to do with killin' her. We could of made one of those anonymous calls and—"

"Are you an idiot?" Doyle's voice rose with frustration. "That lady had a rock-solid alibi. She wasn't even in the state, and her car was still in our lot. She should have just been grateful I got her car cleaned. I just don't understand why the hell she needed to write that damn review? And who was that blond woman who came in and asked me about it?" His voice took on an ominous tone. "I'm telling you, Manny, someone isn't letting this go. You should be worried, too. How long do you think it takes before they figure out—"

"Wow, bro. When you become so soft?"

"Oh, yeah? Why don't you sit in jail for a little while and see how it feels, you—"

Sounds of a scuffle sounded on the other side of the bay door.

"Knock it off." The command was given in a low, firm voice as if this wasn't the first tussle the man had needed to referee.

Someone else was inside.

"How long—" Doyle's panting seemed to indicate he needed a moment to catch his breath. "How long before someone connects the dots? You morons know that shipping out of the country is a federal crime, right?"

"What's the matter? Afraid you used up your only get-out-of-jail-free card?" Manny was taunting Doyle.

A chorus of grunts and groans followed, and it was clear their scuffle had resumed. Something—or someone—struck the other side of the door. Maggie flinched and scooted backward.

There was a loud aggravated groan. "You idiots want someone to call the cops?"

Maggie tipped her head as she listened to the man speak.

"I should just let you two kill each other—would make my job easier, that's for sure. Unfortunately, we promised Ronan his delivery."

Things quieted down again.

"Trust me, he's not a man you want to make angry. So, both of you, go get that shit from the clearing and get it ready to ship out of here. Now."

That voice. Maggie recognized it.

"I'm telling you, we need to hit the pause button," Doyle said again, more insistent this time.

His plea didn't get very far. "I'll tell you when we need to stop," the man said, a steely edge in his voice. "There's still a lot of money to be made."

"We're the ones getting our hands dirty." Doyle's voice escalated. "We're the ones taking all the risks."

"Really?" The third voice dripped with contempt. "You think the two of you could have pulled any of this off without my help? Someone had to be the brains of the operation. You were both living paycheck to paycheck before you met me."

"You're the brains?" Doyle asked. "How, when you're too stupid to realize you're in just as deep as us. You think you're immune? If we get caught, we're all getting locked up." He let loose an almost maniacal laugh. "You'd never survive prison. You know that, right? They'd eat you up in there."

There was a moment of silence before the voice responded, and Doyle's comment was ignored. "No one's going to prison, and I'm not leaving money on the table." There was the sound of something heavy hitting the floor. "Like I said, take this up to the clearing, and get the rest of it ready to go."

A moment later, there was the metallic click of the bay door being unlocked.

When it began to rise, Maggie was only halfway up the grassy incline.

26

As Maggie stumbled up the small hill, her ankle rolled. She clenched her teeth and reached down for only a second. At that moment, feeling pain was a luxury she couldn't afford.

She hobbled across the parking lot, yanked open her car door, and leaped into the driver's seat. She jerked her head up and checked her rearview mirror, convinced she'd see they'd followed her. All she saw was a dimly lit empty parking lot.

Maggie jabbed the button to lock the doors and ducked down in her seat. She waited one minute. Then two. She expected to hear voices calling out to each other as the men attempted to figure out where she'd gone. She heard nothing but the wild thudding of her heart.

She inched up slightly in her seat and stole a furtive glance around the parking lot. An older woman clutching an oversized package of paper towels strolled toward her car parked in front of the drug store. There was no sign of anyone else.

Maggie's shoulders lowered as relief whooshed through her.

She started up her car and dialed Robin's number as she pulled onto the main road. "I'm sorry I said I was going to bail on the podcast, but oh, man. Our listeners are never going to believe what I just heard."

"What are you talking about? Where are you?"

Maggie took one last look out her passenger window. "Just leaving Doyle's body shop."

"You're what?"

"Okay, technically, I'm just leaving the drug store next to the body shop. But about five minutes ago, I was on the side of Doyle's building hiding behind his truck."

"Why? Wait a minute. Did you get the message I left you about the note on my car?"

Maggie's head bobbed. "Yeah, I listened to your voicemail."

"And that didn't make you nervous? You said you couldn't investigate the case anymore, and then you went by yourself?" Robin's voice escalated. "Are you crazy? What if Doyle saw you?"

"Well, I hid first in some bushes, and then I took cover behind his truck. At first, I didn't think he was there, but he was. Robin, he wasn't alone. They did almost see me, but I took off. Just in time." Maggie's ankle throbbed, hot like it was on fire inside her sock. "Except I tripped running up that little hill that leads to the drug store. I think my ankle might be sprained."

Robin let out a loud breath. "I'll meet you at the ER. You should probably get it X-rayed."

"You have to finish packing, and I—I can't go to the ER." The reality of being fired smacked Maggie square in the face. "I don't know if I have my health insurance anymore."

"Did they tell you they canceled your insurance? You usually get till the end of the month."

Maggie tried to remember, but the meeting with HR had been a blur. It didn't even feel like it had only happened earlier that day. "To be honest, I wasn't paying attention. I was in shock. I remember the lady from HR saying they were going to mail paperwork to me." She groaned. "Great. They're probably going to send it to Todd's house because I never gave them my new address." At least Maggie had informed her ex about her situation.

She couldn't bring herself to tell her friend about the visit to her ex-husband's house. Maggie wanted to pretend the whole thing had never happened. It was humiliating.

"You need to get your ankle checked out," Robin insisted.

"I'll go to the doctor tomorrow. It'll be cheaper than the ER."

"Okay, at least come to my house, and I'll wrap it for you. I'm used to Charlie's sports injuries, so I've got a stockpile of ACE bandages. And hurry up. I want to hear *everything*."

"WHY IN THE world did you go to the body shop so late?" Robin asked as she pulled supplies from the closet beside her bathroom.

"Matt was convinced Doyle put the tracker on my car."

Robin sat cross-legged on the floor and gestured for Maggie to sit. "So, he found it?"

Maggie hobbled over and stood on her good leg as she lowered herself onto the edge of the bed. "I met him at the police station. A detective came out and helped us." She scooted back slightly, and Robin reached for her ankle. "He found the Air Tag behind my license plate."

Robin whipped her head up, her mouth hung open. "Are you kidding?"

"I wish I was. At least it's disabled now, but after I left Todd's—"

Robin held the ACE bandage roll in the air as she gave Maggie a pointed stare. "Why were you at Todd's?"

"Matt and I were dealing with the Air Tag situation, and I—I lost track of time." Guilt warmed her face. "I forgot to pick up Jake and his friend at the movies."

Robin's attention was back on Maggie's ankle as she resumed wrapping. "Why didn't you call me? I could have picked him up."

"I didn't even realize I'd forgotten until it was too late." Maggie pressed her hand against her forehead. "Jake had to call Todd."

"Okay, so his dad went and picked him up. Good for him. Does he need an award or something?"

"The bigger problem is that Jake was mad. Really mad. He left me a message—" Maggie's throat tightened, and she choked out the words. "He wants to live with Todd."

Robin's eyes were filled with compassion. "He's a teenager. Just give him time to cool off. You know he'll be back."

"I hope so," Maggie's eyes welled up. "Because if not, Todd's planning on me paying *him* child support. Of course, I'll have no way to do that since I got fired and won't have an income."

Robin grunted as she got up from the floor. She strolled over to her vanity and reached for the tissues. "He really told you he expects you to pay him child support?" she asked over her shoulder. "On the day you got fired?" She shook her head as she handed the box to Maggie. "Wow, he's a real peach."

"He's not even worth talking about." Maggie ran a tissue under her eyes and then grabbed another one to blow her nose. She had no intention of telling her friend that Todd has offered to take her back so she wouldn't have to pay him. She certainly wasn't going to mention that for a split-second she'd almost considered it. "I just hope Jake comes to his senses."

Robin knelt on the floor in front of Maggie and offered a reassuring nod. "He will. He's a good kid, and he loves you."

Maggie slid her cell phone from her back pocket. No new

calls or texts from Jake or Matt. "Well, he hasn't changed his mind yet."

"Give him a little time." Robin tapped the leg that had the ACE bandage. "See if you can stand on your ankle."

Maggie moved herself to the edge of the bed and put both feet on the floor. Robin held her arm as she carefully stood and put weight on it. "It's not too bad."

"Do you think you can make it to our podcast room? I'm sure David's going to want to go to sleep soon."

Maggie glanced behind her. "Yeah, I think so. I just need my purse."

Robin grabbed it from the bed and tossed the strap over her shoulder. "I got it." As they walked, she leaned in close to Maggie in case her assistance was needed. "So, what did Matt say about the Air Tag?"

Maggie limped down the hallway on her own but exhaled loudly when she dropped into her leather chair. It was a relief to give her ankle a break. "He was convinced Doyle put the tracker on my car as a warning to stay out of his business." She couldn't make herself share Matt's parting words to her. If Maggie mentioned the choice he'd forced on her, the tears would start again, and she'd left the box of tissues behind in the bedroom.

"Well, yeah," Robin's shoulders lifted and dropped matter-of-factly. "Same reason he left the note on my car. He wants us to stop investigating him."

"But why would Doyle care what we do unless he has something to hide?"

Robin's forehead wrinkled as she tried to make sense of the point Maggie was trying to make. "Well, we know he does. He killed Grace."

"But think about what he wrote in the note. *You can't do anything about it now.*" Earlier, those words had played over and over in Maggie's head and left her with only one conclusion. "To me, the note references double jeopardy, which doesn't make sense. If he can't be charged, why does he need us to give up?"

Robin gave her a quizzical look. "So, what are you saying?"

"Remember the video we saw from the night before Grace was killed? The one that showed her leaving her house with the plastic bag?"

"Yeah. And she came back with the same bag."

Maggie bobbed her head. "Right. But why would Grace bring it with her—go out at that time of night—only to come back with it about thirty minutes later?"

Robin hesitated, then shrugged. "Maybe she left with one thing in the bag but brought back something else."

"I don't think so." Maggie reached into her purse and pulled out her small notebook. "I took notes when we watched the recordings from the Henry's camera." She opened to the timeline she'd drawn and laid it down on the table so that it faced Robin. "Ron left at 10:02 p.m. Then Grace left her house with the plastic grocery bag at 10:09 p.m. She pulled back into her driveway at 10:43 p.m." Maggie pointed to the circled note she made with the total elapsed time from when Grace left until she returned. "She was gone for a total of thirty-four minutes." Maggie stayed quiet a moment to let Robin study the timeline. When she glanced up, she gave her friend a long look before stating what she now thought was obvious. "I think—I'm pretty sure she had Doyle's football jersey in that bag."

Robin's expression turned dubious. "But even at that time of night, Doyle lives at least twenty minutes from Grace. She wouldn't have been able—"

Maggie waved her index finger in the air. "She didn't go to Doyle's house. I think she went to the body shop. It's almost exactly the amount of time it would have taken her to get there and back."

"But it doesn't make sense. Why would she go to his job so late?"

Maggie crossed her arms on the table in front of her and perched on the edge of her chair. "A couple of weeks ago, Matt and I went to dinner, and we ate at the same Mexican place where Grace had her date with Ron. On the way home, I asked him to take Branson Boulevard."

Robin gazed off thoughtfully and then nodded. "The way you'd go if you were heading to Grace's house."

"Uh, huh." Maggie pressed her lips together as she waited to see if Robin would connect the dots. "They would have gone right past the body shop."

Robin closed her eyes tight and groaned. "I should have known that. The salon where I get my hair done is right behind the mall."

"I can't believe I didn't think of it either. But let's say they drove by that night and Grace saw that Doyle's truck was there. She assumes he's working late. We know, according to Ron, that they had a great first date. Maybe Grace just wants to put the whole Doyle thing behind her so she can move on. She figures the sooner, the better."

Robin bobbed her head as if she was starting to see the logic in Maggie's theory. "She probably didn't want to take a chance that Doyle would stop by her house to get his jersey when Ron was there."

"Right. So, Grace tosses it in that grocery bag and heads out to the body shop to drop it off."

Robin took in a deep breath as her brow furrowed. "But if that's true, she came back with it, so she never actually gave the jersey to him."

"But *why* didn't she give it to him?" Maggie's head dipped as she gave her friend an expectant stare. She was certain she now knew the answer but wanted to see if Robin would reach the same conclusion.

"Maybe Doyle was gone by the time she got there. I mean, she did sit in Ron's car for a while after they got to her house."

"Even if that was the case, Grace could have tied the bag with the jersey on the door handle or something. Doyle would have found it the next morning." Maggie shook her head slowly. "I don't think she had a chance to leave it because she saw or overheard something—"

Robin finished her thought. "Something that freaked her out. That's why she wanted to talk to Pam that night. To figure out if she was overreacting about something that happened when she went to the body shop."

Maggie eased out a long breath. "I'm pretty sure Grace discovered something illegal was going on that night. Maybe she even threatened to tell the authorities."

"And if Doyle knew she was there, he probably decided he needed to kill her to keep her from telling anyone." Robin's hand flew to her forehead. "Now, do you think going there tonight might have been a stupid idea?"

Maggie held up her hands as her shoulders scrunched against her neck. "Well, I don't know for sure that's what happened."

"It's a decent theory. It explains the note and why he'd be so nervous about us investigating Grace's murder. Even though he can't be arrested for it again, he's worried we'll turn up something else that could still land him in prison."

"Karma," Maggie said with a wistful smile. Matt had been right. But there was more to this story Robin hadn't heard. Much more. "The reason I went to the body shop tonight was to put an Air Tag on Doyle's truck. I went by his house first, but it wasn't there. I figured maybe he took the motorcycle home, and the pickup was still at the shop."

Robin arched an eyebrow. "You were going to track *him*?"

Maggie shrugged but a slight smile tugged at the corners of her mouth. "I wanted to turn the tables. Keep an eye on him in case he had any ideas about coming to my apartment."

"Oh, I guess that makes sense. So, can you see where Doyle is now?"

Maggie shifted in her seat and slid her phone from her back pocket. She pulled up the app to locate the tracker and studied her screen. "Well, he left the shop, but I have no idea where he could be heading." She squinted at her phone and then used her fingers to zoom in on his location. "He's on Forbes Road."

"Forbes Road?" Robin frowned. "There's nothing out there. Just woods on one side and strawberry fields on the other until it connects with the interstate. Are you sure the tracker's working?"

Maggie cocked her head thoughtfully. "Unless there's a clearing in those woods."

"What?"

"When you took your car to the body shop, did you notice how far back the building went?"

Robin shook her head. "Not really. I parked in the lot right there in the front. I mean, I saw they were working on a few cars because I could see through the glass behind the front counter."

"Well, there are more bays than you probably thought. The last two—the panes of glass are painted black."

Robin's eyes narrowed. "That way, no one on the outside can see in. You think they're trying to hide whatever's back there?"

"I absolutely do. Tonight, the building was dark, like everyone was gone. From the outside, the place looked closed for the night, but they were behind those painted doors. I heard Doyle and his partner—"

"Manny?"

"Right, Manny. They were fighting. Whatever they were talking about, Doyle said they needed to hit the pause button."

"Pause button for what?" Robin asked.

"I'm not sure. He said something about shipping stuff out of the country and how it was a federal crime."

"Maybe it's drugs."

"They didn't say. Just that they had to get whatever needed to go out from the clearing."

"So, that's where Doyle's heading." Robin nodded slowly as his location began to make sense. "To some clearing in the woods off Forbes Road."

"But while I was there, they were arguing. Doyle sounded angry, like he'd had enough. He said they'd all get locked up if they got caught, and he brought up the murder trial. He said, and I quote—" Maggie caught Robin's eye as she made quotation marks in the air with her fingers. "You're not the one who almost went to prison for something you didn't do."

Robin slammed both palms down on the table so hard Maggie's mic tipped over. "Stop it right now." She shot her friend a look of disbelief. "How is it possible you didn't lead with this information? Like the minute you walked in the door." She rolled her eyes. "I guess you actually hopped in the front door but still."

"Sorry," Maggie said, lifting her mic back into its upright position. "My head's been spinning since I left there." A sly smile spread across her face. "Besides, what Doyle said might not even be the biggest headline of the night."

Robin huffed loudly. "Uh, if Doyle's telling the truth, that's a huge revelation. But wait a minute," she said, scowling. "Does this mean he was also telling the truth about buying a second jersey? Otherwise, how did he get his back?"

"That came up tonight, too," Maggie said. "Manny told Doyle he'd been an idiot to take it from Grace's house. Said if he hadn't, the cops never would have arrested him." She tipped her head to the side and gave Robin a knowing look. "Apparently, it was still in that plastic grocery bag, which explains why they didn't find blood or gunpowder when they tested it."

"So, Doyle was there when Grace was killed. He just wasn't the one who pulled the trigger," Robin said matter-of-factly. "Still guilty as far as—"

Maggie shook her head. "From what I heard tonight, she was already dead when Doyle got there."

"His partner beat him to it?"

"I'm pretty sure Doyle suspects that's the case, but Manny claims he didn't do it. They sounded like they were going to go to blows over it."

"Well, Doyle did almost spend his life in prison for it. I can imagine that would make someone a bit salty." Robin leaned back in her chair and folded her arms against her chest. "But if neither one of them murdered Grace, then who did?"

"Well, I couldn't see the people who were inside, but it wasn't just Doyle and Manny. I heard a third person." Maggie's lips twitched with a slight smile. "And he sounded familiar."

"You recognized the voice?" Robin's eyes lit up. "Is it someone I know, too?"

"This person told them both to calm down, but Doyle told him he'd be in just as deep if they got caught. He said—"

Robin groaned and dropped her head dramatically on the table. "You're *killing* me. Who else was there?"

Maggie leaned back in her chair with a satisfied smile on her face. "See, I told you. This story is podcast gold. Our listeners are going to feel the same way when—"

"You have my permission to torture them all you want, but right now, you need to spill it." Robin pressed her palms together in front of her and gave Maggie a hard stare. "I'm begging you to tell me. Who was it?"

27

"The other voice at the body shop belonged to none other than Harrison Korman."

Robin appeared disappointed with this revelation. "Who?" she asked, a blank expression on her face.

"Harry. My boss. Well, my ex-boss."

Robin's hand flew to her mouth. "Oh, Mr. Nobody! I can't believe he's in on whatever Doyle and Manny are doing that's illegal."

"Oh, but there's more." Maggie's tone was intentionally mysterious, but she was about to give her friend the last missing piece of the puzzle. "I was sure I recognized his voice, but I knew I was right when I saw his Mercedes parked at the body shop." She studied Robin's face waiting for her to make the connection. "You saw his car the day you picked me up at the office. Do I need to remind you what color—"

Robin inhaled sharply. "White," she yelled, her voice full of excitement. "His car was white."

"Yup. Not only is Harry a bully and a jerk, he's also a cold-blooded killer." Just saying the words out loud sent a shiver down Maggie's back. "I can't believe I was wrong about Doyle.

But he was there. I have no doubt he went to Grace's house to kill her." She gave a shrug. "Harry just beat him to it."

Robin gazed off thoughtfully. "So, both witnesses were right about the white car. Melody Kaplan saw Harry's Mercedes, and Roy Jenkins saw Doyle a half an hour later in the Camry he borrowed from Meredith Brinkley."

Maggie gulped down a breath. "Melody Kaplan. Do you think Harry ..."

"Killed her too?" Robin shook her head. "Her daughter called me back and apologized for being so short with me on the phone. She died in her sleep. They're pretty sure it was a heart attack."

Maggie gave a slow nod. "So, he wasn't smart enough to find Melody's statement, not that it matters at this point. If Grace was already dead when Doyle got there, then Harry killed her. I hate to say it, but it makes sense. If he's doing something shady with their books and it blows up, there goes his gravy train. Not to mention he goes to prison a disgrace. His ego could never handle that." She remembered what Doyle had said as he taunted him. "Can you just imagine Harry's condescending attitude in prison? He'd probably get the stuffing kicked out of him."

Robin pursed her lips as she stared at Maggie. "Harry confessed to killing Grace, right? You heard him say it?"

Was Robin saying she didn't see what was right in front of them? "No, but why would he?" Maggie asked. "Doyle is convinced it was Manny. It sounded like Manny's not positive Doyle didn't really kill her. Neither one of them is pointing the finger at Harry."

"I guess that makes sense," Robin said, but she didn't sound entirely convinced.

Maggie rubbed her hands together. "C'mon, you have to admit, this case just took a huge turn. And no one else will be able to tell it the way we can. Harry will go on trial and be convicted, and Pam and her family will finally get justice. And it's because of us. We'll have the inside scoop to share with our listeners."

Robin let out a breath. "Let's hope no one tries to kill us before we have a chance to record the ending to this story. I'm glad you're not working for Harry anymore. If he really did do it—"

The door opened, and Robin's husband stuck his head in the open crack. "Hey, I couldn't figure out where you went." He flinched when he saw Maggie. "Sorry. Are you two recording?"

Robin shook her head. "No, we're just we're planning the next few episodes."

"Oh, okay. I put your suitcase in my truck, and I'm going to take a quick shower and go to bed." He cocked his head to the side and gave his wife a pointed look. "It's getting late, hon. Don't forget we have an early flight in the morning."

She nodded. "I know. We're almost done here."

When the door shut behind him, Robin gave Maggie a hard stare. "You're positive Harry killed Grace? He's the one stalking us, not Doyle?"

"I'm sure he wanted us to think it was Doyle, but it would have been easy for Harry to hide the Air Tag on my car." Maggie crossed her arms on the table in front of her and leaned toward Robin. "Think about it. Harry knows we're friends because he was there that day we went to lunch." She couldn't help but remember the look on her boss's face as he'd watched them pull out of the parking lot. "When you picked me up, you saw what Harry drove, but he also saw your car." She held Robin's gaze. "And your dented bumper."

Robin reeled back in her seat. "You think Doyle said something to him about me bringing my car into the body shop?"

"Doyle brought it up tonight—how you knew about Mered-

ith's car being detailed. He's worried someone's on to them."
Maggie threw up her hands. "All he had to do was mention to
the others that the person asking all the questions was a pretty
blond with a dent in the bumper of her black Lexus. How long
do you think it would take for Harry to put two and two together?" She pressed her lips together and her shoulders lifted. "It
would explain why he's targeting both of us."

"But how would Harry have known where my car would be
to leave that note?"

A twinge of guilt raced through Maggie. "The Air Tag.
Unfortunately, I led him right to you." She offered her friend a
hesitant smile. "But hey, it's not like he can follow you to
Cancun, right?"

Robin didn't respond to Maggie's lighthearted sentiment.
Instead, her face pinched with worry. "But what about you? You
need to call the police to tell them what you know."

Maggie hesitated. "Right now, I don't have any actual proof.
It would be Harry's word against mine, and he could claim—I
mean, he did just fire me."

"But all they have to do is investigate him," Robin insisted.
"They'll find evidence he committed the murder."

Maggie was quiet, and her cheeks burned as she considered
admitting out loud what she was thinking. "You know that if we
turn this over to the police, we'll be out," she said softly. "We'd
have no way—the podcast—" Her words hung in the air.

Robin heaved a sigh. "I know, but I'm finally starting to see
Matt's point. Maybe we are out of our league. This is starting to
feel dangerous."

Maggie didn't disagree, but she knew her ex-boss better than
the police. "The Air Tag's disabled now, and I'll be careful. I just
want to figure out what else Harry is up to, and then—then I'll
tell Matt, and we'll bring in the police." Maggie's pulse quickened as she made the promise. At that point, she had no idea

where she stood with him. She didn't know if he'd even be willing to help her.

"Doyle and Manny are clearly doing something illegal that Harry's benefitting from, and he doesn't want that to end. Mr. Nobody finally feels like he's important." Robin closed her eyes as she rubbed the back of her neck. "There's still one thing that's bothering me," she said when she opened them. "Did Grace know Harry? If there was no forced entry, how did he get into her house? Pam was sure Grace wouldn't have opened the door for a stranger."

Maggie had wondered the same thing and had formulated a theory. "I have a hunch I know the answer. I just need a little help to figure out if I'm right."

Robin's bottom lip jutted out. "I suppose it can't wait until I get back?"

"I guess that depends on what I find out."

The last thing Maggie wanted to do was make this final push without her, but things were spiraling out of control. Being tracked. The note on Robin's car.

If Harry was responsible for it all, there was no telling what he would do next. To keep his secret, he'd already killed one person. Maggie was sure of it. Now she just needed to find the proof.

28

After she left Robin's house, Maggie went back home. It wasn't like she had any choice.

She tried to get some sleep—her large kitchen knife under her pillow—but she tossed and turned before slugging back a sleeping pill left over from the early days of her divorce. When she awoke, she stared at the clock in disbelief. On her first official day of being unemployed, she'd slept in later than she had in years.

She reached for her phone on the nightstand and let out a sigh of relief. Jake had responded to the message she'd sent before she went to bed.

> OK. talk 2 u tonight.

As she stared at his message on the screen, her heart filled with hope. Unless Todd shared her news, her son had no idea she'd been fired. It was Spring Break, so he didn't have school. Most likely, he'd said they'd speak that night because he assumed Maggie would be at work all day.

There was also a text from Robin.

Heading to the airport now. Keep me posted &
be careful. Let Matt help you! Mr. Nobody needs
to pay.

Maggie's pulse ramped up. Could she really do this without
her friend?

She had no choice. It was now her against Harry, and she
was determined to take him down. For her and for Grace. She
put her good foot on the ground and stood on one leg before
placing any weight on her injured ankle to try and walk. It didn't
feel too bad. She limped into the kitchen and brewed herself a
cup of coffee.

She sat at the table, pulled out an extra chair, and set her bad
foot on the seat cushion. As she slowly sipped her Morning
Blend, she planned her day.

First up, she had a call to place. As she'd told Robin, she
needed help if she was going to prove her theory was correct.

"Hey, it's me, Maggie," she said when Charlene answered the
phone.

"Oh, hey." She lowered her voice. "What happened
yesterday?"

"I, uh, got fired."

"Are you kidding?" Maggie's co-worker sounded genuinely
surprised. "I'm so sorry."

"Don't be. Harry set me up, but it's okay. You know what they
say about payback."

Charlene let out a loud huff. "I don't blame you for wanting
revenge. He's such a jerk. So, what are you going to do to him?"

"Oh, I'm not going to do anything to him. Trust me, he's done
it all to himself." Maggie leaned forward and unwrapped the
ACE bandage. It was a sign of weakness she couldn't afford as
she put her plan in motion. "I'm about to blow the lid off the
truth, but I need your help." She tipped her head and scruti-

nized her ankle. It didn't look as swollen as it had the night before.

"Me?" There was hesitation in Charlene's voice. "What can I do?"

Maggie stood carefully and shuffled slowly to the cabinet where she kept her medicine. "I need the master client list from the shared drive. If you can't access it, ask Ernie's assistant. I'm sure she can get it for you, but you can't tell her it's for me. Also, there's a green folder on my desk. I need that, too."

As she presented her needs, Maggie leaned against the kitchen counter and hoped she sounded more confident than she felt. "I know it's asking a lot, but can you bring the file and the list down to me in the parking lot this morning? I'll come by the building, but I can't come in." She snorted. "For obvious reasons."

"The folder isn't there anymore." Charlene took a deep breath and exhaled slowly as if she dreaded what she was about to say. "Your desk—it's empty, Maggie. Harry must have moved everything into his office last night. When I came in, it was all sitting on the conference table in his office."

"Really?" Maggie shook her head in disbelief as she reached for the ibuprofen. "My chair's barely cold. Is he in this morning?"

"Yeah, he just went into a client meeting with Andy."

"Then he should be gone for a bit." Maggie made her way back to the table with the pain relief bottle in her hand. "*Please.*" She wasn't above begging at this point. "I really need what's in that folder." She told Charlene what was written on the label. "You're the only shot I have at getting my hands on it."

"Oh, Maggie. I don't know how I can get that for you now." Her former co-worker sounded apprehensive. "What if he catches me looking through the stuff in his office? I heard he caught you snooping in there yesterday. Is that why you lost your job?"

So, there had been office gossip about her departure after all. Just wait until the news about Harry's arrest circulated.

"That wasn't the only reason, but I can't explain it all just yet." Maggie shook two pills into her hand and slugged them down with her lukewarm coffee. "I can make you a promise, though. If you help me find what I'm looking for, you won't have to worry about Harry reporting you to HR or trying to get you fired. He won't be working for the firm anymore. He'll be in prison."

Two hours later, Maggie hugged Charlene and pulled out of the parking lot of her old office with everything she needed to take down her ex-boss. At least, she hoped what she now would confirm her suspicions.

She took the client list and the file to a nearby coffee shop. As she pored over the pages she needed, she scribbled on a new timeline she'd created in her notebook. Her heart pounded as the pieces began to fall into place. It was hard to believe Harry had been so careless, but before Maggie moved forward with her plan, she had a few last pieces to fact check.

Maggie glanced down at her phone and noted the time. Robin was already in Mexico. This was now her battle to fight. She'd win—or lose—by herself.

After one final sip of her latte, she stood carefully on her bad ankle and walked gingerly toward the trash can. The ibuprofen and additional caffeine seemed to be helping. Maggie tossed in her empty cup and pushed open the door to the parking lot. She was off to her next stop.

She was shocked when over and over she found assistance

she didn't expect. It was almost as if the Universe or some higher power had been sent out with her that day to locate the answers she needed. Proof of Harry's guilt. Deep down, Maggie wanted to believe somehow Grace had a hand in it all—her attempt to give her family some peace.

As the picture of what had happened slowly came together, Maggie couldn't help but feel a sense of satisfaction. Her boss had always considered her to be inferior. Incapable of success. She could only imagine if she'd asked Harry if he considered her a worthy adversary. He would have laughed in her face as tiny pieces of his spittle sprayed her skin and made her gag. It wouldn't be long before Harrison Korman realized just how wrong he'd been about her.

Several hours later, the story of what had happened to Grace was complete. Maggie no longer had a single lingering doubt about Harry's guilt.

As she sat in her car outside the pawn shop that had provided the final clue, Maggie typed a text to Robin and hit send.

> Are you on the beach yet? I was right about everything. Harry's going down. I really wish you were here.

Maggie's phone pinged seconds later with a response, and it included a picture of her friend holding up a fruity cocktail by an enormous swimming pool.

> Good for you! Go show that piece of garbage you're the boss now. Cheers!

She couldn't resist a smile as she read her friend's message. It quickly faded. Maggie's excitement over uncovering the truth about Grace's murder was tempered by her nagging fear that it was going to destroy any chance of a future with Matt. He'd given her an ultimatum, and instead of him, she'd chosen to chase the fulfillment she now felt for honoring her promise to Pam. Grace's family was finally going to get the justice they deserved.

Maggie could only hope she hadn't destroyed her relationship in the process but ignoring what she'd discovered wasn't an option. Maggie had uncovered the truth about everything Harry had been hiding.

Still, her internal voice nagged at her. It tried to insist she keep her word to Robin and go to the police with what she'd found. She pushed down her conscience, because Maggie could almost taste the validation that she'd done what the police couldn't. It was proof that her obsession with true crime had laid the foundation for her to uncover the truth. She'd solved Grace's murder. It would crush her to have to hand her victory off to some detective to claim as his own. This was *her* success. She'd earned it.

More than anything, Maggie was desperate to deliver the news to Harry herself. After the way he'd treated her all these years, she needed to hear the fear in his voice when he realized he'd underestimated her. She'd followed the trail he'd been cocky enough to leave behind, and it was going to cost him his freedom.

She started up her car. It wasn't that she felt uncomfortable sitting in front of the pawnshop, but she needed to get home.

As she thought about Robin's message, her smile returned. It wouldn't be long now. Harry was about to learn who was really in charge. It was Maggie.

29

B ack in her apartment, Maggie grabbed a water bottle and took two more ibuprofen. She lowered herself onto the couch and hesitated as she held her phone. The confidence she'd felt earlier now wavered. She took in several stuttered breaths and brushed the sweat off her upper lip. Could she really do this?

If she didn't, she'd be forced to live in constant fear. That tracker had been hidden on her car, and just as easily, another one could be placed. She might be none the wiser until it was too late. Not to mention, she was sure Jake would come home eventually. Maggie would have to constantly worry about someone showing up at her front door. Her son could get caught in the middle.

She considered calling Matt, but what would she say? He'd already warned her that choosing the case over him would mean they were through. If Maggie called the police on her own, she'd most likely have to turn over her findings to them. She couldn't forfeit the satisfaction of knowing she was the reason for the panic in Harry's voice.

It was time to put him in his place once and for all.

Maggie's heart slammed against her ribs as the phone rang. She drummed her fingers on the coffee table and waited for him to answer.

"Mr. Korman's office."

Maggie caught her breath and regrouped. "Charlene? Harry's got you answering his phone?"

"Yeah. He had it transferred to one of my lines."

"Does he know you took the folder from his office?" Maggie gripped her phone tightly. "Everything okay on your end?"

"Yeah, it's fine. The client meeting ran longer than I thought, and then he and Andy went out to get a late lunch." Charlene let out an aggravated puff of air. "Lucky for him because I have no intentions of becoming his delivery girl. He will need to learn that I don't work for him. Especially now that you're gone. And I plan to warn—"

"Are they back yet?" Maggie cut in. The longer she prolonged the inevitable, the more her nerves tried to convince her to hang up. "I need to talk to him."

She drew in a deep breath and gave herself an internal pep talk. Harry would be able to smell the fear in her voice. Maggie had the truth on her side, and she needed to sound—and be—confident, or this was never going to work.

"You—you want to talk to Harry?"

"Oh, do I ever," Maggie said with such zealous enthusiasm she surprised herself.

"Does that mean—" Charlene lowered her voice a notch. "Did you find what you needed?"

"And then some. Harrison Korman is going down, so get ready. Tell him I'm on the line, and if he says he doesn't want to talk to me, you can tell him it's about Grace."

"Grace? Who's Grace?"

"Don't worry. Harry knows exactly who she is."

Maggie laid her phone on the table and tapped the speaker button.

A moment later, her ex-boss was on the line. "What do you want, Margaret? You no longer work for me. Or this company. From here on out, you need to direct your calls to human resources."

"Oh, okay, sure." She deliberately made her tone breezy and casual. Maggie wanted to lull Harry into a false sense of security before she dropped her bombshell—the real reason for her call. "Do you want to transfer me so I can tell them you killed Grace Hutchinson?"

There was silence on the line for a moment. "Who?" Harry sounded disinterested, as if the conversation was boring him.

"Really? You murdered a woman in cold blood while she ran for her life, and you don't even know her name?"

His defense came quicker this time. "I have no idea what you're talking about."

"Oh, then let me enlighten you. I'll start with Martin Freight. Not a real company, Harry."

Maggie imagined him bristling at her use of his nickname. In all the years she'd worked for him, she'd never called him that to his face. This was starting to be fun.

"You set it up to ship parts from stolen cars. Seems odd that you took Martin Freight on as a client just about the same time as RC's Luxury Car Parts and D & M Body Shop. Even stranger that I never handled the paperwork for any of them. In fact, for some reason, I was restricted from accessing their files."

"I'm a busy man, Margaret. I don't have time for this nonsense."

"Too bad." Maggie was done letting Harry push her around. "Buckle up because I'm just getting started. I know Grace came by the body shop the night before she died. She had Doyle's football jersey to return. But she saw something she wasn't supposed to see, didn't she? You all knew she was there and decided she needed to die so she wouldn't tell anyone what she suspected."

"What is it you want?" Harry's words were crisp and sharp. "You want your job back? Is that it?"

Maggie ignored the interruption and continued. "Grace was supposed to be Doyle's problem to take care of. But much like everything else, you didn't trust him to handle it, so you decided to take matters into your own hands. You went to the florist. You got a cheap bouquet of flowers and then stopped to pick up a bottle of red wine. You went to Grace's house under the guise of making a delivery to her. You used your props as a way to get her to open the door. Which she did."

Maggie paused to take a sip of water and let what she'd said so far sink in.

"She had her purse in her hands, probably planning to give your skanky ass a tip," she continued. "But then you tried to push your way in, and it fell from her grip. I'm going to go out on a limb and say you're a perfect match to the palm print on her front door. But don't worry, I'm sure the police can confirm that."

"So what." Harry's voice now sounded less confident than before. "That doesn't prove anything."

"Oh, but it will."

"Unfortunately, this entire tale is a product of your imagination." He gave an exaggerated sigh. "It's gone wild, I'm afraid. I mean, it's understandable you'd concoct this story and direct your anger at me since I had you fired." There was now an eerie calm to his voice. "Anyone will realize that."

Maggie swallowed hard as she considered he could be right but then reminded herself there could be no disputing what she'd found. "I don't need to make up anything," she said with conviction. "The evidence will tell the story for me."

She consulted the notes she'd written for herself and leaned down toward her phone. Maggie wanted to ensure Harry heard what she said next. "Did you realize that Grace Hutchinson's property borders a nature preserve? There was a study going on at the time she was killed." She was bluffing, but Harry would have no way of knowing that. "Cameras set up to capture the plant life caught the audio of the gun going off. After killing her, you set up the wine, played around with her computer to make it look like she was still alive, and then raced out of Grace's neighborhood. Did you know the woman you nearly smashed into spoke to the police? She told them all about your expensive white sedan running the stop sign at 8:05 p.m."

Harry's silence told Maggie she had his attention. "At 8:14 p.m., you were at the convenience store less than a mile from Grace's house. You went inside and bought a pack of cigarettes." Maggie clucked her tongue in disapproval. "I really thought you'd quit, but I guess killing someone set your nerves on edge." She paused to let the hook set deeper. "I showed the manager your picture, you know, the one on the company website." She could imagine Harry's scowl. He'd made the photographer retake his photo several times, but the partners had used the first shot anyway. He detested it. "Oh, you don't have to worry, he was working the register that night, and he remembered you. He said you lit up before you were even out of the store, and he was annoyed he had to tell you to take your cigarette outside. Way to fly under the radar, Harry."

Maggie took a quick swallow of water and then continued. "After you left, he followed you on the security camera. Watched as you drove around the back of the building and tossed a bouquet of flowers in his dumpster. You know what's funny? Well, not haha funny. More coincidence funny. It was actually the guy's anniversary. He hadn't gotten flowers for his wife, so after you left, he went and plucked that bouquet right out of the dumpster. Apparently, she didn't mind the cheap daisies."

"What's your point?" Harry asked in a gruff voice. "It's not a crime to throw something in the trash."

"No, you're absolutely right." Maggie's head bobbed in agreement even though he couldn't see her. "But the manager said something about you seemed off. You see, when you paid for your cigarettes, he was convinced he saw drops of *blood* on your shirt. Blood, Harry. Makes sense, I guess. I mean, how could you shoot someone from such a close distance and not get a single drop on you?"

Maggie waited to see if he would respond, but Harry remained quiet.

"The next day, when the manager heard there had been a murder nearby, he decided to save the video footage of you. Just. In. Case." She enunciated each word and could imagine the beads of sweat pooling on Harry's forehead.

The part about the footage was true. The manager had seemed almost relieved when Maggie asked to speak to him about Grace's murder earlier that day.

"I always felt like someone would come looking for this footage," he'd said. "Thought for sure I was onto something until I saw on the news someone else had been arrested."

"He's still got your video. Isn't that great?" Maggie filled her voice with overblown enthusiasm. "He let me watch it, and I agree. It definitely looks like blood. I mean, if I can see it on the guy's phone, I'm sure when they show it on one of those big monitors in the courtroom, a jury will be able to see the same thing."

Harry didn't say a word, not that she expected him to. She was sure the clothes he wore that night were long gone, but Maggie couldn't resist a satisfied smile as she imagined his hand curled into a tight fist against his thin, puckered lips.

"I'll bet you didn't give that guy behind the counter a second thought after you left." Her expression turned serious again. "Or Grace, for that matter. You were too busy taking yourself to pick up an expensive steak dinner. You slapped it right on your corporate card. Because why wouldn't you let the company pick up the tab for your morbid celebration?"

By now, Maggie was positive her ex-boss was revisiting his decisions from that night. Harry had been so overly confident he wouldn't get caught that he hadn't considered the trail he'd left for her to find. He'd laid out the events of the entire night on his company credit card.

"You forget I've done your expense reports all these years. And you know, there was one specific charge that always stood out to me like a sore thumb. The one from the pawnshop." Maggie rubbed her index finger against her lips. "What would a man with your money buy at a place like that? Do you remember me asking where I should classify it?"

Harry didn't respond, so Maggie answered for him.

"Office supplies. You claimed you bought artwork for your office. Odd, since you never hung anything new, but that's because it was a lie. There was no painting." She paused to let Harry wonder if she'd discovered the truth. "There was, however, the purchase of a 22-caliber gun." It was a guess. The guy behind the counter at the pawnshop told her he wasn't permitted to provide specifics since she wasn't the police. But when Maggie had asked him if it was possible, his head had bobbed in an almost imperceptible nod. He'd confirmed that the amount Harry had charged on his card was in line with what the weapon would cost. Maggie was convinced her theory was correct as she allowed her words to sink in. "I wonder how HR will feel about your egregious misuse of your corporate card. But since I'm sure the weapon you purchased will be a perfect match to the bullet that killed Grace, I suppose that's the least of your worries right now."

Though he was silent, Harry hadn't hung up on her. Maggie heard his breathing, labored like he was starting to realize he'd underestimated his meek assistant.

"What's the matter, Harry? Cat got your tongue?"

"What do you want?" He spat the words out. "Is it money you're looking for? How much?"

Maggie now knew with absolute certainty that Harry had killed Grace Hutchinson. He wouldn't have offered to throw her a bribe for any other reason.

A smile tugged at her lips. "I'll let you know my terms when I see you. Meet me at the body shop at seven, and I'll tell you what else I know. You should probably invite Manny and Doyle to the party."

"Who? And what body shop are you referring to?"

"Don't play dumb, Harry." Maggie's tone turned angry. "I've been to the clearing. But if you'd rather skip the meeting, I'll just go right to the police."

"Fine." The word was punctuated with a frustrated growl. "I'll be there at seven."

"Don't be late," Maggie said in a sing-song voice. "And don't even think about doing anything stupid. All the evidence I uncovered is in a safe place. If anything happens to me, don't think for a second the police won't find it and have what they need to prove you're a murderer. Among other things."

She had no need to say goodbye. Maggie ended their call, then jabbed at the stop button on the small tape recorder.

She leaned against the back of her couch and released a long, deep breath. Their conversation wouldn't be admissible in court, but at least now maybe the police would listen to her. Not to mention, Robin would be able to listen to the tape when she got back from her vacation. Maybe eventually they'd even be able to play it on their podcast.

As the adrenaline of the confrontation with Harry subsided, nausea set in. Maggie had set the wheels in motion.

There'd be no turning back now.

30

Maggie's heart raced as she stared down at the notification on her phone. While she was talking to Harry, she'd missed a call from Matt. Conflicting emotions surged through her. She was relieved that he'd reached out to her, but she couldn't help but worry that any hope of a future together would be short-lived when he found out what she'd done.

He had explicitly told her to let the investigation go—that their relationship couldn't continue otherwise. Maggie had gone in the other direction. She'd stepped over the line with both feet, stomping on the other side like she had fresh snow on her shoes. She desperately needed Matt's help now, but how could she tell him she'd ignored his warning?

Maggie held her breath as she pressed the button to play his voicemail.

Hi, it's me. Listen, I feel terrible about the way you left here yesterday. I know you were upset about Jake and getting fired. I didn't mean to add to your problems. It's just—I know things—things you don't. I couldn't stand it if anything bad happened to you because I'm —I'm falling in love with you.

Maggie sucked in a gulp of air as her hand flew to her mouth.

Damn. See what you did? You made me tell your voicemail because you didn't answer the phone. I love you, Maggie. Where are you? See, now I'm worried you're not answering. Please call me back.

Matt had admitted he loved her, but was it unconditional? She was about to find out.

Maggie's stomach rolled when he answered the phone.

Her voice was soft and hesitant. "Hey, it's me."

"Hey." His tone matched hers. "I'm glad you called me back. I wanted to call yesterday after you left, but my shift got crazy." He paused. "Listen, I'm sorry about what I said. About forcing you to make a choice. It just all feels so ... complicated."

"It's not, really." Maggie ran her tongue over her lips and took a sip from her water bottle before making her admission. "I'm falling in love with you, too."

"You are?" There was relief in his voice. "My divorce made me realize I don't want to leave anything unsaid. I don't want to lose you."

Maggie let out a stuttered breath. "I don't want to lose you either."

It was too late to change what she'd done, but she hoped it wouldn't leave him feeling like she'd left him with no choice but to walk away.

"Is your son at school?" Matt asked. "Can I come over?"

"It's actually Spring Break, but he—he's not here." Maggie wasn't prepared to share what Jake had said in his angry voicemail to her. Besides, she was sure when they spoke that night, her son would tell her he wanted to come home. "And since I'm unemployed, I'm free as a bird. I would love to see you." She bit down on her bottom lip. "I have something I need you to listen to."

∾

MATT SAT rigid as he listened to the tape Maggie had made of her call with Harry. When it ended, he set his elbows on his thighs and wrapped his hands around his head.

As he stared at the floor, Maggie felt sick. She'd blown it. When his silence became unbearable, she tugged at his arm. "Say something. Anything."

He lifted his eyes to meet hers. "Is all of that true?"

She gave a slow nod, then lifted one shoulder in a half-shrug. "Most of it. I bluffed on some of the evidence I said I had, but Harry wouldn't know that."

Matt eased out a long breath. "I do believe you've uncovered the truth about Grace's murder. Unofficially, I'm impressed. *Unofficially.*" The flicker of a smile played on his lips, but then just as quickly, it fell away. "But here's the problem. As interesting as it is, that tape doesn't prove a thing. Harry never admits he killed Grace, and even if he did, that recording is completely inadmissible—"

"I figured it couldn't be used in court. I just wanted to—"

Matt's exasperated moan interrupted her. "Why, Maggie? Why didn't you just let the police handle this?"

She bowed her head. He was right. She had acted impulsive and reckless calling Harry on her own. "I know," she said in a soft voice as she brought her eyes back up to meet his. "I should have, but can't they still—"

"You've shown your hand now." Matt gave her a hard stare. "If this were a poker game, Harry would know exactly what cards you're holding." His voice escalated. "Not only that, but what about Doyle and Manny? Don't you think Harry's going to tell them you're on to their operation? That you know about the stolen cars. The clearing."

"But that doesn't change the fact—"

Matt threw his hands in the air. "It does." He was yelling now, frustrated he couldn't make Maggie understand. He locked his eyes on hers and lowered his voice. "It changes *everything*." His face softened slightly, and he aimed his chin at the chair across from him. "Sit down."

She lowered herself slowly into the seat, her eyes glued to his face. Their relationship was over, and she had only herself to blame. When she'd considered backing out of the investigation and the podcast, she told Robin it was because she didn't want to risk losing Matt over a guy like Doyle. Then she found out Harry was involved, and Maggie had allowed her hatred for her ex-boss to propel her forward. Her need to get even with him for the way he'd treated her was going to cost her the man she loved.

"You remember Franklin?" Matt asked.

"Detective Franklin? The guy with the Air Tag?"

"Yeah." His shoulders lifted and dropped matter-of-factly. "We just call him Franklin. Anyway, he's been working on a case for a couple of years. Stolen cars. The thieves use Air Tags to track the expensive cars they want to take. They figure out where the person lives and steal the vehicle from the person's driveway in the middle of the night. For a while, it seemed the thefts had stopped." Matt crossed his arms on the table and leaned in as if he had something important to tell her. "It appears their operation halted while Doyle was fighting the murder charge. Cars started disappearing again right after the trial ended."

Maggie nodded slowly as it all came together. It wasn't about drugs. They were stealing cars. This was the pause button Doyle had wanted to press.

"Did you tell Franklin I was on the jury that let him off?"

"I did. I mentioned Doyle's name when I talked to him about the Air Tag—that's when I found out he could be involved. Franklin told me the task force has had their eye on him and

Manny for a while." Matt reached for Maggie's hand and his eyes pleaded with her to understand. "That's why I was so adamant—why I gave you the ultimatum. I wasn't trying to tell you what to do—well, I guess I was, but it was because I was trying to protect you. I was worried enough when I thought Doyle might have killed Grace over a breakup." He shook his head. "Once I knew there was more to this ..." He held her gaze, a crease of concern between his eyebrows. "Criminals who are cornered turn desperate. Just look at how Harry reacted when he thought Grace might blow their cover. She's dead because she knew too much."

"I'm sorry." Maggie meant it. She should have known Matt wasn't trying to control her, that he had a good reason for telling her to let the case go. "I didn't know. I just thought—"

"I couldn't just come out and share information about an active investigation." Matt drew in a deep breath, then exhaled it as a loud sigh. "But I guess you're part of it now." He perched himself on the edge of his chair and leaned toward her. "Doyle and Manny would have a difficult time with the stolen vehicles because VIN numbers make them easy to trace. Franklin's sure they're using them for parts. He just hasn't figured out who they're selling to or where they're disassembling them."

"Oh, wait." There was excitement in Maggie's voice. "I think I might have an idea where they're taking them. I put an Air Tag on Doyle's pickup truck last night."

Matt reeled back in his chair. "You what?"

A guilty heat burned her face. "I know you said to let it go, but I didn't know what was going on and—" Maggie dipped her head. "I'm sorry, but I couldn't drop it. Grace's family deserves answers. I just kept thinking about how I would feel if it had been my sister. I would want someone fighting to uncover the truth."

She opened the app on her phone and pulled up the Air

Tag's location. "I guess it hasn't notified him yet, or he hasn't figured out this Air Tag isn't one of theirs. Doyle's truck is at the body shop now. But last night, it was on Forbes Road."

Matt's gaze drifted for a moment as if he was trying to picture the area. Then, the realization crossed his face. "He was heading to the clearing."

"My thought, too. I don't know exactly where it is, but my guess is that somewhere along that stretch, you'll find an open area in the woods where they're taking the stolen cars."

"On the tape, you said you'd been there."

Maggie offered a sheepish shrug. "A little white lie, but Harry doesn't know it's not true. Besides, I'm sure if I had a little time, I could figure out where it is."

"I don't know about that." He shot her a skeptical look. "It's a long stretch of woods. That's a lot of ground to cover."

Maggie remembered a show she'd watched on the ID channel where the image of two men had been captured outside a woman's house the day she was robbed and attacked. "What if we looked it up on Google Earth?"

Matt pressed his lips together and gave a soft chuckle. "Sure. Go ahead."

As she used her phone to search, Maggie chewed on her bottom lip. She squinted at the screen, and when she glanced up and saw Matt studying her, she huffed out a breath. "Give me a break. You need to give me a little time to figure it out."

He leaned back in his chair and fought a smile. "Take all the time you need."

Maggie scowled when she saw her efforts were amusing him, but she turned her attention back to the screen. Ten minutes later, she dipped her chin. Without saying a word, she handed him her phone.

Matt sat up straight, his eyes wide as he stared at what she'd found. "I can't believe—wow. You're really good at this." He gestured at the tape recorder sitting on her kitchen table. "So, you have this recording you can't use. You told Harry to meet you tonight. Does that mean you have a plan of some sort?"

"I was kind of hoping you'd be willing to help me." Maggie had set up the meeting hoping it might help ensure her a role in taking them all down. "Just call Franklin and tell him what I found out. Before I go to the body shop, he can wire me, and I'll get Harry to confess to Grace's murder. I'll get them to admit to the stolen cars, shipping out the parts. All of it."

Matt stared at her as if she'd lost her mind. "And what if they shoot you instead?" He shook his head firmly. "There's no way I'm letting you put yourself on the line like that."

"Ask Franklin if he's willing." Maggie jabbed her finger against the table. "With my help, his case could be closed today. For so many reasons, Harry needs to rot in prison, but Doyle went to Grace's house the night of the murder, too. He tried to set up an alibi to cover his butt, so I know he went with the intention of killing her. He just didn't get the chance. Grace's family deserves to see them both locked up."

She reached for Matt's hand and her eyes bore into his. "What if you'd been given the chance with your sister's boyfriend? Wouldn't you have taken any opportunity you could to put him behind bars where he couldn't hurt anyone else?" Maggie knew she was fighting dirty, but he'd done the same when he wanted her to drop the case.

Matt sucked in a breath, and Maggie wondered if she'd made a dent in his steely resolve to keep her safe at all costs. Finally, he expelled a defeated groan, then bobbed his head. "You need to tell me everything you found out." His face turned stern. "Everything. Don't try to protect me. Or yourself. I need to know it all."

Maggie relayed how she'd lurked next to the body shop and heard Doyle and his partner behind the painted panes of glass at the back of the building. "I never expected Harry to be there, but as soon as I heard his voice, I knew." She explained how Manny and Doyle both suspected the other of killing Grace. "Then, I realized Harry drives a white car. It was his Mercedes the first witness saw racing away from the scene. It was why the timeline never worked against Doyle. He showed up later."

"Sounds like you're probably right."

"But I still couldn't figure out how Harry could have gotten into Grace's house." She explained what Pam had told her about finding the daisy under the couch. "I suspected if I checked his credit card statements, I might find answers. He uses his company card for everything." Maggie let out a disgusted huff. "Even to fund his plot to commit murder."

Matt shook his head in disbelief. "I can't believe he'd be so stupid."

"Oh, you have no idea. I'm sure the murder was meant to silence Grace about what she must have seen. Whatever they're all involved with, a big part of it is happening at the clearing—"

"That's got to be where they're taking the cars to dismantle them."

"Probably, but part of their operation must be taking place at the body shop. Otherwise, why black out the windows so no one can see in?"

Matt ran the tip of his thumb across his lips. "That could be where they're boxing up the parts to ship."

"If Franklin's team busts into the two bays in the back, I'm sure they'll find a treasure trove of evidence. Not to mention my old office. He'll find information on the fake company Harry set up to launder the money from the stolen parts. Which, by the way, I'm pretty sure he also represents the international buyer."

Matt cocked his head. "Do you know who that is?"

Maggie stared off as she tried to remember what she'd overheard at the body shop. "I'm pretty sure Harry said his name is

Ronan. Supposedly, he's not a man you want to mess with. He didn't mention his last name, but the company's name is RC Luxury Auto Parts. They're out of Canada."

"Let me ask Franklin. It's possible he knows who this guy is. You might have uncovered enough for him to wrap up his investigation."

"But what about Grace's murder?" Maggie reached for Matt's arm as he stood. "I can get Harry to talk. I know his fragile ego better than anyone. If I handle him right, he won't be able to resist bragging to me."

"You think Doyle and Manny are just going to let him run his mouth?"

"That's the thing. Harry thinks he's the brains of the operation. Even though Doyle wanted to pause what they were doing, he still did what Harry told him to do." Maggie held Matt's gaze, her eyes pleading with him. "Please. After all this, let me be part of this. For Grace."

Matt hesitated and then released a weary sigh. "I may regret this, but let me call Franklin. He's going to need to get some search warrants."

31

"You're positive you want to do this?" Franklin gave Maggie a hard stare.

Her legs shook as she stood in front of him in the drug store parking lot beside the body shop.

If she wanted out, this seemed like the moment to speak up. Maggie was far from sure, but she was past the point of changing her mind. She swallowed hard and gave an affirmative nod.

Franklin dipped his chin at a female officer, and she approached with something in her hand.

Maggie took a step back as her brow wrinkled. "What's that?"

"There's a microphone in the stone. It emits a signal we can pick up."

"Really? You don't have to tape wires to me or anything like that?"

Franklin gave her a slight smile. "You've been watching too many old movies."

The officer held what appeared to be a necklace. Maggie held up her hair so she could connect the clasp. "That's it?"

"You need this, too." Franklin held up a key fob for a vehicle. It had several keys attached.

Maggie shot Matt a look and frowned. "I thought I was going to take my own car. Won't Harry be suspicious if I show up for the meeting in something else?"

Matt placed his hand on her arm. "It's not real, Maggie."

"It's not?" In the darkness, she leaned forward to take a closer look. "Then why do I need it?"

"It's the power source for the mic. They're connected by Bluetooth."

"Oh." She studied the fob in Franklin's hand again. "I can't believe it's not real."

"That's the idea," he said. "Leave your purse and the keys to your car behind when you go in. Tuck this into your front pocket. You can even leave the fake keys sticking out a little bit, so they won't suspect it's anything more." He pressed the button meant to unlock the car door. "This turns it on."

Franklin directed his gaze at a non-descript white sprinter van. "Testing, two, three. Hey, Maxwell, you got audio?"

An officer leaned out and gave him a thumbs up.

He gave Maggie a reassuring nod. "Okay, it's working. My guys will be able to hear and record everything that's happening as long as you stay in range." He tapped a button and handed her the fob. "Remember, the unlock button turns on the microphone. I just hit the lock button, which turns the power off."

"You good with how it works?" Matt had a worried crease between his eyebrows.

Maggie took in a stuttered breath and gave a hesitant nod. "I think so." Her stomach was already in knots. What if her nerves got the best of her in the heat of the moment and she forgot which button was which?

"She'll be fine. It's not rocket science." Franklin gestured with his hand for them to follow him.

"All this is for me?" Maggie asked as he pulled open the door of the van.

"Our plan is to make sure nothing happens to you." He aimed his chin in Matt's direction. "That guy made me promise to keep you safe." He gestured at the group of SWAT officers. "That's where they come in. Once you go inside the building, they'll move into position." Franklin pointed toward the pitch-dark corner of the drug store parking lot. "My team will head down from there. They'll make their way down that grassy hill and onto the body shop property. There's a door located at the rear of the building. Half the team will set up there, and the other half will stand ready to break through the panes of glass on the last bay door. Once you're inside the building, stay away from the other side of that door as much as possible."

Maggie drew in a long breath, then released it slowly as she tried to calm her anxiety. "How will I know when they're going to burst in?"

"Just try to keep the guys inside talking. When we've got enough, I'll give them the signal, and we'll make the arrests."

She bobbed her head nervously. "But what if—"

"If it sounds like it's going sideways or something goes wrong, they'll be in the building in a flash to render assistance." Franklin dipped his head and gave her a reassuring squeeze on her shoulder. "Don't worry. You're working for us now. We won't bail on you."

As the time of the meeting approached, Matt leaned in her car window. The muscle in his jaw twitched as he gave her a long look. "I know you want to help get these guys, but I'm begging you to be careful."

Maggie took several deep breaths, but it did nothing to ease the tightness gripping her insides like a vice. If someone had told her several months ago that she'd be heading into a meeting with car thieves and a murderer, she would have said they were crazy. She remembered how nervous she'd been simply sitting outside Doyle's house with Robin. Now, she'd volunteered to head into a locked building with him. To stand opposite Harry while she tried to get him to confess to Grace's murder.

For a fleeting moment, she wished she'd taken Robin up on her offer to go to Mexico. If she had, she'd be drinking a fruity cocktail under a tiki hut instead of sitting in her car wiping nervous sweat from her forehead.

Maggie hit the unlock button on the fob to turn on the microphone and aimed her gaze at the sprinter van. "Can you hear me?"

Franklin stepped out and gave her a thumbs up.

Maggie studied Matt's face, determined to memorize every feature before they parted. Just in case. "Wish me luck."

He leaned in to kiss her, but when he pulled back, his face was pinched with worry. "I know you want to do this, but please be safe. I'm not going to breathe easy until you're back."

She resisted the urge to stare up into her rearview mirror, to take one last look at him as she drove off. Seeing Matt's concern would only make her more nervous. Her heart was already thudding so hard her chest hurt.

A few moments later, Maggie pulled into the body shop parking lot and drove toward the back of the building. She could see the small sliver of light behind the second bay door from the end, but there was no sign of Doyle's truck or Harry's white Mercedes. She had no idea what kind of car Manny drove, but she didn't see anything out of the ordinary. It appeared she was the first to arrive.

"They're not here yet." Her loud whisper was meant to provide an update to Franklin and his team.

Maggie remained in the safety of her car, but as she stared at the building, the hair on her arms stood up. What if they were inside waiting to ambush her?

By seven-twenty, she had started to question her memory. She'd told Harry seven o'clock. She was sure of it.

Maggie turned off the microphone and called Matt from her cell phone. "I'm not sure what to do. There's still no sign of them."

"You're sure they're not inside the building?"

"I guess they could be." Her gaze raked over the property again. "But the only cars I see are ones that need to be repaired."

"Why don't you drive around the building and see if maybe they parked somewhere else?"

"Okay." Maggie pulled around the rear of the building and saw the door Franklin had mentioned. "There aren't any cars in the back, and I can't really pull around to the other side. There's a fence there."

She turned her car around. As she drove back to the other side of the building, Maggie jerked back against her seat. In the dark shadows of the bushes, something moved. Or did it? Her nerves had her eyes seeing things and imagining the worst.

"I'm scared, Matt." Maggie took in several rapid, shallow breaths. "Do you think Harry's messing with me? I feel like he's trying to get me to let down my guard, and the minute I do, he's going to jump out at me."

"I don't like this either. Hang tight. Let me talk to Franklin, and I'll call you right back."

Maggie pointed her headlights at the entrance and watched for a familiar vehicle to turn in from the main road. Nothing.

When her phone vibrated, she nervously jabbed the speaker button.

"Franklin has a bad feeling about this."

Maggie's heart raced into her throat. "What do you mean?"

"They're almost thirty minutes late. Something's not right.

He doesn't want to take any chance they're setting you up somehow. It would have been nice to get them to make the admissions on tape, but his team has a search warrant. The SWAT team is getting into position to go in."

She swung her gaze toward the hill Franklin had said they would use. "Now?"

"As soon as you're safely out of there. Come on back to the drug store parking lot."

She frowned. "I don't get to watch?"

"Maggie." The way Matt said her name made it clear she'd already pushed her luck as far as he was concerned.

When she pulled her car beside the sprinter van, she saw it was empty inside. The team was already gone.

Matt was there waiting, and he yanked open her car door. "He just gave the order for them to enter the building."

He grabbed Maggie's hand and they rushed toward the small group of officers huddled around Franklin. The walkie he held in his hand crackled, followed by a deep male voice. "Standby."

Maggie's chest heaved, and it seemed an eternity before there was any additional communication from the team inside.

Finally, a message came over Franklin's walkie. "Building's clear."

Her eyes frantically searched Matt's for an explanation.

He shook his head. "They're not there. No one's inside."

Franklin scowled as he reached for his cell. "What do you mean, nothing?" He rubbed his temple as he held the phone against his ear. "Okay. Thanks."

Maggie spun to face him. "I don't understand. What happened?"

"The space behind the last two bay doors was empty. As in nothing but walls and floors." Franklin's chest deflated with his defeated sigh. "If there was anything there before, it's gone now."

This was all her fault.

"I'm sorry." Maggie stared at the ground, guilt pressing down on her shoulders. Matt had been right. She'd played this all wrong and given them a warning that they needed to clear out.

But what about her accusation that Harry had killed Grace? Even with everything she'd told him on the phone, he hadn't shown up. He was still underestimating her, as if he was convinced she didn't have the guts to do anything with her so-called evidence. Maggie's hands clenched into fists as anger raged through her.

She stormed to her car and yanked her phone from her purse.

Before Matt could stop her, she'd dialed Harry's cell number. "I don't appreciate being stood up," she said tersely into the phone when he answered.

As Matt waved Franklin over, she lowered the phone and pressed the speaker button.

"Sorry we all had to deviate from your little meeting." Harry sounded smug, like he knew he now had the upper hand. "There were important matters that needed to be taken care of."

Maggie shot Matt and Franklin an aggravated grimace. No doubt that involved moving whatever had been in the building.

"Well, since you couldn't be bothered to show up, now I have things to take care of, too." Maggie's hand flew to her hip. "Looks like I need to turn over the evidence I have to the police."

Harry chuckled as if she'd said something amusing. "If I were you, Margaret, I wouldn't be so hasty. Soon enough, you'll discover I have something you want. What if we could work out a trade? You wouldn't want to leave yourself with nothing to barter with, would you?"

For a moment, Maggie was stunned into silence. "What are you talking about?"

As she held her breath and waited for an answer, Harry disconnected the call.

She whipped around to face Matt. "What the hell does that mean? Where could he be?"

"Maybe he's with Doyle. Can you search his location?"

Her hands shook as she pulled up the Air Tag. She could see his current location was surrounded by green. "Looks like Doyle's truck is at the clearing. That's probably where they moved the stuff from the building."

Franklin reached for Maggie's phone and showed the screen to one of the officers. "Take a couple of guys and head up there. See if you can figure out who owns the property."

Maggie tossed her hands helplessly in the air. "Just because Doyle's there doesn't mean he's got Harry with him. What could he have meant about making a trade? It's not like I'm going to give him the evidence I have in exchange for a stolen car."

Matt pursed his lips. "It's too bad you didn't put the Air Tag on Harry's vehicle."

Maggie's eyes flew open, and she gestured wildly at Franklin. "My phone. I need my phone back." As he handed it to her, she nodded at Matt. "I might have something just as good." She pulled up the photo of the passwords she'd taken at Harry's desk and bit down on her bottom lip. "I'm pretty sure I have a way to find him."

She pulled up the app to locate a phone and logged in using Harry's information.

Her brow furrowed when it showed his location. "I don't understand how—" Maggie pinched the screen to make it larger, to try to make sense of what she was seeing. "This shows Harry's at my house. My old house," she said to clarify, her gaze bouncing between Matt and Franklin. "My ex-husband still lives there."

"Do you think your ex—maybe he's in on this somehow?" Matt looked as confused as she was.

Maggie's shoulders lifted in a slight shrug. "No. Maybe. I

don't know what to think. I can't understand what other reason he would have to be—" She clasped her hand over her mouth. "Jake." Her eyes went wide with horror. "My son is there. Harry would know he's my weak spot." Maggie's chest tightened, and she tried to swallow past the lump in her throat. "What he said about a trade ..."

"But how would he have known your son would be at your ex's house?" Franklin asked.

"He wouldn't, but Harry didn't care about my personal life. I never even told him I got divorced or that I moved. He could have easily gotten my old address through human resources."

Franklin eyed the phone Maggie gripped in her hand. "Can you call your ex-husband? See if he's home?"

"I can try." She dialed Todd's number, but it rang several times and went to voicemail.

"Maybe he's just not answering." Matt gave a sheepish shrug. "Can't say I always pick up when my ex-wife calls."

Maggie considered the awkward way she'd left Todd the night before. "I suppose it's possible he's ignoring me. Let me try Jake's phone." As it rang, she muttered under her breath. "Please pick up, Jake. Please pick up." A whimper slipped from her throat when she heard the familiar voicemail. She pressed her lips together to keep from crying. "He's not answering either."

"What about a neighbor?" Matt asked. "Not that we can go busting into your ex's house looking for Harry, but at least maybe they can tell us if they saw anything out of the ordinary or if his car is there. Same for your ex's vehicle. They might be able to confirm if he's home but just not answering your calls."

Maggie shrugged helplessly. She'd never been very close with the neighbors even when she lived there. "I'm not sure who I could—oh, there's a camera on the front door. It's still there. I just saw it last night."

When Matt flinched, Maggie averted her gaze. When this

was over, she'd explain, but now was not the time. Her fingers trembled as she pulled up the Ring app and switched from the apartment account to the one at her old house.

She glanced over at Matt and nodded. "There's a motion alert from an hour ago."

As he perched over her shoulder, she watched the footage of Todd's car pulling out of the driveway.

"This looks like my ex-husband went out, which means Jake's alone at the house." Maggie scanned the rest of the notifications. "Oh, wait, there's another one after that." She eased out a deep breath and hit the play button. "Maybe he came back."

What she saw instead felt like someone took a baseball bat to her insides. "That's Harry," she said, her voice breaking.

Franklin moved quickly to stand beside Matt. They all watched as her ex-boss stood on Todd's front porch with a McDonald's bag in his hand. He knocked on the front door once, then again. "Uber Eats," he said in a loud voice before putting his ear against the door. "I have a food delivery for you."

Maggie tossed her head back and forth, an ache in the back of her throat. "No, Jake. Don't answer the door," she yelled even though she knew her warning was of no use.

She held her breath as her heart thudded wildly. The next thing she saw was Harry pulling a wad of gum from his mouth. His hand moved closer to the camera lens until the screen went white and the video ended.

Maggie stumbled backward. "I need to go there." Dazed, she glanced around the parking lot for her car.

Matt grabbed her arm and shook his head. "You're in no condition to drive."

She turned, and her eyes pleaded with him. "Please. You need to take me to my son."

"We're all going," Franklin said, already pulling keys from his pocket. "I'll meet you there. Give me the address."

As Matt drove, Maggie dialed Todd's number again and her chest heaved as she listened to it ring. Relief swept through her when he finally answered.

He didn't even say hello. "What do you want?" he asked, sounding annoyed.

"Where are you?"

"Out."

Maggie heard a voice in the background ask, "Who are you talking to?" It was Stephanie.

Clearly, being rejected the night before had sent her ex-husband running to beg his girlfriend for a second chance.

She heard the dismissive response he gave. "It's just Maggie."

Just Maggie. To think, for even a fleeting second, she had believed he was sincere the night before.

"I don't know, Stephanie." Her ex-husband's voice sounded weary as if the call had interrupted a serious conversation that wasn't going the way he'd hoped. "She probably just wants—"

Maggie didn't have time to play games with him. "Todd, listen to me." She pounded the heel of her hand against the car seat. "It's important."

"Calm. Down." Just the familiar way her ex said those two words, she knew he was speaking to her again. "I know you're upset, but Jake's fifteen. He's old enough—"

Maggie emitted a groan of frustration. "Stop. This isn't about where Jake wants to live. I'm calling to say—" She hesitated. What could she say? "Don't go home."

He huffed. "Oh, yeah. Why's that? You gonna try and force our son to go back to your apartment? You can't—"

"Listen to me," Maggie said, her voice rising with frustration. "I don't want you to go home because I'm afraid if you do, you could get Jake killed." She paused, then added, "And maybe yourself."

That got his attention.

"What the hell are you talking about?" Todd asked in a sharp voice.

Maggie's eyes filled with tears. "My boss. He's at your house. I don't know if he went there looking for me, but Jake—he tried to trick him into opening the front door. I don't know—I'm not sure if Jake let him in."

"*Your* boss is at *my* house? Why the hell would he be looking for *you* at *my* house?" The exaggerated amount of confusion in Todd's voice made it clear he hadn't mentioned to Stephanie that his ex-wife had been there the night before. "What's he got, a thing for you or something?"

"What?" Maggie's forehead wrinkled. "No," she said, exasperated. Her ex-husband could be infuriating. "The reason I got fired—my boss is involved in some illegal stuff." She hesitated. "Including murder. I found—"

"What the hell kind of mess did you drag Jake into? I will never forgive you if something happens to our son."

Her throat tightened. "I'll never forgive myself."

"I'm leaving Stephanie's place right now. Where are you?"

"Please, don't try to be a hero. I'm heading to the house now. I'll—I'll fix this. I'll make it right." Even as Maggie said the words, she prayed she could make them true.

After she hung up, Matt reached for her hand and gave it a reassuring squeeze.

"I'm going to try Harry again." Maggie's stomach twisted when the call went directly to voicemail. She wrapped her arm around her middle and shook her head. "It didn't even ring."

"He probably turned off his phone. So now we have no way of knowing if he's still there."

Maggie pressed the button for the Ring app, but there was nothing new. Even if Harry was still there, his gum had covered the motion sensor.

They entered her old neighborhood, and Matt pulled

Maggie's car up behind Franklin's vehicle. The sprinter van pulled in behind her car.

Franklin was at the passenger door before she even had a chance to get out. "Any luck getting a hold of your ex-husband?"

"Yeah, but he's not home."

Franklin gave her a hopeful look. "Any chance you're still on the deed?"

Maggie shook her head as she got out of the car. "No. Todd refinanced after the divorce when he bought me out. I don't even have a key anymore." She still remembered throwing it down on their kitchen table the day she signed the lease for the apartment. "At least I don't have to live here anymore," she'd screamed before storming out to collapse in a fit of tears in her car.

"Let me try Jake again." When he didn't answer, Maggie pressed her lips together and tried to keep from crying. "No answer." Her frantic gaze volleyed between Matt and Franklin. "I need to get inside the house. I need to make sure he's okay."

Franklin's gaze drifted down the street. "Do you know what Harry's car looks like?"

Maggie nodded and she glanced around but there was no sign of it. "I don't see it, but that doesn't mean he isn't here." Harry wasn't a man who simply gave up. "A witness spotted his car in Grace's neighborhood the night of her murder." She regretted now that she had informed her boss of this fact. "Maybe he just decided to be more careful this time."

Franklin hesitated and then shook his head apologetically. "We had a warrant for the body shop but not your ex-husband's house. Unless we suspect a crime is being committed, we can't just break down the front door. Is your ex on his way home?"

Maggie gave a clipped nod and fought back tears.

Franklin wicked sweat from his temple. "Let's say he did park somewhere else and didn't just leave. Any idea if Harry would have been able to find a way into the house? If your son didn't answer the door, that is." His gaze drifted toward the house, but nothing seemed amiss. "Your ex lock up when he's gone?"

Maggie gave a helpless shrug. "Maybe. I don't know. When we were married, he locked himself out all the time when he went running. He hid an extra key under one of those fake rocks. We had it by the back door, so it wasn't so obvious, but I have no idea if it's still there."

She jerked her head toward the side of the house. "We used to have a dog, and there's a doggie door that leads into the laundry room. When he passed away a couple of years ago, Todd was too lazy to replace the door and take it out."

"Are you saying you think Harry could have used it to get inside?" Matt asked.

Maggie snorted at the vision of her ex-boss on his hands and knees crawling through it, the plastic flap covered in dog slobber smacking him in the head. "I doubt he'd ever be that desperate."

"So, what are you saying?" Matt asked. "You think one of the guys should try to get in that way? You heard Franklin. We don't know for sure Harry's inside the house. Or your son, for that matter."

Maggie sized up the officers on the scene. "I'm not sure any of the guys could fit through it anyway."

Matt nudged Franklin's arm. "You saw the footage of him knocking on the front door, and we know he doesn't deliver for Uber Eats. Maggie can't get her son on the phone. What he said to her about making a trade—come on, you can't get probable cause from that? Even if his car's not here, the guy's a suspected murderer."

Maggie sucked in a breath at the reminder that her son could be inside with a killer.

Franklin was quiet as he took in the concern on her face. He opened his mouth as if he was tempted to agree, but then subtly shook his head. His gaze cut back to Matt. "We're not even positive either one of them is in the house. But let's say they are. What if we ... made it worse?" He lowered his voice. "After what happened in Temple Terrace, we need to be careful how we proceed."

Matt gave a side glance in Maggie's direction. "I get it, but—"

"What happened in Temple Terrace?" Her anxious gaze flew between the two men. When neither responded, she stamped her foot against the ground. "*Tell me.*" Her high-pitched shriek demanded an answer.

Matt reached for her, but she yanked herself out of his grasp.

"Just tell me what happened," she said with a whimper. "Please."

"It wasn't the same thing at all, Maggie. That was a domestic situation—a pending divorce. The woman tried to get her soon-to-be-ex arrested. She tipped off the police that he dealt drugs out of his house, and a big deal was about to go down."

Maggie inhaled sharply. "She thought her son was at school, but he got sick, and the father picked him up early, right?"

She bent at the waist, convinced she was going to be sick as she recalled the story from the news. When the police broke down the door, the father shot at them. The bullet ricocheted and killed the little boy who'd come out of his room to see what all the noise was about. In the end, the police found three joints in the house, but that was it. The media had crucified the police department.

"I get why you'd be nervous," Matt said to Franklin. "I know this isn't something you face every day dealing with car thieves, but I still think there's a way—"

"I'd feel better if we waited for the ex-husband. He's got to be here soon, and he can give us permission to enter the residence." Franklin rubbed the back of his neck and the deep crease between his eyes showed the struggle he was having with his decision. "It's just—we could have a hard time justifying that we were convinced a crime was being committed. We're not even sure they're both inside."

Maggie scowled. "I'm telling you, Harry wouldn't have just given up and left." She waved her hands in the air around her. "Clearly, he's not out here, so he must have found a way inside." She gave Franklin a hard stare. "Isn't breaking and entering a crime?"

"Well, yeah. But we wouldn't know he'd broken in until we busted down your ex's door ourselves."

Maggie squeezed her eyes shut. She didn't have time for them to figure out if Jake was in trouble. By then, it could be too late.

She turned to Matt and her eyes locked on his. "Let's say it was me inside, and you knew for a fact Harry was also in the house. You could break down the door if you thought it was necessary to save my life, right?"

He wore a guarded expression as he studied her. "If I believed someone in the house was in danger, then yes. We could argue it was an exigent circumstance."

Maggie didn't know what that meant, and she didn't care. He'd already given her the answer she needed.

She reached for his hand and squeezed it. "I love you."

Maggie then took off running toward the back of the house.

32

The rock in the backyard was flipped over, the key gone. Whether Harry found it, or it had been that way since the last time Todd locked himself out, she had no way of knowing.

Maggie dug in her pocket. She hit the unlock button on the key fob and said a quick prayer they'd be able to hear her.

A few months ago, she wouldn't have stood a prayer of fitting through the doggie door. She sucked in a deep breath and stuck her head through the opening. Her arm scraped against the side of the heavy flap as she wiggled through it, and she clenched her jaw tightly to keep a yelp from escaping.

Once inside, she rubbed at the raw, reddish swipe on her arm. There was no time to feel pain.

Maggie crawled along the tile floor of the laundry room until she got to the door. She inched her way upward, then slowly twisted the knob. When the latch released, she pulled on the door until it opened slightly. It squeaked with a high-pitched protest she'd never noticed when she lived there. Now the sound seemed deafening. She winced, waited a moment, then slipped through the narrow opening.

She scanned her surroundings, and her gaze landed on the kitchen floor—littered with the contents of the drawers and cabinets. She was right. Harry had to be in the house. No doubt he figured he could find the evidence she'd hidden and took great satisfaction in breaking whatever he found instead. He had no idea she didn't even live here anymore.

She crept toward the living room, but there was still no sign of Harry or Jake.

Maggie couldn't help herself as she rushed toward the coffee table in the living room. Todd's empty beer bottles from the night before had been replaced by Jake's controller for his game and a crumpled wrapper from a protein bar. A moan slipped from her lips when she noticed what else was there. Jake's cell phone. She snatched it up and saw the home screen was filled with notifications of missed calls and texts from her and Todd. Her son hadn't seen any of them.

The stairs creaked, and she whipped around.

"Well, look who's home." Harry sneered at her from the middle of the staircase.

"Where is he?" Maggie asked through gritted teeth. "What did you do to my son?"

"Did you have fun at the body shop?" He strolled down the remaining steps as if he was in no hurry and posed on the landing at the bottom. "I don't know who you think you are, Margaret. A person like you doesn't get to make demands of a man like me."

Her eyes blazed with hatred as she glared at Harry. "If you laid one finger on him, I swear I'll kill you."

"If you had just kept your nose out of my business, neither of us would be here right now."

Harry was right. If she'd just gone back to her everyday life after the trial, Jake would be at her apartment right now. But if she had let it go, he would have gotten away with Grace's murder. Maggie couldn't allow that to happen. Her days of saying "yes, sir" to Harrison Korman were over.

She squared her shoulders and moved in his direction. It was now or never. "You must have thought you'd committed the perfect murder. Doyle blamed Manny. Manny blamed Doyle. Neither bothered to look at you because—" Maggie snorted and hoped she sounded braver than she felt. "Let's be real. You're not exactly the toughest guy out there."

Harry flinched at her insult, then his eyes narrowed into thin slits. "People who underestimate me end up being very disappointed."

"I get it." Maggie bobbed her head in false solidarity. "You were worried someone would blow up that sweet little scam you've got going. I mean, a man like you deserves that kind of money, right? An expensive stolen car of your very own." She gestured at his hand as it held onto the end of the banister. "That fancy watch you bought so no one could question your success. You thought you had it made." She cocked her head to the side as she stared at him. "You must have been furious to think Grace Hutchinson had the power to take it all away." She held up her fist, then snapped her hand open. "Poof. All gone."

Harry pressed his lips tightly together as if he wanted to keep his response from escaping.

His ego would kick in. If Maggie pushed hard enough, he wouldn't be able to resist the opportunity to brag. "You went to her house and pretended to have a delivery for her. Wine and flowers. So smart. What woman wouldn't open the door for that?"

His thin lips curled upward into a satisfied smile. "It *was* brilliant, wasn't it?"

Maggie played along, hoping he'd reveal more information about the night Grace was killed. No matter how this ended,

Pam deserved to know the truth about what had happened to her sister.

"It certainly was," she said with a nod. "So, how long did it take before she knew she was in trouble?"

Harry clammed up again, but his cocky smirk remained as if he had a secret he had no intention of sharing.

She needed to keep him talking. "Grace made a run for the back door, but then she tripped. I'm guessing she had a sneezing fit. Did you know she was allergic to those cheap daisies you bought?"

"Sometimes you just get lucky."

Maggie had to work to keep the disgust from her face. "While she was down, you stood over her and shot her in the back of the head. Then, while she lay there bleeding, you set up the wine you'd brought. Was that your plan? To make it look like someone stopped by to have a drink?"

"Perhaps someone else was there that night." Harry's eyebrows lifted. "A mysterious man with no fingerprints or DNA."

"So, tell me then, how did *you* end up with the cork from that bottle of wine? To me," Maggie placed her palm on her chest, "that seems like something the person who killed her would take as a souvenir."

When she'd picked up the file from Charlene, Maggie had peeked in the driver's side window of Harry's Mercedes, shocked at how overconfident he was to leave evidence out in the open. "Odd that you'd leave it in the cup holder of your stolen car. Were you that sure they'd never come for you? Or was it for the confidence boost? I'm sure you needed a daily reminder that you're a tough guy capable of killing an innocent woman."

Harry pursed his lips. "You really have stuck your nose where it doesn't belong."

He stepped off the landing and sauntered in Maggie's direction.

Her legs wobbled underneath her, but she stood firm as she glared at him. "Grace Hutchinson didn't do anything to deserve to cross paths with the likes of you."

Harry's shoulders lifted in a shrug of indifference. "Sometimes there's collateral damage on the way to the top."

"She had a family that loved her."

"And I had business to take care of." His casual tone told her he felt no remorse for what he'd done.

"With Martin Freight, the fake company you set up?" Maggie asked. "Or RC's Luxury Car Parts? Were you afraid Ronan would decide *you* were collateral damage if his shipments stopped?" Her eyes narrowed with contempt. "You were really working both sides of the equation, weren't you?"

"What would someone like you know about achieving success?"

"But is it really success if it's illegal?" Maggie gave him a hard stare. She was done letting him intimidate her. "Didn't you just take the easy way out because you knew you didn't have what it takes to really make it? Inside those expensive suits, you're still the skinny little nerd who got beat up after school." She was playing with fire, but oh, it felt good to finally tell him what she thought about him. "Money can't change who you are inside, Harry. You're still the same loser you've been your whole life. It's no wonder you're alone. Who in their right mind would want to be with a miserable man like you?"

His face turned stone cold. "Shut up, Margaret."

Success. She'd hit a nerve. "The only way you're going to shut me up is to kill me. I mean, you've already murdered one person. Or are there more?"

Harry reached behind his back. Maggie sucked in a breath when his hand reappeared holding a small pistol.

Her chest tightened as he pointed the gun at her. Confronting him had been a gamble, but Maggie couldn't give up now. This only proved he had the capacity to kill. She tucked her fear deep down and offered him a disappointed shake of her head. "See, you're always looking to take the easy way out, Harry. Pulling a trigger doesn't make you tough. It means you're weak. A coward." She let the words settle over him, and when his eyes went dark, she knew she'd hit a bullseye. Clearly, it wasn't the first time in his life someone had described him that way. "At least the police will know to get you for two murders when my bullet matches the one you used to kill Grace."

Harry glowered at her. Maggie could almost see him calculating his next move, the anger he felt for her simmering just below the surface. She'd now given him something to prove. He set the gun on the end table and as his eyes narrowed to crinkled slits, he moved toward her. "You have no idea how much I'm going to enjoy squeezing the life out of you. Watching you gasp for your last breath until I'm finally rid of you."

Maggie swallowed hard, but this was what she'd been working toward. She said a silent prayer that Matt and Franklin had heard his threat. "Really?" She forced an amused laugh from her throat. "You think you can kill me with your bare hands?" she asked, baiting him. "We both know you don't have what it takes." Her eyes bore into his. "You should have sent a real man like Doyle to do the hard stuff."

Harry growled, and in several long strides, he was standing over her. When his hands reached for her neck, Maggie released a bloodcurdling scream.

It almost drowned out the sound of the front door being kicked in.

33

As a police officer cuffed Harry, Maggie rubbed at her neck.

Now that she was out of danger, she couldn't resist one final self-serving jab at her ex-boss. "By the way, loser, people who underestimate *me* end up being very disappointed. Or locked up for the rest of their life." She released a disgusted hiss. "I hope you rot in prison."

Matt put his arm around Maggie and led her to the couch. "Don't worry. He'll get what he has coming to him. You did great."

"What about Jake?" Her eyes pleaded with his for good news.

Matt hesitated for a moment, then gave his head a slight shake. "No sign of him yet."

Maggie's gaze flew to Harry, and she leaped from the couch and rushed toward him. Matt bolted forward and blocked her from reaching the only person who knew where her son was.

"Where is he?" She attempted to lunge at Harry, but Matt had a firm grip on her arm.

"Don't give him the satisfaction," he said. "Franklin's guys will find Jake."

Maggie stood frozen, unable to give up on the idea that her ex-boss might say something that would provide a clue as to her son's whereabouts.

"Oh, Margaret." Harry peered over Matt's shoulder to give her a knowing smile. "Are you an optimist now? At the office, you were always such a downer."

"I'm absolutely an optimist." Maggie's hands were squeezed into fists by her side, but a tight smile twitched her lips. "I'm *confident* you're going to spend the rest of your miserable life staring at the walls of a dirty cell. And I have *no doubt* that each and every time they let your skinny ass out for your one hour of fresh air, you'll have to watch your back that someone doesn't stick a homemade knife in it. Because trust me, they're not going to like you in there any more than anyone liked you out here. I am *positive* you won't get anything even close to medium rare filet mignon on your lunch tray." She leveled an unflinching stare at him. "And the one thing I know for damn certain is that I can't wait to be called to the stand to testify against you. For Grace's murder, and let's now add attempted murder to the long list of charges that will make sure you never see the light of day again."

Harry's brows came together as he gave her an exaggerated look of confusion. "Murder? Attempted murder? I'm sure I have no idea what you're talking about. I know I terminated your employment for inadequate job performance. It's also noted in your file that you tend to have a wild imagination and an attitude that leans toward being vengeful."

Maggie laughed at his lackluster attempt to convince her he was still on top. "The evidence will speak for itself. I've got the truth about Grace on my side, and I'm looking forward to telling the police everything I know about what you've been up to."

Franklin nodded at one of the officers. "Take him outside."

With Harry out of Maggie's line of sight, the detective placed a reassuring hand on her shoulder. "My team is searching the house and the property. If your son's here, we'll find him."

She bit down on her lower lip and grabbed his arm when he turned to join his officers. "Let me help look for him. Please."

Matt leaned in close. "Maggie, leave this to the police," he said softly. "I'm begging you."

Her eyes nervously searched his face. "But Jake has to be okay, right? I mean, Harry didn't say he wasn't." Her legs wobbled underneath her as she stood there seeking reassurance from him. "He's got to be here somewhere."

"The guys are trained for this sort of thing. Don't worry. They'll find him." Matt took her hand and led her back to Todd's couch. "C'mon, sit down." He ran his thumb over the mark on her neck and then eyed the scrape on her arm. "You sure you're okay? Let me call the paramedics to check you out."

With all the adrenaline Maggie had rushing through her, nothing hurt. Not even her ankle. "I'm fine, but I can't say I'm not extremely grateful for your impeccable timing. I turned on the microphone before I went in. Were you able to hear everything Harry said, or did you just hear my scream?"

"We heard it all. We also got word the other team made it to the clearing and arrested Doyle, Manny, and a handful of guys they had helping out." He nudged her arm. "All because of you. You're a big deal around the station today."

Earlier that day, his statement would have made Maggie's insides burst with pride. Now, her success was meaningless until she knew her son was safe. "That's good," she said, but her voice was void of enthusiasm. "I mean I'm happy for Franklin that his case is solved, but right now, I can't think about anything but Jake."

He wrapped his arm around her, and she sat in silence, a vacant stare on her face.

"Anything?" Matt asked a few minutes later when one of the officers entered the living room.

He shook his head. "Not yet."

Maggie swung her gaze toward Matt and her bottom lip started to quiver. "This is all my fault. Jake didn't ask to be dragged into this. To be used as Harry's pawn ..."

He pulled her close. "Don't think like that. They haven't found anything yet, so it's still possible he's fine." He used his thumb to wipe away the tears that had dripped down her cheek. "You don't even know for sure he was in the house when Harry got here. He could be at a friend's. Maybe he's blissfully unaware of what happened tonight."

Maggie gave a single nod, but in her gut, she knew. Jake wouldn't have gone out without telling Todd, and her teenage son would never have left without his phone. He had to be in the house somewhere, but it seemed impossible the officers couldn't find a single trace of him. It was almost like he didn't want to be found, as if—

Maggie pulled herself out of Matt's embrace and scrambled off the couch.

"Wait," she called out to the officer as he started to ascend the stairs to the second floor. She rushed over to him and tugged on his arm. "Use the word broccoli."

He spun around, a baffled expression on his face. "I'm sorry. I don't understand."

"While you're searching—call out the word broccoli. It was our—my son Jake and I had a code word. He'll know it's safe for him to come out if he hears it. Maybe he's just hiding and not ..." Maggie's voice broke.

"Okay, ma'am." He gave a nod meant to reassure her. "We'll try that."

"Broccoli?" Matt asked as the officer made his way up the stairs.

"When Jake was little, there was this missing persons case. A man approached a little boy on the school playground. He told the boy his mommy had been in an accident, and he'd been sent to pick him up to bring him to the hospital to see her. Of course, the boy didn't know any better." Maggie drew in a deep breath. "He went off with this guy and was never seen again. I couldn't stop thinking about what Jake would do if that happened. I drilled it into his head that he shouldn't ever go anywhere with a stranger. I reassured him that I would never send someone to pick him up, but if I absolutely had to, the person would say the word broccoli to him. That would be Jake's way of knowing it was safe. It was our code word." Her shoulders lifted as Matt stared at her. "No bad guy's going to lure a child away by mentioning a vegetable."

"You really do watch a lot of true crime, don't you?"

Maggie gave a sad nod. "I've always found it fascinating. I like to try to guess what happened, but I never really thought about what the family went through. But now that it's my kid, my story—"

Her phone pinged. She lunged for it, but it was the Ring app notification.

She let out a wail, then read what was on the screen to Matt. "Potential hostage situation in the area of 56th Drive. Heavy police presence and SWAT." Todd's house was dead center in the shaded circle that indicated the approximate area of the event.

She shoved her phone at him. "Look what someone wrote. *I heard it's a child.* How do they even know that?" Maggie bowed her head, helpless to stop the tears from falling.

He nudged her shoulder. "Hey."

"All the times I've seen those stupid notifications and now it's—"

"Maggie." Matt put his finger under her chin to force her to look up at him. When he had her attention, he ran his thumbs under her eyes to wipe her tears. A slow smile spread across his face, and he gestured toward the top of the stairs.

"Mom." Jake's voice was soft and meek. His hair was plastered to his forehead, his T-shirt and shorts soaked as they clung to his body.

Relief raced through Maggie as she propelled herself from the couch. She raced up the stairs and swooped him into a hug.

Her teenager was taller than her, but he wrapped his arms around his mom's waist and embraced her back. "Sorry. I'm a little sweaty."

Maggie hugged him tighter. "I couldn't care less. I was so worried." She pulled back to study him. "What—how—"

"All that stuff you drilled into me came in handy today."

Her head tipped to the side. "What do you mean?"

"This guy came to the door and said he had a food delivery. I thought maybe Dad told you he went out, so you sent me something for dinner. But then I looked through the peephole and saw he had McDonald's. We haven't been eating fast food, so it seemed strange that's what you'd send. Not to mention, the guy didn't look like he should be delivering food." His eyebrows shot up and he let out an appreciative puff of air. "The watch he was wearing was fire. It looked super expensive."

"I guess fire is a good thing, but you're right about what it costs. It's a Rolex." Pride swelled up inside Maggie that her son had been smart enough to assess the situation before he opened the door. "That was a great observation."

"The whole time, I kept thinking about what you always say about not trusting anyone. Being a little paranoid."

"Careful, not paranoid," Maggie said, parroting back her own words before rolling her eyes at herself. "Sorry. Go on."

"Well, I was both. But then I heard him try to open the front door, and I freaked. No delivery guy's gonna break in just to drop off food. I knew something wasn't right, so I remembered what they teach us at school. Escape if you can. My first instinct was to get out of the house, so I ran for the kitchen. But then I heard the guy outside talking to someone. He said he would try the back door to see if he could jimmy it. I didn't know if someone else was waiting out front, so I made a split-second decision to hide."

So, he *had* been hiding.

"Where?" she asked.

"In the attic."

Maggie's forehead wrinkled. "The attic? What would make you think—"

"Remember when we moved into the apartment? You told me you were going to have to come up with a new place to hide my Christmas presents this year."

Maggie nodded and a smile tugged at her lips. "Because here I always hid them in the attic."

"And I never found them. Every year, I checked every closet. Under every bed. But I never even thought about looking up there." His shoulders hitched up. "I figured it was as good a place as any. I even pulled the ladder up with me."

She hugged him again. "You're brilliant."

"I had no idea what was going on, but I was afraid to come out. Then I heard someone scream."

"It was me." Maggie gestured at the couch and waved. "That's Matt. He saved me."

"After I heard that, there was no way I was moving. I figured I'd just stay put until—" Jake let out a deep sigh. "Actually, I had no idea how I'd know when it was safe to come out."

"Broccoli," Maggie said in a soft voice.

He nodded. "Broccoli. I couldn't believe it when I heard someone calling out our code word. I figured it couldn't be a coincidence." His head bobbed as he fought a smile. "Pretty smart, Mom. I'm starting to think I didn't give your true crime watching enough credit. You knew what you were talking about. You just forgot one thing."

She cocked her head and studied him. "Oh, yeah, what's that?"

"You never drilled into me to grab my phone before I hid. That would have been helpful advice. I left in on the coffee table."

Jake's gaze drifted down the stairs toward the living room and he eyed the front door Matt had kicked in. "Wow. Has Dad seen that?"

34

———

"So, you two are dating?" Jake asked after he was officially introduced to Matt.

Maggie offered a hesitant nod. "We are. He's a cop."

Her son seemed to consider this information and gave a nod of approval. "Cool. You guys are a good match, I guess." He turned to Maggie and smiled. "He fights crime. You're obsessed with it."

She opened her mouth to protest but eyed Matt giving Jake a subtle wink.

"What?" he asked with feigned innocence. "Your son's not wrong."

"No, I suppose he's not. We are a good match."

"Jake, did your mom tell you we went to high school together in New Jersey?" Matt asked. "We've known each other for almost thirty years."

"That's crazy."

The simplistic response of a teenage boy.

As Maggie sat on the couch sandwiched between her boyfriend and her son, her phone buzzed.

"It's Grace's sister," she announced, then stood to take the call. "Hey, Pam." Maggie slipped away with the phone at her ear. "You have perfect timing."

"Oh yeah? I just called to tell you I talked to Ron. He didn't bring flowers to my sister's house."

"I know." Maggie glanced back at the couch and smiled when she observed Matt and Jake engaged in small talk.

"You talked to him, too?"

"No, but I found out how the flowers got inside Grace's house. It was a ruse to get her to open the door." Maggie stared out the front window at the commotion still going on outside. "We got him," she choked out, her eyes wet. She'd dreamed of this moment, of telling Pam that her sister's murderer wouldn't go unpunished. "The police just took him away."

Pam sucked in a breath. "You got him? But what about double jeopardy? Does this mean—"

"We were wrong. Doyle didn't kill your sister. His accountant did." Maggie shook her head. The reality of the situation still seemed surreal. "My old boss."

Pam was silent for a moment. "But I don't understand," she said finally. "Why would Doyle's accountant, your boss—why in the world would he want to kill my sister? You're sure it was him?"

"This time, I'm positive. I'll explain everything when I see you. But just know, the guy who did it is going to go away for a long time. He's also facing possession of a stolen vehicle, fraud, attempted murder—"

Pam inhaled sharply. "Who else did he try to kill?"

"Um, me."

"What? Maggie, are you okay?"

"I'm fine. I'm glad he didn't succeed, but I needed him to prove he was capable of it. And even though I won't be on the jury this time around, you don't have to worry." A grin spread across Maggie's face. "I'm going to make a rock-star witness for the prosecution. This time I'll make sure there's a guilty verdict."

"I can't thank you enough for—for caring enough about my sister to never give up." Pam voice was thick with emotion. "You know, the reward for information about Grace's killer was never claimed, but you and Robin earned it. I need to give my parents the news."

"I'll call you tomorrow, and we'll make a plan to get together." Maggie jerked up her head as Todd rushed through the front door. "I can tell all of you what happened at the same time."

She hung up and set her phone on the coffee table, then watched her ex-husband hug Jake.

When he pulled back, he leveled an angry glare in Maggie's direction. "What the hell is going on here? You'd better believe a judge is going to hear about this. You'll be lucky if you ever—"

Matt interrupted her ex-husband's tirade by stepping forward and extending his hand. "You must be Todd. Nice to meet you. I'm Matt, Maggie's boyfriend." He winced as he aimed his chin at the broken door frame. "Sorry about your front door, man."

Maggie didn't even attempt to hide the smile that tugged at her lips. Their status was apparently official.

"You—you kicked in my door?" Todd's gaze cut sideways to his ex-wife as he looked for an explanation.

Jake spoke up instead. "Mom's boyfriend's a cop."

"Yeah, I had no choice." Matt lifted his shoulders in a casual shrug and reached for Maggie's hand. "Someone was trying to strangle the woman I love. I wasn't about to let that go down."

Todd grunted a response Maggie couldn't understand, but she no longer cared what he thought.

"She's quite the crime-fighting dynamo." Matt glanced over at her and nodded before his gaze landed back on Todd. "Not only did she figure out who really killed Grace Hutchinson, but she helped break up a chop shop for stolen cars our auto theft task force has been trying to bust for a couple of years."

Jake slung his arm around Maggie's shoulders and bobbed his head. "Yeah, Mom's kind of a hero."

Todd ignored his proclamation and aimed an incredulous stare first at his ex-wife and then at his son. "But at what cost? You could have been hurt or worse."

Jake dismissed his concern. "I'm fine. She taught me well and—"

He was interrupted when Maggie's phone vibrated loudly and skipped across Todd's coffee table.

She hitched up a shoulder. "Sorry." Maggie scooped it up to find a text from Robin.

> Anything go down yet?

Maggie stepped out of the circle and smiled as she typed her reply:

> Oh, it went down all right. (But don't worry, I fed and walked Duke before the you-know-what hit the fan.)

She then typed a second text.

> Matt told me he loved me. Harry got arrested, and Pam said we might even get the reward that was offered.

She watched as the blinking dots told her Robin was typing a response.

Not we. YOU. You're the one who solved the
case. Can we record the minute I get back? I
need to hear every last detail! (And that includes
the love stuff!!)

Maggie rejoined the group and tugged on Matt's arm. "That
was Robin. I feel bad she had to miss all the fun, but I'm sure the
beach in Mexico isn't such a bad place to be instead." She hesitated and raised her eyes to meet his. "When she gets back, she
wants to pick up where we left off. You know, the podcast."

"I figured she might." Matt gave her a slow nod. "If that's
what you want to do, then I think you should."

Her eyebrows shot up. "Really? You're—"

"Podcast?" Todd cut in as if their private conversation
included him.

"Yeah, my friend Robin and I started a podcast." Maggie
couldn't resist the chance to clarify. "A *true-crime* podcast."

"You? What are you, like the host of it?" Her ex snorted
dismissively as if the idea was ridiculous.

"As a matter of fact, I am." The pride that surged through her
was a feeling her ex's putdown could no longer shatter. "Well,
co-host, actually."

Todd didn't have a chance to respond before Maggie's phone
rang again.

She held up her index finger when she saw Charlene's name
on the screen. "Excuse me. Apparently, I'm very popular today."
She stepped away to answer the call. "Hey, is everything okay?"

"A bunch of cops showed up at the office," Charlene said in a
loud whisper. "They shoved some papers at Andy, and now they're
ransacking Harry's office. They just packed up his computer."

"Oh, really?" A slow smile spread across Maggie's face. Her
one regret was that she hadn't been there to see Franklin's guys
storm her ex-boss's office for herself. "Well, it's not like he'll need

his computer where he's going. Last I saw him, he was sporting a pair of handcuffs and ducking his head as the cops shoved him into the back seat of a police car."

"Oh, wow." Charlene giggled. "I would have loved to see that. He was probably all freaked out that the handcuffs would scratch his precious Rolex. Can you fill me in yet on what he did?"

"Absolutely, but it's a bit crazy right now. Let me call you tomorrow, and I'll tell you everything."

Maggie hung up and returned to Matt's side. "Looks like Franklin's guys are making the rounds. They're turning Harry's office upside down as we speak." She could only imagine the chaos at the firm. "I wonder if any of the partners knew what he was up to."

"Maybe in light of this news, you can get your job back."

Maggie shook her head. "Nah. I think you were right." She swung her gaze toward Todd, who had moved to the kitchen to assess the broken dishes strewn across the tile. "About a lot of things. It does take two people to make a marriage fall apart, but the divorce was my chance at a fresh start. And I'm not just talking about you."

"Oh, really?" Matt studied her as if he was trying to determine what she had planned.

"Yeah, I think I'm going to try to jump off that ledge you talked about." She hadn't tried to solve Grace's murder for the reward, but it would certainly help. Maggie put her arms around him and looked into his eyes. "Someone very smart once told me that the only thing that matters is the score at the end. I'm ready to make the second half count."

"Good for you. I have no doubt you can do anything you set your mind to." Matt glanced around the house and laughed. "I think you proved that today."

"Thanks, Coach." A warm feeling of contentment enveloped her. This was what unconditional love was supposed to feel like.

Matt leaned over and kissed her. "Any idea what you want to do next?"

"Well, I absolutely want to continue to do the podcast, but I need something that will pay the bills. Remember when you said you became a cop because you wanted to help people?"

His eyes went wide, and worry slid across his face. "Uh, you want to be a cop like me?"

Maggie patted his arm to reassure him. "Not exactly. Franklin's job would probably be more my speed, but I think I've decided—I want to go back to school. That day in the crime lab, I told the investigator she had my dream job. I wasn't kidding. Back then, it was because I thought it would be fun to be part of the true crime stuff I was always watching. Now, I realize how desperate families are to know the truth. I want to make a difference, too. I want to be the reason someone like Harry doesn't get away with murder."

Matt placed his hand on the side of her face. "I have no doubt you'll be amazing at it. But if you change your mind—" He aimed his chin in Franklin's direction. "I'm not so sure you couldn't eventually steal his job from underneath him."

Maggie felt a tap on her shoulder. When she turned around, Jake stood there. In an instant, gratitude and relief swept through her again. This day could have had a very different ending. The crime story on the evening news had almost been about her family.

"Hey, Mom, any chance we can get out of here and go home? I'd love to take a shower and change out of these sweaty clothes."

Home. The word sounded so sweet. Maggie called out to her ex-husband. "Todd, Jake wants to go home. To my apartment," she added hastily in case there was any doubt. After he gave a begrudging nod, she wrapped her arms around her son. "Sure, we can go."

Jake eyed Matt. "You coming?"

He shot Maggie a look, then smiled as he shrugged. "If you'll both have me."

"I wouldn't have it any other way." Maggie leaned into him and lowered her voice. "Besides, it's not like you even have your car here. I wouldn't feel right abandoning you at my ex-husband's house."

Matt hesitated and pursed his lips. "Actually, let me talk to Franklin real quick. I'm sure you need to give a statement about what transpired tonight, and another detective will probably need to go over what you uncovered about Grace's murder. Considering the whole thing was recorded, your statement can probably wait until tomorrow, but let me make sure." He held up his index finger and his gaze bounced between Maggie and Jake. "Give me one minute, okay?"

As Maggie watched, Matt trotted over to speak to Franklin. When he was finished, instead of coming back to them, he strolled over to talk to Todd.

Jake's eyebrows shot up, and he flashed Maggie a questioning stare.

She was just as confused as her son. "I have no idea what he could be talking to Dad about."

Matt reappeared at her side a few minutes later. "Okay, we're good to go."

"What was that about? Why were you talking to my ex-husband?"

"Oh, I just told him to send me the bill for the broken door." He gave a casual shrug. "I figured it was the least I could do."

"Wow." Jake bobbed his head in an appreciative nod. "Well played, dude. My dad's really cheap, and now he can't say anything bad about you."

Maggie admonished her son, but she couldn't help but laugh. Whether the move was strategic or not didn't matter. Unless it concerned Jake, she had no interest in Todd's opinions anymore.

When he'd first told her he wanted a divorce, Maggie imagined her life was over. Now, as she stepped over the splintered frame of the front door, she realized her marriage and her divorce had made her who she was. They'd taught her what she wanted in life. She was sure she'd make mistakes with Matt, too, but Maggie was prepared to learn from them so they could move forward. Together.

She thought back to what he'd said on their first date and finally accepted he'd been right. Maggie wasn't too old for a fresh start. It was now time to do something she enjoyed—something she knew she'd be good at. She reached for Matt's hand. There wasn't anyone else she wanted by her side as she began her second half.

There were murders to be solved—bad guys to lock up. Families deserved to know the truth. Maggie couldn't wait to play her part.

FROM THE AUTHOR

Thank you for reading *Burden of Doubt*. If you've enjoyed this book, a rating or review would be much appreciated. Reviews and referrals help other readers find my books and allow me to keep writing them.

Please also consider checking out my other novels:

Where the Truth Hides – Investigation Duo Series, Book 1
The Dark Inheritance – Investigation Duo Series, Book 2
Memory Hunter – Investigation Duo Series, Book 3
When Wings Flutter

ABOUT BURDEN OF DOUBT

The idea for this book took root while I was serving as a juror on a murder trial. Not only did I find the process fascinating, but it changed the way I look at some of the true crime cases I read about.

We found our defendant not guilty. At the time, I absolutely thought there was the possibility he did it, but the prosecution just didn't prove their case. Some key pieces of evidence that would have pushed us all over the line to a guilty verdict were never presented. Like Maggie, I couldn't quite let it go. I had a strong need to know if we'd made the right decision. Had we let a murderer go free?

What I learned after the trial is that everything related to the case becomes public record, including witness statements. And several of those statements? Well, they went a long way toward planting doubt for me that our defendant had indeed committed the crime. While I was relieved that I felt we'd delivered the right verdict, it bothered me that we never heard from these witnesses because they didn't help the prosecution's case. We only learned what those in charge wanted us to know. There was also never any discussion of these witnesses in the newspaper articles about the murder. Remember that next time you're reading up on a true-crime case and you think you know the whole story.

If you've read my Investigation Duo series, you know I also have a passion for utilizing DNA. It's the perfect marriage for my true-crime addiction as more and more cold cases are being solved using investigative genetic genealogy. From the time I started writing this book to it being published, there was an update to the Delphi murders and there are rumblings of hope for answers in the JonBenét Ramsey case. (Don't come for me about the family...) My newest obsession is a podcast called DNA:ID. What I see time and again is that DNA reveals the truth about cases that have been cold for years, and it's not always the answer everyone expects.

While I've always been obsessed with true crime, I do know that sometimes people need a reminder that these stories are about real people and families who've faced the worst situations imaginable. I tried to have Maggie come to the same realization as well when it was her family in peril. She's going to embark on a new career in crime scene investigation. Could there be a new series in the works? Might she join forces with Jules and Becky in the Investigation Duo series? Time will tell.

ACKNOWLEDGMENTS

To my editor, **Jonas Saul**, you are always my strongest advocate and I'm not sure where I would be without you. Thank you for always championing my writing and for sharing my belief that things happen exactly the way they are meant to.

To **Robin Lubetkin**, my equally obsessed true crime friend. So much of Robin in this book came from you. I'm grateful to have someone to share my addiction and thank you for always keeping me on your verdict-alert radar.

Thank you to **Peyton Regalado** and family for our invaluable plotting session around a fire pit on what was probably one of the few cold nights in Florida.

I'm most appreciative to **Joe Torok**, Retired Sergeant with the Broward County Sheriff's Office. From Air Tags to stolen auto parts to wiring a confidential informant, I couldn't write it without your valuable insight. Well, I could, but it probably wouldn't be accurate!

To **Stacy Ostrau** for being the kind of friend who understands that arranging a trip to the County Crime Lab is the perfect birthday present for someone like me, and a big thank you to **Roberto Caceres**, Crime Scene Detective, for being one of our official tour guides. Like Maggie, I was enthralled with the entire experience.

A big thank you to **Stephanie Juergens Kravetz** for being my Tampa Bay Buccaneers resource. At the time I wrote this book, Tom Brady mania had taken over Florida. It was impossible to find a fan who *didn't* have his jersey!

To **Sarah Henry,** thanks for letting me use your name and sharing my belief that the title of Crazy Cat Lady isn't such a bad thing! There was a little too much truth in Maggie and Robin's podcast episode. At the time I wrote it, the Ring camera from my front door was in my spare room awaiting a foster cat's delivery of kittens. Good thing nobody across the street got murdered!

I'm grateful for **Woody Kamena, Stacey Halpin, and Peyton Regalado** for agreeing to read this book ahead of the curve to provide feedback. The early drafts aren't always pretty!

ABOUT THE AUTHOR

Liane Carmen is the author of *Burden of Doubt*, *When Wings Flutter*, and the Investigation Duo Series. Her goal is to write novels that keep mystery lovers guessing, and if her Google searches ever come into question, she'd be grateful if her readers could vouch for her.

She's an avid reader and a genealogy buff who's been known to lose large blocks of time researching her family tree. Obsessed with both DNA and true crime, Liane is thrilled that investigative genetic genealogy is now solving cold cases.

She lives in Florida with a houseful of pets and relishes her new title of grandmother.

For more information about her upcoming books, visit her website at www.lianecarmen.com.

Printed in Great Britain
by Amazon

59806590R00199